The Complet

The Complete Ringer

The Adventures of Fiction's Nemesis and Master of Disguise

The Ringer
and
Again the Ringer

Edgar Wallace

LEONAUR

The Complete Ringer
The Adventures of Fiction's Nemesis and Master of Disguise
The Ringer
and
Again the Ringer
by Edgar Wallace

FIRST EDITION

First published under the titles
The Ringer
and
Again the Ringer

Leonaur is an imprint of Oakpast Ltd

Copyright in this form © 2019 Oakpast Ltd

ISBN: 978-1-78282-830-3 (hardcover)
ISBN: 978-1-78282-831-0 (softcover)

http://www.leonaur.com

Contents

The Ringer

Contents

Chapter 1

The Assistant Commissioner of Police pressed a bell on his table, and, to the messenger who entered the room a few seconds after: "Ask Inspector Wembury if he will be good enough to see me," he said.

The commissioner put away into a folder the document he had been reading. Alan Wembury's record both as a police officer and as a soldier was magnificent. He had won a commission in the war, risen to the rank of Major and had earned the Distinguished Service Order for his fine work in the field. And now a new distinction had come to him.

The door opened and a man strode in. He was above the average height. The commissioner looked up and saw a pair of good-humoured grey eyes looking down at him from a lean, tanned face.

"Good morning, Wembury."

"Good morning, sir."

Alan Wembury was on the sunny side of thirty, an athlete, a cricketer, a man who belonged to the out-of-doors. He had the easy poise and the refinement of speech which comes from long association with gentlemen.

"I have asked you to come and see me because I have some good news for you," said the commissioner.

He had a real affection for this straight-backed subordinate of his. In all his years of police service he had never felt quite as confident of any man as he had of this soldierly detective.

"All news is good news to me, sir," laughed Alan.

He was standing stiffly to attention now and the commissioner motioned him to a chair.

"You are promoted divisional inspector and you take over 'R' Division as from Monday week," said the chief, and in spite of his self-control, Alan was taken aback. A divisional inspectorship was one of the prizes of the C.I.D. Inevitably it must lead in a man of his years to a central inspectorship; eventually inclusion in the Big Four, and one knows not what beyond that.

"This is very surprising, sir,'" he said at last. "I am terribly grateful. I think there must be a lot of men entitled to this step before me—"

Colonel Walford shook his head.

"I'm glad for your sake, but I don't agree," he said. And then, briskly: "We're making considerable changes at the Yard. Bliss is coming back from America; he has been attached to the Embassy at Washington—do you know him?"

Alan Wembury shook his head. He had heard of the redoubtable Bliss, but knew little more about him than that he was a capable police officer and was cordially disliked by almost every man at the Yard.

"'R' Division will not be quite as exciting as it was a few years ago," said the commissioner with a twinkle in his eye; "and you at any rate should be grateful."

"Was it an exciting division, sir?" asked Alan, to whom Deptford was a new territory.

Colonel Walford nodded. The laughter had gone out of his eyes; he was very grave indeed when he spoke again.

"I was thinking about The Ringer—I wonder what truth there is in the report of his death? The Australian police are almost certain that the man taken out of Sydney Harbour was this extraordinary scoundrel."

Alan Wembury nodded slowly.

The Ringer!

The very name produced a little thrill that was unpleasantly like a shiver. Yet Alan Wembury was without fear; his courage, both as a soldier and a detective, was inscribed in golden letters. But there was something very sinister and deadly in the very name of The Ringer, something that conjured up a repellent spectacle. . .the cold, passionless eyes of a cobra.

Who had not heard of The Ringer? His exploits had terrified London. He had killed ruthlessly, purposelessly, if his motive were one of personal vengeance. Men who had good reason to hate and fear him, had gone to bed, hale and hearty, snapping their fingers at the menace, safe in the consciousness that their houses were surrounded by watchful policemen. In the morning they had been found stark and dead. The Ringer, like the dark angel of death, had passed and withered them in their prime.

"Though The Ringer no longer haunts your division, there is one man in Deptford I would like to warn you against," said Colonel Walford, "and he—"

"Is Maurice Meister," said Alan, and the commissioner raised his eyebrows in surprise.

"Do you know him?" he asked, astonished. "I didn't know Meister's reputation as a lawyer was so widespread."

Alan Wembury hesitated, fingering his little moustache.

"I only know him because he happens to be the Lenley's family lawyer," he said.

The commissioner shook his head with a laugh. "Now you've got me out of my depth: I don't even know the Lenleys. And yet you speak their name with a certain amount of awe. Unless," he said suddenly, "you are referring to old George Lenley of Hertford, the man who died a few months ago?"

Alan nodded.

"I used to hunt with him," mused the commissioner. "A hard-riding, hard-drinking type of old English squire. He died broke, somebody told me. Had he any children?"

"Two, sir," said Alan quietly.

"And Meister is their lawyer, eh?" The commissioner laughed shortly. "They weren't well advised to put their fortune in the hands of Maurice Meister."

He stared through the window on to the Thames embankment. The clang of tram bells came faintly through the double windows. There was a touch of spring in the air; the bare branches along the Embankment were budding greenly, and soon would be displayed all their delicate leafy splendour. A curious and ominous place, this Scotland Yard, and yet human and kindly hearts beat behind its grim exterior.

Walford was thinking, not of Meister, but of the children who were left in Meister's care.

"Meister knew The Ringer," he said unexpectedly, and Wembury's eyes opened.

"Knew The Ringer, sir?" he repeated.

Walford nodded.

"I don't know how well; I suspect too well—too well for the comfort of The Ringer if he's alive. He left his sister in Meister's charge—Gwenda Milton. Six months ago, the body of Gwenda Milton was taken from the Thames." Alan nodded as he recalled the tragedy. "She was Meister's secretary. One of these days when you've nothing better to do, go up to the Record Office—there was a great deal that didn't come out at the inquest."

13

"About Meister?"

Colonel Walford nodded.

"If The Ringer is dead, nothing matters, but if he is alive"—he shrugged his broad shoulders and looked oddly under the shaggy eyebrows at the young detective—"if he is alive, I know something that would bring him back to Deptford—and to Meister."

"What is that, sir?" asked Wembury.

Again, Walford gave his cryptic smile.

"Examine the record and you will read the oldest drama in the world—the story of a trusting woman and a vile man."

And then, dismissing The Ringer with a wave of his hand as though he were a tangible vision awaiting such a dismissal, he became suddenly the practical administrator.

"You are taking up your duties on Monday week. You might like to go down and have a look round, and get acquainted with your new division?"

Alan hesitated.

"If it is possible, sir, I should like a week's holiday," he said, and in spite of himself, his tanned face assumed a deeper red.

"A holiday? Certainly. Do you want to break the good news to the girl?" There was a good-humoured twinkle in Walford's eyes.

"No, sir." His very embarrassment seemed to deny his statement. "There is a lady I should like to tell of my promotion," he went on awkwardly. "She is, in fact—Miss Mary Lenley."

The commissioner laughed softly.

"Oh, you know the Lenleys that much, do you?" he said, and Alan's embarrassment was not decreased.

"No, sir; she has always been a very good friend of mine," he said, almost gently, as though the subject of the discussion were one of whom he could not speak in more strident tones. "You see, I started life in a cottage on the Lenley estate. My father was head gardener to Squire Lenley, and I've known the family ever since I can remember. There is nobody else in Lenley village"—he shook his head sadly—"who would expect me—I—" He hesitated, and Walford jumped in.

"Take your holiday, my boy. Go where you jolly well please! And if Miss Mary Lenley is as wise as she is beautiful—I remember her as a child—she will forget that she is a Lenley of Lenley Court and you are a Wembury of the gardener's cottage! For in these democratic days, Wembury,"—there was a quiet earnestness in his voice—"a man is what he is, not what his father was. I hope you will never be obsessed

14

by a sense of your own unworthiness. Because, if you are"—he paused, and again his eyes twinkled—"you will be a darned fool!"

Alan Wembury left the room with the uneasy conviction that the assistant commissioner knew a great deal more about the Lenleys than he had admitted.

Chapter 2

It seemed that the spring had come earlier to Lenley village than to grim old London, which seems to regret and resist the tenderness of the season, until, overwhelmed by the rush of crocuses and daffodils and yellow-hearted narcissi, it capitulates blandly in a blaze of yellow sunshine.

As he walked into the village from the railway station, Alan saw over the hedge the famous Lenley Path of Daffodils, blazing with a golden glory. Beyond the tall poplars was the roof of grey old Lenley Court.

News of his good fortune had come ahead of him. The bald-headed landlord of the Red Lion Inn came running out to intercept him, a grin of delight on his rubicund face.

"Glad to see you back, Alan," he said. "We've heard of your promotion and we're all very proud of you. You'll be Chief of the Police one of these days."

Alan smiled at the spontaneous enthusiasm. He liked this old village; it was a home of dreams. Would the great, the supreme dream, which he had never dared bring to its logical conclusion, be fulfilled?

"Are you going up to the court to see Miss Mary?" and when he answered yes, the landlord shook his head and pursed his lips. He was regret personified. "Things are very bad up there, Alan. They say there's nothing left out of the estate either for Mr. John or Miss Mary. I don't mind about Mr. John: he's a man who can make his way in the world—I wish he'd get a better way than he's found."

"What do you mean?" asked Alan quickly. The landlord seemed suddenly to remember that if he was speaking to an old friend, he was also speaking to a police officer, and he became instantly discreet.

"They say he's gone to the devil. You know how people talk, but there's something in it. Johnny never was a happy sort of fellow; he's forgotten to do anything but scowl in these days. Poverty doesn't come easy to that young man."

"Why are they at the court if they're in such a bad way? It must be an expensive place to keep up. I wonder John Lenley doesn't sell it?"

"Sell it!" scoffed the landlord. "It's mortgaged up to the last leaf on the last twig! They're staying there whilst this London lawyer settles the estate, and they're going to London next week, from what I hear."

This London lawyer! Alan frowned. That must be Maurice Meister, and he was curious to meet the man about whom so many strange rumours ran. They whispered things of Maurice Meister at Scotland Yard which it would have been libel to write, slander to say. They pointed to certain associations of his which were unjustifiable even in a criminal lawyer, whose work brought him into touch with the denizens of the underworld.

"I wish you'd book me a room, Mr. Griggs. The carrier is bringing my bag from the station. I'll go to up the court and see if I can see John Lenley."

He said "John," but his heart said "Mary." He might deceive the world, but he could not deceive his own heart.

As he walked up the broad oak-shaded drive, the evidence of poverty came out to meet him. Grass grew in the gravelled surface of the road; those fine yew hedges of the Tudor garden before which as a child he had stood in awe had been clipped by an amateur hand; the lawn before the house was ragged and unkempt. When he came in sight of the court his heart sank as he saw the signs of general neglect. The windows of the east wing were grimy—not even the closed shutters could disguise their state; two windows had been broken and the panes not replaced.

As he came nearer to the house, a figure emerged from the shadowy portico, walked quickly towards him, and then, recognising, broke into a run.

"Oh, Alan!"

In another second, he had both her hands in his and was looking down into the upturned face. He had not seen her for twelve months. He looked at her now, holding his breath. The sweet, pale beauty of her caught at his heart. He had known a child, a lovely child; he was looking into the crystal-clear eyes of radiant womanhood. The slim, shapeless figure he had known had undergone some subtle change; the lovely face had been moulded to a new loveliness.

He had a sense of dismay. The very fringe of despair obscured for the moment the joy which had filled his heart at the sight of her. If she had been beyond his reach before, the gulf, in some incomprehensible manner, had widened now.

With a sinking heart he realised the gulf between this daughter of the Lenleys and Inspector Wembury.

"Why, Alan, what a pleasant sight!" Her sad eyes were brightened with laughter. "And you're bursting with news! Poor Alan! We read it in the morning newspaper."

He laughed ruefully.

"I didn't know that my promotion was a matter of world interest," he said.

"But you're going to tell me all about it." She slipped her arm in his naturally, as she had in the days of her childhood, when the gardener's son was Mary Lenley's playmate, the shy boy who flew her kite and bowled and fielded for her when she wielded a cricket bat almost as tall as herself.

"There is little to tell but the bare news," said Alan. "I'm promoted over the heads of better men, and I don't know whether to be glad or sorry!"

He felt curiously self-conscious and gauche as they paced the untidy lawn together.

"I've had a little luck in one or two cases I've handled, but I can't help feeling that I'm a favourite with the commissioner and that I owe my promotion more to that cause than to any other."

"Rubbish!" she scoffed. "Of course, you've had your promotion on merit!"

She caught his eyes looking at the house, and instantly her expression changed.

"Poor old Lenley Court!" she said softly. "You've heard our news, Alan? We're leaving next week." She breathed a long sigh. "It doesn't bear thinking about, does it? Johnny is taking a flat in town, and Maurice has promised me some work."

Alan stared at her.

"Work?" he gasped. "You don't mean you've got to work for your living?"

She laughed at this.

"Why, of course, my dear—my dear Alan. I'm initiating myself into the mysteries of shorthand and typewriting. I'm going to be Maurice's secretary."

Meister's secretary!

The words had a familiar sound. And then in a flash he remembered another secretary, whose body had been taken from the river one foggy morning, and he recalled Colonel Walford's ominous words.

"Why, you're quite glum, Alan. Doesn't the prospect of my earning

17

a living appeal to you?" she asked, her lips twitching.

"No," he said slowly, and it was like Alan that he could not disguise his repugnance to the scheme. "Surely there is something saved from the wreck?"

She shook her head.

"Nothing—absolutely nothing! I have a very tiny income from my mother's estate, and that will keep me from starvation. And Johnny's really clever, Alan. He has made quite a lot of money lately—that's queer, isn't it? One never suspected Johnny of being a good business man, and yet he is. In a few years we shall be buying back Lenley Court."

Brave words, but they did not deceive Alan!

Chapter 3

He saw her look over his shoulder, and turned. Two men were walking towards them. Though it was a warm day in early summer, and the Royal Courts of Justice forty miles away, Mr. Meister wore the conventional garb of a successful lawyer. The long-tailed morning coat fitted his slim figure faultlessly, his black cravat with its opal pin was perfectly arranged. On his head was the glossiest of silk hats, and the yellow gloves which covered his hands were spotless. A sallow, thin-faced man with dark, fathomless eyes, there was something of the aristocrat in his manner and speech. "He looks like a duke, talks like a *don* and thinks like a devil," was not the most unflattering thing that had been said about Maurice Meister.

His companion was a tall youth, hardly out of his teens, whose black brows met at the sight of the visitor. He came slowly across the lawn, his hands thrust into his trousers pockets, his dark eyes regarding Alan with an unfriendly scowl.

"Hallo!" he said grudgingly, and then, to his companion: "You know Wembury, don't you, Maurice—he's a sergeant or something in the police."

Maurice Meister smiled slowly.

"Divisional Detective Inspector, I think," and offered his long, thin hand. "I understand you are coming into my neighbourhood to add a new terror to the lives of my unfortunate clients!"

"I hope we shall be able to reform them," said Alan good-humouredly. "That is really what we are for!"

Johnny Lenley was glowering at him. He had never liked Alan, even as a boy and now for some reason, his resentment at the presence

18

of the detective was suddenly inflamed.

"What brings you to Lenley?" he asked gruffly. "I didn't know you had any relations here?"

"I have a few friends," said Alan steadily.

"Of course, he has!" It was Mary who spoke. "He came to see me, for one, didn't you, Alan? I'm sorry we can't ask you to stay with us, but there's practically no furniture left in the house."

John Lenley's eyes snapped at this.

"It isn't necessary to advertise our poverty all over the kingdom, my dear," he said sharply. "I don't suppose Wembury is particularly interested in our misfortunes, and he'd be damned impertinent if he was!"

He saw the hurt look on his sister's face, and his unreasonable annoyance with the visitor was increased. It was Maurice Meister who poured oil upon the troubled water.

"The misfortunes of Lenley Court are public property, my dear Johnny," he said blandly. "Don't be so stupidly touchy! I, for one, am very glad to have the opportunity of meeting a police officer of such fame as Inspector Alan Wembury. You will find your division rather a dull spot just now, Mr. Wembury. We have none of the excitement which prevailed when I first moved to Deptford from Lincoln's Inn Fields."

Alan nodded.

"You mean, you're not bothered with The Ringer?" he said.

It was a perfectly innocent remark, and he was quite unprepared for the change which came to Meister's face. He blinked quickly as though he had been confronted with a brilliant light. The loose mouth became in an instant a straight, hard line. If there was not fear in those inscrutable eyes of his, Alan Wembury was very wide of the mark.

"The Ringer!" His voice was husky. "Ancient history, eh? Poor beggar, he's dead!"

He said this with almost startling emphasis. It seemed to Alan that the man was trying to persuade himself that this notorious criminal had passed beyond the sphere of human activity.

"Dead. . . .drowned in Australia."

The girl was looking at him wonderingly.

"Who is The Ringer?" she asked.

"Nobody you would know anything about, or ought to know," he said, almost brusquely. And then, with a little laugh: "We're all talking 'shop,' and criminal justice is the worst kind of 'shop' for a young lady's ears."

"I wish to heaven you'd find something else to talk about," growled John Lenley fretfully, and was turning away when Maurice Meister asked: "You are at present in a West End division, aren't you, Wembury? What was your last case? I don't seem to remember seeing your name in the newspapers."

Alan made a little grimace.

"We never advertise our failures," he said. "My last job was to inquire into some pearls that were stolen from Lady Darnleigh's house in Park Lane on the night of her big Ambassadors' party."

He was looking at Mary as he spoke. Her face was a magnet which lured and held his gaze. He did not see John Lenley's hand go to his mouth to check the involuntary exclamation, or the quick warning glance which Meister shot at the young man. There was a little pause.

"Lady Darnleigh?" drawled Maurice. "Oh, yes, I seem to remember. . .as a matter of fact, weren't you at her dance that night, Johnny?"

He looked at the other and Johnny shook his shoulder impatiently.

"Of course, I was. . .I didn't know anything about the robbery till afterwards. Haven't you anything else to discuss, you people, than crimes and robberies and murders?"

And, turning on his heel, he slouched across the lawn.

Mary looked after him with trouble in her face.

"I wonder what makes Johnny so cross in these days—do you know, Maurice?"

Maurice Meister examined the cigarette that burnt in the amber tube between his fingers. "Johnny is young; and, my dear, you mustn't forget that he has had a very trying time."

"So have I," she said quietly. "You don't imagine that it is nothing to me that I am leaving Lenley Court?" Her voice quivered for a moment, but with a resolution that Alan could both understand and appreciate, she was instantly smiling. "I'm being very pathetic; I shall be weeping on Alan's shoulder if I am not careful. Come along, Alan, and see what is left of the rosery—perhaps when you have seen its present condition, we will weep together!"

Chapter 4

Johnny Lenley looked after them until they had disappeared from view. His face was pale with anger, his lips trembled.

"What brings that swine here?" he demanded.

Maurice Meister, who had followed across the lawn, looked at him

20

oddly.

"My dear Johnny, you're very young and very crude. You have the education of a gentleman and yet you behave like a boor!"

Johnny turned on him in a fury.

"What do you expect me to do—shake him cordially by the hand and bid him welcome to Lenley Court? The fellow's risen from the gutter. His father was our gardener—"

Maurice Meister interrupted him with a chuckle of malicious enjoyment.

"What a snob you are, Johnny! The snobbery wouldn't matter," he went on in a more serious tone, "if you would learn to conceal your feelings."

"I say what I think," said Johnny shortly.

"So does a dog when you tread on his tail," replied Maurice. "You fool!" he snarled with unexpected malignity. "You half-wit! At the mention of the Darnleigh pearls you almost betrayed yourself. Did you realise to whom you were talking, who was probably watching you? The shrewdest detective in the C.I.D.! The man who caught Hersey, who hanged Gostein, who broke up the Flack Gang."

"He didn't notice anything," said the other sulkily, and then, to turn the conversation to his advantage: "You had a letter this morning, was there anything about the pearls in it—are they sold?"

The anger faded from the lawyer's face; again, he was his suave self.

"Do you imagine, my dear lad, that one can sell fifteen thousand pounds' worth of pearls in a week? What do you suppose is the procedure—that one puts them up at Christie's?"

Johnny Lenley's lips tightened. For a while he was silent. When he spoke, his voice had lost some of its querulous quality.

"It was queer that Wembury was on the case—apparently they've given up hope. Of course, old Lady Darnleigh has no suspicion—"

"Don't be too sure of that," warned Meister. "Every guest at No. 304, Park Lane, on that night is suspect. You, more than any, because everybody knows you're broke. Moreover, one of the footmen saw you going up the main stairs just before you left."

"I told him I was going to get my coat," said Johnny Lenley quickly, and a troubled look came to his face. "Why did you mention that I was there to Wembury?"

Maurice laughed.

"Because he knew; I was watching him as I spoke. There was the faintest glint in his eyes that told me. I'll set your mind at ease; the

21

person at present under suspicion is her unfortunate butler. Don't imagine that the case has blown over—it hasn't. Anyway, the police are too active for the moment for us to dream of disposing of the pearls, and we shall have to wait a favourable opportunity when they can be placed in Antwerp."

He threw away the end of the thin cigarette, took a gold cigarette-case from his waistcoat pocket, selected another with infinite care and lit it, Johnny watching him enviously.

"You're a cool devil. Do you realise that if the truth came out about those pearls it would mean penal servitude for you, Maurice?"

Maurice sent a ring of smoke into the air.

"I certainly realise it would mean penal servitude for you, my young friend. I fancy that it would be rather difficult to implicate me. If you choose for your amusement to be a robber baron, or was it a Duke of Padua?—I forget the historical precedent—and engage yourself in these Rafflesish adventures, that is your funeral entirely. Because I knew your father and I've known you since you were a child, I take a little risk. Perhaps the adventure of it appeals to me—"

"Rot!" said Johnny Lenley brutally. "You've been a crook ever since you were able to walk. You know every thief in London and you've 'fenced'—"

"Don't use that word!" Maurice Meister's deep voice grew suddenly sharp. "As I told you just now, you are crude. Did I instigate this robbery of Lady Darnleigh's pearls? Did I put it into your head that thieving was more profitable than working, and that with your education and entry to the best houses you had opportunities which were denied to a meaner—thief?"

This word was as irritating to Johnny Lenley as "fence" had been to the lawyer.

"Anyway, we are in, the same boat," he said. "You couldn't give me away without ruining yourself. I don't say you instigated anything, but you've been jolly helpful, Maurice. Someday I'll make you a rich man."

The dark, sloe-like eyes turned slowly in his direction. At any other time, this patronage of the younger man would have infuriated Meister; now he was only piqued.

"My young friend," he said precisely, "you are a little over-confident. Robbery with or without violence is not so simple a matter as you imagine. You think you're clever—"

"I'm a little bit smarter than Wembury," said Johnny complacently.

22

Maurice Meister concealed a smile.

It was not to the rosery that Mary led her visitor but to the sunken garden, with its crazy paving and battered statuary. There was a cracked marble bench overlooking a still pool where water-lilies grew, and she allowed him to dust a place for her before she sat down.

"Alan, I'm going to tell you something. I'm talking to Alan Wembury, not to Inspector Wembury," she warned him, and he showed his astonishment.

"Why, of course. . ." He stopped; he had been on the point of calling her by name. "I've never had the courage to call you Mary, but I feel—old enough!"

This claim of age was a cowardly expedient, he told himself, but at least it was successful. There was real pleasure in her voice when she replied: "I'm glad you do. 'Miss Mary' would sound horribly unreal. In you it would sound almost unfriendly."

"What is the trouble?" he asked, as he sat down by her side.

She hesitated only a second.

"Johnny," she said. "He talks so oddly about things. It's a terrible thing to say, Alan, but it almost seems as though he's forgotten the distinction between right and wrong. Sometimes I think he only says these things in a spirit of perversity. At other times I feel that he means them. He talks harshly about poor, dear father, too. I find that difficult to forgive. Poor daddy was very careless and extravagant, but he was a good father to Johnny—and to me," she said, her voice breaking.

"What do you mean when you say Johnny talks oddly?"

She shook her head.

"It isn't only that: he has such strange friends. We had a man here last week—I only saw him, I did not speak to him—named Hackitt. Do you know him?"

"Hackitt? Sam Hackitt?" said Wembury in surprise. "Good Lord, yes! Sam and I are old acquaintances!"

"What is he?" she asked.

"He's a burglar," was the calm reply. "Probably Johnny was interested in the man and had him down—"

She shook her head.

"No, it wasn't for that." She bit her lip. "Johnny told me a lie; he said that this man was an artisan who was going to Australia. You're sure this is your Sam Hackitt?"

Alan gave a very vivid, if brief, description of the little thief.

"That is he," she nodded. "And, of course, I know he was an unpleasant sort of man. Alan, you don't think that Johnny is bad, do you?"

He had never thought of Johnny as a possible subject for police observation. "Of course not!"

"But these peculiar friends of his—?"

It was an opportunity not to be passed.

"I'm afraid, Mary, you're going to meet a lot of people like Hackitt, and worse than Hackitt, who isn't a bad soul if he could keep his fingers to himself."

"Why?" she asked in amazement.

"You think of becoming Meister's secretary—Mary, I wish you wouldn't."

She drew away a little, the better to observe him.

"Why on earth, Alan . . .? Of course, I understand what you mean. Maurice has a large number of clients, and I'm pretty sure to see them, but they won't corrupt my young mind!"

"I'm not afraid of his clients," said Alan quietly. "I'm afraid of Maurice Meister."

She stared at him as though he were suddenly bereft of his senses.

"Afraid of Maurice?" She could hardly believe her ears. "Why, Maurice is the dearest thing! He has been kindness itself to Johnny and me, and we've known him all our lives."

"I've known you all your life, too, Mary," said Alan gently, but she interrupted him.

"But, tell me why?" she persisted. "What do you know against Maurice?"

Here, confronted with the concrete question, he lost ground.

"I know nothing about turn," he admitted frankly. "I only know that Scotland Yard doesn't like him."

She laughed a low, amused laugh.

"Because he manages to keep these poor, wretched criminals out of prison! It's professional jealousy! Oh, Alan," she bantered him, "I didn't believe it of you!"

No good purpose could be served by repeating his warning. There was one gleam of comfort in the situation; if she was to work for Meister she would be living in his division. He told her this.

"It will be rather dreadful, won't it, after Lenley Court?" She made a little face at the thought. "It will mean that for a year or two I shall have no parties, no dances—Alan, I shall die an old maid!"

"I doubt that," he smiled, "but the chances of meeting eligible young men in Deptford are slightly remote," and they laughed together.

Chapter 5

Maurice Meister stood at the ragged end of a yew hedge and watched them. Strange, he mused, that never before had he realised the beauty of Mary Lenley. It needed, he told himself, the visible worship of this policeman to stimulate his interest in the girl, whom in a moment of impulse, which later he regretted, he had promised to employ. A bud, opening into glorious flower. Unobserved, he watched her; the contour of her cheek, the poise of her dark head, the supple line of her figure as she turned to rally Alan Wembury. Mr. Meister licked his dry lips. Queer that he had never thought that way about Mary Lenley. And yet. . .

He liked fair women. Gwenda Milton was fair, with a shingled, golden head. A stupid girl, who had become rather a bore. And from a bore she had developed into a sordid tragedy. Maurice shuddered as he remembered that grey day in the coroner's court when he had stood on the witness stand and had lied and lied and lied.

Turning her head, Mary saw him and beckoned him, and he went slowly towards them.

"Where is Johnny?" she asked.

"Johnny at this moment is sulking. Don't ask me why, because I don't know."

What a wonderful skin she had—flawless, unblemished! And the dark grey eyes, with their long lashes, how adorable! And he had known her all her life and been living under the same roof for a week, and had not observed her values before!

"Am I interrupting a confidential talk?" he asked.

She shook her head, but she did not wholly convince him. He wondered what these two had been speaking about, head to head. Had she told Alan Wembury that she was coming to Deptford? She would sooner or later, and it might be profitable to get in first with the information.

"You know, Miss Lenley is honouring me by becoming my secretary?"

"So, I've heard," said Alan, and met the lawyer's eyes. "I have told Miss Lenley"—he spoke deliberately; every word had its significance—"that she will be living in my division. . .under my paternal eye, as it were."

There was a warning and a threat there. Meister was too shrewd a man to overlook either. Alan Wembury had constituted himself the girl's guardian. That would have been rather amusing in other circumstances. Even as recently as an hour ago he would have regarded Alan Wembury's chaperonage as a great joke. But now. . .

He looked at Mary and his pulse was racing.

"How interesting!" his voice was a little harsh and he cleared his throat. "How terribly interesting! And is that duty part of the police code?"

There was the faintest sneer in his voice which Alan did not miss.

"The duty of a policeman," he said quietly, "is pretty well covered by the inscription over the door of the Old Bailey."

"And what is that?" asked Meister. "I have not troubled to read it."

"'Protect the children of the poor and punish the wrongdoer,'" said Alan Wembury sternly.

"A noble sentiment!" said Maurice. And then: "I think that is for me."

He walked quickly towards a telegraph messenger who had appeared at the end of the garden.

"Is Maurice annoyed with you?" asked Mary.

Alan laughed.

"Everybody gets annoyed with me sooner or later. I'm afraid my society manners are deplorable."

She patted the hand that lay beside hers on the stone bench.

"Alan," she said, half whimsically, half seriously, "I don't think I shall ever be annoyed with you. You are the nicest man I know."

For a second their hands met in a long, warm clasp, and then she saw Maurice walking back with the unopened telegram in his hand.

"For you," he said jovially. "What a thing it is to be so important that you can't leave the office for five minutes before they wire for you—what terrible deed has been committed in London in your absence?"

Alan took the wire with a frown. "For me?" He was expecting no telegram. He had very few personal friends, and it was unlikely that his holiday would be curtailed from headquarters.

He tore open the envelope and took out the telegram. It was closely written on two pages. He read:

Very urgent stop return at once and report to Scotland Yard stop be prepared to take over your division tomorrow morning stop Australian police report Ringer left Sydney four months ago and is believed to be in London at this moment message ends.

The wire was signed "Walford."

Alan looked from the telegram to the smiling old garden, from the garden to the girl, her anxious face upturned to his.

"Is anything wrong?" she asked.

He shook his head slowly.

The Ringer was in England!

His nerves grew taut at the realisation. Henry Arthur Milton, ruthless slayer of his enemies—cunning, desperate, fearless.

Alan Wembury's mind went back to Scotland Yard and the commissioner's office. Gwenda Milton—dead, drowned, a suicide!

Had Maurice Meister played a part in the creation of that despair which had sent her young soul unbidden to the judgment of God? Woe to Maurice Meister if this were true!

Chapter 6

The Ringer was in London!

Alan Wembury felt a cold thrill each time the thought recurred on his journey to London.

It was the thrill that comes to the hunter, at the first hint of the man-slaying tiger he will presently glimpse.

Well named was The Ringer, who rang the changes on himself so frequently that police headquarters had never been able to circulate a description of the man. A master of disguise, a ruthless enemy who had slain without mercy the men who had earned his hatred.

For himself, Wembury had neither fear nor hatred of the man he was to bring down; only a cold emotionless understanding of the danger of his task. One thing was certain—The Ringer would go to the place where a hundred bolts and hiding places were ready to receive him.

To Deptford. . .?

Alan Wembury gave a little gasp of dismay. Mary Lenley was also going to Deptford—to Meister's house, and The Ringer could only have returned to England with one object, the destruction of Maurice Meister. Danger to Meister would inevitably mean danger to Mary Lenley. This knowledge took some of the sunlight of the spring sky and made the grim facade of Scotland Yard just a little more sinister.

Though all the murderers in the world were at large, Scotland Yard preserved its equanimity. He came to Colonel Walford's room to find the assistant commissioner immersed in the particulars of a minor robbery.

"You got my wire?" said Walford, looking up as Alan came in. "I'm awfully sorry to interrupt your holiday. I want you to go down to Deptford to take charge immediately und get acquainted with your new division."

"The Ringer is back, sir?"

Watford nodded. "Why he came back, where he is, I don't know— in fact, there is no direct information about him and we are merely surmising that he has returned."

"But I thought—"

Walford took a long cablegram from the basket on his table. "The Ringer has a wife. Few people know that," he said. "He married her a year or two ago in Canada. After his disappearance, she left this country and was traced to Australia. That could only mean one thing. The Ringer was in Australia. She has now left Australia just as quickly as she left this country; she arrives in England tomorrow morning."

Alan nodded slowly.

"I see. That means that The Ringer is either in England or is making for this country."

"You have not told anybody?" the commissioner asked. "I'd forgotten to warn you about that. Meister was at Lenley Court, you say? You didn't tell him?"

"No, sir," said Alan, his lips twitching. "I thought, coming up in the train, that it was rather a pity I couldn't—I would like to have seen the effect upon him!"

Alan could understand how the news of The Ringer's return would flutter the Whitehall dovecotes, but he was unprepared for the extraordinarily serious view which Colonel Walford took of the position.

"I'll tell you frankly, Wembury, that I would much rather be occupying a place on the pension list than this chair at Scotland Yard when that news is published."

Alan looked at him in astonishment; the commissioner was in deadly earnest.

"The Ringer is London's favourite bogy," Colonel Walford said, "and the very suggestion that he has returned to England will be quite sufficient to send all the newspaper hounds of Fleet Street on my track. Never forget, Wembury, he is a killer, and he has neither fear nor appreciation of danger. He has caused more bolts to be shot than any other criminal on our list! The news that this man is at large and in London will arouse such a breeze that even I would not weather it!"

"You think he'll be beyond me?" smiled Alan.

"No," said Walford surprisingly, "I have great hopes of you—and great hopes of Dr. Lomond. By the way, have you met Dr. Lomond?"

Alan looked at him in surprise. "No, sir, who is he?"

Colonel Walford reached for a book that lay on his table, "He is one of the few amateur detectives who have impressed me," he said. "Fourteen years ago, he wrote the only book on the subject of the criminal that is worth studying. He has been in India and Tibet for years and I think the Under-Secretary was fortunate to persuade him to fill the appointment."

"What appointment, sir?"

"Police surgeon of 'R' Division—in fact, your new division," said Walford. "You are both making acquaintance with Deptford at the same time."

Alan Wembury turned the closely-set pages of the book. "He is a pretty big man to take a fiddling job like this," he said and Walford laughed.

"He has spent his life doing fiddling jobs—would you like to meet him? He is with the chief constable at the moment."

He pressed a bell and gave instructions to the messenger who came. "Lomond is rather a character—terribly Scottish, a little cynical and more than a little pawky."

"Will he help us to catch The Ringer?" smiled Alan and he was astonished to see the commissioner nod.

"I have that feeling," he said.

The door opened at that moment and a tall bent figure shuffled in. Alan put his age at something over fifty. His hair was grey, a little moustache drooped over his mouth and the pair of twinkling blue eyes that met Alan's were dancing with good-humour. His homespun suit was badly cut, his high-crowned felt hat belonged to the seventies.

"I want you to meet Inspector Wembury who will be in charge of your division," said Walford and Wembury's hand was crushed in a powerful grip.

"Have ye any interesting specimens in Deptford, inspector? I'd like fine to measure a few heids."

Alan's smile broadened.

"I'm as ignorant of Deptford as you—I haven't been there since before the war," he said.

The doctor scratched his chin, his keen eyes fixed on the younger man, "I'm thinkin' they'll no' be as interesting as the Lolos. Man, there's a wonderful race, wi' braci-cephalic heads, an' a queer develop-

29

ment of the right parietal. . ."

He spoke quickly, enthusiastically when he was on his favourite subject.

Alan seized an opportunity when the doctor was expounding a view on the origin of some mysterious Tibetan tribe to steal quietly from the room. He was not in the mood for anthropology.

An hour later as he was leaving Scotland Yard, he met Walford as he was coming out of his room and walked with him to the Embankment, "Yes—I got rid of the doctor," chuckled the colonel, "he's too clever to be a bore, but he made my head ache!" Then suddenly: "You're handing over that pearl case to Burton—the Darnleigh pearls I mean. You have no further clue?"

"No, sir," said Alan. He had almost forgotten that there was such a case in his hands.

The commissioner was frowning. "I was thinking, after you left, what a queer coincidence it was that you were going to Lenley Court. Young Lenley was apparently at Lady Darnleigh's house on the night of the robbery," and then, seeing the look that came to his subordinate's face, he went on quickly: "I'm not suggesting that he knew anything about it, of course, but it was a coincidence. I wish we could clear up that little mystery. Lady Darnleigh has too many friends in Whitehall for my liking and I get a letter from the Home Secretary every other day asking for the latest news."

Alan Wembury went on his way with an uneasy mind. He had known that Johnny was at the house on the night of the robbery but he had never associated "the Squire's son" with the mysterious disappearance of Lady Darnleigh's pearls. There was no reason why he should, he told himself stoutly. As he walked across Westminster Bridge he went over again and again that all too brief interview he had had with Mary.

How beautiful she was! And how unapproachable! He tried to think of her only, but against his will a dark shadow crept across the rosy splendour of dreams: Johnny Lenley.

Why on earth should he, and yet—the Lenleys were ruined. . . Mary was worried about the kind of company that Johnny was keeping. There was something else she had said which belonged to the category of unpleasant things. Oh, yes, Johnny had been "making money" Mary told him a little proudly. How?

"Rot!" said Alan to himself as an ugly thought obtruded upon his mind. "Rubbish!"

The idea was too absurd for a sane man to entertain. The next morning, he handed over all the documents in the case to Inspector Burton and walked out of Scotland Yard with almost a feeling of relief. It was as though he had shaken himself clear of the grisly shadow which was obscuring the brightness of the day.

The week which followed was a very busy one for Alan Wembury. He had only a slight acquaintance with Deptford and its notables. The grey-haired Scots surgeon he saw for a minute or two, a shrewd old man with laughing eyes and a fund of dry Scottish humour, but both men were too busy in their new jobs to discuss The Ringer.

Mary did not write, as he had expected she would, and he was not aware that she was in his district until one day, walking down the Lewisham High Road, somebody waved to him from an open taxicab and turning, he saw it was the girl. He asked one of his subordinates to find out where she and Johnny were staying and with no difficulty located them at a modern block of flats near Malpas Road, a building occupied by the superior artisan class. What a tragic contrast to the spacious glories of Lenley Court! Only his innate sense of delicacy prevented his calling upon her, and for this abstention at least one person was glad.

Chapter 7

"I saw your copper this morning," said Johnny flippantly. He had gone back to lunch and was in a more amiable mood than Mary remembered having seen him recently.

She looked at him open-eyed.

"My 'copper'?" she repeated.

"Wembury," translated Johnny. "We call these fellows 'busies' and I've never seen a busier man," he chuckled. "I see you're going to ask what 'busy' means. It is a thieves' word for detective."

He saw a change come to her face.

"'We' call them?" she repeated. "You mean 'they' call them, Johnny."

He was amused as he sat down at the table.

"What a little purist you're becoming, Mary," he said. "We, or they, does it matter? We're all thieves at heart, the merchant in his Rolls and the workman on the tram, thieves every one of them!"

Very wisely she did not contest the extravagant generalisation.

"Where did you see Alan?"

"Why the devil do you call him by his Christian name?" snapped

Johnny. "The man is a policeman, you go on as though he were a social equal."

Mary smiled at this as she cut a round of bread into four parts and put them on the bread plate.

"The man who lives on the other side of the landing is a plumber, and the people above us live on the earnings of a railway guard. Six of them, Johnny—four of them girls."

He twisted irritably in his chair. "That's begging the question. We're only here as a temporary expedient. You don't suppose I'm going to be content to live in this poky hole all my life? One of these days I'll buy back Lenley Court."

"On what, Johnny?" she asked quietly.

"On the money I make," he said and went back to his *bête noire*. "Anyway, Wembury isn't the sort of fellow I want you to know," he said. "I was talking to Maurice about him this morning, and Maurice agrees that it is an acquaintance we ought to drop."

"Really?" Mary's voice was cold. "And Maurice thinks so too—how funny!"

He glanced at her suspiciously.

"I don't see anything amusing about it," he grumbled. "Obviously, we can't know—"

She was standing facing him on the other side of the table, her hands resting on its polished surface.

"I have decided to go on knowing Alan Wembury," she said steadily. "I'm sorry if Maurice doesn't approve, or if you think I'm being very common. But I like Alan—"

"I used to like my valet, but I got rid of him," broke in Johnny irritably.

She shook her head.

"Alan Wembury isn't your valet. You may think my taste is degraded, but Alan is my idea of a gentleman," she said quietly, "and one cannot know too many gentlemen."

He was about to say something sharp, but checked himself, and the matter had dropped for the moment.

The next day Mary Lenley was to start her new life. The thought left her a little breathless. When Maurice had first made the suggestion that she should act as his secretary the idea had thrilled her, but as the time approached, she had grown more and more apprehensive. The project was one filled with vague unpleasant possibilities and she could not understand why this once pleasing prospect should now have such an effect upon her.

Johnny was not up when she was ready to depart in the morning, and only came yawning out of his bedroom when she called him.

"So, you're going to be one of the working classes," he said almost jovially. "It will be rather amusing. I wouldn't let you go at all, only—"

"Only?" she waited.

Johnny's willingness that she should accept employment in Maurice's office had been a source of wonder to her, knowing his curious nature.

"I shall be about, keeping an eye on you," he said good-humouredly.

A few minutes later she was hurrying down crooked Tanners Hill toward a neighbourhood the squalor of which appalled her. Flanders Lane has few exact parallels in point of grime and ugliness, but Mr. Meister's house was most unexpectedly different from all the rest.

It stood back from the street, surrounded by a high wall which was pierced with one black door which gave access to a small courtyard, behind which was the miniature Georgian mansion where the lawyer not only lived but had his office.

An old woman led her up the worn stairs, opened a heavy ornamental door and ushered her into an apartment which she was to know very well indeed. A big panelled room with Adam decorations, it had been once the drawing-room of a prosperous City merchant in those days when great gentlemen lived in the houses where now the poor and the criminal herded like rats.

There was an air of shabbiness about the place and yet it was cheerful enough. The walls were hung about with pictures which she had no difficulty in recognising as the work of great masters. But the article of furniture which interested her most was a big grand piano which stood in an alcove. She looked in wonder at this and then turned to the old woman.

"Does Mr. Meister play this?"

"Him?" said the old lady with a cackle of laughter. "I should say he does!"

From this chamber led a little doorless ante-room which evidently was used as an office, for there were deed boxes piled up against one wall and a small desk on which stood a covered typewriter.

She had hardly taken her survey when the door opened and Maurice Meister came quickly in, alert and smiling. He strode toward her and took both her hands in his.

"My dear Mary," he said, "this is delightful!"

His enthusiasm amused her.

"This isn't a social call, Maurice," she said. "I have come to work!"

She drew her hands free of his. Had they always been on these affectionate terms, she wondered. She was puzzled and uneasy. She tried to reconstruct from her memory the exact relationship that Maurice Meister had stood to the family. He had known her since she was a child. It was stupid of her to resent this subtle tenderness of his.

"My dear Mary, there's work enough to do—title deeds, evidence," he looked vaguely round as though seeking some stimulant to his imagination.

And all the time he looked he was wondering what on earth he could find to keep her occupied.

"Can you type?" he asked.

He expected a negative and was amazed when she nodded.

"I had a typewriter when I was twelve," she smiled. "Daddy gave it to me to amuse myself with."

Here was relief from a momentary embarrassment. Maurice had never wished or expected that his offer to employ the girl should be taken seriously—never until he had seen her at Lenley Court and realised that the gawky child he had known had developed so wonderfully.

"I will give you an affidavit to copy," he said, searching feverishly amongst the papers on his desk. It was a long time before he came upon a document sufficiently innocuous for her to read. For Maurice Meister's clientele was a peculiar one, and he, who through his life had made it a practice not to let his right hand know what his left hand did, found a difficulty in bringing himself to the task of handing over so much of his dubious correspondence for her inspection. Not until he had read the paper through word by word did he give it to her.

"Well, Mary, what do you think of it all?" he demanded, "and do, please, sit down, my dear!"

"Think of it all? This place?" she asked, and then, "You live in a dreadful neighbourhood, Maurice."

"I didn't make the neighbourhood. I found it as it is," he answered with a laugh. "Are you going to be very happy here, Mary?"

She nodded. "I think so. It is so nice working for somebody one has known for so long—and Johnny will be about. He told me I should see a lot of him."

Only for a second did the heavy eyelids droop. "Oh," said Maurice Meister, looking past her. "He said you'd see a lot of him, eh? In business hours, by any chance?"

She did not detect the sarcasm in his tone.

"I don't know what are your business hours, but it is rather nice, isn't it, having Johnny?" she asked. "It really doesn't matter working for you because you're so kind, and you've known me such a long time, but it would be rather horrid if a girl was working for somebody she didn't know, and had no brother waiting on the doorstep to see her home."

He had not taken his eyes from her. She was more beautiful even than he had thought. Hers was the type of dainty loveliness which so completely appealed to him. Darker than Gwenda Milton, but finer. There was a soul and a mind behind those eyes others; a latent passion as yet unmoved; a dormant fire yet to be kindled. He felt her grow uncomfortable under the intensity of his gaze, and quick to sense this, he was quicker to dispel the mist of suspicion which might soon gather into a cloud.

"I had better show you the house," he said briskly, and led her through the ancient building.

Before one door on the upper floor he hesitated and finally, with an effort, slipped the key in the lock and threw open the door.

Looking past him, Mary saw a room such as she had not imagined would be found in this rather shabby old house. In spite of the dust which covered everything it was a beautiful apartment, furnished with a luxury that amazed her. It seemed to be a bed and sitting-room, divided by heavy velvet curtains which were now drawn. A thick carpet covered the floor, the few pictures that the room contained had evidently been carefully chosen. Old French furniture, silver light brackets on the walls, every fuse and every fitting spoke of lavish expenditure.

"What a lovely room!" she exclaimed when she had I recovered her breath.

"Yes. . .lovely." He stared gloomily into the nest which had once known Gwenda Milton, in the days before tragedy had come to her. "Better than Malpas Mansions, Mary, eh?" The frown had vanished from his face; he was his old smiling self. "A little cleaning, a little dusting, and there is a room for a princess—in fact, my dear, I shall put it entirely at your disposal."

"My disposal!" she stared at him. "How absurd, Maurice! I am living with Johnny and I couldn't possibly stay here, ever."

He shrugged.

"Johnny? Yes. But you may be detained one night—or Johnny may be away. I shouldn't like to think you were alone in that wretched flat."

He closed and locked the door and followed her down the stairs.

"However, that is a matter for you entirely," he said lightly. "There is the room if you ever need it."

She made no answer to this, for her mind was busy with speculation. The room had been lived in, she was sure of that. A woman had lived there—it was no man's room. Mary felt a little uneasy. Of Maurice Meister and his private life, she knew nothing. She remembered vaguely that Johnny had hinted of some affair that Meister had had, but she was not curious.

Gwenda Milton!

She remembered the name with a start. Gwenda Milton, the sister of a criminal. She shivered as her mind strayed back to that gorgeous little suite, peopled with the ghost of a dead love, and she had the illusion that a white face, tense with agony, was peering at her as she sat at the typewriter. She looked round with a shudder, but the room was empty and from somewhere near at hand she heard the sound of a man humming a popular tune.

Maurice Meister did not believe in ghosts.

Chapter 8

On the afternoon of the day that Mary Lenley went to Meister's house the *Olympic* was warped into dock at Southampton. The two Scotland Yard men who had accompanied the ship from Cherbourg, and who had made a very careful scrutiny of the passengers, were the first to land and took up their station at the foot of the gangway. They had a long time to wait whilst the passport examinations were taking place, but soon the passengers began to straggle down to the quay.

Presently one of the detectives saw a face which he had not seen on the ship. A man of middle height, rather slight, with a tiny pointed beard and a black moustache appeared at the ship's side and came slowly down.

The two detectives exchanged glances and as the passenger reached the quay one of them stepped to his side and said: "Excuse me, sir, I did not see you on the ship."

For a second the bearded man surveyed the other coldly. "Are you making me responsible for your blindness?" he asked.

They were looking for a bank robber who had crossed from New York, and they were taking no chances. "May I see your passport?"

The bearded passenger hesitated, then slipping his hand into his inside pocket pulled out, not a passport but a leather note-case. From this he extracted a card. The detective took it and read:

CENTRAL INSPECTOR BLISS.

C.I.D. SCOTLAND YARD. ATTACHED WASHINGTON EMBASSY.

"I beg your pardon, sir."

The detective pushed the card back into the other's hand and his attitude changed.

"I didn't recognise you, Mr. Bliss. You hadn't grown a beard when you left the Yard."

"Who are you looking for?" he asked harshly.

The second detective gave a brief explanation.

"He's not on the ship, I can tell you that," said Bliss, and with a nod turned away.

He did not carry his bag into the Customs, but depositing it at his feet, he stood with his back to the wall of the Custom House and watched the passengers disembark. Presently he saw the girl for whom he had been looking.

Slim, svelte, immensely capable, entirely and utterly fearless—this was the first impression Inspector Bliss had received. He never had reason to revise his verdict. Her olive skin was faultless, the dark eyes under delicately pencilled eyebrows were insolent, knowledgeable. Here was a girl not to be tampered with, not to be fooled; an exquisite product of modernity. Expensively and a little over-dressed, perhaps. One white hand glittered with diamonds. Two large stones flashed on the lobes of her pink ears. As she brushed past him there came to the sensitive nostrils of Mr. Bliss the elusive fragrance of a perfume that was strange to him.

She had come on board at Cherbourg, and it was, he thought, a remarkable coincidence that they should have travelled to England on the same boat, and that she had not recognised him. Following her into the Custom House, he watched her thread her way through piles of luggage under the indicator M. His own customs examination was quickly finished. He handed his bag to a porter and told him to find a seat in the waiting train, and then he strolled toward where the girl, now hidden in the little crowd of passengers, was pointing out her baggage to the customs officer.

As though she were aware of his scrutiny she looked over her shoulder twice, and on the second occasion their eyes met, and he saw a look of wonder—or was it apprehension?—come into her face.

When her head was turned again, he approached nearer, so near that looking round, she almost stared into his face, and gasped.

"Mrs. Milton, I believe?" said Bliss.

Again, that look. It was fear, beyond doubt.

"Sure! That's my name," she drawled. She had the soft cultured accent of one who had been raised in the Southern States. "But you certainly have the advantage of me."

"My name is Bliss. Central Inspector Bliss of Scotland Yard," he said.

Apparently, the name had no significance, but as he revealed his calling, he saw the colour leave her cheeks, to flow back again instantly.

"Isn't that interesting?" she said, "and what can I do for—Central Inspector Bliss of Scotland Yard?"

Every word was like a pistol shot. There was no doubt about her antagonism.

"I should like to see your passport."

Without a word she took it from a little hand-bag and handed it to him. He turned the leaves deftly and examined the embarkation stamps.

"You've been in England quite recently?"

"Sure! I have," she said with a smile. "I was here last week. I had to go to Paris for something. From there I made the trip from Cherbourg—I was just homesick to hear Americans talking."

She was looking hard at him, puzzled rather than frightened.

"Bliss?" she said thoughtfully, "I can't place you. Yet, I've got an idea I've met you somewhere."

He was still examining the embarkation marks.

"Sydney, Genoa, Domodossola—you're a bit of a traveller, Mrs. Milton, but you don't move quite so fast as your husband."

A slow smile dawned on the beautiful face.

"I'm too busy to tell you the story of my life, or give you a travelogue," she said, "but maybe you want to see me about something more important?"

Bliss shook his head. In his sour way he was rather amused.

"No," he said, "I have no business with you, but I hope one day to meet your husband."

Her eyes narrowed.

"Do you reckon on getting to heaven too?" she asked sardonically. "I thought you knew Arthur was dead?"

38

His white teeth appeared under his bearded lips for a second. "Heaven is not the place I should go to meet him," he said.

He handed back her passport and turning on his heel walked away.

She followed him with her eyes until he was out of sight, and then with a quick little sigh turned to speak to the customs officer. Bliss! The ports were being watched.

Had The Ringer reached England? She went cold at the thought. For Cora Ann Milton loved this desperate man who killed for the love of the killing, and who was now an Ishmael and a wanderer on the face of the earth with the hands of all men against him and a hundred police packs hot on his trail.

As she walked along the platform, she examined each carriage with a careless eye. After a while she found the man she sought. Bliss sat in the corner of the carriage, apparently immersed in a morning newspaper.

"Bliss!" she said to herself. "Bliss!"

Where had she seen his face before? Why did the sight of this dour looking man fill her soul with terror? Cora Ann Milton's journey to London was a troubled one.

Chapter 9

When Johnny Lenley called at Meister's house that afternoon, the sight of his sister hard at work with her typewriter was something of a shock to him. It was as if he recognised for the first time the state of poverty into which the Lenleys had fallen.

She was alone in the room when he came and smiled up at him from a mass of correspondence.

"Where's Maurice?" he asked, and she indicated the little room where Meister had his more important and confidential interviews which the peculiar nature of his clientele demanded.

"That's a rotten job, isn't it?"

He hoped she would say "no" and was relieved when she laughed at the question.

"It is really very interesting," she said, "and please don't scowl, Johnny, this is less boring than anything I have done for years!"

He looked at her for a moment in silence; he hated to see her thus —a servant. Setting his teeth, he crossed the room and knocked at the door of Meister's private bureau.

"Who is there?" asked a voice.

Johnny tried to turn the handle but the door was locked. Then he heard the sound of a safe closing, the bolt slipped back and the lawyer appeared.

"What is the secret?" grumbled Johnny as he entered the private apartment.

Meister closed the door behind him and motioned him to a chair.

"I have been examining some rather interesting pearls," he said meaningly, "and naturally one does not invite the attention of all the world to stolen property."

"Have you had an offer for them?" asked Johnny eagerly.

Maurice said he had. "I want to get them off to Antwerp tonight," he said.

He unlocked the little safe in the corner of the room, took out a flat cardboard box, and removing the lid he displayed a magnificent row of pearls embedded in cotton wool.

"There are at least twenty thousand pounds worth," said Johnny, his eyes brightening.

"There is at least five years' penal servitude," said Maurice brutally, "and I tell you frankly, Johnny, I'm rather scared."

"Of what?" sneered the other. "Nobody is going to imagine that Mr. Meister, the eminent lawyer, is 'fencing' Lady Darnleigh's pearls." Johnny chuckled as the thought occurred to him. "By gad! You'd cut a queer figure in the dock at the Old Bailey, Maurice, can't you imagine the evening newspapers running riot over the sensational arrest and conviction of Mr. Maurice Meister, late of Lincoln's Inn Fields, and now of Flanders Lane, Deptford."

Not a muscle of Maurice's face moved, only the dark eyes glowed with a sudden baleful power.

"Very amusing," he said evenly. "I never credited you before with an imagination." He carried the pearls to the light and examined them, before he replaced the cardboard lid.

"You have seen Mary?" he asked in a conversational tone.

Johnny nodded.

"It is beastly to see her working, but I suppose it is all right. Maurice—"

The lawyer turned his head.

"Well?"

"I've been thinking things over. You had a girl in your service named Gwenda Milton?"

"Well?" said Maurice again.

"She drowned herself, didn't she? Have you any idea why?"

Maurice Meister was facing him squarely now. Not so much as a flicker of an eyelid betrayed the rising fury within him.

"The jury said—" he began.

"I know what the jury said," interrupted Johnny roughly, "but I have my own theory."

He walked slowly to the lawyer and touched him lightly on the shoulder as he emphasised every word.

"Mary Lenley is not Gwenda Milton," he said. "She is not the sister of a fugitive murderer, and I am expecting a little better treatment for her than Gwenda Milton received at your hands."

"I don't understand you," said Meister. His voice was very low and distinct.

"I think you do." Johnny nodded slowly. "I want you to understand that there will be very serious trouble if Mary is hurt! They say that you live in everlasting fear of The Ringer—you would have greater cause to fear me if any harm came to Mary!"

Only for a second did Maurice drop his eyes.

"You're a little hysterical, Johnny," he said, "and you're certainly not in your politest mood this morning. I think I called you crude a week ago, and I have no reason to revise that description. Who is going to harm Mary? As for The Ringer and his sister, they are dead!"

He picked up the pearls from the table, again removed the lid and apparently his eyes were absorbed in the contemplation of the pearls again.

"As a jewel thief—"

He got so far when there came a gentle tap at the door.

"Who's there?" he asked quickly.

"Divisional Inspector Wembury!"

Chapter 10

Maurice Meister had time hastily to cover the pearls, toss them back into the safe and lock it before he opened the door. In spite of his iron nerve, the sallow face of the lawyer was drawn and white, and even his companion showed signs of mental strain as Alan appeared. It was Johnny who made the quicker recovery.

"Hallo, Wembury!" he said with a forced laugh. "I don't seem to be able to get away from you!"

There was evidence of panic, of deadly fear, something of breathless terror in the attitude of these men. What secret did they hold in common? Alan was staggered by an attitude which shouted "guilt" with a tongue of brass.

"I heard Lenley was here," he said, "and as I wanted to see him—"

"You wanted to see me?" said Johnny, his face twitching. "Why on earth should you want to see me?"

Wembury was well aware that Meister was watching him intently. No movement, no gesture, no expression was lost on the shrewd lawyer. What were they afraid of? Alan wondered, and his heart sank when, looking past them, he saw Mary at her typewriter, all unconscious of evil. "You know Lady Darnleigh, don't you?" he asked.

John Lenley nodded dumbly.

"A few weeks ago, she lost a valuable string of pearls," Alan went on, "and I was put in charge of the case."

"You?" Maurice Meister's exclamation was involuntary.

Alan nodded. "I thought you knew that. My name appeared in the newspapers in connection with the investigations. I have handed the case over to Inspector Burton, and he wrote me this morning asking me if I would clear up one little matter that puzzled him."

Mary had left her typewriter and had joined the little group. "One little matter that was puzzling him?" repeated John Lenley mechanically. "And what was that?"

Wembury hesitated to put the question in the presence of the girl. "He wanted to know what induced you to go up to Lady Darnleigh's room."

"And I have already given what I think is the natural explanation," snapped Johnny.

"That you were under the impression you had left your hat and coat on the first floor? His information is that one of the footmen told you, as you were going upstairs, that the coats and hats were on the ground floor."

John Lenley avoided his eyes. "I don't remember," he said. "I was rather rattled that night. I came downstairs immediately I recognised my mistake. Is it suggested that I know anything about the robbery?" His voice shook a little.

"Of course, no such suggestion is put forward," said Wembury with a smile, "but we have to get information wherever we can."

"I knew nothing of the robbery until I read about it in the newspapers and—"

"Oh, Johnny," Mary gasped the words, "you told me when you came home there had been a—"

Her brother stared her into silence. "It was two days after, you remember, my dear," he said slowly and deliberately. "I brought the newspaper in to you and told you there had been a robbery. I could not have spoken to you that night because I did not see you."

For a moment Alan wondered what the girl was going to say, but with a tremendous effort of will she controlled herself. Her face was colourless, and there was such pain in her eyes that he dared not look at her.

"Of course, Johnny, I remember...I remember," she said dully. "How stupid of me!"

A painful silence followed.

Alan was looking down at the worn carpet; his hand was thrust into his jacket pocket. "All right," he said at last. "That, I think, will satisfy Burton. I am sorry to have bothered you." He did not look at the girl: his stern eyes were fixed upon Johnny Lenley. "Why don't you take a trip abroad, Lenley?" He spoke with difficulty. "You are not looking quite as well as you might."

Johnny shifted uneasily under his gaze. "England is good enough for me," he said sulkily. "What are you, Wembury, the family doctor?"

Alan paused. "Yes," he said at last, "I think that describes me," and with a curt nod he was gone.

Mary had gone back to her typewriter but not to work. With a gesture Maurice led the young man back to his room and closed the door quietly.

"I suppose you understand what Wembury meant?" he said.

"Not being a thought reader, I didn't," replied Johnny. He was hovering between rage and amusement. "He has got a cheek, that fellow! When you think that he was a gardener's boy..."

"I should forget all that," said Mr. Meister savagely. "Remember only that you have given yourself away, and that the chances are from today onward you will be under police observation—which doesn't very much matter, Johnny, but I shall be under observation, too, and that is very unpleasant. The only doubt I have is as to whether Wembury is going to do his duty and communicate with Scotland Yard. If he does you will be in serious trouble."

"So will you," replied Johnny gruffly. "We stand or fall together over this matter, Maurice. If they find the pearls where will they be? In your safe! Has that occurred to you?"

Maurice Meister was unruffled, could even smile.

"I think we are exaggerating the danger to you," he said lightly. "Perhaps you are right and the real danger is to me. They certainly have a down on me, and they'd go far to bring me to my knees." He looked across at the safe. "I wish those beastly things were a thousand miles away. I shouldn't be surprised if Mr. Wembury returned armed with a search warrant, and if that happened the fat would be in the fire!"

"Why not post them to Antwerp?" asked the other.

Meister smiled contemptuously.

"If I am being watched, as is very likely," he said, "you don't suppose for one moment that they would fail to keep an eye on the post office? No, the only thing to do with those wretched pearls is to plant them somewhere for a day or two."

Johnny was biting his nails, a worried look on his face.

"I'll take them back to the flat," he said suddenly. "There are a dozen places I could hide them."

If he had been looking at Maurice, he would have seen a satisfied gleam in his eyes.

"That is not a bad idea," said the lawyer slowly. "Wembury would never dream of searching your flat—he likes Mary too much."

He did not wait for his companion to make up his mind, but, unlocking the safe, took out a box and handed it to the other. The young man looked at the package dubiously and then slipped it into his inside pocket.

"I'll put it into the box under my bed," he said, "and let you have it back at the end of the week."

He did not stop to speak to Mary as he made his way quickly through the outer room. There was a sense of satisfaction in the very proximity of those pearls, for which he had risked so much, that gave him a sense of possession, removed some of the irritable suspicion which had grown up in his mind since Meister had the handling of them.

As he passed through crowded Flanders Lane a man turned out of a narrow alley and followed him. As Johnny Lenley walked up Tanners Hill, the man was strolling behind him, and the policeman on point duty hardly noticed him as he passed, never dreaming that within reach of his gloved hand was the man for whom the police of three continents were searching—Henry Arthur Milton, otherwise known as The Ringer.

Chapter 11

Long after Lenley had taken his departure Maurice Meister strode

44

up and down his tiny sanctum, his hands clasped behind him.

A thought was taking shape in his mind—two thoughts indeed, which converged, intermingled, separated and came together again—Johnny Lenley and his sister.

There had been no mistaking the manner in Lenley's voice. Meister had been threatened before and now, so far from moving him from his half-formed purpose, it needed only the youthful and unbalanced violence of Johnny Lenley to stimulate him in the other direction. He had seen too much of Johnny lately. Once there was a time when the young man was amusing—then he had been useful. Now he was becoming not only a bore but a meddlesome bore. He opened the door gently and peeped through the crack. Mary was sitting at her typewriter intent upon her work.

The morning sun flooded the little room, and made a nimbus about her hair. Once she turned her face in his direction without realising that she was being watched. It was difficult to find a fault in the perfect contour of her face and the transparent loveliness of her skin. Maurice fondled his chin thoughtfully. A new interest had come into his life, a new chase had begun. And then his mind came uneasily back to Johnny.

There was a safe and effective way of getting rid of Johnny, with his pomposity, his threats and his stupid confidence.

That last quality was the gravest danger to Maurice. And when Johnny was out of the way many difficulties would be smoothed over. Mary could not be any more adamantine than Gwenda had been in the earliest stages of their friendship.

Inspector Wembury!

Maurice frowned at the thought. Here was a troublemaker on a different plane from Lenley. A man of the world, shrewd, knowledgeable, not lightly to be antagonised. Maurice shrugged his shoulders. It was absurd to consider the policeman, he thought. After all, Mary was not so much his friend as his patroness. She was wholly absorbed in her work when he crossed the room and went softly up the stairs to the little suite above.

As he opened the door he shivered. The memory of Gwenda Milton and that foggy coroner's court was an ugly one. A little decoration was needed to make this room again as beautiful as it had been. The place must be cleaned out, decorated and made not only habitable but attractive. Would it attract Mary—supposing Johnny were out of the way? That was to be discovered. His first task was to settle with John

Lenley and send him to a place where his power for mischief was curtailed. Maurice was a wise man. He did not approach or speak to the girl after the interview with her brother, but allowed some time to elapse before he came to where she was working.

The little lunch which had been served to her was uneaten.

She stood by the window, staring down into Flanders Lane, and at the sound of his voice she started.

"What is the matter, my dear?" Maurice could be very fatherly and tender. It was his favourite approach.

She shook her head wearily. "I don't know, Maurice. I'm worried —about Johnny and the pearls."

"The pearls?" he repeated, in affected surprise. "Do you mean Lady Darnleigh's pearls?"

She nodded. "Why did Johnny lie?" she asked. "It was the first thing he told me when he came home, that there had been a robbery in Park Lane and that Lady Darnleigh had lost her jewels."

"Johnny was not quite normal," he said soothingly. "I shouldn't take too much notice of what he said. His memory seems to have gone to pieces lately."

"It isn't that." She was not convinced. "He knew that he had told me, Maurice: there was no question of his having forgotten." She looked up anxiously into his face. "You don't think—" She did not complete the sentence.

"That Johnny knew anything about the robbery? Rubbish, my dear! The boy is a little worried—and naturally! It isn't a pleasant sensation to find yourself thrown on to the world penniless as Johnny has. He has neither your character nor your courage, my dear."

She sighed heavily and went back to her desk, where there was a neat little pile of correspondence which she had put aside. She turned the pages listlessly and suddenly withdrew a sheet.

"Maurice, who is The Ringer?" she asked.

He glared back at the word.

"The Ringer?"

"It's a cablegram. You hadn't opened it. I found it amongst a lot of your old correspondence."

He snatched the paper from her. The message was dated three months before, and was from Sydney. By the signature he saw it was from a lawyer who acted as his agent in Australia, and the message was brief:

Man taken from Sydney Harbour identified, not Ringer, who is believed to have left Australia.

Mary was staring at the lawyer. His face had gone suddenly haggard and drawn; what vestige of colour there had been in his cheeks had disappeared.

"The Ringer!" he muttered. . . . "Alive!"

The hand that held the paper was shaking, and, as though he realised that some reason for his agitation must be found, he went on with a laugh: "An old client of mine, a fellow I was rather keen on—but a scoundrel, and more than a scoundrel."

As he spoke, he tore the form into little pieces and dropped the litter into the wastepaper basket. Then unexpectedly he put his arm about her shoulder.

"Mary, I would not worry too much about Johnny if I were you. He is at a difficult age and in a difficult mood. I am not pleased with him just now."

She stared at him wonderingly.

"Not pleased with him, Maurice? Why not?"

Maurice shrugged his shoulders.

"He has got himself mixed up with a lot of unpleasant people—men I would not have in this office, and certainly would not allow to associate with you."

His arm was still about her shoulder, and she moved slightly to release herself from this parental embrace. She was not frightened, only a little uncomfortable and uneasy, but he allowed his arm to drop as though his gesture had been born in a momentary mood of protection, and apparently did not notice the movement by which she had freed herself.

"Can't you do something for him? He would listen to you," she pleaded.

But he was not thinking of Johnny. All his thoughts and eyes were for the girl. She was holding his arms now, looking up into his face, and he felt his pulses beating a little faster. Suppose Johnny took the detective's advice and went off to the Continent with the pearls—and Mary! He would find no difficulty in disposing of the necklace and would secure a sum sufficient to keep him for years. This was the thought that ran through Meister's mind as he patted the girl's cheek softly.

"I will see what can be done about Johnny," he said. "Don't worry your pretty head anymore."

In his private office Meister had a small portable typewriter. Throughout the afternoon she heard the click-click of it as he laboriously wrote his message of betrayal.

That evening, when Inspector Wembury came back to Flanders Lane Police Station, he found a letter awaiting him. It was typewritten and unsigned and had been delivered by a district messenger from a West Central office. The message ran:

> The Countess of Darnleigh's pearl necklace was stolen by John Lenley of 37, Malpas Mansions. It is at present in a cardboard carton in a box under his bed.

Alan Wembury read the message and his heart sank within, him, for only one course was open to him, the course of duty.

Chapter 12

Wembury knew that he would be well within his rights if he ignored this typewritten message, for anonymous letters are a daily feature of police life. Yet he realised that it was the practice that, if the information which came thus surreptitiously to a police station coincided with news already in the possession of the police, or if it supported a definite suspicion, inquiries must be set afoot.

He went to his little room to work out the problem alone. It would be a simple matter to hand over the inquiry to another police officer, or even to refer it to. . .But that would be an act of moral cowardice.

There was a small sliding window in the door of his office which gave him a view of the charge room, and as he pondered his problem a bent figure came into his line of vision and, acting on an impulse, he jumped up from the table, and, opening the door beckoned Dr. Lomond. Why he should make a confidant of this old man who was ignorant of police routine he could not for the life of him explain. But between the two men in the very short period of their acquaintance there had grown a queer understanding.

Lomond looked round the little room from under his shaggy brows.

"I have a feeling that you're in trouble, Mr. Wembury," he said, his eyes twinkling.

"If that's a guess, it's a good one," said Alan.

He closed the door behind the police surgeon and pushed forward a chair for him. In a few words he revealed the problem which was exercising his mind, and Lomond listened attentively.

"It's verra awkward." He shook his head. "Man, that's almost like a drama! It seems to me there's only one thing for you to do, Mr. Wembury—you'll have to treat John Lenley as though he were John Smith or Thomas Brown. Forget he's the brother of Miss Lenley, and I think," he said shrewdly, "that is what is worrying you most—and deal with this case as though it were somebody you had never heard of."

Alan nodded slowly.

"That, I'm afraid, is the counsel I should give myself, if I were entirely unprejudiced in the matter."

The old man took a silver tobacco box from his pocket and began slowly to roll a cigarette.

"John Lenley, eh?" he mused. "A friend of Meister's!"

Alan stared at him. The doctor laid significant emphasis on the lawyer's name.

"Do you know him?"

Lomond shook his head.

"Through my career," he said, "I have followed one practice when I come to a strange land—I acquire the local legends. Meister is a legend. To me he is the most interesting man in Deptford, and I'm looking forward to meeting him."

"But why should Johnny Lenley's friendship with Meister—" began Alan, and stopped. He knew full well the sinister importance of that friendship.

Maurice Meister was something more than a legend: he was a sinister fact. His acquaintance with the criminal law was complete. The loopholes which exist in the best drawn statutes were so familiar to him that not once, but half a dozen times, he had cleared his clients of serious charges. There were suspicious people who wondered how the poor thieves who employed him raised the money to pay his fees. There were ill-natured persons who suggested that Meister paid himself out of the proceeds of the robbery and utilised the opportunities he had as a lawyer to obtain from his clients the exact location of the property they had stolen. Many a jewel thief on the run had paused in his flight to visit the house in Flanders Lane, and had gone on his way, leaving in the lawyer's hands the evidence which would have incriminated him. He acted as a sort of banker to the larger fry, and exacted his tribute from the smaller.

"Let me see your anonymous letter," said the doctor.

He carried the paper to the light and examined the typewritten

49

characters carefully.

"Written by an amateur," he said. "You can always tell amateur typists, they forget to put the spaces between the words; but, more important, they vary the spaces between the lines."

He pursed his lips as though he were about to whistle.

"Hum!" he said at last. "Do you rule out the possibility that this letter was written by Meister himself?"

"By Meister?" That idea had not occurred to Alan Wembury. "But why? He's a good friend of Johnny's. Suppose he were in this robbery, do you imagine he would trust John Lenley with the pearls and draw attention to the fact that a friend of his was a thief?"

The doctor was still frowning down at the paper.

"Is there any reason why Meister should want John Lenley out of the way?" he asked.

Alan shook his head.

"I can't imagine any," he said, and then, with a laugh: "You're taking rather a melodramatic view, doctor. Probably this note was written by some enemy of Lenley's—he makes enemies quicker than any man I know."

"Meister," murmured the doctor, and held the paper up to the light to examine the watermark. "Maybe one day you'll have an opportunity, inspector, of getting a little of Mr. Meister's typewriting paper and a specimen of lettering."

"But why on earth should he want Johnny Lenley out of the way?" insisted Alan. "There's no reason why he should. He's an old friend of the family, and although it's possible that Johnny has insulted him, that's one of Johnny's unpleasant little habits. That's no excuse for a civilised man wanting to send another to penal servitude—"

"He wishes Mr. John Lenley out of the way"—Lomond nodded emphatically. "That is my eccentric view. Inspector Wembury, and if I am an eccentric, I am also a fairly accurate man!"

After the doctor left, Alan puzzled the matter over without getting nearer to the solution. Yet he had already discovered that Dr. Lomond's conclusions were not lightly to be dismissed. The old man was as shrewd as he was brilliant. Alan had read a portion of his book, and although twenty years old, this treatise on the criminal might have been written a few weeks before.

He was in a state of indecision when the telephone bell in his room shrilled. He took up the instrument and heard the voice of Colonel Walford.

"Is that you, Wembury? Do you think you can come up to the Yard? I have further information about the gentleman we discussed last week."

For the moment Alan had forgotten the existence of The Ringer. He saw now only an opportunity of taking counsel with a man who had not only proved a sympathetic superior, but a very real friend.

Half an hour later he knocked at the door of Colonel Walford's room, and that moment was one of tragic significance for Mary Lenley.

Chapter 13

John Lenley, after a brief visit to his house, where, behind a locked door, he packed away carefully a small cardboard box, had gone to town to see a friend of the family.

Mary came home to an empty flat. Her head was aching, but that was as nothing to the little nagging pain at her heart. The little supper was a weariness to prepare—almost impossible to dispose of.

She had eaten nothing since breakfast, she remembered, and if she had failed to recall the fact, the queer and sickly sensation of faintness which had come over her as she was mounting the stone steps of Malpas Mansions was an unpleasant reminder of her abstinence.

She forced herself to eat, and was brewing her second cup of tea when she heard a key turn in the lock and John Lenley came in. His face was as black as thunder, but she had ceased to wonder what drove Johnny into those all too frequent tempers of his. Nor was there need to ask, for he volunteered the cause of his anger.

"I went out to the Hamptons' to tea," he said, as he sat down at the table with a disparaging glance at its meagre contents. "They treated me as though I were a leper—and those swine have been entertained at Lenley Court times without number!"

She was shocked at the news, for she had always regarded the Hamptons as the greatest friends of her father.

"But surely, Johnny, they didn't—they weren't horrible because of our—I mean because we have no money?"

He growled something at this.

"That was at the back of it," he said at last. "But I suspect another cause."

And then the reason flashed on her, and her heart thumped painfully.

"It was not because of the Darnleigh pearls, Johnny?" she faltered. He looked round at her quickly.

"Why do you ask that?—Yes, it was something about that old fool's jewellery. They didn't say so directly, but they hinted as much." She felt her lower lip trembling and bit on it to gain control.

"There is nothing in that suggestion, is there, Johnny?" It did not sound like her voice—it was a sound that was coming from far away— a strange voice suggesting stranger things.

"I don't know what you mean!" he answered gruffly, but he did not look at her.

The room spun round before her eyes, and she had to grasp the table for support.

"My God! You don't think I am a thief, do you?" she heard him say. Mary Lenley steadied herself.

"Look at me, Johnny!" Their eyes met. "You know nothing about those pearls?"

Again, his eyes wandered. "I only know they're lost! What in hell do you expect me to say?" He almost shouted in a sudden excess of weak anger. "How dare you, Mary...cross-examine me as though I were a thief! This comes from knowing cads like Wembury. . . !"

"Did you steal Lady Darnleigh's pearls?"

The tablecloth was no whiter than her face. Her lips were blood-less. He made one effort to meet her eyes again, and failed.

"I—" he began.

Then came a knock at the door. Brother and sister looked at one another.

"Who is that?" asked Johnny huskily.

She shook her head.

"I don't know; I will see."

Her limbs were like lead as she dragged them to the door; she thought she was going to faint. Alan Wembury stood in the doorway, and there was on his face a look which she had never seen before.

"Do you want me, Alan?" she asked breathlessly.

"I want to see Johnny."

His voice was as low as hers and scarcely intelligible. She opened the door wider and he walked past her into the dining-room. Johnny was standing where she had left him, by the little round table covered with the remains of the supper, and the clang of the door as Mary closed it came to his ears like the knell of doom.

"What do you want, Wembury?" John Lenley spoke with difficulty.

His heart was beating so thunderously that he felt this man must hear the roar and thud of it.

"I've just come from Scotland Yard." Alan's voice was changed and unnatural. "I've seen Colonel Walford, and told him of a communication I received this afternoon. I have explained the"—he sought for words—"the relationship I have with your family and the regard in which I hold it, and just why I should hesitate to do my job."

"What is your job?" asked Lenley after a moment of silence.

"Immediately, I have no business."—Wembury chose his words deliberately and carefully. "Tomorrow I shall come with a warrant to search this house for the Darnleigh pearls."

He heard the smothered sob of the girl, but did not turn his head.

John Lenley stood rigid, his face as white as death. He was ignorant of police procedure, or he would have realised how significant was Alan's statement that he did not possess a search warrant. Wembury sensed this ignorance, and made one last desperate effort to save the girl he loved from the tragic consequences of her brother's folly.

"I have no search warrant and no right to examine your flat," he said. "The warrant will be procured by tomorrow morning."

If John Lenley had a glimmering of intelligence, and the pearls were hidden in the flat, here was a chance to dispose of them, but the opportunity which Alan offered was not taken.

It was sheer mad arrogance on Lenley's part to reject the chance that was given to him. He would not be under any obligation to the gardener's son!

"They are in a box under the bed," he said. "You knew that or you wouldn't have come. I am not taking any favours from you, Wembury, and I don't suppose I should get any if I did. If you feel any satisfaction in arresting a man whose father provided the cottage in which you were born, I suppose you are entitled to feel it."

He turned on his heel, walked into his room, and a few seconds later came back with a small cardboard box which he laid on the table. Alan Wembury was momentarily numbed by the tragedy which had overwhelmed this little household. He dared not look at Mary, who stood stiffly by the side of the table. Her pallid face was turned with an agonised expression of entreaty to her brother, and it was only now that she could find speech.

"Johnny! How could you!"

He wriggled his shoulders impatiently.

"It is no use making a fuss, Mary," he said bluntly. "I was mad!"

Turning suddenly, he caught her in his arms, and his whole frame shook as he kissed her pale lips.

"Well, I'll go," he said brokenly, and in another instant had wrenched himself free of her kiss and her clinging hands, and had walked out of the room a prisoner.

Chapter 14

Neither Alan Wembury nor his prisoner spoke until they were approaching Flanders Lane Police Station, and then Johnny asked, without turning his head.

"Who gave me away?"

It was only the rigid discipline of twelve years' police work that prevented Alan from betraying the betrayer.

"Information received," he answered conventionally, and the young man laughed.

"I suppose you've been watching me since the robbery," he said. "Well, you'll get promotion out of this, Wembury, and I wish you joy of it."

When he faced the desk sergeant his mood became a little more amiable, and he asked if Maurice Meister could be intimated. Just before he went to the cell he asked, "What do I get for this, Wembury?"

Alan shook his head. He was certain in his mind that, though it was a first offence, nothing could save Johnny Lenley from penal servitude.

It was eleven o'clock at night, and rain was falling heavily, when Alan came walking quickly down the deserted stretch of Flanders Lane, towards Meister's house. From the opposite side of the road he could see above the wall the upper windows; one window showed a light. The lawyer was still up, possibly was interviewing one of his queer clients, who had come by a secret way into the house to display his ill-gotten wares or to pour a tale of woe into Meister's unsympathetic ear. These old houses near the river were honeycombed with cellar passages, and only a few weeks before, there had been discovered in the course of demolition a secret room which the owner, who had lived in the place for twenty years, had never suspected.

As he crossed the road, Alan saw a figure emerge from the dark shadow of the wall which surrounded the lawyer's house. There was something very stealthy in the movements of the man, and all that was police officer in Wembury's composition, was aroused by this furtiveness. He challenged him sharply, and to his surprise, instead of turning and running, as the Flanders Laner might be expected to do in the circumstances, the man turned and came slowly towards him and stood revealed in the beam of Inspector Wembury's pocket lamp, a slight man with a dark, bearded face. He was a stranger to the detective, but that was not remarkable. Most of the undesirables of Deptford were as yet unknown to Alan.

"Hallo! Who are you, and what are you doing here?" he asked, and immediately came the cool answer:

"I might ask you the same question!"

"I am a police officer," said Alan Wembury sternly, and he heard a low chuckle.

"Then we are brothers in misfortune," replied the stranger, "for I am a police officer, too. Inspector Wembury, I presume?"

"That is my name," said Alan, and waited.

"I cannot bother to give you my card, but my name is Bliss—Central Detective Inspector Bliss—of Scotland Yard."

Bliss? Alan remembered now that this unpopular police officer had been due to arrive in England on that or on the previous day. One fact was certain: if this were Bliss, he was Alan's superior officer.

"Are you looking for something?" he asked.

For a while Bliss made no reply.

"I don't know what I'm looking for exactly. Deptford is an old division of mine, and I was just renewing acquaintance with the place. Are you going to see Meister?"

How did he know it was Meister's house, Alan wondered? The lawyer had only gone to live there since Bliss had left for America. And what was his especial interest in the crook solicitor? As though he were reading the other's thoughts, Bliss went on quickly: "Somebody told me that Meister was living in Deptford. Rather a 'come down' for him. When I knew him first, he had a wonderful practice in Lincoln's Inn."

And then with an abrupt nod he passed on the way he had been going when Wembury had called him back. Alan stood by the door of Meister's house and watched the stranger till he was out of sight, and only then did he ring the bell. He had some time to wait, time for thought, though his thoughts were not pleasant. He dared not think of Mary, alone in that desolate little flat, with her breaking heart and her despair. Nor of the boy he had known, sitting on his plank bed, his head between his hands, ruin before him.

Presently he heard a patter of slippered feet coming across the courtyard, and Meister's voice asked: "Who is that?"

"Wembury."

A rattle of chains and a shooting of bolts, and the door opened. Though he wore his dressing-gown, Wembury saw, when they reached the dimly lit passage, that Meister was fully dressed; even his spats had not been removed.

"What is the trouble, Mr. Wembury?"

Alan did not know how many people slept in the house or what could be overheard. Without invitation he walked up the stairs ahead of the lawyer into the big room. The piano was open, sheets of music lay on the floor. Evidently Meister had been spending a musical evening. The lawyer closed the door behind him.

"Is it Johnny?" he asked.

Was it imagination on Alan's part, or was the lawyer's voice strained and husky.

"Why should it be Johnny?" he demanded. "It is, as a matter of fact. I arrested him an hour ago for the Darnleigh pearl robbery. He has asked me to get into communication with you."

Maurice did not reply: he was looking down at the floor, apparently deep in thought.

"How did you come to get the information on which he was arrested, or did you know all the time that Johnny was in this?" he asked at last.

Alan was looking at him keenly, and under his scrutiny the lawyer shuffled uneasily.

"I am not prepared to tell you that—if you do not know!" he said. "But I have promised Lenley that I will carry his message to you, and that ends my duty so far as he is concerned."

The lawyer's eyes were roving from one object in the room to another. Not once did he look at Wembury.

"It is curious," he said, shaking his head sorrowfully, "but I had a premonition that Johnny had been mixed up in this Darnleigh affair. What a fool! Thank God his father is dead—"

"I don't think we need bother our heads with pious wishes," said Alan bluntly. "The damnable fact is that Lenley is under arrest for a jewel robbery."

"You have the pearls?"

Alan nodded.

"They were in a cardboard box—there was also a bracelet stolen, but that is not in the box," he said slowly. "Also I have seen a sign of an old label, and I think I shall be able to trace the original owner of the box."

And then, to his astonishment, Meister said: "Perhaps I can help you. I have an idea the box was mine. Johnny asked me for one a week ago. Of course, I had no notion of why he wanted it, but I gave it to him. It may be another box altogether, but I should imagine the carton is mine."

Momentarily Alan Wembury was staggered. He had had a faint hope that he might be able to connect Meister with the robbery, the more so since he had discovered more than he had told. The half-obliterated label had obviously been addressed to Meister himself, yet the lawyer could not have been aware of this fact. It was one of the slips that the cleverest criminals make. But so quick and glib was he that he had virtually destroyed all hope of proving his complicity in the robbery—unless Johnny told. And Johnny was not the man who would betray a confederate.

"What do you think he will get?" asked Maurice.

"The sentence? You seem pretty certain that he is guilty."

Maurice shrugged. "What else can I think—obviously you would not have arrested him without the strongest possible evidence. It is a tragedy! Poor lad!"

And then all the dark places in this inexplicable betrayal were lit in one blinding flash of understanding. Mary! Wembury had scoffed at the idea that Meister wished to get her brother out of the way. He could see no motive for such an act of treachery. But now all the hideous possibilities presented themselves to him, and he glared down at the lawyer. He knew Meister's reputation; knew the story of Gwenda Milton; knew other even less savoury details of Meister's past life. Was Mary the innocent cause of this wicked deed? Was it to gain domination over her that Johnny was being sent into a living grave? This time Meister met his eyes and did not flinch.

Chapter 15

"I don't think you need trouble about Miss Lenley." Alan's voice was deadly cold. "Fortunately, she lives in my division, and she trusts me well enough to come to me if she's in any trouble."

He saw the slow smile dawn upon the lawyer's face.

"Do you think that is likely. Inspector Wembury?" Meister asked. His voice had a quality of softness which was almost feline. "As I understand, you had the unhappy task of arresting her brother: is she likely to bring her troubles to you?"

Alan's heart sank. The thought of Mary's attitude towards him had tortured him since the arrest. How could she continue to be friendly with the man who was immediately responsible for the ruin and disgrace of her brother?

"The Lenleys are an old family," Meister went on. "They have their modicum of pride. I doubt if poor Mary will ever forgive you for arresting her brother. It will be terribly unjust, of course, but women are illogical. I will do what I can for Miss Lenley, just as I shall do what I can for Johnny. And I think my opportunities are more obvious than yours. Can I see Johnny tonight?"

Alan nodded.

"Yes, he asked me if you would see him at once, though I'm afraid you can do very little for him. No bail will be granted, of course. This is a felony charge."

Maurice Meister hurried to the door that led to his room, slipping off his dressing-gown as he went.

"I will not keep you waiting very long," he said. Left alone in the big room, Alan paced up and down the worn carpet, his hands behind him, his chin on his breast. There was something subtly repulsive in this atmosphere. The great piano, the faded panelling, the shabby richness of the furnishing and decoration. The room seemed to be over-supplied with doors: he counted four, in addition to the curtain which hid the alcove. Where did all these lead to? And what stories could they tell, he wondered.

Particularly interested was he in one door which was heavily bolted and barred, and he was staring at this when, to his amazement, above the frame glowed suddenly a long red light. A signal of some kind—from whom? Even as he looked, the light died away and Meister came in, struggling into his overcoat.

"What does that light mean, Mr. Meister?"

The lawyer spun round. "Light? Which light?" he asked quickly, and following the direction of the detective's finger, he gasped. "A light?" incredulously. "You mean that red lamp? How did you come to notice it?"

"It lit up a few minutes ago and went out again." It was not imagination on his part: the lawyer's face had gone a sickly yellow.

"Are you sure?" And then, quickly: "It is a substitute for a bell—I mean, if you press the bell on the outer door the lamp lights up; bells annoy me."

He was lying, and he was frightened too. The red lamp had another

58

significance. What was it?

In those few seconds Meister had become ill at ease, nervous; the hand that strayed constantly to his mouth trembled. Glancing at him out of the corner of his eye, when he thought he was free from observation, Alan saw him take a small golden box from his pocket, pinch something from its contents and sniff at his thumb and finger. "Cocaine," guessed Wembury, and knew that his theory was right when almost immediately the lawyer became his old buoyant self.

"You must have imagined it—probably a reflection from the lamp on the table," he said.

"But why shouldn't there be somebody at the front door?" asked Alan coolly, and Meister made an effort to correct his error.

"Very probably there is," He hesitated. "I wonder if you would mind, inspector—would it be asking you too much to go down to the front gate and see? Here is the key!"

Alan took the key from the lawyer's hand, went downstairs across the courtyard and opened the outer gate. There was nobody there. He suspected, indeed he was sure, that the lawyer had asked him to perform this service because he wished to be alone in the room for a few minutes, possibly to investigate the cause of and reason for that signal.

As he went up the stairs, he heard a sharp click as though a drawer had closed, and when he came into the room, he found Meister pulling on his gloves with an air of nonchalance.

"Nobody?" he asked. "It must have been your imagination, inspector, or one of these dreadful people of Flanders Lane playing a trick."

"The lamp hasn't lit since I left the room?" asked Alan, and when Meister shook his head, "You are sure?"

"Absolutely," said the lawyer, and too late saw he was trapped.

"That is very curious." Wembury looked hard at him. "Because I pressed the front door bell, and if the lamp was what you said it was, it should have lit up again, shouldn't it?"

Meister murmured something about the connections being out of order, and almost hustled him from the room.

Alan was not present at the interview at the police station. He left Meister in the charge of the station sergeant, and went home to his lodgings in Blackheath Road with a heavy heart. He could do nothing for the girl; not so much as suggest a woman who would keep her company. He could not guess that at that moment, when his heart ached for her, Mary had a companion, and that companion a woman.

Chapter 16

Long after Johnny Lenley had been taken away Mary Lenley sat numbed, paralysed to inaction by the overwhelming misfortune which had come to her. She sat at the table, her hands clasped before her, staring down at the white cloth until her eyes ached. She wished she could weep, but no tears had come. The only reminder she had of the drama that had been played out under that roof was the empty feeling in her breast, it was as though her heart had been taken from her.

Johnny a thief! It wasn't possible, she was dreaming. Presently she would wake up from this horrible nightmare, hearing his voice calling her from the lawn. . . .But she was not at Lenley Court: she was in a block of industrial flats, sitting on a cheap chair, and Johnny was in a prison cell. The horror of it made her blood run cold. And Alan— what vicious trick of fate had made him Johnny's captor? She had a vivid memory of that scene which had preceded Johnny's arrest. Every word Alan had spoken had been burnt into her brain. Too well she realised that Wembury had risked everything to save her brother. He had given him a chance. Johnny had only to keep silence and spend the night in getting rid of those pearls, and he would have been with her now. But his fatal *hauteur* had been his undoing. She had no bitterness in her soul against Alan Wembury, only a great sorrow for him, and the memory of his drawn face hurt her almost as much as Johnny's mad folly.

She heard the bell tinkle faintly. It rang three times before she understood that somebody was at the front door. Alan perhaps, she thought, and, getting up stiffly, went out into the hall and opened the door. A woman stood there dressed in a long black mackintosh; a black hat enhanced the fairness of her hair and skin. She was beautiful, Mary saw, and apparently a lady.

"You've made some mistake—" she began.

"You're Mary Lenley, aren't you?" An American, noted Mary, and looked her astonishment. "Can I see you?"

The girl stood aside, and Cora Ann Milton walked into the room and looked round. There was a faint hint of disparagement in her glance, which Mary was too miserable to resent.

"You're in trouble, aren't you?"

Uninvited, she sat down by the half-opened drawer of the table, took a jewelled case from her bag and lit a cigarette.

"Yes, I'm in trouble—great trouble," said Mary, wondering how this woman knew, and what had brought her here at such an hour.

"I guessed that. I hear Wembury pulled your brother for a jewel theft—he caught him with the goods, I guess?"

Mary nodded slowly. "Yes, the pearls were in this house. I had no knowledge that they were here."

She wondered in a dim way whether this American was Lady Darnleigh; so many members of the aristocracy have been recruited from the United States that it was possible.

"My name's Milton—Cora Ann Milton," said the woman, but the name meant nothing to Mary Lenley. "Never heard of me, kid?"

Mary shook her head. She was weary in body and soul, impatient that this intruder into her sorrow should leave her.

"Never heard of The Ringer?"

Mary looked up quickly.

"The Ringer? You mean the criminal who is wanted by the police?"

"Wanted by everybody, honey." Despite the flippancy of her tone, Cora Ann's voice shook a little. "By me more than anybody else—I'm his wife!"

Mary got up quickly from her chair. It was incredible! This beautiful creature the wife of a man who walked everlastingly in the shadow of the gallows!

"I'm his wife," nodded Cora Ann. "You don't think it's a thing to boast about? That's where you're wrong." And then, abruptly: "You're working for Meister, aren't you?"

"I am working for Mr. Meister," said Mary quietly; "but really, Mrs.—"

"Mrs. Milton," prompted Cora.

"Mrs. Milton, I don't quite understand the object of your visit at this time of night."

Cora Ann Milton was regarding the room with shrewd, appraising eyes.

"It's not much of an apartment you've got, but it's better than that cute little suite of Meister's."

She saw the colour come into the girl's face and her eyes narrowed.

"He's shown it to you eh? Gosh, that fellow's a quick worker!"

"I don't understand what you mean." Mary was slow to anger, but now she felt her resentment merging into anger. At the back of her mind was a confused idea that, but for Johnny's misfortune, this woman would never have dared to see her. It was as though his arrest had qualified her for admission to the confidence of the underworld.

"If you don't know what I mean, I won't say much more about it," said the woman coolly. "Does Meister know I'm back?"

Mary shook her head. Mrs. Milton was sitting by the table, and was taking a handkerchief from the little bag on her lap: she was very deliberate and self-possessed. "I don't think he's very much interested in your movements, Mrs. Milton," said Mary wearily. "Do you mind if I ask you not to stay? I've had a great shock this evening and I'm not in a mood to discuss Mr. Meister or your husband or anybody."

But Cora Ann Milton was not easily abashed. "I guess when all this trouble is over, you'll be working late at Meister's house," she said, "and I'm wondering whether you'd like to have my address?"

"Why on earth—" began Mary.

"Why on earth!" mimicked the other. "I guess this is an age of freedom when the only place you see a chaperon is a museum. But I should like you to get in touch with me if. . .anything happens. There was another girl once. . . .but I guess you don't want any awful example. And, say, I'd be much obliged to you if you'd not mention the fact to dear Maurice that The Ringer's wife is in town."

Mary hardly listened to the latter part of the speech. She walked to the door and opened it suggestively. "That means I've got to go," said Cora Ann with a good-natured smile. "I'm not blaming you, kid. I guess I'd feel that way myself if some dame came floating in on me with all that guardian angel stuff."

"I don't require guardianship, thank you. I have a number of friends—"

She stopped. A number of friends! Not in all London, in all the country, was there any to whom she could turn in her trouble, except to—Alan Wembury. And Maurice?

Why did she hesitate at Maurice? In the last day or two a subtle change had come over their relationship. He was no longer the natural refuge and adviser to whom she would go in her distress.

Cora Ann was watching her from the doorway; keen, shrewd eyes seemed to be reading her every thought. "That man Wembury's a decent fellow. I hope you're not going to be sore at him for pinching your brother?"

Mary made a weary gesture: she had reached almost the end of her tether.

Long after the girl had gone, she sat by the table, trying to understand just what this visit of Cora Ann Milton's meant. Had she followed the woman down the stairs, she might have discovered.

Cora turned into the dark, deserted street, walked a few paces, and then, as if by magic from some mysterious underground trap, a man appeared by her side, so unexpectedly and silently that she started and took a step away from him.

"Oh!. . .you scared me!" she breathed.

"Did you see the girl?"

"Yes, I saw her. Arthur"—her voice was broken and agitated—"why do you stay here? Don't you realise, you fool, what danger. . ."

She heard his low chuckle.

"Cora Ann, you talk too much," he said lightly. "By the way, I saw you this afternoon."

"You saw me?" she gasped. "Where were you?" Suddenly: "Arthur, how am I to know you when I see you? I've got that spookish feeling that you're round me all the time, and I'm forever peering into people's faces as I pass them—I'll be pinched for being too fresh one of these days!"

Again, he chuckled.

"Surely my own loving wife would know me?" he said ironically. "The eyes of love could penetrate any disguise."

He heard her teeth snap in anger. Arthur Milton had the trick of infuriating this beautiful wife of his.

"I'll know what you look like now," she said.

Suddenly there was a click and a white beam of light flashed in his face.

"You're a fool!" he said roughly, as he knocked the lamp down. "When you can see, others can see."

"I wish 'em joy!" she whispered. For she had looked into a face that was covered from forehead to chin by a square of black silk, through which a pair of wide-set eyes stared down at her.

"Did you get my letter?" he demanded.

"Yes—the code, you mean. I thought the newspapers did not publish code messages?"

He did not answer and mechanically she felt in her bag. The envelope she had put there was gone.

"What is it?" he asked quickly and when she told him: "Cora, you're a goop! You must have dropped it in this girl Lenley's flat! Go and get it!"

Cora Ann hurried up the stairs and knocked at the door. It was immediately answered by Mary.

"Yes, I've come back," said the woman breathlessly. "I dropped a letter here somewhere: I've only just missed it."

Mary turned back and together they searched the flat, turning up carpets and shaking out curtains, but there was no sign of the letter.

"You must have lost it elsewhere." The woman was so agitated that she was sorry for her. "Did it have any money—"

"Money? No," said Cora Ann impatiently. "I wish it had."

She looked round the room in bewilderment. "I know I had it before I came in."

"Perhaps you left it at your own home?" suggested Mary, but Cora Ann shook her head, and after another thorough search she began to doubt whether she had brought it out with her.

Mary Lenley closed the door upon her finally with heartfelt thanksgiving, walked listlessly back to the table and sat down. Her tea was cold and bitter. She pulled open a little drawer in the table where the spoons were kept, and looked down in amazement. The letter for which they had sought lay on top of a miscellaneous collection of spoons and forks. It was simply inscribed on the envelope "Cora Ann", and had no address. Perhaps the address was inside, she thought, and after some hesitation pulled out its contents, a square white card covered with groups of letters and figures, written in an almost microscopic hand. It did not need any very great acumen on her part to know that she was looking at a code: if she had been more experienced in such matters, she would have realised how ingenious a code it was.

She replaced the card, put it again in the drawer and waited for the woman to return. What had happened was obvious: when she had taken her handkerchief from the bag, the letter had slipped into the drawer, which had been slightly open, and in moving she must have closed the drawer, which ran very easily, without noticing the fact.

That night, before she went to bed, Mary took the letter into her room and locked it away in one of the drawers of her dressing-table where she kept her few trinkets, and, having locked it away, forgot all about it.

Chapter 17

It was a month later that Mary Lenley sat in the marble hall of the Central Criminal Court and waited with folded hands and a set, tragic face for the jury's finding. She had gone into court and had heard the preliminaries of the evidence, but the sight of that neat figure in the dock was more than she could bear, and she had gone out to wait with fatalistic resignation for the final curtain of the drama.

The door leading to the court opened and Alan Wembury came out and walked over to her.

"Is it—ended?" she asked huskily.

Wembury shook his head. "Very soon now, I think," he said quietly. He looked as if he had not slept, he was hollow-eyed, haggard, a man distracted.

"I'm sorry, Alan." She put out her hand and gently touched his. The touch of her hand almost brought the tears to his eyes.

"You don't know how I feel about this, Mary; and the horrible thing is that I am getting the credit for the arrest—I had a letter from the commissioner yesterday congratulating me!"

She smiled faintly.

In every tragedy there is a touch of grotesque comedy, and it seemed to be supplied in this case by the unsought honour that had come to this reluctant police officer.

He sat by her side and tried to comfort her, and if his efforts were a little awkward, a little gauche, she understood. And then Maurice came into the hall, his old, immaculate self. His silk hat was more shiny than ever, his spats were like the virgin snow. He might have come straight from a wedding party but for his lugubrious countenance.

"The judge is summing up," he said. "I wish you'd go into court, Wembury, so that you can bring news of what happens."

It was a crude request, which Alan diagnosed as a wish on the part of the lawyer to be alone with Mary.

"There goes a very clever young man," said Meister, as he watched the broad-shouldered figure of the detective disappear through the swing doors. "Unscrupulous, but then all police officers are unscrupulous. A climber, but all police officers are ambitious."

"I've never found Alan unscrupulous," said Mary.

Maurice Meister smiled. "That is perhaps a strong word to employ," he agreed carelessly. "After all, the man had to do his duty, and he was very ingenious in the method he employed to trap poor Johnny."

"Ingenious? Trap?" She frowned at him.

"That did not come out in the evidence. Nothing that is detrimental to the police force ever comes out in police court evidence, my dear," said Maurice with a meaning smile. "But I am on the inside of things, and I happen to know that Wembury has been on Johnny's trail ever since the robbery was committed. That was why he came down to Lenley Court."

She stared at him. "Are you sure? I thought—"

"You thought he came down to see you, to get your congratulations on his promotion?" said Maurice. "That is a natural error. My dear, if you think the matter over, you will realise that a detective officer must always pretend to be doing something other than he actually is doing. If you were to tax Wembury with his little act of duplicity, he would of course be indignant and deny it."

She thought a while. "I don't believe it," she said. "Alan told me that he had not associated Johnny with the crime until he received an anonymous letter."

"S-sh!" said Meister warningly.

Alan had come out of the court and was walking towards them.

"The judge will be another ten minutes," he said, and then, before Meister could warn her, the girl asked: "Alan, is it true that you have been watching Johnny for a long time?"

"You mean in connection with this offence? No, I knew nothing about it. I did not suspect Johnny until I had a letter, written by somebody who was in a very favourable position to know all about the robbery."

His eyes were on Maurice Meister.

"But when you came down to Lenley Court—"

"My dear,"—it was Maurice who interrupted hastily—"why ask the inspector these embarrassing questions?"

"It doesn't embarrass me," said Alan curtly. "I went to Lenley Court to see Miss Lenley and to tell her of my promotion. You're not suggesting that my visit had anything to do with the robbery, are you?"

Maurice shrugged his shoulders.

"I was probably giving you credit that you did not deserve," he said, with an attempt to pass the matter off humorously. "As a solicitor I am not unacquainted with these mysterious letters which the police are supposed to receive, and which cover the operations of their—noses, I think is the word for police informer."

"You know it's the word for police informer, Mr. Meister," said Alan. "And there was nothing mysterious about the letter which betrayed Lenley, except the writer. It was written on typewriting paper, Swinley Bond No. 14."

He saw Meister start.

"I have made a few inquiries amongst the stationers of Deptford, and I have discovered that that particular paper is not supplied locally. It comes from a law stationer's in Chancery Lane and is their own especial property. I tell you that in case you would like to take the inquiry any further."

With a nod he left them together. "What does he mean?" asked the girl, a little worried.

"Does anyone know what any police officer means?" asked Maurice, with a forced laugh.

She was thoughtful for a while, and sat for a long time without speaking.

"He suggested that Johnny had been betrayed by—by somebody—"

"Somebody who did not live in Deptford, obviously," said Maurice quickly. "Really, my dear, I shouldn't take too much notice of that cock-and-bull story. And it would be well if you did not see too much of Wembury in the future."

"Why?" she asked, looking at him steadily.

"There are many reasons," replied Maurice slowly. "In the first place, I have a clientele which would look a little askance at me if my secretary were a friend of a police officer. Of course," he went on hurriedly, as he saw the look in the girl's face, "I have no wish to dictate to you as to your friends. But I want to be of help to you, Mary. There are one or two matters which I would like to discuss after this unpleasant business is over. You can't live alone in Malpas Mansions."

"Johnny will be sent to prison, of course?" she nodded.

It was not the moment for delicacy.

"Johnny will be sent to penal servitude," said Meister: "you've got to get that fast in your mind. This may mean seven years for him, and you must reconcile yourself to that possibility. As I say, you can't live alone—"

"I can't live anywhere else but Malpas Mansions," she said. The note of determination in her voice was unmistakable. "I know you mean to be kind, Maurice, but there are some things which I cannot do. If you care to employ me, I'll be pleased to work for you. I don't think I'm sufficiently competent to work for anybody else, and I'm sure no other employer would give me the wages you have offered. But I'm living at Malpas Mansions until Johnny returns."

There came a dramatic interruption. The swing door opened and Alan Wembury walked out. He stood stock still for a moment, looking at her, and then slowly paced across the tiled floor.

"Well?" she asked breathlessly.

"Three years penal servitude," said Alan. "The judge asked if anything was known of him and I went into the box and told the Bench all I knew."

"And what did you know?" asked Meister. He was on his feet now, facing the detective.

"I know that he was a decent boy who has been ruined by associating with criminals," said Wembury between his teeth; "and someday I am going to take the man who ruined Johnny Lenley, and put him in that court." He pointed back to the swing door. "And when I go into the box it will not be to plead for the prisoner but to tell the judge a story that will send the man who betrayed John Lenley to a prison from which he will never come out!"

Chapter 18

To Maurice Meister, The Ringer was dead. He treated as a jest, or as one of those stupid legends which to the criminal mind is gospel, all the stories of Henry Arthur Milton's presence in England. The three months which followed Johnny's sentence were too full to allow him time even to consider with any seriousness the whispered hints which came to him from his unsavoury clients.

Scotland Yard, which acts only on definite knowledge, had taken no step to warn him, and that was the most comforting aspect of the situation. Mary came regularly to work, and from being an ornament to the establishment, developed into a most capable typist. She often wondered whether it would not be fair to Maurice to tell him of the interview she had had with Cora Ann Milton; but since The Ringer's name was never again mentioned, she thought it wisest to let the matter drop. If she had not severed all association with Alan Wembury, she saw very little of him. Twice she had almost met him in the street, but he had obviously avoided her. At first, she was hurt, but then she realised that it was Alan's innate delicacy which was responsible. One day in the High Street she saw him and before he could escape intercepted him.

"Alan, you're being very unkind," she said, and added mischievously: "People think that you will not know me because of my dubious relations!"

He went red and white at this, and she was instantly sorry. There was something childlike about Alan.

"Of course, I meant nothing of the sort. But you're being I rather a pig, aren't you? You've avoided me like the plague."

"I thought I was being rather delicate," he said ruefully, and, grasping the nettle firmly: "Have you heard from Johnny?"

She nodded. "He is quite cheerful, and already making plans for the future," she said, and added: "Won't you take me to tea somewhere on Wednesday—that is my early day?"

It was a very happy, man who went back to the station house. Indeed, he was so cheerful that old Dr. Lomond, busy at the sergeant's desk writing a report upon a drunken motorist, looked over his glasses and rallied him in his dour way.

"Have ye had money left ye?"

"Something better than that," smiled Alan. "I've rid myself of a dull ghost."

Lomond clucked his lips derisively as he signed his name with a flourish and blotted the report.

"That means that you've had a quarrel with a girl, and she's suddenly decided to make it up," he said. He had an uncanny habit of getting into the mind of his audience. "I'm no' saying that matrimony is no' a good thing for any man. But it must be terribly risky for a police officer."

"I'm not contemplating matrimony," laughed Alan.

"Then I wonder ye're not ashamed of yourself," said the doctor as he shuffled down to the fire and shook off the ash of his cigarette into the grate.

"You ought to be a happy man," said Alan. "Colonel Walford told me he had written you a letter of thanks for the work you did in the Prideaux case."

The old man shook his head.

"Man, I'm no' proud of my work. But poisoners I abominate, and Prideaux was the most cold-blooded poisoner I have ever known. A strange man with a queer occiput. Have you ever noticed the occiput of poisoners? It juts oot from the back of the heid."

As he was talking a stocky, poorly dressed man had come into the charge room. There was a grin on his unshaven face as he made his way to the sergeant at the desk. He had all the aplomb of a man in familiar surroundings, and as he laid his ticket of leave on the desk, he favoured the sergeant with a friendly nod.

"Why, Hackitt!" said Wembury. "I didn't know you were out."

He shook hands with the ex-convict and Sam Hackitt's grin broadened.

"I got my brief last Monday," he said. "Old Meister's giving me a job."

"What, Sam, are you going into the law?"

The idea tickled Hackitt.

"No, I'm going to clean his boots! It's a low job for a man of my ability, Mr. Wembury, but what can you do when the police are 'ounding you down all the time?"

"Hounding grandmothers!" said Alan, with a smile "You fellows hound yourselves down. So, you're going to valet Meister, are you? I wish you luck."

Sam Hackitt scratched his unshaven chin thoughtfully.

"They tell me Johnny Lenley's been put away, Mr. Wembury? That's bad luck."

"Did you know him?" asked Alan.

Sam Hackitt hesitated.

"Well, I can't say that I know him. I went down to the country to see him once, when he was a swell. I knew he was on the crook then, and somebody put up a joke for him and me."

Alan knew what "a joke" meant in the argot of the criminal classes: it meant a robbery, big or small.

"But I didn't take it on," said Sam. "It was a bit too dangerous for me, and I don't like working with amachoors. They're bound to give you away if they're a bit too impetuous. Especially as this gentleman who was putting up the money for the joke wanted us to carry a shooter—not for me, thank you!"

Alan was acquainted with the professional burglar's horror of firearms. But surely the man who had planned the robbery was as well aware of the dangers of a burglar being captured with firearms in his possession?

"Who is the Big Fellow, Sam?" he asked, never for one moment expecting a truthful reply; for only in a moment of direst necessity would a thief betray his "big fellow" or employer.

"Him? Oh, he's a chap who lives in Sheffield," said Sam vaguely. "I didn't like the job, so I didn't take it on. He's a nice boy—that young Lenley, I mean. It's a pity he went crook, a gentleman of his education."

And then he changed the subject abruptly.

"Mr. Wembury, what's this yarn about The Ringer being in London? I heard about it when I was in Maidstone, and I sent a letter to your boss."

Alan was surprised. The Ringer belonged to another plane, and although the little criminals were greatly intrigued by the operations of this super-criminal, he had not connected any of them with the man for whom the police were searching.

"He's drowned, as a matter of fact," said Sam comfortably. "I read about it when I was in 'stir' (prison)."

"Did you know him, Sam?"

Again, the ex-convict scratched his chin.

"I'm one of the few people who've seen him without his make-up," he grinned. "The Ringer, eh? What a lad! There never was a bloke who could disguise himself like that bird!"

The sergeant had copied particulars of Sam Hackitt's brief into a book, and now handed the ticket of leave back to the man.

"We may be asking to see you one of these days, Hackitt, if The Ringer turns up," said Wembury.

Sam shook his head.

"He'll never turn up: he's drowned. I believe the newspapers."

Dr. Lomond watched the stocky figure disappear through the doorway and shook his head.

"There goes a super-optimist," he said, "and what a heid! Did you notice, Wembury, the flattening of the skull? Man, I'd like to measure him!"

Chapter 19

The days that intervened before Wednesday were very long days and each seemed to consist of much more than twenty-four hours. Alan had a note from the girl in the morning, asking him to meet her at a little teashop in the West End, and he was at the rendezvous a quarter of an hour before she was due to arrive. She came at last, a trim, neat figure in blue serge, with just a little more colour in her cheeks than was ordinary.

"I'm being a dutiful servant," she said. "I would have met you at Blackheath, only I was afraid that some of Mr. Meister's clients might have seen you and thought I was in secret communication with the police over their grisly pasts!"

He laughed at this. He had never seen her so light-hearted since the old Lenley Court days.

The teashop was only sparsely patronised. It was an hour before the rush of shoppers filled each seat and occupied every table, and he found a quiet corner where they could talk. She was full of hopeful plans for the future. Maurice (he hated to hear her call Meister by his Christian name) was going to start Johnny on a poultry farm: she had worked out to a day the end of Johnny's period of imprisonment.

"He has three months remitted for every year if he is on his best behaviour," she said. "And Johnny is being very sensible. When he wrote the other day, he told me he was going to earn his full marks. That will be wonderful, won't it, Alan?"

He hesitated to ask the question that was in his mind, but presently he put it to her, and she nodded.

"Yes, he writes about you, and he has no resentment at all. I think you could be a very good friend to him when he comes out."

Her own days were so filled, she told him, that the time was passing rapidly, more rapidly than she had dared hope. Maurice was most kind. (How often she repeated that very sentence!) And life at Malpas Mansions was moving smoothly. She had been able to employ a little maid-of-all-work.

"A queer little thing who insists upon telling me all the horrors of Deptford." She smiled quietly. "As though I hadn't enough horrors of my own! Her favourite hero is The Ringer—do you know about him?"

Alan nodded.

"He's the hero of all the funny-minded people of Deptford," he said. "They love the thought of anybody outwitting the police."

"He is not in England, is he?" Alan shook his head. "Are you terribly interested in The Ringer?" she went on. "Because, if you are, I can tell you something—I have met his wife."

He opened his eyes wide at this.

"Cora Ann Milton?" he said incredulously, and she laughed at the impression her words had made on him.

She told him of Cora Ann's visit, and yet for some reason, which she did not understand herself, she did not give a faithful account of that interview, or even hint that Cora Ann had warned her against Meister. It was when she came to the code letter that he was more interested.

"I've only just remembered it!" she said penitently; "it is in my bureau and ought to be sent to her."

"A code card—that is very important," said Alan. "Do you think you could bring it to me tomorrow?"

She nodded.

"But why on earth did she come—the night Johnny was arrested, you say?" said Alan. "Have you seen her since?"

Mary shook her head. "Don't let's talk about The Ringer. It's shop to you, isn't it? It's shop to us both—ugh!" She shivered.

They strolled through Green Park together and dined at a little restaurant in Soho. He told her of his new *bête noir*—the black-bearded Inspector Bliss, and was so vehement on the subject that she dissolved into laughter. It was the day of days in Alan Wembury's life, and when he left her, after seeing her on a tramcar bound southward, something of the colour of life went with her.

Meister had asked the girl to call at his house on her way home, but mentally Mary had laid down a formula which was subsequently to serve her well. She had fixed nine o'clock as the utmost limit she could work in the house, and as it was past that hour when she reached New Cross, she went straight to Malpas Mansions. One little luxury had been introduced into the flat: Maurice had insisted that she should be connected with the telephone system, and this was a great comfort to her.

The bell was ringing as she unlocked the door, and, lighting the gas, hurried to the little table where the instrument stood. As she expected, it was Meister.

"My dear girl, where have you been?" he asked testily. "I have been waiting for you since eight o'clock."

She glanced at the watch on her wrist: it was a quarter to ten.

"I'm sorry, Maurice," she said, "but I didn't definitely promise I'd call."

"Have you been to a theatre or something?" he asked suspiciously. "You didn't tell me anything about it?"

"No, I've been to see a friend."

"A man?"

Mary Lenley possessed an almost inexhaustible fund of patience, but the persistence of this cross-examination irritated her, and he must have guessed this, for, before she could reply, he went on: "Forgive my curiosity, my dear, but I am acting in *loco parentis* to you whilst poor Johnny is away, and I'd like to know—"

"I went to dinner with a friend," she interrupted shortly. "I'm sorry I have put you to any inconvenience, but I did not exactly promise, did I?"

A pause.

"Can't you come round now?"

Her "No" was very decisive.

"It is much too late, Maurice. What is it you want doing?"

If he had answered right away, she might have believed him, but the pause was just a little too long.

"Affidavits!" she scoffed. "How absurd, at this time of night! I'll come down earlier in the morning."

"Your friend was not by any chance Alan Wembury?" asked Meister's voice.

Mary considered that a very opportune moment to hang up the receiver.

She went into her little bedroom to change whilst the kettle was boiling, and the draught from the open window slammed the door behind her. She lit the gas, and closed the window with a thoughtful frown. She had given her servant a holiday, and the girl had left before her. Because of a threatening rainstorm, Mary had gone round the flat closing every window. Who had opened it? She looked round the room and a chill crept down her spine. Somebody had been in the room: one of the drawers in her chest had been forced open. As far as she could see, nothing had been stolen. Then with a gasp she remembered the code letter—it was gone! The wardrobe had been opened also; her dresses had been moved, and the long drawer beneath had been searched. By whom? Not by any ordinary burglar, for nothing except the letter had been taken.

She went back to the window and, pulling it open, looked down. There was a sheer drop into the yard of fifty feet. To the right was the tiny balcony jutting out from her kitchenette, and by its side a balance lift by which the households in Malpas Mansions could obtain their supplies from the tradesmen in the yard below. The lift was at the bottom, and she could see the long steel ropes swaying gently in the stiff breeze that was blowing. A nimble man could climb to the level of the balcony without any superhuman effort. But what man, nimble or otherwise, would risk his neck for the sake of turning over her few poor possessions and extracting Cora Ann's letter?

She had an electric torch in the kitchen, and she brought this to make a closer inspection. It was then she found the wet footprints on the carpet. It was a new carpet and had the disadvantage of showing every stain. Two muddy footprints were so clearly on view that she wondered she had not seen them when she came into the room.

She made another discovery: the dressing-table where she had left a number of brushes neatly arranged was all disarranged. She found one of the clothes brushes at the foot of the bed, and it had evidently been used to brush somebody who was very untidy, for it was wet and had a smear of mud at the end of the bristles. Nor had the cool intruder been satisfied with a rough toilet: he had used her hair-brushes; in the white bristles she saw a coarse black hair. She had seen its kind before: her father had a trick of straightening his beard with any brush that was handy. Somebody with a beard, a black beard, had tidied himself before the glass. She began to laugh; the idea was so absurd; but it was not long before she was serious again.

She heard the bell ring in the kitchen, and opened the front door to find the man who acted as porter to the block.

"I'm sorry to bother you, miss, but has anybody been in your flat whilst you have been out?"

"That's just what I was wondering, Jenkins," she answered, and led him into the room to show him the evidence of the visit.

"There has been a man hanging around the block all the evening," said the porter, scratching his head; "a fellow with a little black beard. One of the tenants saw him in the back courtyard just before dark, having a look at the tradesmen's lift, and the lady who lives on the opposite landing says before that he was knocking at this door for ten minutes, trying to make somebody hear. That must have been about eight o'clock Have you lost anything, miss?"

She shook her head.

"Nothing valuable." She could not explain the exact value of The Ringer's code card.

Chapter 20

A man with a beard! Where had she heard about a man with a beard? And then she suddenly remembered her talk with Alan. Inspector Bliss! That idea seemed too fantastic for words.

She took the telephone directory, and turned the pages until she found the Flanders Lane police station. A gruff voice answered her. Mr. Wembury had not returned. He had been out all day but was expected at any minute. She gave her name and telephone number, and insisted upon the private nature of the call. An hour later the telephone bell rang and Alan's voice greeted her. She told him in a few words what had happened, and she heard his gasp of astonishment.

"I don't think it could possibly have been the person you think," he said, and she realised he was probably speaking in a room where other people were. "But if it's not too late, may I come round?"

"Do, please," she said without hesitation.

Alan came after such a remarkably short interval that she suggested he must have flown.

"A taxi," he explained. "One doesn't often see them in High Street, Deptford, but I was fortunate."

It was the first time he had been in the flat since Johnny's arrest. The very arrangement of the furniture aroused ugly memories. She must have divined this, for she led him straight to her room, and showed him the evidence of the visitor's presence.

"Bliss?" he frowned. "Why on earth should Bliss come here? What on earth did he expect to find?"

"That is what I should like to know." She could smile now. It was rather wonderful how comforting was the presence of Alan Wembury. "If it were the letter, he could have come and asked for it."

But he shook his head. "Have you anything here of Meister's—any papers?" he asked suddenly.

She shook her head.

"Keys?" he suggested.

"Why, yes, of course!" she remembered. "I've the keys of the house. His old cook is rather deaf, and Maurice is seldom up when I arrive, so he has given me a key of the outer gate and the door."

"Where do you keep them?" asked Alan.

She opened her bag.

"I carry them about with me. Besides, Alan, why on earth should Mr. Bliss want the keys? I suppose he can see Mr. Meister whenever he wishes."

But Alan's mind was on another trail. Did Bliss know of the visit of Cora Ann Milton to this girl? Supposing he had set himself the task of hunting down The Ringer—and Alan Wembury had not been notified that the Central Office were playing a lone hand—would he make this difficult entry in order to test his suspicions? And suppose he were after the letter; how would he have heard of it?

"Only one man would have come after that letter—and that man is The Ringer," he said with conviction.

He had left the front door open when he came in, and now, as they returned to the dining-room, the porter appeared in the hall.

"Here you are, miss," he called eagerly. "The fellow's outside. What about calling a policeman?"

"Which fellow?" asked Wembury quickly. "Do you mean the bearded man?"

Evidently the porter did not know Alan for a police officer.

"Yes, sir. Don't you think we ought to call a policeman? There's one on point duty at the end of the road."

Wembury brushed past him and ran down the stairs. Emerging into the night, he saw a man standing on the opposite side of the road. He made no attempt to conceal himself: indeed, he was standing in the full light of the street lamp, but drew aside as Wembury crossed the road, and long before he reached the stranger, he knew that Mary's surmise had been correct. It was Bliss.

"Good evening. Inspector Wembury," was the cool greeting.

Without preliminary, Alan made his accusation.

"Somebody has broken into Miss Lenley's flat tonight, and I have reason to believe it is you, Bliss."

"Broken into Miss Lenley's flat, eh?" The central inspector was rather amused. "Do I look like a burglar?"

"I don't know what you look like, but you were seen in the court-yard just before dark, examining the food lift. There's no doubt that the man who entered Miss Lenley's room gained admission by that means."

"In that case," said Bliss, "you had better take me down to your funny little police station and charge me. But before you do so, I will make your job a little easier by confessing that I did climb that infernal rope, that I did force the window of Miss Lenley's bedroom, that I did inspect the flat. But I did not find what I expected to find. The man who was there before me got that."

"Is that your explanation?" asked Wembury, when the other had finished, "that there was another man in the flat?"

"Exactly—a perfect explanation, though it may not satisfy you. I did not climb the rope until I had seen somebody else go up that way, and open the window. It was just before dusk. Your friends will doubtless tell you that I immediately went up the stairs and knocked at Miss Lenley's door, and, receiving no answer, decided to make my entrance the same way as the unknown intruder. Does that satisfy you, Mr. Wembury, or do you think that as a police officer I exceeded my duty in chasing a burglar?"

Alan was in a quandary. If the story the man told was true, he had perfect justification for his action. But was it true?

"Did you turn out the contents of the drawers by any chance?"

Bliss shook his head.

"No, I'm afraid our friend forestalled me there. I opened one drawer and gathered from its confusion that my predecessor had made a search. I don't think he found what he wanted, and that he will very likely come again tonight. That is why I am here. Have you any further questions, inspector?"

"No," said Alan shortly.

"And you're not thinking of inviting me to meet your superintendent? Good! Then I think my presence for the moment is a little superfluous." And, with a jerk of his shoulder, he turned and strolled at a leisurely pace along the sidewalk.

Going back to the girl, Alan told her of his interview, and loyalty to his cloth prevented his giving his own private views on the matter.

"He may be speaking the truth," he said. "Of course, it was his duty to follow a burglar. If he is lying, we shall hear no more of it, but if he is telling the truth he will have to report the matter."

He left her half an hour later, and as he went out of the flat, he looked round for Bliss, but there was no sign of him. When he returned to the police station, he was taken aback to learn that Bliss had indeed reported the burglary, given times and full particulars, and had added a note to his report to the effect that Divisional Inspector Wembury had charge of the case.

Alan was baffled. If Bliss's account was true, who could have been the first man to climb up the rope? And what other object had he in burgling Mary Lenley's flat than a search for the code? It brought The Ringer too near for comfort. Here was a mystery, which was never solved until that night of horror when The Ringer came to Meister's house.

Two little problems were recurring to Mary Lenley from day to day. Not the least important of these was contained in the formula, "Shall I tell Maurice?" Should she tell Maurice that she had been to tea with Alan Wembury…should she tell him of the burglary that had been committed the night before? On the whole she felt the least unpleasant confession, the one which would absorb him to the exclusion, was the second of her adventures.

Maurice was not down when she arrived, and Mr. Samuel Hackitt, newly installed in the Meister household, was polishing wearily the window that looked out on to the leads. He had made his appearance a few days before, and in spite of his unpleasant past Mary liked the little man.

"Good morning, miss." He touched an invisible cap. "The old man's still up in bed, bless his old heart!"

"Mr. Meister had a heavy night," she said primly.

"'Thick' is the word I'd use," said Sam, wringing out a leather cloth at his leisure.

Very wisely Mary did not encourage any further revelations.

"Funny old house, this, miss." Sam knocked with his knuckle at one of the panels. "Holler. It's more like a rabbit warren than a house." Mr. Meister's residence had been built in the days when Peter the Great was still living in Deptford. She passed this news of historical interest on to the wholly unimpressed man.

"I never knew Peter. . .King, was he? That sounds like one of Meister's lies."

"It's history, Sam," she said severely, as she dusted her typewriter.

"I don't take any notice of history—that's lies, too," said Hackitt, calmly. "Lor' miss, you don't know all the his'try books I've read—'Ume, Macaulay, Gibbons, the feller that wrote all about Rome."

She was astounded.

"You've read them?"

He nodded. "Studied 'em," he said solemnly, so solemnly that she laughed.

"You're quite a student: I didn't realise that you were such a well-read man."

"You have to do something in 'stir'," said Sam, and she realised that this reading of his had whiled away some period of his incarceration.

He had an extraordinary stock of knowledge on unlikely subjects. Possibly this was gained under similar circumstances. Once or twice he strayed to the piano, although this had been dusted and polished, as she could see in her face reflected in the black top; but the piano fascinated him, and probably he had a higher respect for Mr. Meister because of his musical qualities than for his knowledge of the law. He depressed a key that tinkled sharply and apologised.

"I'm going up to Scotland Yard tomorrow, miss," he said, and she thought it had something to do with his recent imprisonment, and expressed only a polite interest. "Never been there before," said Sam complacently, "but I suppose it's like every other busy's office—one chair, one table, one pair of handcuffs, a sergeant and forty-five thousand perjuring liars!"

The entrance of Meister at that moment cut short his speculations. Maurice looked shaky and ill, she thought. After he had gruffly dismissed his new servitor, he told her he had slept badly.

"Where did you go—" he began.

She thought it was an excellent moment to tell him of her burglar.

And because she did not wish to talk of Cora Ann she made no reference to the stolen letter. He listened in amazement, until she came to the interview which Alan had had with Inspector Bliss.

"Bliss! That's queer!"

He stood up, his eyes tightened, as though he were facing a bright light.

"Bliss. . . .I haven't seen him for years. He's been in America. A clever fellow. . . .Bliss. . .humph!"

"But don't you think it was extraordinary, Maurice, that he should climb up into my flat, or that there should have been anybody there before him—what profit can they find in burgling my poor little apartment?"

Maurice shook his head.

"I don't believe it. Bliss wanted to find something in your room. The yarn about another man having gone up is all bunk."

"But what could he find?" she insisted, and Maurice Meister was not prepared to offer a convincing reason.

Bliss! He had no right in Deptford, unless—Maurice was both puzzled and apprehensive. The advent of a Central man to Deptford could only indicate some extraordinary happening, and in his mind, he went over the various events which might be calculated to interest that exalted policeman. Strangely enough, Deptford at this moment was unusually well behaved. There had been no serious charges in the division for three months, and Meister, who had his finger in more lawless pies than his worst enemy gave him credit for, knew that there had been no steal of such importance that Scotland Yard would send one who was reputedly its most promising officer to conduct an independent examination.

By some extraordinary process, peculiarly his own, he decided that there was nothing sinister in this attention. Probably Headquarters were trying out the new divisional inspector, and had sent this wise and experienced officer to discover the extent of his acquaintance with the Lenleys.

Meister's breakfast was not an elaborate meal, and was usually served in his little bureau. This morning it consisted, as usual, of a cup of coffee, a small plate of fruit and a biscuit. He unfolded the newspaper by the side of his table and glanced at it idly. His life was so full that he had little time for, or interest in, the great events of the world; but a news item at the top of the columns caught his eye.

"Prison Riot Convict Saves the Life of Deputy Governor"

He glanced through the description, expecting to find a name with which he was familiar, but, as is usual in these cases, a strict anonymity was preserved as to the identity of the prisoner concerned. There had been a riot in a county jail; the ringleaders had struck down a warder and taken possession of his keys, and would have killed the deputy governor, who happened to be in the prison hall at the time, but for the bravery of a convict who, with the aid of a broom handle, defended the official till armed warders came on the scene. Maurice pursed his lips and smiled. His regard for the criminal was a very low one. They were hardly human beings; he speculated idly on what reward the heroic convict would receive. Something more than he deserved.

Opening the box of cigars that was on the table, he bit off the end and lit a long, black cheroot, and as he smoked his mind vacillated between Mary and her peculiar experience. What was Bliss doing in Deptford, he wondered; he tried to recall the man as he had known him years before, but he was unsuccessful.

Hackitt came in to clear away the breakfast things, and, glancing familiarly over Meister's shoulder, read the account.

"That deputy's a pretty nice fellow," he volunteered. "I wonder what made the boys get up against him. But the screws are bad."

Meister raised his cold eyes.

"If you want to keep this job, you'll not speak unless you're spoken to, Hackitt."

"No offence," said Hackitt, quite unperturbed. "I'm naturally chatty."

"Then try your chattiness on somebody else!" snapped Maurice.

The man went out of the room with the tray, and had gone a few minutes before he returned, bearing a long yellow envelope. Meister, snatching it from his hand, glanced at the superscription. It was marked "Very Urgent and Confidential" and bore the stamp of Scotland Yard.

"Who brought this?" he asked.

"A copper," said Sam.

Maurice pointed to the door.

"You can go."

He waited till the door had closed upon his servant before he tore open the flap, and his hand shook as he drew out the folded typewritten paper.

Sir, I have the honour to inform you that the deputy commissioner, Colonel Walford, C.B., wishes to see you at his office at

Scotland Yard at 11.30 in the forenoon tomorrow. The matter is of the greatest importance, and the deputy commissioner wishes me to say that he trusts you will make every effort to keep this appointment, and notify him by telegram if you cannot be at Scotland Yard at the hour named.

I have the honour to be, sir, (etc.)

A summons to Scotland Yard! The first that Meister had ever received. What did it portend?

He rose to his feet, opened a little cupboard and took out a long bottle of brandy, and splashed a generous portion into a glass, and he was furious with himself to find that his hand was shaking. What did Scotland Yard know? What did they wish to know? His future, his very liberty, depended on the answer to those questions. The morrow! The very day he had chosen to put into execution certain plans he had formulated. Unconsciously Scotland Yard had given Mary Lenley a day of respite!

Chapter 21

At the lawyer's request, Mary came early to work the following morning, and she was surprised to find Maurice up and dressed. He was one of those men who usually was meticulously careful as to his dress, and indeed was almost a dandy in this respect. But he was usually a slow dresser and liked to lounge about the house in his pale green dressing-gown until the arrival of clients or the necessity for a consultation with counsel, made him shed that garment.

When she came in, he was walking up and down the room with his hands clasped behind him. He looked as if he had not slept very well, and she remarked upon this.

"Yes, I slept all right." He spoke jerkily, nervously, and he was obviously labouring under some very strong emotion. It never occurred to Mary Lenley that that emotion might be fear. "I have to go to Scotland Yard, my dear," said Meister, "and I was wondering"—he forced a smile—"whether you would like to come up with me—not into the Yard," he added hastily, when he saw the look of repugnance on her face. "Perhaps you would like to stay at a—at a tearoom or somewhere until I came out?"

"But why, Maurice?" The request was most unexpected.

He was not patient to answer questions.

"If you don't wish to come, don't, my dear—" he said sharply, but altered his tone. "There are one or two things I would like to talk to you about—business matters in which I may need a little—clerical assistance."

He walked to her desk and took up a paper.

"Here are the names and addresses of a number of people: I wish you to keep this paper in your bag. The gentlemen named should be notified if anything—I mean, if it is necessary."

He could not tell her that he had passed that night in a cold sweat of fear, alternating snatches of bad dreams with an endless cogitation on the unpleasant possibilities which the morrow held. Nor could he explain that the names which he had written down and chosen with such care, were men of substance who might vouch for him in certain eventualities. He might have confessed with truth that he wanted her company that morning for the distraction he needed during the hours that preceded his interview with the commissioner; and if the worst happened, for somebody to be at hand whom he could notify and trust to work in his interests.

"I don't know what they want me for at Scotland Yard," he said, with an attempt at lightness. "Probably some little matter connected with one of my clients."

"Do they often send for you?" she asked innocently.

He looked at her quickly. "No, I have never been before. In fact, it is a most unusual procedure. I have never heard of a solicitor being sent for."

She nodded at this. "I thought so," she said. "Alan told me that they ask you to come to Scotland Yard either to 'pump' you or catch you!"

He glowered at this. "I beg of you not to give me at second hand the vulgarities of your police officer friend. 'To pump you'—what an expression! Obviously, they have asked me to go because I've defended some rascal about whom they want information. Possibly the man is planning to rob me."

The point was such a sore one that Mary very wisely refrained from carrying it any further.

Maurice possessed no car of his own, and it was characteristic of him that the local garage could supply no machine of sufficient magnificence to support his state. The Rolls which came to him from a West End hirer was the newest and shiniest that could be procured, and to the admiration and envy of the Flanders Laners, who stood in their doorways to watch the departure, Mary drove off with her employer. His nervousness seemed to increase rather than diminish as Deptford was left behind. He asked her half a dozen times if she had the paper with the names of his influential friends. Once, after an interregnum of gloomy silence on his part, she had tried to make conversation by asking him if he had seen an item in the newspaper.

"Riot in a prison?" he answered abstractedly. "No—yes, I did. What about it?"

"It is the prison Johnny is in," she said, "and I was rather worried —he is such an impetuous boy, and probably he has done something foolish. Is there any way of finding out?"

Meister was interested.

"Was Johnny in that jail? I didn't realise that. Yes, my dear, we'll find out if you wish."

He evidently brooded upon this aspect of the prison riot, for as the car was crossing Westminster Bridge he said: "I hope Johnny is not involved: it would mean the loss of his marks."

She had hardly digested this ominous remark before the car turned on to the Thames Embankment and pulled up just short of the entrance to Scotland Yard.

"Perhaps you would like to sit in the car and wait?"

"How long will you be gone?" she asked.

Mr. Meister would have given a lot of money to have been able to answer that question with any accuracy.

"I don't know. These official people are very dilatory. Anyway, you can amuse yourself as you wish."

As he was talking, he saw a man drop nimbly from a tram-car and slouch across the road towards the arched entrance of police head-quarters.

"Hackitt?" he said incredulously. "He didn't tell me he was coming. He served me my breakfast half an hour before you arrived at the house."

His face was twitching. She was amazed that so small a thing could have so devastating an effect.

"All right," he nodded and scarcely looking at her, strode away.

He stopped at the entrance to the Yard as some creature of the wild might halt at the entrance of a trap. What did Hackitt know about him? What could Hackitt say? When he had taken the man into his employ, he had not been actuated by any sense of charity—on the contrary, he felt he was securing a bargain. But was Hackitt in the pay of the police—a "nose," sent into his house to pry amongst his papers, unearth his secrets, reveal the mysteries of locked cellars and

84

boarded-up attics?

Setting his teeth, he walked down the gentle slope and turned into Scotland Yard.

Chapter 22

Mary elected to spend the first part of her time of waiting in the car with a newspaper, but the printed page was a poor rival to the pageant of life that was moving past. The clanging trams crowded with passengers, the endless procession of vehicles crossing the beautiful bridge, the panorama of London which was visible through the front windows of the car. She wondered if business would call Alan Wembury to headquarters, and had dismissed this possibility when he made a very commonplace appearance. Somebody walked past the car with long strides: she only saw the back of him, but in an instant, she was out on the sidewalk. He heard her voice and spun round.

"Why, Mary!" he said, his face lighting up. "What on earth are you doing this side of the world? You haven't come with Meister?"

"Did you know they've sent for him?"

Alan nodded.

"Is it anything very important? He is a little worried, I think."

Wembury might have told her that Meister's worry before he went to Scotland Yard was as nothing to what it would be after.

"You didn't bring Mr. Hackitt by any chance?" he smiled, and she shook her head.

"No, Maurice didn't know that Hackitt was coming—I think that rather distressed him. What is the mystery, Alan?"

He laughed. "The mystery is the one you're making, my dear." And then, as he saw the colour come to her face, he went on penitently: "I'm awfully sorry. That's terribly familiar."

"I don't mind really," she laughed. "I'm pretending that you're a very old gentleman. Do you often have these important conferences? And who is that, Alan?"

A beautiful little coupe had drawn noiselessly to the kerb just ahead of their own car. The chauffeur jumped down, opened the lacquered door, and a girl got out, looked up at the facade of Scotland Yard and passed leisurely under the arch. Though it was early in the morning, and the place was crowded, a cigarette burnt between her gloved fingers and she left behind her the elusive fragrance of some eastern perfume.

"She's a swell, isn't she? And an old acquaintance of yours."

"Not Mrs. Milton!" said the girl in amazement.

"Mrs. Milton it is. I must run after her and shepherd her into a nice airy room."

She dismissed him with a nod. He took her hand in his for a moment and looked down into her eyes.

"You know where to find me, Mary?" he said in a low voice, and before she could answer this cryptic question, he was gone.

At the request of a policeman, the driver of her car moved the car beyond the gateway and came to a halt at a place where she had a more comprehensive view of the building. It did not look like a police headquarters: it might have been the head office of some prosperous insurance company, or a Government building on which a usually staid architect had been allowed to give full play to his Gothic tendencies. What was happening behind those windows? What drama or tragedy was being played out in those rooms which look upon the Embankment? She thought of Johnny and shivered a little. His record was somewhere in that building, tabulated in long cabinets, his finger-prints, body-marks, colouring. It was dreadfully odd to think of Johnny as a number in a card index. Did they have numbers in jail also? She seemed to remember reading about such things.

She was suddenly conscious that somebody was staring in at the car, and, turning her head, she met a pair of humorous blue eyes that twinkled under shaggy grey eyebrows. A tall, bent figure in a homespun suit, with an impossible brown felt hat on the back of his white head, and he was obviously wishing to speak to her. She opened the door of the car and came out.

"Ye'll be Miss Lenley, I think? My name's Lomond."

"Oh, yes, you're Dr. Lomond," she smiled. "I thought I recognised you."

"But, my dear leddy, you've never seen me!"

"Alan—Mr. Wembury says you look like every doctor he has ever known."

This seemed to please him, for his shoulders shook with silent laughter.

"Ye're no' curious, or you'd ask me how I knew you," he said. And then he looked up at Scotland Yard. "A sad and gloomy-faced place, young leddy." He shook his head dolefully. "You've no' been called here professionally?"

As he spoke, he fumbled in his pockets, produced a silver tobacco-box and rolled a cigarette.

"They've dragged me from my studies to examine a poor wee body," he said, and at first, she took him literally, and thought he had been brought to identify some drowned or murdered man, and the look of antipathy in her face was not lost on the doctor.

"She's alive," he gurgled, "and no' so unattractive!" He held out his long hand. "I'd like to be meeting you more often, Miss Lenley. Mebbe I'll come along and see you one day, and we'll have a bit chat."

"I should love it, doctor," she said truthfully.

She liked the old man: there was a geniality and a youthfulness in that smile of his that went straight to her heart. She watched him shuffling laboriously, the cigarette still twisting and rolling in his hand, until the grey pillars of the gateway hid him for view. Who was the poor wee body? She knew that he referred to a forthcoming cross-examination, for Alan had told her of his exploit with the poisoner Ann Prideaux. And then it flashed upon her—Cora Milton! She felt rather sorry for Dr. Lomond: he was such a nice, gentle soul; he would find Cora Ann Milton a particularly difficult lady.

Chapter 23

Mary did not see Central Detective Inspector Bliss walk quickly through the stone doorway of Scotland Yard. He scarcely acknowledged the salute of the constable on duty, and passed along the vaulted corridor to the chief constable's room. A slight, bearded man, pale of face, brusque of manner, he might hold the respect of his subordinates, but he had no place in their affections.

"That's Mr. Bliss," said the officer to a younger constable. "Keep out of his way. He was bad enough before he went to America—he's a pig now!"

Mr. Maurice Meister, sitting on a hard form in one waiting-room, saw him pass the open door and frowned. The walk of the man was oddly familiar.

Sam Hackitt, ex-convict, lounging in the corridor in charge of a plain clothes police officer, scratched his nose thoughtfully and wondered where he had seen the face before. Mr. Bliss opened the door of the chief constable's room, walked in and slammed the door. Wembury, gazing abstractedly through the double windows which gave a view of the Embankment, turned his head and nodded. Every time he had met Central Inspector Bliss, he had liked him less.

The bearded man made for the desk in the centre of the room, picked up a sheet of paper, read it and grunted. A trim messenger came in and handed him a letter, he read the address and dropped the envelope on the table. Turning his head with an impatient growl, he asked: "Why is the assistant commissioner holding this inquiry, anyway? It's not an administration job. Things have changed pretty considerably since I was here."

Alan withdrew his attention from the new County Council building. "The chief constable had the case in hand," he said, "but he's away ill, so Colonel Walford is taking it for him."

"But why Walford?" snarled Bliss. "He has about as much knowledge of the job as my foot!"

Alan was very patient. He knew that he would be meeting Bliss that morning and had it in his mind to ask him about that mysterious visit he had paid to Malpas Mansions, but Bliss seemed hardly in a communicative mood.

"This is a pretty big thing. If The Ringer is really back—and headquarters is pretty certain that he is—"

Bliss smiled contemptuously. "The Ringer!" And then, remembering: "Who is this man who wrote from Maidstone Prison?"

"Hackitt—a fellow who knew him."

Bliss laughed harshly. "Hackitt! Do you think that Hackitt knows anything about him? You're getting pretty credulous at Scotland Yard in these days!"

The whole attitude of the man was offensive. It was as though he wished deliberately to antagonise the other.

"He says he'd recognise him."

"Bosh!" said Bliss scornfully. "It's an old lag's trick. He'd say anything to make a sensation."

"Dr. Lomond says—" began Alan, and was stopped by an explosive snort from the bearded detective.

"I don't want to know what any police surgeon says! That fellow's got a hell of a nerve. He wanted to teach me my business."

It was news to Wembury that the pawky old police surgeon had ever crossed swords with this querulous man.

"Lomond's a clever fellow!" he protested.

Bliss was turning the leaves of a book he had taken from the table.

"So, he admits in this book of his. I suppose this sort of thing impresses you, eh? I've been two years in America, the home of all this anthropology sort of muck. I've met madmen who could give points to Lomond. Suppose Hackitt says he knows The Ringer, who else is going to identify him?" he asked, throwing down the volume.

"You, for one. I understand you tried to arrest him after the Atta-man case."

Bliss looked at him sharply. "I? I never saw the swine. He had his back to me the day I went to pinch him. I just laid my hands on him when—bingo! I was on the ground with four inches of good knife in me. Who's seen him?"

"Meister?" suggested Alan.

The other man frowned. "Meister! Will he ever have a chance of talking? That is what I want to know!"

It was the second surprise of the morning for Wembury. "Why shouldn't he?"

But Inspector Bliss avoided the question. "I'll bet Meister never saw him plainly in his life. Too full of dope, for one thing. The Ringer's clever. I hand it to him. I wish to God I'd never left Washington—I had a soft job there."

"You don't seem very happy," smiled the younger man.

"If you'd been there, they'd have kept you there," snapped the other. "They wanted me back at the Yard."

In spite of his annoyance Wembury laughed. "I like your manners, but I hate your modesty," he said. "And yet we seem to have been catching 'em all right. I haven't noticed very much depression amongst the criminal classes since you returned."

But Bliss was not to be drawn. He was studying the title page of the book in his hand, and was on the point of making some sarcastic reference to Dr. Lomond and his anthropological studies when Colonel Walford came in and the two men stiffened to attention.

"Sorry, gentlemen, to keep you waiting," he said cheerfully. "Good morning, Bliss."

"Good morning, sir."

"There's a letter for you, sir," said Wembury.

"Yes," growled Bliss impatiently. "The assistant commissioner can see that for himself."

"The man who wrote to you from Maidstone is here, sir," reported Alan.

"Oh, Hackitt?"

"You don't think he knows The Ringer, do you, sir?" asked Bliss with a contemptuous smile.

"Honestly, I don't. But he comes from Deptford. There's just a remote chance that he's speaking the truth. Have him up, Wembury—I'll go along and tell the chief commissioner I am taking the inquiry."

When he had gone: "Hackitt!" said Bliss. "Huh! I remember him. Five-six years ago I got him eighteen months at the London Sessions for housebreaking. A born liar!"

Two minutes later, in response to Alan's telephoned instructions, the "born liar" was ushered into the room.

Mr. Samuel Cuthbert Hackitt had the pert manner of the irrepressible Cockney. He stood now, in no wise abashed by the surroundings or awed by the imponderable menace of Scotland Yard.

Alan Wembury smiled a greeting.

"Hallo, Mr. Wembury!" said Sam cheerfully. "You're looking bright an' 'ealthy."

He was looking hard at Alan's companion.

"You remember Mr. Bliss?"

"Bliss?" Sam frowned. "You've changed a bit, ain't yer? Where did yer get your whiskers from?"

"You shut your ugly mouth," snapped Bliss, and Sam grinned.

"That's more like yer."

"Remember where you are, Hackitt," warned Wembury.

The ex-convict showed his white teeth again. "I know where I am, sir. Scotland Yard. You don't 'arf do yourselves well, don't you? Where's the grand planner? Meister's got one! Look at the flowers—love a duck, everything the 'eart can desire."

If looks could kill, the scowl on the face of Bliss would have removed one law breaker from the world. What he might have said is a matter for conjecture as the commissioner came back at that moment.

"Good mornin', sir," said Sam affably. "Nice pitch you've got here. All made out of thieving and murder!"

Colonel Walford concealed a smile. "We have a letter from you when you were in prison, Hackitt." He opened a folder and, taking out a sheet of blue note-paper, read:

Dear Sir: This comes hoping to find you well, and all kind friends at Scotland Yard—

"I didn't know Bliss was back," interjected Sam.

The Colonel continued:

There's a lot of talk about The Ringer down here—him that was drowned in Australia. Dear sir, I can tell you a lot about him now that he's departed this life, as I once see him though only for a second and I knew where he lodged.

"Is that true?"

"Yes, sir," nodded Sam. "I lodged in the same 'ouse."

"Oh, then, you know what he looks like?"

"What he looked like," corrected Sam. "He's dead."

Colonel Walford shook his head, and the man's jaw dropped. Looking at him, Alan saw his face change colour.

"Not dead? The Ringer alive? Good morning, thank you very much!" He turned to go.

"What do you know about him?"

"Nothing!" said Hackitt emphatically. "I'll tell you the truth, sir, without any madam whatsoever, (telling the tale). Nosing on a dead man's one thing," said Sam earnestly; "nosing on a live Ringer is another, I give you my word! I know a bit about The Ringer—not much, but a bit. And I'm not goin' to tell that bit. And why? Because I just come out of 'stir' and Meister's give me a job. I want to live peaceable without any trouble from anybody."

"Now don't be foolish, Hackitt," said the commissioner "If you can help us, we may be able to help you."

Sam's long lip curled in a sardonic smile.

"If I'm dead, can you help me to get alive?" he asked sarcastically. "I don't nose on The Ringer. He's a bit too hot for me."

"I don't believe you know anything," sneered Bliss.

"What you believe don't interest me," growled the convict.

"Come on—if you know anything, tell the commissioner. What are you afraid of?"

"What you're afraid of," snapped Hackitt. "He nearly got you once! Ah! That don't make you laugh! I'm very sorry; I come up here under what is termed a misapprehension. Goodbye, everybody."

He turned to go.

"Here, wait," said Bliss.

"Let him go—let him go!" The commissioner waved Sam Hackitt out of existence.

"He never saw The Ringer," said Bliss when the man had gone.

Walford shook his head. "I don't agree. His whole attitude shows that he has. Is Meister here?"

"Yes, sir—he's in the waiting-room," replied Alan.

Chapter 24

A few seconds later came Maurice Meister, his debonair self, yet not wholly at his ease. He strode into the room, examined his wristwatch ostentatiously, and looked from one to the other.

"I think there must be some mistake," he said. "I thought I was going to see the chief constable."

Walford nodded. "Yes, but unfortunately he's ill; I'm taking his place."

"I was asked to call at eleven-thirty; it is now"—he consulted his watch—"twelve-forty-nine. I have a case to defend at the Greenwich Police Court. God knows what will happen to the poor devil if I'm not there."

"I am sorry to have kept you waiting," said Colonel Walford coldly. "Take a seat."

As he went to sit, putting his stick and hat on the desk, he looked at Bliss. "Your face is vaguely familiar," he said.

"My name is Bliss," replied the detective. The eyes of the two men met.

So, this was Bliss: Maurice averted his eyes from that defiant stare. "I'm sorry—I thought I knew you."

He seated himself carefully near the desk, placed his hat on the table and drew off his gloves.

"It is a little unusual, is it not, to summon an officer of the Royal Courts of Justice to Scotland Yard?" he asked.

The assistant commissioner settled himself back in his chair: he had dealt with men far cleverer than Maurice Meister.

"Now, Mr. Meister, I am going to speak very frankly—that is why I brought you here."

Meister's brows met. "'Brought' is not a word I like, Mr. Walford."

"Colonel Walford," prompted Alan. The Colonel took up a minute paper and read a line or two.

"Mr. Meister," he began, "you are a lawyer with a large clientele in Deptford?" Meister nodded. "There isn't a thief in South London who doesn't know Mr. Meister of Flanders Lane. You are famous both as a defender of hopeless cases—and—er—as a philanthropist." Again, Meister inclined his head as though at a compliment. "A man commits a burglary and gets away with it. Later he is arrested; none of the stolen property is found—he is apparently penniless. Yet you not only defend him personally in the police court, and through eminent counsel at the Old Bailey, but during the time the man is in prison you support his relatives."

"Mere humanity! Am I—am I to be suspect, as it were, because I—I help these unfortunate people? I will not see the wives and the wretched children suffer through the faults of their parents," said Maurice Meister virtuously.

Bliss had stepped out of the room. Why, he wondered, in some apprehension?

"Oh, yes; I'm sure of that," answered the Colonel dryly. "Now, Mr. Meister, I haven't brought you here to ask you about the money that you distribute from week to week, or where it comes from. I'm not even going to suggest that somebody who has access to the prisoner in a professional capacity has learnt where the proceeds of the robbery are hidden, and has acted as his agent."

"I am glad you do not say that, Colonel." Meister had recovered his nerve by now; was his old urbane self. There was danger here, deadly, devastating danger. He had need for a cool head. "If you had said that, I should have been extremely—"

"I'm not insisting on it, I tell you. The money comes from somewhere, Meister. I am not curious. Sometimes you do not support your clients with money—you take their relatives into your employment?"

"I help them in one way or another," admitted Meister.

The Colonel was eyeing him closely.

"When a convict has a pretty sister, for example, you find it convenient to employ her. You have a girl secretary now, a Miss Lenley?"

"Yes."

"Her brother went to prison for three years on information supplied to the police—by you!"

Meister shrugged his shoulders. "It was my duty. In whatever other respect I fail, my duty as a citizen is paramount."

"Two years ago," said Walford slowly, "she had a predecessor, a girl who was subsequently found drowned." He paused, as though waiting for a response. "You heard me?"

Maurice sighed and nodded. "Yes, I heard you. It was a tragedy. I've never been so shocked in my life—never. I don't like even to think about it."

"The girl's name was Gwenda Milton." Walford spoke deliberately. "The sister of Henry Arthur Milton—otherwise known as—The Ringer!"

There was something in his tone which was significant. Meister looked at the Colonel strangely.

"The most brilliant criminal we have in our records—and the most dangerous."

Two spots of dull red came into the sallow face of the lawyer.

"And never caught. Colonel—never caught!" he almost shouted. "Although the police knew that he was passing through Paris—knew the time to a minute—he slipped through their fingers. All the clever policemen in England and all the clever policemen in Australia have never caught him."

He gained control of his voice; was his old urbane self in an instant.

"I'm not saying anything against the police. As a ratepayer, I am proud of them—but it wasn't clever to let him slip. I don't mind saying this to you because you're new to the business."

The commissioner overlooked the implied insolence of this reference to his recent appointment.

"He should have been taken, I admit," he said quietly. "But that is beside the point. The Ringer left his sister in your care. Whether he trusted you with his money I don't know—he trusted you with his sister."

"I treated her well," protested Meister. "Was it my fault that she died? Did I throw her into the river? Be reasonable. Colonel!"

"Why did she end her life?" asked Walford sternly.

"How should I know? I never dreamt that she was in any kind of trouble. As God is my judge!"

The Colonel checked him with a gesture. "And yet you made all the arrangements for her at the nursing home," he said significantly.

Meister's face paled. "That's a lie!"

"It didn't come out at the inquest. Nobody knows but Scotland Yard and—Henry Arthur Milton!"

Maurice Meister smiled. "How can he know—he's dead. He died in Australia."

There was a pause, and then Walford spoke.

"The Ringer is alive—he's here," he said, and Meister came to his feet, white to the lips.

Chapter 25

Maurice Meister faced the assistant commissioner with horror in his eyes.

"The Ringer here! Are you serious?"

The commissioner nodded.

"I repeat—he's alive—he's here."

"That can't be true! He wouldn't dare come here with a death sentence hanging over him. The Ringer! You're trying to scare me—ha! ha!" He forced a laugh. "Your little joke, Colonel."

"He's here—I've sent for you to warn you."

"Why warn me?" demanded Meister. "I never saw him in my life, I don't even know what he looks like. I knew the girl he used to run around with an American girl. She was crazy about him. Where is she? Where she is, he is."

"She's in London. In this very building at this very moment!"

Meister's eyes opened wide.

"Here? The Ringer wouldn't dare do it!" And then, with sudden violence: "If you know he's in London, why don't you take him? The man's a madman. What are you for? To protect people—to protect me! Can't you get in touch with him? Can't you tell him that I knew nothing about his sister, that I looked after her and was like a father to her? Wembury, you know that I had nothing to do with this girl's death?"

He turned to Alan.

"I know nothing about it," said the detective coldly. "The only thing I know is that if anything happens to Mary Lenley, I'll—"

"Don't you threaten me!" stormed Meister.

"I don't know what women see in you, Meister! Your reputation is foul!"

Meister's lips were trembling. "Lies, more lies! They tear a man's character to rags, these scum! There have been women—naturally. We're men of the world. One isn't an anchorite. The Ringer!"—he forced a smile. "Pshaw! Somebody has been fooling you! Don't you think I should have heard? Not a bird moves in Deptford but I know it. Who has seen him?"

"Meister, I've warned you," said Walford seriously as he rang a bell. "From now on your house will be under our observation. Have bars put on your windows; don't admit anybody after dark and never leave the house by night except with a police escort."

Inspector Bliss came in at that moment.

"Oh, Bliss—I think Mr. Meister may need a little care taken of him—I put him in your charge. Watch over him like a father." The dark eyes of the detective fell upon the lawyer as he rose. "The day you take him I'll give a thousand pounds to the Police Orphanage," said Meister.

"We don't want money so badly as that. I think that is all. It is not my business to pass judgment on any man. It is a dangerous game that you are playing. Your profession gives you an advantage over other receivers—"

It was the one word above all others that Meister hated.

"Receiver! You hardly realise what you are saying."

"Indeed, I do. Good morning."

Meister polished his hat on his sleeve as he walked to the door. "You will be sorry for that statement, Colonel. For my own part, I am unmoved by your hasty judgment." He looked at his watch. "Five minutes to one—"

He had left behind his walking stick. Bliss picked it up. The handle was loose, and with a twist he drew out a long steel blade. "Your swordstick, Mr. Meister—you seem to be looking after yourself pretty well," he said with an unholy grin.

Meister shot one baleful look at him as he went out of the room.

He scarcely remembered leaving the chief constable's office, but walked down the corridor and into the yard like a man in a dream. It was not possible. The Ringer back in London! All these stories at which he had scoffed were true. A terrible miracle had happened. Henry Arthur Milton was here, in this great city, might be this man or that . . .he found himself peering into the faces he met between the Yard and the sidewalk where his car was parked.

"Is anything wrong, Maurice?" asked Mary anxiously, as she came to meet him.

"Wrong?" His voice was thick, unnatural; the eyes had a queer, glazed expression. "Wrong? No, nothing is wrong—why? What can be wrong?"

All the time he was speaking, his head turned nervously left and right. Who was that man walking towards him, swinging a cane so light-heartedly? Might he not be The Ringer? And that pedlar, shuffling along with a tray of matches and studs before him, an unkempt, grimy, dirty-looking old man—it was such a disguise as The Ringer would love to adopt. Bliss? Where had he seen Bliss before? Somewhere. . .his voice, too, had a familiar sound. He racked his brains to recall. Even the chauffeur came under his terrified scrutiny: a burly man with a long upper lip and a snub nose. That could not be The Ringer. . .

"What is the matter, Maurice?"

He looked at her vacantly. "Oh, Mary!" he said. "Yes, of course, my dear, we ought to be getting home."

He stumbled past her into the car, dropped on to the padded seat with a little groan.

"Do you want to go back to Deptford, Maurice?"

"Yes—back to Deptford."

She gave instructions to the chauffeur and, entering the car after

96

him, closed the door. "Was it something awful, Maurice?"

"No, my dear." He roused himself with a start. "Awful?. . .No, a lie, that's all! Tried to scare me. . .tried to scare Maurice Meister!" His laugh was thin and cracked and wholly unnatural. "They thought it would rattle me.You know what these police commissioners are. . . . . . . .jumped up army officers who have been jobbed into a soft billet, and have to pretend they understand police work to keep it!" His face changed.

"That man Bliss was there—the fellow you told me about. I can't quite place him, Mary. Did your—did Wembury tell you anything about him?" She shook her head.

"No, Maurice, I only know what I told you."

"Bliss!" he muttered. "I've never seen a detective with a beard before. They used to wear them years ago: it was quite the ordinary thing, but nowadays they're clean-shaven. . . .he comes from America, too. Did you see Hackitt?"

She nodded. "He came out about ten minutes before you and got on a tram."

He heaved a deep and troubled sigh. "I wish I'd seen him. I'd like to know what they asked him about. Of course, I know now: they brought him there for an altogether different reason.They're sly, these fellows; you never know what they're after.The truth isn't in them!"

He was feeling in his pocket for the little cushion-shaped gold box, and Mary pretended not to see. She had guessed the nature of the stimulant which Maurice took at frequent intervals, and of late he had made no disguise of his weakness. He snuffled at a pinch of white, glittering powder, dusted his face with a handkerchief, and a few seconds later was laughing at himself—another man. She had often wondered at the efficacy of the drug, not realising that every week he had to increase the dose to produce the desired effect, and that one day he would be a cringing, crawling slave to the glittering white powder which he now regarded as his servant.

"Wembury threatened me, by gad!" His tone had changed: he was now his pompous self. "A wretched hireling police officer threatened me, an officer of the High Court of Justice!"

"Surely not, Maurice? Alan threatened you?" He nodded solemnly, and was about to tell her the nature of the threat when he thought better of it. Even in his present mood of exaltation he had no desire to raise the subject of Gwenda Milton.

"I took no notice, of course. One is used to dealing with that kind of creature. By the way, Mary, I have made inquiries and I've discovered that Johnny was not involved in the prison riot."

She was so grateful for this news, that she did not for one moment question its authenticity. Mary did not know that Scotland Yard was as ignorant of what happened in the prison as the Agricultural and Fisheries Board. But when he was under the influence of the drug, Maurice lied for the pleasure of lying: it was symptomatic of the disease.

"No, he was not in any way connected with the trouble. It was a man named—I forget the name, but it doesn't matter—who was the ringleader. And, my dear, I've been thinking over that burglary at your house." He half-turned to face her, the drug had transformed him: he was the old loquacious, debonair and carefree Meister she knew. "You can't stay any longer at Malpas Mansions. I will not allow it. Johnny would never forgive me if anything happened to you."

"But where can I go, Maurice?"

He smiled.

"You're coming to my house. I'll have that room put in order and the lights seen to. You can have a maid to look after you..."

She was shaking her head already. "That is impossible," she said quietly. "I am not at all nervous about the burglary, and I am quite sure that nobody intended harming me. I shall stay at Malpas Mansions, and if I get too nervous, I shall go into lodgings."

"My dear Mary!" he expostulated.

"I'm determined on that, Maurice," she said, and he was a picture of resignation.

"As you wish. Naturally, I would not suggest that you should come to a bachelor's establishment without rearranging my household to the new conditions; but if you're set against honouring my little hovel, by all means do as you wish."

As they approached New Cross, he woke from the reverie into which he had fallen and asked: "I wonder who is on the rack at this moment?"

She could not understand what he meant for a moment.

"You mean at Scotland Yard?"

He nodded. "I'd give a lot of money," he said slowly, "to know just what is happening in Room C 2 at this very second, and who is the unfortunate soul facing the inquisitors."

Chapter 26

Dr. Lomond could neither be described as an unfortunate soul, nor the genial assistant commissioner as an inquisitor. Colonel Walford for the moment was being very informative, and the old doctor listened, rolling one of his interminable cigarettes, and apparently not particularly interested in the recital.

Lomond was possessed of many agreeable qualities, and he had the dour humour of his race. Alert and quick-witted, he displayed the confidence and assurance of one who was so much master of his own particular subject that he could afford to mock himself and his science. His attitude towards the commissioner was respectful only so far as it implied the deference due to an older man, but an equal.

He paused at the door.

"I'll not be in the way, will I?"

"Come along in, doctor," smiled the commissioner.

"Poor old Prideaux!" he shook his head sadly. "Man, it's on my conscience sending a man to be hanged in the suburbs! There was a dignity about Newgate and an historical value to being hanged at Tyburn. I wish I didn't know so much about criminology. Have ye ever noticed Wembury's ears, sir? He exhibited these appendages of the embarrassed Wembury in the manner of a showman. A tee-pical criminal ear! In conjunction with the prognathic process of the jaw suggests a rabid homicide! Have ye ever committed a murder?"

"Not yet," growled Alan.

Lomond finished rolling his cigarette, and the commissioner, who had been waiting patiently for this operation to be concluded, spoke: "I wanted to have a little chat with you, doctor."

"About a woman," said Lomond, without looking up.

"How the devil did you guess that?" asked the surprised Walford.

"I didn't guess; I knew. You see, you're a broadcaster—most people are. And I'm terribly receptive. Telepathic. It's one of the animal things left in me."

Bliss was watching, his lips lifted in derision.

"Animal?" he growled. "I always thought telepathy was one of the signs of intellect. That's what they say in America."

"They say so many things in America that they don't mean. Telepathy is just animal instinct which has been smothered under reason. What would you have me do for the lady?"

"I want you to find out something about her husband," said Walford, and the doctor's eyes twinkled.

"Would she know? Do wives know anything about their husbands?"

"I'm not so sure that he is her husband," said Bliss.

The old man chuckled.

"Ah! Then she would! She'd know fine if he was somebody else's husband. Who is she?"

The commissioner turned to Wembury.

"What is her real name?"

"Cora Ann Milton—she was born Cora Ann Barford."

Lomond looked up suddenly.

"Barford—Cora Ann? Cora Ann! That's a coincidence!"

"Why?"

"I was hearing a lot about a Cora Ann, a few months ago," said the doctor, lighting his limp cigarette.

"You don't want me, sir?" said Bliss. "I've got some real work to do!" He walked to the door. "Doctor, here's a job after your own heart. A man with your wisdom ought to catch him in a week."

"I ignore that," said the doctor, smoking placidly, and the sound of his chuckle pursued Bliss down the corridor.

And now Lomond was to hear the police story of The Ringer. The commissioner opened a dossier.

"The history of this man is a most peculiar one, and will interest you as an anthropologist. In the first place, he has never been in our hands. The man is an assassin. So far as we know, he has never gained a penny by any of the murders of which we suspect him. We know almost for certain that during the war he was an officer in the Flying Corps—a solitary man with only one friend, a lad who was afterwards shot on an ill-founded charge of cowardice made by his colonel— Chafferis-Wisman. Three months after the war ended Chafferis-Wisman was killed. We suspect; indeed, we are certain, the murderer was The Ringer, who had disappeared immediately after the Armistice was signed—didn't even wait to draw his gratuity."

"He was no Scotsman," interjected Lomond.

"He had refused the D.S.O.—every decoration that was offered to him," Walford went on. "He was never photographed in any of the regimental groups. We have only one drawing of him, made by a steward on a boat plying between Seattle and Vancouver. It was on this boat that Milton was married."

"Married?"

Walford explained.

"There was a girl on the ship, a fugitive from American justice; she had shot a man who had insulted her in some low-down dancehall in

Seattle. She must have confided in Milton that she would be arrested on her arrival in Vancouver, for he persuaded a parson on board to marry them. She became a British subject and defeated the extradition law," he continued. "It was a foolish, quixotic thing to do."

Lomond's eyes twinkled.

"Ah, then, he must be a Scotsman. He's really a terror, eh?"

"If people knew this man was in England, there would be trouble," said the Colonel. "He certainly killed old Oberzhon, who ran a South American agency of a very unpleasant character. He killed Attaman, the moneylender. Meister, by the way, was in the house when the murder was committed. There has been method in every killing. He left his sister in Meister's charge when he had to fly the country over the Attaman affair. He did not know that Meister was giving us information about his movements. And, of course, Meister being the brute he is..." He shrugged.

"The Ringer knows?" Lomond moved his chair nearer to the desk. "Come that's interesting."

"We know he was in Australia eight months ago. Our information is that he is now in England—and if he is, he has come back with only one object: to settle with Meister in his own peculiar way. Meister was his solicitor—he was always running around with Gwenda Milton."

"You say you have a picture of him?"

The commissioner handed a pencil sketch to Lomond, and the doctor gasped.

"You're joking—why—I know this man!"

"What!" incredulously.

"I know his funny little beard, emaciated face, rather nice eyes—good Lord!"

"You know him—surely not?" said Wembury.

"I don't say I know him, but I have met him."

"Where—in London?"

Lomond shook his head.

"No. I met this fellow in Port Said about eight months ago. I stepped off there on my way back from Bombay. I was staying at one of the hotels, when I heard that there was a poor European who was very sick in some filthy caravanserai in the native quarter. Naturally I went over and saw him—the type of creature who pigs with natives interests me. And there I found a very sick man; in fact, I thought he was going to peg out." He tapped the picture. "And it was this gentleman!"

"Are you certain?" asked Walford.

"No man with a scientific mind can be certain of anything. He had come ashore from an Australian ship—"

"That's our man, sir!" exclaimed Wembury.

"Did he recover?"

"I don't know." Lomond was dubious. "He was delirious when I saw him. That is where I heard the names 'Cora Ann'. I saw him twice. The third time I called, the old lady who ran the show told me that he had wandered out in the night—the Lord knows what happened to him; probably he fell into the Suez Canal and was poisoned. Would he be The Ringer? No, it's not possible!"

The commissioner looked at the sketch again.

"It almost seems like it. I've an idea that he is not dead. Now you may be useful, doctor. If there is one person who knows where The Ringer is to be found, it is Mrs. Milton."

"Cora Ann. Yes?"

"Doctor, I was more than impressed by your examination of Prideaux. I want you to try your hand on this woman. Bring her up, inspector."

When the door closed on Wembury he drew another paper from the folder. "Here are the ascertainable facts about her movements. She returned to this country on a British passport three weeks ago. She is staying at the Marlton."

Lomond adjusted his glasses and read. "She came overland from Genoa —British passport, you say. Is she—er—married?"

"Oh, there's no doubt about that; he married her on the boat, but they were only a week together."

"A week? Ah, then she may still be in love with him," said the cynical Lomond. "If my Egyptian friend is The Ringer, I know quite a lot about this woman. He was rather talkative in his delirium, and I'm beginning to remember some of the things he told me. Now, let me think! Cora Ann. . ." He turned suddenly. "Orchids! . . .I've got it!"

Chapter 27

It was at that moment that Cora Ann was ushered in. She was brightly and expensively dressed, and for a moment she stood look-ing from one to the other, poising the cigarette she held between her gloved fingers.

"Good morning, Mrs. Milton." The commissioner rose. "I asked you to come because I rather wanted my friend here to have a little talk with you."

Cora scarcely looked at the shabby doctor: her attention was for the moment concentrated on the military-looking commissioner.

"Why, isn't that nice!" she drawled. "I'm just crazy to talk to somebody." She smiled round at Wembury. "What's the best show in London, anyway? I've seen most of 'em in New York, but it was such a long time ago—"

"The best show in London, Mrs. Milton," said Lomond, "is Scotland Yard! Melodrama without music, and you are the leading lady."

She looked at him for the first time.

"Isn't that cute! What am I leading?" she asked.

"Me, for the moment," said the cheerful Scot. "You haven't seen much of London lately, Mrs. Milton—it is Mrs. Milton, isn't it?"

She nodded.

"You've been abroad, haven't you?"

"I certainly have—all abroad!" she replied slowly.

Lomond's voice was very bland. "And how did you leave your husband?" he asked.

She was not smiling now. "Say, Wembury, who is this fellow?" she demanded.

"Doctor Lomond, police surgeon, 'R' division."

The news was reassuring. There was a note of amusement in her voice when she replied. "You don't say? Why, you know, doctor, that I haven't seen my husband in years, and I'll never see him again. I thought everybody had read that in the newspapers. Poor Arthur was drowned in Sydney Harbour."

Dr. Lomond's lips twitched and he nodded at the gaily attired girl. "Really? I noticed that you were in mourning."

She was baffled: something of her self-confidence left her. "Why, that's not the line of talk I like," she said.

"It's the only line of talk I have." He was smiling now. "Mrs. Milton, to revert to a very painful subject—"

"If it hurts you, don't talk about it."

"Your husband left this country hurriedly three"—he turned to Wembury—"or was it four years ago. When did you see him last?"

Cora Ann was coolness itself. She did not answer the question. Here was a man not to be despised. A crafty, shrewd man of affairs, knowledge in the deeps of his grey-blue twinkling eyes.

"You were in Sydney three months after he reached there," Lomond continued, consulting the paper which Walford had given him.

"You called yourself Mrs. Jackson, and you registered at the Harbour Hotel. You had suite No. 36, and whilst you were there you were in communication with your husband."

The corners of her mouth twisted in a smile. Cora's sarcasm was a tantalising thing.

"Isn't that clever! Suite No. 36 and everything! Just like a real little sleuth!" Then, deliberately: "I never saw him, I tell you."

But Lomond was not to be put off.

"You never saw him, I guess that. He telephoned. You asked him to meet you—or didn't you? I'm not quite sure." He paused, but Cora Ann did not answer. "You don't want to tell me, eh? He was scared that there was somebody trailing you—scared that you might lead the police to him."

"Scared!" she repeated scornfully. "Where did you get that word? Nothing would scare Arthur Milton—anyway, he's dead!"

"And now has nothing to be scared about—if he was a Presbyterian," said Lomond—it was Lomond at his pawkiest. "Let's bring him to life, shall we?" He snapped his fingers. "Come up. Henry Arthur Milton, who left Melbourne on the steamship *Themistocles* on the anniversary of his wedding—and left with another woman."

Up to this moment Cora Ann had remained cool, but at the mention of the name of the ship she stiffened, and at his last words she came to her feet in a fury.

"That's a lie! There never was another woman." Recovering herself, she laughed. "Aw, listen! You put a raw one over there! I'm a fool to get sore with you! I don't know anything, that's all. You've got nothing on me —I needn't answer a single question. I know the law; there's no third degree in England, don't forget it. I'm going."

She moved towards the door, Wembury waiting to open it, his hand upon the knob.

"Open the door for Mrs. Milton," said Lomond, and added innocently: "It is Mrs. Milton, isn't it?"

She flung round at this. "What do you mean?"

"I thought it might be one of those artistic marriages that are so popular with the leisured classes," suggested Lomond, and she walked slowly back to him.

"You may be a hell of a big doctor," she said, a little breathlessly, "but your diagnosis is all wrong!"

"Really—married and everything?" Scepticism was in his voice.

She nodded. "First on the ship by a parson, and that's legal, and

104

then at St. Paul's Church, Deptford, to make sure. Deptford is a kind of home town to me. Next to an ash-pit I don't know any place I'd hate worse to be found dead in. Folks over home talk about Limehouse and Whitechapel—they're garden cities compared with that hell-shoot! But I was married there by a real reverend gentleman. There was nothing artistic about it—except my trousseau!"

"Married, eh?" The old Scot's voice spoke his doubts. "Liars and married men have very short memories—he forgot to send you your favourite orchids."

She turned suddenly in a cold fury—a fury which had grown out of her increasing fear of this old man.

"What do you mean?" she asked again.

"He always sent you orchids on the anniversary of your wedding," said Lomond carefully, and never once did his eyes leave hers. "Even when he was hiding in Australia, he in one town, you in another—when he was being watched for, and you were shadowed, he sent you flowers. But this year he didn't. I suppose he forgot, or possibly he had other use for orchids?"

She came nearer to him, almost incoherent in her rage.

"You think so!" She almost spat the words. "That's the kind of thought a man like you would have! Can't get that bug out of your head, can you? Another woman! Arthur thought of nobody but me—the only thing that hurt him was that I couldn't be with him. That's what! He risked everything just to see me—just to see me. I must have met him on Collins Street but didn't know him—he took the chance of the gallows just to stand there and see me pass."

"And well worth the risk. So, he was in Melbourne when you were there —but he did not send you your orchids?"

She flung out her hand impatiently.

"Orchids! What do I want with orchids? I knew when they didn't come—" She stopped suddenly.

"That he had left Australia," accused Lomond. "That is why you came away in such a hurry. I'm beginning to believe that you are in love with him!"

"Was I?" she laughed. "I kind of like him," Cora took up her bag. "Well, that is about all, I guess." She nodded to the Colonel and walked a step nearer the door. "You're not going to arrest me or anything?"

"You are at liberty to go out, when you wish, Mrs. Milton," said Walford.

"Fine!" said Cora Ann, and made a little curtsy. "Good morning, everybody."

"Love is blind." The hateful voice of the inquisitor arrested her. "You met him and didn't recognise him! You want us to believe that he was so well disguised that he could venture abroad in Collins Street in daylight—oh no, Cora Ann, that won't do!"

She was very near the end of her control. Rage shook her as she turned back to her tormentor.

"On Collins Street? He'd walk on Regent Street—in daylight or moonlight. Dare? If he felt that way, he'd come right here to Scotland Yard—into the lions' den, and never turn a hair. That's the fool thing he would do. You could guard every entrance and he'd get in and get out! You laugh—laugh, go on, laugh, but he'd do it—he'd do it—"

Bliss had come into the room.

Looking past the doctor, she might see him. Alan Wembury did not follow the direction of her eyes—only he saw her face go white, saw her sway and caught her in his arms as she fell.

Chapter 28

No woman is wholly saint, or, in this enlightened age, innocent of the evil which rubs elbows with men and women alike in everyday life. Mary Lenley had passed through all the stages of understanding where Maurice Meister was concerned, beginning with the absolute trust which was a legacy of her childhood, and progressing by a series of minor shocks to a clearer appreciation of the man as he really was, and not as she, in her childish enthusiasm, had pictured him. And with this understanding ran a nice balance of judgment. She was neither horrified nor distressed when there dawned upon her mind the true significance of Gwenda Milton's fate. Nobody spoke to her plainly of that unhappy girl. She had perforce to piece together from extrinsic evidence, the scraps of information so grudgingly given, and fill in the gaps from her imagination.

It was a curious fact that she did not regard herself as being in any danger from Maurice. They had been such good friends; their earlier relationships had been so peculiarly intimate that never once did she suspect that the pulse of Maurice Meister quickened at the sight of her. His offer to place the suite upstairs at her disposal, she had regarded merely as an act of kindness on his part, which, had it been considered, he would have made, and her own refusal was largely based upon her love of independence and a distaste for accepting a hospitality which might prove irksome, and in the end, unworkable. Behind it all, was the instinctive dislike of the woman to place herself under too deep an obligation to a man. Two days after the interview at Scotland Yard, she came one morning to find the house filled with workmen who were fitting a new sash to the large window overlooking the leads.

"Putting some bars up at the window, miss," said one of the workmen. "I hope we're not going to make too much noise for you."

Mary smiled. "If you do, I'll take my work into another room," she said.

Why bars at the window? The neighbourhood was an unsavoury one, but never once had Mr. Meister been subjected to the indignity of harbouring an uninvited guest in the shape of a burglar. There was precious little to lose, so far as she could see, though Mr. Meister's silver was of the finest. Hackitt was never tired of talking about the silver; it fascinated him.

"Every time I polish that milk jug, miss, I get nine months," her told her, and the mention of imprisonment brought her mind back to Scotland Yard.

"Yes, miss," said Sam, "I saw the chief commissioner—it's funny how these coppers can never find anything out, without applying to us lags!"

"What did he want to see you about, Hackitt?"

"Well, miss"—Sam hesitated—"it was about a friend of mine, a gentleman I used to know."

He would tell her nothing but this. She was intrigued. She asked Meister at the first opportunity what the ex-convict had meant, and he also evaded the question.

"It would be wise, my dear, if you did not discuss anything with Hackitt," he said. "The man is a liar and wholly unscrupulous. There's nothing he wouldn't say to make a little bit of a scare. Have you heard from Johnny?"

She shook her head. A letter had been due that morning but it had not arrived, and she was unaccountably disappointed. "Why are you putting these bars up, Maurice?"

"To keep out bad characters," he said flippantly. "I prefer that they should come through the door."

The little jest amused him. His general manner suggested that he had had recourse to his old system of stimulation.

"It's terribly lonely here at night," he went on. "I wonder if you realise how lonely a man I am, Mary?"

"Why don't you go out more?" she suggested.

He shook his head.

"That is the one thing I don't want to do—just now," he answered. "I wouldn't mind so much if I could get somebody to stay later. In fact, my dear Mary, I won't beat about the bush, but I should be very greatly obliged to you if you would spend a few of your evenings here."

He probably anticipated the answer he received.

"I'm sorry, Maurice, but I don't wish to," she said. "That sounds very ungrateful, I know, after all you have done for me, but can't you see how impossible it is?"

He was looking at her steadily from under his lowered lids, and apparently did not accept her refusal in the light of a rebuff.

"Won't you come to supper one night and try me? I will play you the most gorgeous sonata that composer ever dreamt! It bores me to play to myself," he went on, forestalling her reply. "Don't you think you could be very sociable and come up one evening?"

There was really no reason why she should not, and she hesitated.

"I'll think about it," she said.

That afternoon an unusual case came to Mr. Meister, the case of a drunken motorist who was arrested whilst he was driving a car, and she was preparing to go home that night when Mr. Meister came hurrying in from a visit to the unfortunate.

"Don't go yet, Mary," he said. "I have a letter I want to write to Dr. Lomond about this wretched prisoner. Lomond has certified him as being drunk, but I am getting his own doctor down, and I want this old Scotsman to be present at the examination."

He dictated the letter, which she typed and brought to him for his signature.

"How can I get this to Lomond's house?" he asked, and looked up at her. "I wonder if you would mind taking it? It is on your way—he has lodgings in Shardeloes Road."

"I'll take it with pleasure," said Mary with a smile. "I am anxious to meet the doctor again."

"Again? When did you see him last?" he asked quickly.

She told him of the little conversation they had had outside Scotland Yard. Meister pinched his lip.

"He's a shrewd old devil," he said thoughtfully. "I'm not so sure that he hasn't more brains than the whole of Scotland Yard together. Give him your brightest smile, Mary: I particularly want to get this man off a very serious charge. He is a very rich stockbroker who lives at Blackheath."

Mary wondered, as she left the house, what effect her bright smile might have in altering the diagnosis the doctor had made; she very rightly surmised that the police surgeon was not the type of man who was susceptible to outside influence.

Dr. Lomond's rooms were in a dull little house in a rather dull little road, and the landlady who answered her knock seemed to have taken complete control of the doctor's well-being.

"He's only just come in, miss, and I don't think he'll see you."

But Mary insisted, giving her name, and the woman went away, to return immediately to usher her into a very Victorian parlour, where, on the most uncomfortable of horsehair chairs, sat the doctor, an open book on his knees and a pair of steel-rimmed pince-nez gripped to the end of his nose.

"Well, well, my dear," he said, as he closed the book and came cautiously to his feet. "What is your trouble?"

She handed him the letter and he opened it and read, keeping up a long string of comment in an undertone, which she supposed was not intended to reach her.

"Ah. . .from Meister. . .the slimy scoundrel...About the drunk. . .I thought so! Drunk he was and drunk he is, and all the great doctors of Harley Street will no' make him sober . . .Verra well, verra well!"

He folded the letter, put it in his pocket and beamed over his glasses at the girl.

"He's made a messenger of ye, has he? Will ye no' sit down. Miss Lenley?"

"Thank you, doctor," she said, "I am due at my flat in a few minutes."

"Are ye now? And ye'd be a wise young leddy if ye remained in your flat."

What made her tell the doctor, she did not know: before she realised what she was saying, she was halfway through the story of her burglary.

"Inspector Bliss?" he mused. "He was the man—yes, I heard of it. Alan Wembury told me. That's a nice boy, Miss Lenley," he added, looking at her shrewdly. "I'll tell you something. You wonder why Bliss went into your flat? I don't know, I can't tell you with any accuracy, but I'm a psychologist, and I balance sane probabilities against eccentric impulses. That's Greek to you and almost Greek to me too, Miss Lenley. Bliss went into your room because he thought you had something that he wanted very much, and when a police officer wants something very much, he takes unusual risks. You missed nothing?"

She shook her head.

"Nothing except a letter which didn't belong to me. It was left in my place by Mrs. Milton. I found it and put it in the drawer. That was the only thing taken."

He rubbed his stubbly chin.

"Would Inspector Bliss know it was there? And if he knew it was there, would he think it worthwhile risking his neck to get it? And if he got it, what would he discover?"

Lomond shook his head.

"It's a queer little mystery which you've got all to yourself, young leddy."

He walked out into the passage with her and stood in his carpeted feet on the top step, waving her farewell, a limp cigarette drooping from under the white moustache.

Chapter 29

One unpleasant change had come over Maurice Meister since his visit to Scotland Yard: he was drinking heavily; the brandy bottle was never far away from his table. He looked old and ill in the mornings; did what he had never done before—wandered into his big room soon after breakfast, and, sitting down at the piano, played for hours on end, to her great distraction. Yet he played beautifully, with the touch of a master and the interpretation of one inspired. Sometimes she thought that the more dazed he was, the better he played. He used to sit at the piano, his eyes staring into vacancy, apparently seeing and hearing nothing. Hackitt used to come into the room and watch him with a contemptuous grin, speaking to him sometimes, well assured that the mind of Meister was a million years away. Even Mary had to wait by him patiently for long periods before she could obtain any intelligible answer to her questions.

He was afraid of things, jumped at the slightest sound, was reduced to a quivering panic by an unexpected knock on his door. Hackitt, who was sleeping in the house, had dark stories to hint at as to what happened in the night. Once he came and found Maurice's table littered with brandy bottles, all empty save one. Two days after the workmen had left the house, Alan Wembury, dozing in the charge room at Flanders Lane, waiting for the arrival of a prisoner whom he had sent his men to "pull in", heard the telephone bell ring and the exchange between the desk sergeant and somebody at the other end of the line.

"For you, Mr. Wembury," said the sergeant, and Alan, shaking himself awake, took the instrument from his subordinate's hand.

It was Hackitt at the other end, and his voice was shrill with apprehension.

"...I don't know what's the matter with him. He's been raisin' hell since three o'clock this morning. Can't you bring a doctor along to see him, Mr. Wembury?"

"What is the matter with him?" asked Alan.

The scared man at the other end would not vouchsafe an opinion.

"I don't know—he's locked up in his bedroom and he's been shoutin' an' screamin' like a lunatic."

"I'll come along," said Alan, and hung up the 'phone, as Dr. Lomond appeared from the cells.

This was the second time he had been called that night to deal with a case of delirium, and his presence at the police station at that hour of the morning was very providential. In a few words Alan retailed Hackitt's report.

"Drink it may be, dope it certainly is," said Dr. Lomond, pulling on his cotton gloves deliberately. "I'll go along with ye. Maybe I'll save an inquest!"

But Alan was half-way out of the station-house by now, and Dr. Lomond had to run to overtake him.

In a quarter of an hour Wembury was pressing the bell in the black door. It was opened immediately by Hackitt, dressed in shirt and trousers, his teeth chattering, a look of genuine concern on his face.

"This is a new stunt, isn't it, Sam?" asked Wembury sternly. "Ringing up the police station for the divisional surgeon? Why didn't you send for Meister's own doctor?"

Hackitt thought that this was a foolish question but did not say so.

"I didn't know who his doctor was, and he's been shouting blue murder—I didn't know what to do with him."

"I'll step up and see him," said Lomond. "Where is his room?"

Going to a door, Sam opened it.

"Up here, sir."

Lomond looked up and presently the sound of his footsteps treading the stairs grew fainter. "You were afraid you'd be suspected if he died, eh?" asked Wembury. "That's the worst of having a bad record, Hackitt."

He picked up a silver salver from the table—Meister had surprisingly good silver. Sam was an interested spectator.

"That's heavy, ain't it?" said Sam with professional interest. "That'd sell well. What would I get for that?"

"About three years," said Alan coldly, and Mr. Hackitt closed his eyes.

Presently he remembered that he had a communication to make.

"'Ere, Mr. Wembury, what's Bliss doin' on your manor (district)?"

"Bliss? Are you sure, Sam?"

"I couldn't make any mistake about a mug like that," said Sam. "He's been hanging about since I've been here."

"Why?"

"I don't know," confessed the ex-convict. "I found him hiding upstairs yesterday."

"Mr. Bliss?" To say that Wembury was surprised is to describe his emotions mildly.

"I said to him 'What are you doin' up here?'" said Sam impressively.

Wembury shook his head. "You're lying," he said.

"All right," retorted the disgusted Sam. "All you fellers hang together."

The feet of Lomond sounded on the stairs, and presently he came in.

"Is he all right, doctor?" asked Wembury.

"Meister? O, Lord, yes. What a lad! Meister? Good old English family that. Nearly came over with the Conqueror—only the Conqueror lost the war."

Lomond smelt at the decanter that was on the table, and Wembury nodded. "That's the poison that is killing him."

Lomond sniffed again. "It's no' poison, it's Scotch! It's the best way of poisoning yourself I know. No!"—he took a pinch of snuff from an imaginary box. "Cocaine, Wembury—that's the stuff that's settling Meister."

He looked round the room. "This is a queer kind of office, Wembury."

"Yes," said Alan soberly, "and some queer things have happened in this room, I should imagine. Have they put the window bars in?" he asked, addressing Sam, and the man nodded.

"Yes, sir. What are they for?"

"To keep The Ringer out!"

Sam Hackitt's face was a study. "The Ringer!" he gasped. "That's what they're for? Here! I'm through with this job! I wondered why he had the bars put in and why he wanted me to sleep on the premises."

"Oh—you're afraid of The Ringer, are you?" Lomond asked, interested, and Wembury intervened.

"Don't be a fool, Hackitt. They're all scared of The Ringer."

"I wouldn't stay here at nights for a hundred thousand rounds," said Sam fervently, and the doctor sniffed.

"It seems a fearful lot of money for a very doubtful service," was his dry comment. "I'd like you to go away for a while, Mr. Hackitt."

He himself closed the door on the perturbed Sam.

"Come up and look at Meister," he said, and Alan followed the slow-moving doctor up the stairs.

"He's alive all right," said Lomond, standing in the doorway.

Meister lay on his tumbled bed, breathing stertorously, his face purple, his hands clutching at the silken coverlet.

A commonplace sordid ending to what promised to be high tragedy, thought Alan.

And at that moment something gripped his heart, as though an instinctive voice whispered tremendously that in this end to his first scare was the beginning of the drama which would involve not only Maurice Meister, but the girl who was to him something more than the little carriage child who passed and who swung on the gate of his father's cottage, something more than the sister of the man he had arrested, something more than he dared confess to himself.

Chapter 30

Once or twice during the hour of strenuous work which followed, he heard Sam Hackitt's stealthy feet on the stairs, and once caught a glimpse of him as he disappeared in a hurry. When he came down it was nearly seven o'clock. Sam, very businesslike in his green baize apron, with a pail of water and a washleather in his hand, was industriously cleaning the windows, somewhat hampered by the bars.

"How is he, sir?" he asked.

Alan did not reply. He was at the mysterious door, the bolted door that was never opened and led to nowhere.

"Where does this door lead?"

Sam Hackitt shook his head. It was a question that had puzzled him, and he had promised himself the pleasure of an Inspection the first time he was left alone in the house.

"I don't know, I've never seen it open. Maybe it's where he keeps his money. That fellow must be worth millions, Wembury."

Alan pulled up the bolts, and tried the door again. It was locked, and he looked round. "Is there a key to this?"

Sam hesitated. He had the thief's natural desire to appear in the light of a fool.

"Yes, there is a key," he said at last, his anxiety for information overcoming his inclination towards a reputation for innocence. "It's hanging up over the mantelpiece. I happen to know because—"

"Because you've tried it," said Alan, and Sam protested so violently that he guessed that whatever plan he may have formed had not yet been put into execution.

Alan walked to the door leading to the room above and listened: he thought he heard Meister talking. By the time Lomond returned, Alan Wembury was growing a little weary of a vigil which he knew was unnecessary. If he had admitted the truth to himself, he was waiting to see Mary Lenley.

Lomond worried him a little. This enthusiastic amateur in crime detection seemed to have come under the fascinating influence of Cora Ann. He had seen them together twice and had remonstrated.

"She's a dangerous woman, doctor."

"And I'm a fearfully dangerous man," said Lomond. "I like her— I'm sorry for the poor wee thing. That is my pet vice—being sorry for women."

"Mind that you aren't sorry for yourself some day!" said Wembury quietly, and the doctor chuckled.

"Eh? What is that? A warning to young lads?" he asked, and changed the subject.

Wembury was standing outside the house when the police surgeon returned.

"I'll go up and see this poor laddie," he said sardonically. "Are ye waiting for somebody?"

"Yes—no. I'm waiting for one of my men," said Alan, and the doctor grinned to himself—he had at last succeeded in making a police officer blush.

Meister was dozing when he looked in at him, and he came downstairs to inspect again the room which was both office and drawing-room of Meister's establishment.

Sam came in and watched the doctor's inspection with interest.

"I saw Wembury outside," he said, with the easy familiarity of his class. "I suppose he's waiting to see Miss Lenley."

The doctor looked round.

"Who is Miss Lenley?"

"Oh, she's the typewriter," said Sam, and the doctor's eyebrows rose.

"Typewriter? They have a sex, have they? What a pretty idea!" He lifted the cover of the machine. "What's that one—male or female?"

"I'm talking about the young lady, sir—the lady who works it," said the patient Sam.

"Oh, the typist? Who is she?" Lomond was interested. "Oh, yes! She's the sister of the man in prison, isn't she?"

"Yes, sir—Johnny Lenley. Got three for pinchin' a pearl necklace."

"A thief, eh?" He walked over to the piano and opened it.

"A gentleman thief," explained Sam.

"Does she play this?" The doctor struck a key softly.

"No, sir—him."

"Meister?" Lomond frowned. "Oh, so I've heard!"

"When he's all dopy," explained Sam. "Can't hear nothing! Can't see nothing. He gives me the creeps sometimes."

"Musical. That's bad."

"He plays all right," said Sam with fine contempt for the classics. "I like a bit of music myself, but the things he plays—" He gave a horrible imitation of Chopin's Nocturne—"Lummy, gives you the fair hump!"

The front door bell called the ex-convict from the room, and Dr. Lomond, sitting on the piano stool, his hands thrust into his pockets, continued his survey of the room. And as he looked, a curious thing happened. Above the door, concealed in the architrave, the red light suddenly glowed. It was a signal—from whom? What was its significance? Even as he stared, the light went out. Lomond went on tiptoes to the door and listened. He could hear nothing.

Just then Hackitt returned with half-a-dozen letters in his hand.

"The post—" he began, and then suddenly saw Lomond's face.

"Hackitt," asked the doctor softly, "who else is in this house beside you and Meister?"

He looked at him suspiciously. "Nobody. The old cook's ill."

"Who gets Meister's breakfast?"

"I do," nodded Sam; "a biscuit and a corkscrew!"

Lomond looked up at the ceiling. "What's above here?"

"The lumber-room." Hackitt's uneasiness was increasing. "What's up, doctor?"

Lomond shook his head. "I thought—no, nothing."

"Here! You ain't half putting the wind up me! Do you want to see the lumber room, doctor?"

Lomond nodded and followed the man up the stairs, past Meister's room to a dingy apartment stacked with old furniture. He was hardly out of the room when Wembury came in with Mary Lenley.

"You're getting me a bad name, Alan," she smiled. "I suppose I shouldn't call you Alan when you are on duty? I ought to call you Inspector Wembury."

"I'd be sorry if you didn't call me Alan. Now it does require an effort to call you Mary. Never forget that I was brought up to call you Miss Mary and take off my cap to your father!"

Mary sighed.

"Isn't it odd—everything?"

"Yes—it's queer." He watched her as she took off coat and hat. "People wouldn't believe it if you put it in a book. The Lenleys of Lenley Court, and the Wemburys of the gardener's cottage!"

She laughed aloud at this.

"Don't be stupid. Heavens, what a lot of letters!"

There was only one which interested her: it was addressed in pencil in Maurice Meister's neat hand. Evidently its contents were of such engrossing interest that she forgot Alan Wembury's presence. He saw the colour surge to her pale cheek and a new light come to her eyes, and his heart sank. He could not know that Meister had repeated his invitation to supper and that the flush on Mary's cheek was one of anger.

"Mary," he said for the second time, "are you listening?"

She looked up from the letter she was reading.

"Yes."

How should he warn her? All that morning he had been turning over in his mind this most vital of problems.

"Are you all right here?" he asked awkwardly.

"What do you mean?" she asked.

"I mean—well, Meister hasn't the best of reputations. Does your brother know you're working here?"

She shook her head and a shadow came to her face. "No—I didn't want to worry him. Johnny is so funny sometimes, even in his letters."

Alan drew a long breath. "Mary, you know where I am to be found?"

"Yes, Alan, you told me that before." She was surprised.

"Well—er—well, you never know what little problems and difficulties you may have. I want you—I'd like you to—well, I'd rather like to feel that if anything unpleasant occurred—" He floundered on, almost incoherently.

"Unpleasant?" Did he guess, she wondered? She was panic stricken at the thought.

"And you were—well, distressed," he went on desperately, "you know what I mean? Well, if anybody—how shall I put it? . . .If anybody annoyed you, I'd like you to come to me. Will you?"

Her lips twitched. "Alan! You're being sentimental!"

"I'm sorry."

As he reached the door, she called him by name. "You're rather a dear, aren't you?" she said gently.

"No, I think I'm a damned fool!" said Alan gruffly, and slammed the door behind him.

She stood by the table thinking; she had a vague uneasiness that all was not well; that behind the habitual niceness of Maurice Meister was something sinister, something evil. If Johnny was only free—Johnny, who would have sacrificed his life for her.

Chapter 31

There was a way into Meister's house which was known to three people, and one of these, Maurice hoped, was dead. The second was undoubtedly in prison, for John Lenley had surprised the lawyer's secret. Meister's grounds had at one time extended to the bank of a muddy creek, and even now, there was a small ramshackle warehouse standing in a patch of weed-grown grass that was part of Meister's demesne, although it was separated from the house in Flanders Road by a huddle of slum dwellings and crooked passage-ways.

That morning there walked along the canal bank a young man, who stopped opposite the factory, and, looking round to see if he was observed, inserted a key in the weather-beaten door and passed into the rank ground. In one corner was a tiny brick dwelling which looked like a magazine, and the same key that had opened the outer gate opened the door of this, and the stranger slipped inside and locked the door after him before he began to go down a winding staircase that had a been put there in recent years.

At the bottom of the stairs was a brick-vaulted passage, high enough for a short man to walk without discomfort, but not sufficiently elevated to admit the stranger's progress without his stooping. The floor was unlittered, and although there were no lights the newcomer searched a little niche half a dozen steps up the passage and found there the four electric torches which Meister kept there for his own use. The passage had recently been swept by the lawyer's own hands.

He expected that very soon a delicious visitor would pass that way, escaping the observation of the men who guarded the house, and he himself had conducted Mary Lenley through the passage which held none of the terrors that are usually associated with such subterranean ways.

The stranger walked on, flashing his light ahead of him. After three minutes' walk the passage turned abruptly to the left, and finally it terminated in what had the appearance of a cellar, from which there led upward a flight of carpeted steps. The stranger went cautiously and noiselessly up these stairs. Half-way up he felt the tread give and grinned. It was, he knew, a pneumatic arrangement by which a warning lamp was lit in Meister's room. He wondered who was with him now, and whether his forgetfulness of the signal embarrassed the lawyer.

He came to a long panel and listened. He could hear voices: Meister's and—Mary Lenley's. He frowned. Mary here? He thought she had given up the work. Bending his ear close to the panel, he listened.

". . .my dear," Meister was saying, "you're exquisite—adorable. To see your fingers move over that shabby old typewriter's keys is like watching a butterfly flit from flower to flower."

"How absurd you are, Maurice!" said Mary. Then came the slow sound of music as Meister sat at the piano. Mary's voice again, and the sound of a little struggle.

Meister caught her by the shoulders and was drawing her to him when, staring past her, he saw a hand come round the corner of the door.

He only saw this and, in another second, with a scream of terror, Meister had flown from the room, leaving the girl alone.

She stood rooted to the spot terror-stricken. Farther and farther along the wall crept the hand and then the panel swung open and a young man stepped into the room.

"Johnny!"

In another instant, Mary Lenley was sobbing in the arms of her brother.

Chapter 32

It was Johnny Lenley!

"Darling—why didn't you tell me you were coming back? . . . This is a wonderful surprise! Why, I only wrote to you this morning!"

He put her away at arm's length and looked into her face.

"Mary, what are you doing in Meister's office?" he asked quietly, and something in his tone chilled her.

"I'm working for him," she said. "You knew I was, Johnny, before—before you went away." And then her hand went up to his face. "It's wonderful to see you—wonderful! Let me look at you. You poor boy, have you had a bad time?"

To the watchful and interested Mr. Hackitt, who had made an unobtrusive entrance and with whom sentiment was a weak point, this seemed an unnecessary question.

"Not so bad as it might have been," said Johnny carelessly. Then: "Why did you go to work at all? I left money with Maurice and told him I didn't want you to work anymore. It was the last thing I told him at the Old Bailey."

Hackitt clicked his lips impatiently. "Left money with Meister? You're mad!"

But Lenley did not hear. "Did he stop the allowance?" he asked, his anger rising at the thought.

"No, Johnny, he didn't. . .I didn't know there was an allowance even."

The brother nodded. "I see," he said.

"You're not angry with me, are you, Johnny?" She raised her tearful eyes to his. "I can't believe it is you. Why, I didn't expect you home for an awful long time."

"My sentence was remitted," said Lenley. "A half-lunatic convict attacked the deputy governor, and I saved him from a mauling. I had no idea that the authorities would do more than strike off a few days from my sentence. Yesterday at dinner-time the governor sent for me and told me that I was to be released on licence."

Again Mr. Hackitt registered despair. Johnny Lenley's notions had never been as professional as he could have desired them, and here he was admitting without shame that he had saved the life of one of his natural enemies! The girl's hands were on her brother's shoulders, her grave eyes searching his face.

"You're finished with that dreadful life, haven't you?" she asked in a low voice. "We're going somewhere out of London to live. I spoke to Maurice about it. He said he'd help you to go straight. Johnny, you wouldn't have had that terrible sentence if you had only followed his advice."

John Lenley bit his lip. "Meister told you that, did he?" he asked slowly. "Mary, are you in love with Maurice?" She stiffened, and he mistook her indignation for embarrassment. "Do you love him?"

"He has been kind," she said coldly. She struggled hard to think of some favourable quality of Meister.

"I realise that, dear," he nodded, "but how has he been kind?" And then, seeing her distress, he gripped her shoulders and shook her gently, and the hard face softened, and into the grey, deep-set eyes came the old mother look she had loved in him. "Anyway, you'll work no more."

"Then I must work at once." She laughed, but there was a catch in her throat. "And you must be very patient. . .if you want to see Maurice he'll be down soon now—I think you scared him."

He watched her as she went back to her table, and then caught Hackitt's eye and jerked his head. "Sam, what's the idea?" Mr. Hackitt shrugged.

"I've only been here a few days. You're a man of the world, Johnny. Ever seen a tiger being kind to a skinned rabbit? I don't know anything more than that."

Lenley nodded. "Is that so?" he said.

He had come straight to the lawyer's to liquidate old debts and make an end of an unprofitable association. And then London and the stink and grime of Flanders Lane would know him no more: he would find fields where he could work without the supervision of over-armed guards, and with the knowledge that peace and comfort lay at his day's end. He stood by the door, talking to Sam, questioning him, never doubting where Meister's "kindness" would ultimately end. And then the lawyer came into the room. His eyes were all for the girl: her nimble fingers flashing amongst the keys. He went round to her and dropped his hands on her shoulders.

"My dear, forgive me! I'm just as jumpy as I can be, and I'm imagining all sorts of queer things."

"Maurice!"

The lawyer spun round, his colour coming and going. "You!" he croaked. "Out! . . .I thought. . ."

Johnny Lenley smiled contemptuously. "About two years too soon, eh? I'm sorry to disappoint you, but miracles happen, even in prison—and I'm one."

With a tremendous effort the lawyer recovered his balance and was his old genial self.

"My dear fellow"—he offered a wavering hand, but Lenley apparently did not see it—"sit down, won't you? What an amazing thing to happen! So it was you at the panel....Hackitt, give Mr. Lenley a drink. ..you'll find one in the cupboard...well, this is a sight for sore eyes!"

Hackitt offered the drink, but the other shook his head. "I want to see you, Maurice." He looked significantly at Mary, and rising, she left the room.

"How did you get your ticket?" asked Meister, helping himself to the ever handy bottle.

"The remainder of my sentence was wiped out," said Lenley curtly. "I thought you'd have read that."

The lawyer frowned. "Oh! Were you the lag who saved the life of the governor? I remember reading about it—brave boy!"

He was trying to get command of the situation. Other men had come blustering into that office, and had poured a torrent of threats over the table, leaving him unmoved.

"Why did you allow Mary to go on working for you?"

Meister shrugged. "Because, my dear fellow, I can't afford to be charitable," he said blandly.

"I left you the greater part of four hundred pounds," Lenley's voice was stern and uncompromising, "the money I got from my first thefts."

"You were well defended, weren't you?"

"I know the fee," said Lenley quietly. "When you had had that, there was still the greater part of four hundred left. Why did you stop the allowance?"

The lawyer sat down again in the chair he had vacated, lit cigar, and did not speak until he saw the match almost burning his fingertips.

"Well, I'll tell you. I got worried about her. I like you, Johnny, I've always been interested in you and your family. And it struck me that a young girl living alone, with no work to do, wasn't exactly having a fair chance. I thought it would be kinder to you and better for her to give her some sort of employment—keep her mind occupied, you understand, old man? I take a fatherly interest in the kid."

He met the challenging eyes and his own fell before them.

"Keep your fatherly paws to yourself when you're talking to her, will you, Maurice?" The words rang like steel on steel.

"My dear fellow!" protested the other.

"And listen!" Lenley went on. "I know you pretty well; I've known you for a long time, both by reputation and through personal acquaintance. I know just how much there is in that fatherly interest stuff. If there has been any monkey business as there was with Gwenda Milton, I'll take that nine o'clock walk for you!"

Meister jerked up his head.

"Eh?" he rasped.

"From the cell to the gallows," Lenley went on. "And I'll toe the trap with a good heart. You don't misunderstand me?"

Chapter 33

The lawyer got up slowly. Whatever else he was, Maurice Meister was no coward when he had to deal with tangible dangers.

"You'll take the nine o'clock walk, will you?" he repeated with a sneer. "What a very picturesque way of putting things! But you won't walk for me. I shall read the account in bed."

He strolled across to the piano and sat down, his fingers running swiftly over the keys. Softly came the dirge-like notes of "*Mort d'un Cosaque*"—a dreary, heart-stirring thing that Maurice Meister loved.

"I always read those accounts in bed," he went on, talking through the music; "they soothe me. Ever go to the cinema, Johnny?' 'The condemned man spent a restless night and scarcely touched his breakfast. He walked with a firm step to the scaffold and made no statement. A vulgar end to a life that began with so much promise.' Hanged men look very ugly."

"I've told you, Maurice—any monkey business, and I'll get you even before The Ringer." Johnny's voice shook with suppressed passion.

"Ringer!" he laughed. "You have that illusion, too? How amusing!"

The tune changed to "*Ich liebe dich.*"

"The Ringer! Here am I, alive and free, and The Ringer—where is he? That sounds almost poetical! Dead at the bottom of Sydney Harbour. . . .or hiding in some unpleasantly hot little town, or in the bush with the sundowners—a hunted dog."

A man was standing at the barred window behind him, glaring into the room—a bearded face was pressed to the pane.

"The Ringer is in London, and you know it," said Lenley. "How near he is to you all the time. God knows!"

As though the eavesdropper heard, he suddenly withdrew. But for the moment Maurice Meister had no mind for The Ringer. The music intoxicated, enthralled him. "Isn't that lovely?" he breathed. "Is there a woman in the world who can exalt the heart and soul of a man as this—is there a woman worth one divine harmony of the master?"

"Was Gwenda Milton?" snarled Lenley. The music stopped with a crash and Meister, rising, turned to Lenley in a cold fury.

"To hell with Gwenda Milton and Gwenda Milton's brother, alive or dead!" he roared. "Don't mouth her name to me!" He snatched the glass of whisky he had put on the top if the piano and drained it at a draught. "Do you think she is on my conscience—she's not! Any more than you or any other weak whining fool, soaked to the soul with self-pity. That's what's the matter with you, my dear boy—you're sorry for yourself! Weeping over your own miseries. The cream of your vanity's gone sour!" Suddenly his tone changed.

"Ach! Why do you annoy me? Why are you so inexpressibly common? I won't quarrel with you, my dear Johnny. Now what is it you want?"

For answer the caller took from his pocket a small package and opened it on the desk. Inside, wrapped in cotton wool, was a little jewelled bangle. "I don't know how much is due to me; this will make it more."

Meister took the bangle and carried the glittering thing to the light. "Oh, this is the bracelet—I wondered what you had done with it."

"I collected it on my way here: it was left with a friend of mine. That is all I had for my three years," he said bitterly. "Three robberies and I've only touched a profit on one!"

Maurice stroked his upper lip thoughtfully.

"You are thinking of your second exploit: the little affair at Camden Crescent?"

"I don't want to discuss it," said Johnny impatiently. "I'm finished with the game. Prison has cured me. Anyhow, in the Camden Crescent job, the man who you sent to help me got away with the stuff. You told me that yourself."

In that second a plan was born in Meister's mind. "I told you a lie," he said slowly. And then, in a more confidential tone: "Our friend never got away with it."

"What!"

"He hid it. He told me before I got him off to South Africa. There was an empty house in Camden Crescent—where the burglary was committed—there is still. I didn't tell you before, because I didn't want to be mixed up in the business after the Darnleigh affair. I could have got half a dozen men to lift it—but I didn't trust them."

Irresolution showed in Lenley's face; the weak mouth drooped a little. "Let it stay where it is," he said, but he did not speak with any great earnestness.

Meister laughed. It was the first genuine laugh of his that the day had brought forth. "You're a fool," he said in disdain. "You've done your time, and what have you got for it? This!" He held up the trinket. "If I give you twenty pounds for it, I'm robbing myself. There's eight thousand pounds' worth of good stuff behind that tank—yours for the taking. After all, Johnny," he said, adopting a tone of persuasion, "you've paid for it!"

"By God, I have!" said the other between his teeth. "I've paid for it all right!"

Meister was thinking quickly, planning, cross-planning, organising, in that few seconds of time.

"Knock it off tonight," he suggested, and again Lenley hesitated. "I'll think about it. If you're trying to shop me—"

Again, Meister laughed. "My dear fellow, I'm trying to do you a good turn and, through you, your sister."

"What is the number of the house? I've forgotten."

Meister knew the number well enough: he forgot nothing. "Fifty-seven. I'll give you the twenty pounds for this bracelet now."

He opened his desk, took out his cash-box and unlocked it. "That will do to go on with."

Lenley was still undecided; nobody knew that better than the lawyer. "I want full value for the rest if I go after it—or I'll find another 'fence'."

It was the one word that aroused the lawyer to fury. "'Fence'? That's not the word to use to me, Johnny."

"You're too sensitive," said his dour client.

"Just because I help you fellows, when I ought to be shopping you. . . ." The lawyer's voice trembled. "Get another 'fence', will you? Here's your twenty." He threw the money on the table, and Lenley, counting it, slipped it into his pocket. "Going into the country, eh? Taking your little sister away? Afraid of my peculiar fascinations?"

"I'd hate to hang for you," said John Lenley, rising.

"Rather have The Ringer hang, eh? You think he'll come back

with all that time over his head, with the gallows waiting for him? Is he a lunatic? Anyway—I'm not scared of anything on God's Almighty earth."

He looked round quickly. The door that led to his room was opening.

It was Dr. Lomond: Hackitt had left him in the lumber room and had forgotten that he was in the house. The doctor was coming into the room but stopped at the sight of the young man.

"Hallo—I'm awfu' sorry. Am I butting in on a consultation?"

"Come in, doctor—come in. This—is—a friend of mine. Mr. Lenley."

To Meister's surprise the doctor nodded.

"Aye. I've just been having a wee chat with your sister. You've just come back from the—country, haven't you?"

"I've just come out of prison, if that's what you mean," said the other bluntly, as he turned to go. His hand was on the knob when the door was flung open violently and a white-faced Hackitt appeared.

"Guv'nor!" He crossed fearfully to Meister and lowered his voice. "There's a party to see you."

"Me? Who is it?"

"They told me not to give any name," gasped Sam. "This party said: 'Just say I'm from The Ringer'."

Meister shrank back.

"The Ringer!" said Lomond energetically. "Show him up!"

"Doctor!"

But Lomond waved him to silence. "I know what I am doing," he said.

"Doctor! Are you mad? Suppose—suppose—"

"It's all right," said Lomond, his eyes on the door.

Chapter 34

Presently it opened, and there came into view of the white-faced Maurice a slim, perfectly dressed girl, malicious laughter in her eyes.

"Cora Ann!" croaked Meister.

"You've said it! Gave you all one mean fright, eh?" She nodded contemptuously. "Hallo, doc!"

"Hallo, little bunch of trouble. You gave me heart disease!"

"Scared you, too, eh?" she scoffed. "I want to see you, Meister."

His face was still pallid, but he had mastered the panic that the name of The Ringer had evoked.

125

"All right, my dear, Johnny!" He looked hard at Lenley. "If you want anything, my dear boy, you know where you can get it," he said, and Johnny understood, and went out of the room with one backward glance of curiosity at the unexpected loveliness of the intruder.

"Get out, you!" Maurice spoke to Hackitt as though he were a dog, but the little Cockney was unabashed.

"Don't you talk to me like that, Meister—I'm leaving you today."

"You can go to hell," snarled Maurice.

"And the next time I'm pinched I'm going to get another lawyer," said Sam loudly.

"The next time you're pinched you'll get seven years," was the retort.

"That's why I'm goin' to change me lawyer."

Maurice turned on him with a face of fury. "I know a man like you who thought he was clever. He's asked me to defend him at the Sessions."

"I don't call that clever."

"Defend him! I'd see him dead first."

"And he'd be better off!" snapped Sam.

Lomond and the girl made an interested audience.

"That's what you get for helping the scum!" said Meister, when his truculent servant had gone.

Obviously, he wanted to be alone with the girl, and Dr. Lomond, who had good reason for returning, said that he had left his bag upstairs in Meister's room, and made that the excuse for leaving them. Maurice waited until the door closed on the old man before he spoke.

"Why—my dear Cora. Ann. You're prettier than ever. And where is your dear husband?" asked Meister blandly.

"I suppose you think that because you're alive, he's dead?"

He laughed. "How clever of you! Did it take you long to think that out?"

She was staring round the room. "So, this is the abode of love!" She turned fiercely upon the lawyer. "I never knew Gwenda—I wish to God I had! If Arthur had only trusted me as he trusted you! I heard about her suicide, poor kid, when I was on my way to Australia and flew back from Naples by airplane."

"Why didn't you wire me? If I had only known—"

"Mcister—you're a paltry liar!" She went to the door through which the doctor had passed, opened it and listened. Then she came back to where Meister sat lighting a cigar. "Now listen—that Scotch sleuth will be coming back in a minute." She lowered her voice to an intense whisper. "Why don't you go away—out of the country—go somewhere you can't be found—take another name? You're a rich man—you can afford to give up this hole!"

Maurice smiled again.

"Trying to frighten me out of England, eh?"

"Trying to frighten you!" The contempt in her voice would have hurt another man. "Why, it's like trying to make a negro black! He'll get you, Meister! That's what I'm afraid of. That is what I lie in bed and think about—it's awful. . .awful. . .!"

"My dear little girl!"—he tried to lay his hand on her cheek, but she drew back—"don't worry about me."

"You! Say, if I could lift my finger to save you from hell I wouldn't! Get out of the country—it's Arthur I want to save, not you! Get away—don't give him the chance that he wants to kill you."

Maurice beamed at her.

"Ah! How ingenious! He dare not come back himself, But he has sent you to England to get me on the run!"

Cora's fine eyes narrowed. "If you're killed—you'll be killed here! Here in this room where you broke the heart of his sister! You fool!"

He shook his head. "Not such a fool, my dear, that I'd walk into a trap. Suppose this man is alive: in London I'm safe—in the Argentine he'd be waiting for me. And if I went to Australia, he'd be waiting for me, and if I stepped ashore at Cape Town. . .No, no, little Cora Ann, you can't catch me."

She was about to say something when she heard the door open. It was the "Scotch sleuth"; whatever warning she had to deliver must remain unspoken.

"Had your little talk, Cora Ann?" asked Lomond, and in spite of her anxiety the girl laughed.

"Now listen, doctor, only my best friends call me Cora Ann," she protested.

"And I'm the best friend you ever had," said the doctor.

Meister was in eager agreement. "She doesn't know who her best friends are. I wish you'd persuade her."

Neither gave him encouragement to continue. He had the uncomfortable feeling that he was an intruder in his own house, and the arrival of Mary Lenley gave him an excuse to wander to the little office alcove where he was out of sight but not out of hearing.

"I like meeting you, Cora Ann," said the doctor.

She laughed. "You're funny."

"I've brought the smile to the widow's eye," said Lomond unsmilingly.

She shot a swift sidelong glance at the man. "Say, Scottie! That widow stuff—forget it! There are times when I almost wish I was— no, not that—but that Arthur and I had never met."

He was instantly sympathetic. "Arthur was a bad lad, eh?"

She sighed. "The best in the world—but not the kind of man who ought to have married."

"There isn't any other kind," said Lomond, and then, with a cautious look round at Meister: "Were you very much in love with him?"

She shrugged. "Well—I don't know."

"Don't know? My dear young person, you're old enough to know where your heart is."

"It's in my mouth most times," she said, and he shook his head.

"Ye poor wee devil! Still, you followed him to Australia, my dear?"

"Sure, I did. But that kind of honeymoon takes a whole lot of romance out of marriage. You don't have to be a doctor to know that."

He bent over her. "Why don't you drop him, Cora Ann? That heart of yours is going to wear away from being in your mouth all the time."

"Forget him?" Lomond nodded. "Do you think he wants me to forget him?"

"I don't know," said Lomond. "Is any man worth what you are suffering? Sooner or later he will be caught. The long arm of the law will stretch out and take him, and the long leg of the law will boot him into prison!"

"You don't say!" She looked round to where Meister was sitting by Mary Lenley, and her tone grew very earnest. "See here. Dr. Lomond, if you want to know—my Ringer man is in danger, but I'm not scared of the police. Shall I tell you something?"

"Is it fit for me to hear?" he asked.

"That'll worry me!" she answered sarcastically. "I'm going to be frank with you, doctor. I've a kind of hunch there is only one man in God's wide world that will ever catch Arthur Milton—and that man is you!"

Chapter 35

Lomond met her eyes.

"You're just daft!" he said.

"And why?"

"A pretty girl like you—hooking on to a shadow—the best part of your life wasted."

"You don't say!"

"Now, you know it's so, don't you? It's a dog's life. How do you sleep?"

"Sleep!" She threw out her arms in a gesture of despair. "Sleep!"

"Exactly. You'll be a nervous wreck in a year. Is it worth it?"

"What are you trying out?" she asked breathlessly. "What's your game?"

"I'll tell you—shall I? I wonder if you'll be shocked?" She was looking at him intently. "Wouldn't it be a good idea for you to go away and forget all about The Ringer? Cut him out of your mind. Find another—interest." He laughed. "You think I'm being unpleasant, don't you? But I'm only thinking of you. I'm thinking of all the hours you're waiting for something to happen—with your heart in your mouth."

Suddenly she sprang to her feet. "Listen! You've got some reason behind all this!" she breathed.

"I swear to you—"

"You have—you have!" She was in a fury. "You're a man—I know what men are. See here—I've put myself in hell and I'm staying put!"

She picked up her bag from the table.

"I've given you your chance," said Lomond, a little sadly.

"My chance. Dr. Lomond! When Arthur Milton says 'I'm tired of you —I'm sick of you—you're out,' then I'll go. My way—not your way. You've given me my chance—Gwenda Milton's chance! That's a hell of a chance, and I'm not taking it!"

Before he could speak, she had flung from the room.

Meister had been watching, and now he came slowly to where the doctor was standing. "You've upset Cora Ann."

"Aye," nodded Lomond, as he took up his hat and bag thoughtfully. "Aye."

"Women are very strange," mused Meister. "I rather think she likes you, doctor."

"You think so?" Lomond's manner and voice were absent. "I wonder if she'd come out and have a bit of dinner with me?"

"How marvellous it would be if she liked you well enough to tell you a little more about The Ringer," suggested Maurice slyly.

"That's just what I was thinking. Do you think she would?"

Maurice was amused. Evidently there was no age limit to men's vanity. "You never know what women will do when they're in love—eh, doctor?"

Dr. Lomond did not reply; he went out of the room, counting the silver in his hand.

Meister's head was clear now. Johnny was a real menace. . . .he had threatened, and a young fool like that would fulfil his threat, unless. . .Would he be mad enough to go to Camden Crescent that night? From Johnny his mind went to Mary. His love for the girl had been a tropical growth. Now, when it seemed that she was to be taken from him, she had become the most desirable of women. He sat down at the piano, and at the first notes of the "*Liebestraum*," the girl entered.

He was for the moment oblivious of her presence, and it was through a cloud of dreams that her voice brought him to realities.

"Maurice. . . ." He looked at her with unseeing eyes. "Maurice." The music stopped. "You realise that I can't stay here now that Johnny's back?" she was saying.

"Oh, nonsense, my dear!" His tone had that fatherly quality which he could assume with such effect.

"He is terribly suspicious," she said, and he laughed.

"Suspicious! I wish he had something to be suspicious about!"

She waited, a picture of indecision. "You know I can't stay," she said desperately.

He got up from the piano, and coming across to her, laid his hands on her shoulder. "Don't be silly. Anyone would think I was a leper or something. What nonsense!"

"Johnny would never forgive me."

"Johnny, Johnny!" he snapped. "You can't have your life governed and directed by Johnny, who looks like being in prison half his life."

She gasped. "Let us see things as they are," he went on. "There's no sense in deceiving oneself. Johnny is really a naughty boy. You don't know, my dear, you don't know. I've tried to keep things from you and it has been awfully difficult."

"Keep things from me—what things?" Her face had gone pale.

"Well—" his hesitation was well feigned—"what do you think the young fool did—just before he was caught? I've been his best friend, as you know, and yet—well, he put my name to a cheque for four hundred pounds."

She stared at him in horror.

"Forgery!"

"What is the use of calling it names?" He took a pocket-book from

130

his dressing-gown and extracted a cheque. "I've got the cheque here. I don't know why I keep it, or what I'm going to do about Johnny."

She tried to see the name on the oblong slip, but he was careful to keep it hidden. It was, in fact, a cheque he had received by the morning post, and the story of the forgery had been invented on the spur of the minute. Inspirations such as this had been very profitable to Maurice Meister.

"Can't you destroy it?" she asked tremulously.

"Yes—I suppose I could." His hesitation was artistic. "But Johnny is so vindictive. In self-defence I've got to keep this thing." He put the cheque back in his pocket. "I shall never use it, of course," he said airily. And then, in that tender tone of his: "I want to talk to you about Johnny and everything. I can't now, with people walking in and out all the time and these policemen hanging round. Come up to supper—the way I told you."

She shook her head. "You know I can't. Maurice, you don't wish people to talk about me as they are talking about—Gwenda Milton."

The lawyer spun round at the words, his face distorted with fury. "God Almighty! Am I always to have that slimy ghost hanging round my neck? Gwenda Milton, a half-wit who hadn't the brains to live! All right—if you don't want to come, don't. Why the hell should I worry my head about Johnny? Why should I?"

She was terrified by this sudden violence of his.

"Oh, Maurice, you're so unreasonable. If you really want—"

"I don't care whether you do or whether you don't," he growled. "If you think you can get along without me, try it. I'm not going on my knees to you or to any other woman. Go into the country—but Johnny won't go with you, believe me!"

She caught his arm, frantic with the fear his half-threat had roused. "Maurice—I'll do anything you wish—you know I will."

He looked at her oddly. "Come at eleven," he said, and: "If you want a chaperon, bring The Ringer!"

The words were hardly spoken when there came three deliberate raps at the door, and Maurice Meister shrank back, his shaking hand at his mouth. "Who's there?" he asked hoarsely.

The deep tone of a man answered him. "I want to see you, Meister."

Meister went to the door and flung it open. The sinister face of Inspector Bliss stared into his.

"What...what are you doing here?" croaked the lawyer.

Bliss showed his white teeth in a mirthless smile. "Protecting you from The Ringer—watching over you like a father," he said harshly. His eyes strayed to the pale girl. "Don't you think, Miss Lenley—that you want a little watching over, too?"

She shook her head. "I am not afraid of The Ringer," she said; "he would not hurt me."

Bliss smiled crookedly.

"I'm not thinking of The Ringer!" he said, and his menacing eyes wandered to Maurice Meister.

Chapter 36

The return of John Lenley was the most supremely embarrassing thing that had ever happened within Maurice Meister's recollection. If he had resented the attitude of the young man before, he hated him now. The menace in his words, the covert threat behind his reference to Gwenda Milton, were maddening enough, but now there was another factor operating at a moment when it seemed that all his dreams were to be realised, and Mary Lenley, like a ripe plum, was ready to fall into his hands; when even the fear of The Ringer had evaporated in some degree, there must enter upon the scene this young man whom he thought he would not see again for years.

Prison had soured and aged him. He had gone away a weakling, come back a brooding, vicious man, who would stop at nothing—if he knew. There was nothing to know yet. Meister showed his teeth in a smile. Not yet. . .

Maurice Meister was no coward in his dealings with other men: he had all the qualities of his class. Known dangers he could face, however deadly they might be. He could have met John Lenley and without wincing could have told him of his evil plan—if he were sure of Mary. Yet the sight of a door opening slowly and apparently through no visible agency brought him to the verge of hysteria.

The Ringer was alive: the worst of Meister's fear died with the sure knowledge. He was something human, tangible; something against which he could match his brains.

That afternoon, when they were alone, he came in to Mary and, standing behind her, dropped his hands upon her shoulders. He felt her stiffen, and was amused.

"You haven't forgotten what you promised this morning?" he asked. She twisted from his clasp and came round to meet his eyes.

"Maurice, was it true about the cheque? You were not lying?" He nodded slowly. "We're alone now," she said desperately. "Can't we talk.

. .is it necessary that I should come tonight?"

"Very necessary," said Meister coolly. "I suppose you are aware that there are three people in the house besides ourselves? Do, for Heaven's sake, take a sane view of things, Mary; see them as they are, not as you would like them to be. I have to protect myself against Johnny—an irresponsible and arrogant young man—and I am very much afraid of—" he nearly said "fools" but thought better of it—"young men of his peculiar temperament." He saw the quick rise and fall of her bosom: it pleased him that he could stir her even to fear. How simple women were, even clever women! He had long ceased to be amazed at their immense capacity for believing. Credulity was one of the weaknesses of humankind that he could never understand.

"But, Maurice, isn't this as good an opportunity as we can get? Nobody will interrupt you...why, you are here with your clients for hours on end! Tell me about the cheque and how he came to forge it. I want to get things right."

He spread out his hands in a gesture of mock helplessness.

"What a child you are, Mary! How can you imagine that I would be in the mood to talk of Johnny, or plan for you? Keep your promise, my dear!"

She faced him squarely. "Maurice, I'm going to be awfully plain-spoken." What was coming? he wondered. There was a new resolution in her voice, a new courage in her eyes. She was so unlike the wilting, terrified being of the morning that he was for a moment staggered. "Do you really wish me to come tonight. . .just to talk about the cheque that Johnny has forged?"

He was so taken aback by the directness of the question that he could not for the moment answer. "Why, of course," he said at length. "Not only about the forgery, but there are so many other matters which we ought to talk over, Mary. If you're really going into the country, we must devise ways and means. You can't go flying off into Devonshire, or wherever it is you intend settling, at a minute's notice. I am getting some catalogues from one of my—from a house agent I represent. We can look over these together—"

"Maurice, is that true? I want to know. I'm not a child any longer. You must tell me."

She had never looked more lovely to him than in that moment of challenge.

"Mary," he began, "I am very fond of you—"

"What does that mean—that you love me?" The cold-bloodedness of the question took his breath away. "Does it mean, you love me so much that you want to marry me?" she asked.

"Why, of course," he stammered. "I am awfully fond of you. But marriage is one of the follies that I have so far avoided. Does it mean anything, my dear? A few words mumbled by a paid servant of the Church. . ."

"Then you don't want to marry me, Maurice?" she said quietly. "I am right there, aren't I?"

"Of course, if you wish me—" he began hastily.

She shook her head. "I don't love you and I don't wish to marry you, if that is what you mean," she said. "What do you really want of me?" She was standing close to him when she asked the question, and in another instant, she was struggling in his arms.

"I want you—you!" he breathed. "Mary, there is no woman in the world like you. . . .I adore you. .."

Summoning all her strength, she broke free from his grasp and held him breathlessly at arm's length. "I see!" She could hardly articulate the words. "I guessed that. Maurice, I shall not come to this house tonight."

Meister did not speak. The wild rush of passion which had overcome him had left him curiously weak. He could only look at her; his eyes burnt. Once he put up his trembling hand as though to control his lips. "I want you here tonight." The voice was scarcely audible. "You have been frank with me; I will be as frank with you. I want you: I want to make you happy. I want to take away all the dread and fear that clouds your life. I want to move you from that squalid home of yours. You know what has happened to your brother, don't you? He's been released on ticket-of-leave. He has two years and five months to serve. If I prefer a charge of forgery against him, he will get seven years and the extra time he has not served. Nine and a half years. ..you realise what that means? You'll be over thirty before you see him again."

He saw her reel, thinking she was going to faint, caught her by the arm, but she shook off his hand. "That puts the matter in a different light, doesn't it?"

He read agreement in a face which was as white as death.

"Is there no other way, Maurice?" she asked in a low voice. "No service I can render you? I would work for you as a housekeeper, as a servant—I would be your best friend, whatever happened to you, your loyalist helper."

Meister smiled.

"You're getting melodramatic, my dear, and that is stupid. What a fuss over a little supper party, a little flirtation."

Her steady eyes were of his. "If I told Johnny—" she began slowly.

"If you told Johnny, he'd come here, and be even more melodramatic. I should telephone for the police and that would be the end of Johnny. You understand?"

She nodded dumbly.

Chapter 37

At five o'clock Meister told her she could go home for the evening. Her head was aching; she had done practically no work that afternoon, for the letters were blurred and illegible specks of black that swam before her eyes. No further reference was made to the visit of the evening, and she hurried from the house into the dark street. A thin fog lay on Deptford as she threaded a way along the crowded side-walk of High Street.

Suppose she went to Alan? The thought only occurred to be rejected. She must work out her own salvation. Had Johnny been at home when she arrived, she might have told him, even if he had not guessed from her evident distress that something unusual had occurred.

But he was out; had left a note on the table saying that he had gone to town to see a man he knew. She remembered the name after a while; it was a gentleman farmer who had been a neighbour of theirs in the old days at Lenley. It was a dismal thought that all these preparations of Johnny's would come to naught if—She shuddered. Either prospect she did not dare think about.

She went to her room and presently came her little maid-of-all-work with the announcement that a gentleman had called to see her.

"I can't see anybody. Who is it?"

"I don't know, miss. He's a fellow with a beard."

She walked quickly past the girl across the dining-room into the tiny hall.

"You don't know me, I think," said the man at the door. "My name is Bliss."

Her heart sank. Why had this man come from Scotland Yard? Had Maurice, in one of those paroxysms of unreasonable temper, sent him?

"Come in, please."

He walked into the room, a cigarette drooping from his bearded mouth, and slowly took off his hat, as though he were reluctant to pay even this tribute of respect to her.

"I understand your brother's been released from prison today—or was it yesterday?"

"Yesterday," she said. "He came home this morning."

To her surprise, he made no further reference to Johnny, but took from his pocket a morning newspaper and folded it to show a column on the front page. She read the advertisement his finger indicated.

X2Z. LBa4T. QQ57g. LL4i8TS. A79Bf.

"What does it mean?" she asked.

"That is what I want to know," said Bliss, fixing his dark eyes on her. "It is a message either from The Ringer to his wife, or from his wife to The Ringer, and it is in a code which was left at this flat last week. I want you to show me that code."

"I'm sorry, Mr. Bliss"—she shook her head—"but the code was stolen—I thought by—"

"You thought by me?" His lips twisted in a grim smile. "So, you didn't believe that cock-and-bull story I told about my having seen a man climbing into the flat and going up after him? Miss Lenley, I have reason to believe that the code was not taken from your house, but that it is still here, and that you know where it is."

She had a feeling that, insulting as he was, he was merely testing her. His attitude was that of a man who wished to be convinced.

"The code is not here," she said quietly. "I missed it the night I came back and found the flat had been burgled."

She wondered if the peculiar look she saw indicated relief or scepticism.

"I'll have to take your word," he said, and folded up the paper. "If what you say is true, no other person than The Ringer and his wife has this code."

Mary was a trifle bewildered. "Of course," she said, "unless the person whom you saw climb into my room—"

"My theory is that that was The Ringer himself," said Bliss. He had not taken his eyes off her all the time he had been speaking. "Are you scared of The Ringer, Miss Lenley?"

In spite of her trouble she smiled. "Of course not. I told you today. Why should I be scared of him? I have done him no harm, and from what I know of him he is not the kind of man who would hurt any woman."

Again, that fleeting smile. "I'm glad you have such a high opinion of the scoundrel," he said, in a more genial tone. "I am afraid it is one that I do not share. How do you like Meister?"

Everybody asked her that question; it was beginning to get on her nerves; and he must have seen this, for, without waiting for her answer, he went on quickly: "You've got to look after that brother of yours. Miss Lenley. He's a pretty foolish young man."

"So, Maurice Meister thinks," she was stung into replying.

"Does he?" The answer seemed to amuse him. "That is about all. I'm sorry to have disturbed you."

He walked to the door and turned round.

"Rather a nice fellow, Wembury, eh? A bit of an impetuous young fool, but rather nice?" Again, he did not wait for an answer, but pulled the door close behind him, and she opened it in time to see him shut the front door. She herself had to go out again; the shops did not close till seven, and the evening was the only time she had for marketing. She made a list of all the things that Johnny liked; steadfastly kept out of her mind the pitiful possibilities which might disturb this house-keeping of hers.

With a basket on her arm she went out into the Lewisham High Road and shopped for an hour, and she was hurrying back to Malpas Mansions when she saw a tall man walking ahead of her. He wore a grey overcoat, but she could not mistake that shuffling gait and bent shoulders. She intended passing him without speaking, but almost before she came abreast. Dr. Lomond, without turning his head, hailed her. "It's fine to see a lassie with a basket, but the eggs ye bought were no' so good."

She gasped at this and laughed. It was the first time that day she had been genuinely amused.

"I didn't know I was under police observation," she said.

"It's a verra peculiar thing, that few people do," he said drily. "But I was watching ye in the egg shop—lassie, you've a trusting disposition. Those new-laid eggs you bought are contemporaneous with the eggs of the great roc." And then, seeing her rueful face in the light of a shop window, he chuckled. "I tell ye this, Miss Lenley; I'm a verra good obsairver. I obsairve eggs and skulls, jaws, noses, eyes and detectives! Was Mr. Bluss very offensive?" (He always referred to the ill-favoured inspector as "Bluss".) "Or was it merely a social call?"

"Did you know Mr. Bliss had been to see me?" she asked in astonishment.

The old man nodded "He's been around here a' the afternoon.

137

When he came to Malpas Mansions I happened to be passing and gave him goodnight, but he's a sorry fellow wi'oot any milk of human kindness in his dour system."

"Are you watching somebody now?" she asked mischievously, and was staggered when he pointed ahead. "Yon's the fellow," he said.

"Mr. Bliss?" She peered into the night, and at that moment saw in the light of a street standard the dapper figure of the Central Inspector.

"He interests me, that body," admitted Lomond. "He's mysteerious, and mysteerious things are very attractive to a plain, matter-of-fact old man like me."

She left him to his chase and got back to the Mansions just as Johnny returned. He was in excellent spirits; joked with her on her marketing, and uttered gloomy forebodings as to the effect upon his digestion. She could not remember when she had last seen him in that mood. And then he said something which gladdened her heart.

"That fellow Wembury isn't such a bad chap, after all. Which reminds me that I ought to call at Flanders Lane and register myself."

She heard this with a little pang.

"You are on ticket of leave, aren't you, Johnny. If anything happened. . . . I mean, if you were silly again, would you have to serve the full sentence?"

"If I'm silly again?" he asked sharply. "What do you mean?" And then with an air of unconcern: "You're being silly now, Mary. I'm going to lead a highly respectable life."

"But if you were—"

"Of course, I should have to serve the unfinished portion of my sentence in addition to any other I might get; but as I'm most unlikely to be what you call silly, we needn't consider that. I suppose, Meister's finished with you for the day? I hope in a week or two you'll be finished with him for good. I don't like you working there, Mary."

"I know, Johnny, but—"

"Yes, yes, I quite understand. You never work there at night, do you, dear?"

She could say "No" to this truthfully.

"I'm glad. You'll be wise to see Maurice only in business hours."

He lit a cigarette, blew a cloud of smoke into the air. Johnny was trying to frame the lie he must tell her.

"I may be late tonight," he said eventually. "A man I know has asked me to go to supper in the West End. You don't mind, do you?"

She shook her head. "No. What time will you be back?"

He considered this before he answered. "Not before midnight— probably a little later," he said.

Mary found her breath coming more quickly. "I—I may be late myself, Johnny. I've promised to go to a party. ..some people I've met."

Would he be deceived? she wondered. Apparently, he was, for he accepted her story of this mythical engagement without question.

"Get as much fun out of life as you can, old girl," he said, us he stripped his coat and walked into his bedroom. "I suppose it'll be a ghastly party after the wonderful shows we had at Lenley Court in the old days. But wait till we get on to our farm; we're going to do a bit of hunting—keep a horse or two. . . ."

He was in his bedroom now and she did not hear the remainder of his highly coloured plans.

He left the house by eight o'clock, and she sat down to wait for the hours to pass. How would this day end? And what would Alan think about it all? Alan, to whom she was something sacred and apart. She closed her eyes tightly us if to shut out some horrible vision. The world would never again be the same as it was. She had thought that, the day Johnny went away, when she had walked down the broad steps of the Old Bailey, her heart broken, her future wrecked. But now she watched the minute hand of the little American clock move all too quickly towards the hour of fate, she realised that her supreme hour of trial had yet to come.

Chapter 38

The fog which lay over Deptford extended to a wider area. An hour after Mary had had her little talk with Johnny, a powerful two-seater car came whizzing through the mist which shrouded the countryside between Hatfield and Welwyn, turned from the main road into a bumpy cart track and continued till, ahead of the driver, loomed the great arch of an abandoned hangar. The place had been an aerodrome in the days of the war, but it had been sold and re-sold so often that the list of its owners was of considerable length.

Stopping the car, he dimmed the lights and stepped briskly from the machine, walking towards the hangar. He heard a dog bark and the challenge of a man's voice. "Is that you, Colonel?"

The motorist answered.

"I've got your machine ready and it's all tuned up, but you won't be able to take your trip to Paris tonight. The fog's thick, and I've just been on the 'phone to the Cambridge aerodrome. They say that one of their pilots went up and found the fog was two thousand feet deep and extending over the channel."

"What could be nicer?" said the man called "Colonel Dane" cheerfully. "Fog driving is my speciality!"

The keeper of the hangar grunted something about every man to his taste, and walked ahead, swinging a dim lantern. Using all his strength, he rolled back the soft squeaking door of the hangar, and a long propeller and a portion of the fuselage of a Scout machine were revealed in the nickering light of the lantern.

"She's a beauty, Colonel," said the man admiringly. "When do you expect to come back?"

"In a week," said the other.

The collar of his overcoat was turned up and it was impossible to see anything save a pair of keen eyes, and these were only visible at intervals, for his soft felt hat was pulled down over his forehead and afforded a perfect shade.

"Yes, she's a beauty," said the man. "I've been tuning her up all the afternoon."

He was an ex-Air Force mechanic, and was for the moment the tenant of the garage, and the small cottage where he lived. Incidentally, he was the best paid aeroplane mechanic in England at the moment.

"The police were here today, sir," he said. "They came nosing around, wanting to know who was the owner of the 'bus—I told them you were an ex-officer of the Flying Corps who was thinking of running a light aircraft club. I've often wondered what you really are, sir?"

The man whom he called "Colonel" laughed softly.

"I shouldn't do too much wondering, Green," he said. "You're paid to think of nothing but struts and stays, carburettors and petrol supply!"

"I've had all sorts of theories," the imperturbable Green went on. "I thought maybe you were running dope to the Continent. If you are, it's no business of mine." Then he went off at a tangent. "Have you heard about The Ringer, sir? There's a bit in tonight's paper."

"The Ringer? Who on earth is The Ringer?"

"He's a fellow who disguises himself. The police have been after him for years."

Green was the kind of man who had the police news at his fingertips and could give the dates of the conviction and execution of every murderer for the past twenty years. "He used to be in the Air Force, from what they say."

"I've never heard of him," said the Colonel. "Just stand outside, will you. Green?"

He walked into the hangar and, producing a powerful electric lamp from his pocket, made a minute examination of the aeroplane, testing wires, and eventually climbing into the fuselage to inspect the controls.

"Yes, she's all right," he said as he dropped lightly down. "I don't know what time I shall be going, but probably some hour of the night. Have her taken out behind the garage facing the long field. You've been over the ground—I don't want to get her scratched before I start to rise."

"I've combed the ground, sir," said Green complacently.

"Good!"

"Colonel Dane" took from his pocket a flat wad of notes, counted a dozen and placed them in the hand of his assistant.

"Since you are so infernally curious, I will tell you, my friend. I am hoping tonight to be running away with a lady—that sounds a little romantic, doesn't it?"

"She's somebody's wife, eh?" said Green, scenting a scandal.

"She's somebody's wife," agreed the Colonel gravely. "With any kind of luck, I shall be here either at two o'clock tomorrow morning or two o'clock the following morning. The thicker the fog, the better I shall like it. I shall be accompanied by a lady, as I have told you. There will be no baggage, I want to carry as much juice as I can."

"Where are you making for, Colonel?"

The Ringer laughed again. He was easily amused tonight.

"It may be France or Belgium or Norway or the North Coast of Africa or the South Coast of Ireland—who knows? I can't tell you when I shall return, but before I go, I shall leave you enough money to live in comfort for at least a year. If I'm not back in ten days, I advise you to let the garage, keep your mouth shut, and with any kind of luck we shall be meeting again."

He picked his way back to the car, and Green, with all the curiosity of his kind, sought vainly to catch a glimpse of his face. Never once had he seen this strange employer of his, who had engaged him by night, and by night had visited him, choosing always those conditions which made it necessary to wear either a long mackintosh or a heavy ulster.

Green was always under the impression that his employer wore a beard, and in subsequent evidence that he gave adhered to this state-ment. Bearded or clean-shaven, he could not have penetrated beyond the muffling collar even now, as he escorted the "Colonel" back to his car.

"Talking about this Ringer—" began Green.

"I wasn't," said the other shortly, as he stepped into the car and jammed his foot on the self-starter. "And I advise you to follow my example. Green. I know nothing about the fellow, except that he's a dangerous man—dangerous to spy upon, more dangerous to talk about. Keep your mind fixed on aeroplanes. Green; they are less dead-ly!"

In another few seconds the rear light of his car was out of sight.

Chapter 39

Sam Hackitt had other trials than were represented by a vigilant constabulary. There was, for example, a lady whom in a misguided moment he had led to the altar—an act he had spent the rest of his life regretting. She was a loud, aggressive woman, who hated her husband, not for his offences against society but for certain weaknesses of his which led him to neglect his home—a collection of frowsy furniture in a dingy little room off Church Street.

Sam was as easy-going as most criminals, a fairly kind man, but he lived in terror of his wife. Since his release from prison he had very carefully avoided her, but the news of his return had spread, and there had been two scenes, one on Meister's doorstep and one in High Street, Deptford, when a raucous virago had followed him along the street explaining to the world at large the habits, character and delin-quencies of Mr. Samuel Hackitt.

One day, Sam in an off moment had strolled up west, and in a large window in Cockspur Street he had seen many glowing booklets de-scribing the wonder of the life on the western prairies of Canada; and though agriculture was a pursuit which had never wholly attracted him, he became from that instant an enthusiastic pioneer. But to reach Canada, money was needed, and to acquire property required more money. Sam Hackitt sat down cold-bloodedly to consider the prob-lem of transportation and sustenance. He had sufficient money saved to buy his ticket, but this he did surreptitiously, passing the emigration doctor with flying colours. Sam decided that, all being fair in love and war, and his relationships with Mr. Meister being permanently strained, it would be no hurt to his conscience to help himself to a few portable and saleable souvenirs.

That which he most strenuously coveted was a small black metal cash-box, which Meister usually kept in the second drawer of his desk. The lawyer, by reason of the peculiar calls made upon him, generally had a large sum of money in his cash-box, and it was this which Sam most earnestly desired.

There had been no opportunity in the past two days even to look at the box, and now, with the return of Johnny and his own summary ejection—Meister, as an act of grace, had told him he could stay on for the remainder of the week—a moment of crisis had arisen.

He had no grudge against Mary Lenley, but he had found a sense of bitter resentment growing towards the girl that day when, after the sixth attempt to walk into the room and make a quick extraction, he found her covering her typewriter before going home.

"You are leaving us, Hackitt?" she said on this occasion.

Sam thought that he could leave with greater rapidity if she would be kind enough to give him an opportunity of opening the second drawer of Mr. Meister's desk.

"Yes, Miss. I can't stand Meister any longer. I suppose you're glad about your brother coming back, Miss?"

"Very glad. We're going into the country."

"Taking up farming, Miss?" asked Sam, interested.

She sighed.

"I'm afraid we shan't be much use as farmers."

"I thought of going in for farming myself," said Sam. "I've had a bit of experience—I worked in the fields down at Dartmoor."

"Are you going to farm in England?" she asked, surprised out of her mood.

Sam coughed. "I'm not exactly sure. Miss, but I thought of going abroad. Into the great open spaces as it were."

"Sam, you've been to the pictures," she accused him, and he grinned.

"This is no country for a man who's trying to get away from the arm of the police," he said. "I want to go abroad and make a fresh start."

She looked at him oddly.

"Why are your eyes always on Mr. Meister's desk? Is there anything wrong with it?" she asked.

"No, no, Miss," said Sam hastily, "only I thought of giving it a rub up tomorrow. Look here, miss,"—he walked nearer to her and lowered his voice to a confidential tone—"you've known old Meister for years, haven't you?"

She nodded.

"I don't suppose you know very much about him except that he's a snide lawyer," said Sam outrageously. "Don't you think it'd be a good idea if you had another young lady in to help you? This may be my last word to you."

She looked at him kindly: how well he meant. "There isn't enough work for two people," she said.

He nodded knowingly.

"Yes, there is. Miss. You make enough work—do a little bit of miking."

"'Miking'?"

"Slowing up, ca' canny—it's a Scottish expression."

"But why should I do that? It wouldn't be very honest, would it?" she smiled in spite of herself.

The honesty of things never made any very great appeal to Sam Hackitt.

"It mightn't be honesty, but it'd be safe," he said, and winked. "I hope you won't be offended, but if I had a sister, I wouldn't pass her within half a mile of Meister's house."

He saw her expression change and was instantly apologetic, and took the first opportunity of getting out of the room.

There was only one way for Sam: the steel grille which protected the window leading on to the leads was an effective barrier to the average thief, but Sam was above the average. And, moreover, when he cleaned the windows that morning, he had introduced a little appliance to the lock, an appliance which the maker had not foreseen. If Alan Wembury had examined the bars carefully, he would have seen a piece of steel wire neatly wrapped round a bar, and had he followed the wire to its end he would have discovered that it entered the lock in such a way that a person outside the window had only to loosen the wire and pull, to force back the catch. It was an ingenious contrivance and Sam was rather proud of it.

That night, after Alan Wembury had gone, Sam crouched on the leads. He heard Alan come and go. It was an unpleasant experience crouching there, for the fog was alternated with a drizzle which soaked him through and chilled him to the bone. He heard Meister talking to himself as he paced up and down the room, heard the rattle of knife against plate, and then Sam cursed. Meister was at the piano—he might be there for hours. And Sam hated music. But apparently the man was in a fitful mood: the music ceased, and Sam heard the creak of a chair, and after a while his stertorous, regular breathing. The lawyer was asleep and Sam waited no longer. A quick pull and the grille was unfastened. He had greased the window sash and it rose noiselessly.

Meister sat at the piano, his eyes wide open, an unpleasant sight. Sam no more than glanced at the little table, near the settee, which was covered by a cloth. Tiptoeing across the room, he reached for the switch and turned out the lights.

The fire burnt low; but he was a famous night worker, and by touch located the drawer, fitted the little instrument he carried into the lock, and pulled. The drawer opened, and his hand groped in the interior. He found the cash-box instantly, but there were other treasures. A small cupboard under the disused buffet held certain priceless articles of Georgian silver. He went back to the window, lifted inside his portmanteau and packed until the case could hold no more. Lifting the suitcase, he stepped softly back towards safety, and was nearly opposite the mystery door when he heard a faint click and stood, petrified, all his senses alert.

It might have been a cooling cinder in the fire. He moved stealthily, one hand extended before him, an instinctive gesture common to all who work in the dark. He was opposite the mystery door, when suddenly a cold hand closed on his wrist!

He set his teeth, stifled the cry which rose, and then, with a quick jerk, wrenched free. Who was it? He could see nothing, could only hear quick breathing, and darted for the window. In a second, he was on the leads and in another he was racing across the courtyard. The fear of death in his heart.

There could be only one explanation for that cold and deathly hand—The Ringer had come for Meister!

Chapter 40

Early that evening Alan Wembury made a hurried call at Meister's house. The girl was gone but Meister was visible. He came down in his inevitable dressing-gown and was so gloomy and nervous a man that Alan formed the impression that he had been sent for so urgently to soothe the lawyer's nerves.

But in this he was wrong.

"Sorry to bother you, inspector. . ." Meister was, for the first time in his life, at a loss as to how he should proceed. Alan waited. "The fact is. . .I've got a very unpleasant duty to perform—very unpleasant. To tell you the truth, I hate doing it."

Still Alan said nothing to encourage the coming confidence and Meister hardly wanted encouragement.

"It's about Johnny. You understand my position, Wembury? You know what the commissioner said to me? I am under suspicion—unjustly, it is true—but I am suspect by police headquarters."

What was coming next? Alan wondered. This was so unlike the Meister he knew that he might be excused his bewilderment.

"I can't afford to take risks," the lawyer went on. "A few weeks ago, I might have taken a chance, for the sake of Mary—Miss Lenley. But now I simply dare not. If I know of a felony about to be committed or contemplated, I have only one course—to inform the police."

Now Alan Wembury understood. But he still maintained his silence.

Maurice was walking nervously up and down the room. He sensed the antagonism, the contempt of the other man, and hated him for it. Worse than this, he was well aware that Alan knew that he was lying: knew full well that the betrayal was cold-blooded and deliberate.

"You understand?" asked Meister again.

"Well?" said Alan. He was nauseated by this preliminary. "What felony is Lenley committing?"

Meister drew a long breath.

"I think you should know that the Darnleigh affair was not Johnny's first job. He did the burglary at Miss Bolter's about a year ago. You remember?"

Wembury nodded. Miss Bolter was an eccentric maiden lady of great wealth. She had a house on the edge of Greenwich—a veritable storehouse of old jewellery. A robbery had been committed and the thieves had got away with £8,000 worth of jewels.

"Was Lenley in that—is that the information you are laying?"

"I am laying no information," said Maurice hastily. "I merely tell you what I believe to be true. My information, which you will be able to confirm, is that the jewels were never got away from the house—you will remember that the burglars were disturbed at their nefarious work."

Alan shook his head. "I still don't understand what you're driving at," he said.

Meister looked round and lowered his voice. "I understand from some hint he dropped that he is going to Camden Crescent tonight to get the jewels! He has borrowed the key of the house next door, which happens to be my property and is empty. My theory is that the jewels are hidden on the roof of No. 57. I suggest—I do no more than suggest, that you post a man there tonight."

"I see!" said Alan softly.

"I don't want you to think that I intend harm to Johnny—I'd rather have cut off my right hand than hurt him. But I have my duty to do—and I am already under suspicion and deeply involved, so far as John Lenley is concerned."

Alan went back to Flanders Lane police station with a heavy heart. He could do nothing. Meister would report to headquarters that he had given him the information. To warn John Lenley would mean ruin—disgrace—probably an ignominious discharge from the service.

He sent a man to take up a position on the roof of Camden Crescent.

Within an hour he had his report. He was standing moodily before the fire when the telephone bell rang. The sergeant pulled the instrument over to him.

"Hallo!" He looked up at the clock mechanically to time the call in his book. "What's that?" He covered the receiver with his hand. "The night watchman at Cleavers reports there's a man on the roof in Camden Crescent."

Alan thought for a moment. "Yes, of course. Tell him not to worry; it is a police officer."

"On the roof of Camden Crescent?" asked the sergeant incredulously.

Alan nodded, and the officer addressed himself to his unknown vis-à-vis.

"That's all right, son. He's only one of our men...eh? He's sweeping the chimney...yes, we always have policemen sweep chimneys and we usually choose the night." He hung up the receiver. "What's he doing up there?"

"Looking round," said Alan indifferently.

His men were searching for another criminal that night. Sam Hackitt had disappeared from Meister's house, and the slatternly woman who was known as Mrs. Hackitt had been brought in earlier in the evening charged with fighting. It was the old sordid story...a younger woman who had taken the erratic fancy of the faithless Sam. In her fury Mrs. Hackitt had "squeaked"—the story of Sam's plans was told to the station sergeant's desk—and two of Wembury's men were looking for him.

Dr. Lomond had once said that he felt the police were very hard on little criminals, that they sought crime, and grew callous to all the sufferings attendant upon its detection. Alan wondered if he had grown callous. Perhaps he had not. Perhaps no police officer should. They came to be rather like doctors, who have two personalities, in one of which they can dissociate from themselves all sentiment and human tenderness. And then the object of his thoughts appeared and Wembury's heart leapt. John Lenley came into the charge-room, nodding to the sergeant.

"I'm reporting here," he said.

He took some papers out of his pocket and laid them on the desk.

"My name's Lenley. I'm a convict on licence."

And then he caught Wembury's eye and came over to him and shook hands.

"I heard you were out, Lenley. I congratulate you." All the time he was speaking, there was in his mind the picture of that crouching, waiting figure of justice on the roof of Camden Crescent. He had to clench his teeth to inhibit the warning that rose to his lips.

"Yes, I came out yesterday," said Johnny.

"Your sister was glad to see you?"

"Yes," said Lenley curtly, and seemed disinclined to make any further reference to Mary.

"I'd like to find a job for you, Johnny," said Alan, in desperation. "I think I can."

John Lenley smiled crookedly.

"Prisoners' Aid Society?" he asked. "No, thank you! Or is it the Salvation Army you're thinking of? Paper sorting at two pence a hundredweight? When I get a job, it will be one that a waster can't do, Wembury. I don't want helping; I want leaving alone."

There was a silence, broken by the scratching of the sergeant's pen.

"Where are you going tonight?" asked Alan. At all costs this man must be warned. He thought of Mary Lenley waiting at home. He was almost crazy with the fear that she might in some way conceive the arrest of this man as a betrayal on his part.

John Lenley was looking at him suspiciously. "I'm going up west. Why do you want to know?"

Alan's indifference was ill assumed. "I don't wish to know particularly," And then: "Sergeant, how far is it from here to Camden

148

Crescent?"

He saw Johnny start. The man's eyes were fixed on his.

"Not ten minutes' walk," said the sergeant.

"Not far, is it?" Alan was addressing the ticket-of-leave man. "A mere ten minutes' walk from Camden Crescent to the station house!"

Johnny did not answer.

"I thought of taking a lonely stroll up west," Alan went on. "Would you like to come along and have a chat? There are several things I'd like to talk to you about."

Johnny was watching him suspiciously. "No," he said quietly. "I've got to meet a friend."

Alan picked up a book and turned the leaves slowly. He did not raise his eyes when he said: "I wonder if you know whom you're going to meet? You used to be a bit of an athlete in your early days, Lenley—a runner, weren't you? I seem to remember that you took prizes?"

"Yes, I've got a cup or two," he said, in a tone of surprise.

"If I were you"—still Alan did not raise his eyes from the book—"I'd run and not stop running until I reached home. And then I'd lock the door to stop myself running out again!"

The desk sergeant was intrigued.

"Why?" he asked.

Johnny had turned his back on Wembury and was apparently absorbed in the information he was giving to the sergeant. Then he walked to the door.

"Goodnight, Lenley, if I don't see you again," said Wembury.

Johnny spun round. "Do you expect to see me again?" he asked. "Tonight?"

"Yes—I do."

The words were deliberate. It was the nearest to a warning that he could give consistent with his duty; and when, with a shrug, Johnny Lenley went out into the night, the heart of Alan Wembury was sore.

"What fools these people are!" he said aloud.

"And a good job, too!" returned the sergeant. "If they weren't fools, you'd never catch 'em!"

Wembury would have gone out had it not been for his promise to meet Dr. Lomond here. He did not want to be round when the inevitable happened and Johnny Lenley was brought in—unless he had taken the hint. Had he? It seemed impossible of belief that he could have the situation so plainly put before him, and yet ignore the warning.

Chapter 41

Lomond had just shuffled in and was cursing the weather when there was a heavy footfall in the corridor outside and the lawyer lurched in. His overcoat was open, his silk hat was on the back of his head, an unaccustomed cigarette drooped from his lips. The transition from the dark street to the well-lit charge-room temporarily blinded him. He leered for a long time at the doctor.

"The man of medicine and the man of law!" he said thickly and thumped himself on the chest. "My dear doctor, this is almost an historic meeting!"

He turned to Alan. "Have they brought him in? I didn't think he'd be fool enough to do the job, but he's better away, my dear Wembury, very much better."

"Did you come to find out? You might have saved yourself the trouble by telephoning," said Alan sternly.

The whole mien of Meister suddenly changed. The look that Alan had seen in his eyes before reappeared, and when he spoke his voice was harsh but coherent.

"No, I didn't come for that." He looked round over his shoulder. The policeman had come from the door to the sergeant, and was whispering something to him. Even the doctor seemed interested. "Hackitt cleared out and left me alone—the dirty coward! Alone in the house!"

Up went the hand to his mouth.

"It got on my nerves, Wembury. Every sound I heard, the creak of a chair when I moved, a coal falling from the fire, the rattle of the windows—"

Out of the dark beyond the doorway loomed a figure. Nobody saw it. The three men talking together at the desk least of all. Inspector Bliss stared into the charge-room for a second and vanished as though he were part of some magician's trick. The policeman at the desk caught a glimpse of him and walked to the door. The sergeant and the doctor followed at a more leisurely pace.

"Every sound brings my heart into my mouth, Wembury. I feel as though I stood in the very presence of doom."

His voice was a husky whine.

"I feel it now—as though somewhere near me, in this very room, death were at my elbow. Oh, God, it's awful—awful!"

Suddenly he swayed, and Alan Wembury caught him just in time.

Fortunately, the doctor was at hand, and they sat him on a chair whilst Sergeant Carter delved into his desk for an ancient bottle of smelling-salts that had served many a fainting lady, overcome in that room by her temporary misfortunes.

"What's the matter with him?"

"Dope," answered the doctor laconically. "Take him into the in-spector's room, sergeant, he'll be all right in a few minutes!"

He watched the limp figure assisted from the charge-room and shook his head. Then he strolled back to the main door and into the corridor. He was peering out into the night.

"What is it, doctor?" asked Alan.

"There he is again!" Lomond pointed to the dark street.

"Who is it?"

"He's been watching the station ever since Meister came in," said Lomond, as he came back to the charge-room and drew up a chair to the fire.

"Who is the mysterious watcher?" asked Wembury, smiling.

"I don't know. It looked like Bliss to me," said Lomond, rolling a cigarette; "he doesn't like me—I don't know why."

"Do you know anybody he likes—except Bliss?" growled Wembury.

"I heard quite a curious thing about him at the club this after-noon," said Lomond slowly. "I met a man who knew him in Washing-ton—a doctor man. He swears that he saw Bliss in the psychopathic ward of a Brooklyn hospital."

"When was this?"

"That is the absurd part of it. He said he saw him only a fortnight ago."

Wembury smiled. "He has been back months."

"Do you know Bliss very well?"

"No, not very well," admitted Wembury. "I never met him until he returned from America. I had seen him—he's a much older man than I, and my promotion was rather rapid. He was a sub-inspector when I was only a constable—hallo!"

A man strode into the charge-room and walked straight to the sergeant's desk. It was Inspector Bliss.

"I want a gun," he said shortly.

"I beg pardon?" Carter stared at him.

"I want an automatic."—louder.

Wembury chuckled maliciously.

"That's right, sergeant—Central Inspector Bliss from Scotland Yard wants an automatic. What do you want it for, Bliss? Going ratting?"

Bliss favoured him with a crooked smile.

"Yes, but you needn't be afraid, though. What's it to do with you?"

"Quite a lot," said Wembury, quietly, as the sergeant produced an automatic. "This is my division."

"Any reason why I shouldn't have it?" demanded the bearded man.

"None," said Wembury, and as the other made for the door: "I should sign for it, though. You seem to have forgotten the routine, Bliss."

Bliss turned with a curse. "I've been away from this damned country, you know that."

The doctor's eyes were twinkling. "Good evening, Mr. Bliss."

For the first time it seemed Bliss noticed the police surgeon's presence. "'Evening, Professor. Caught The Ringer yet?"

"Not yet," smiled Lomond.

"Huh! Better write another book and then perhaps you will!"

"We are amused," responded Lomond dryly. "No, I haven't caught The Ringer, but I dare say I could put my hand on him."

Bliss looked at the other suspiciously. "Think so? You've got a theory, eh?"

"A conviction, a very strong conviction," said Lomond mysteriously.

"Now you take a tip from me. Leave police work to policemen. Arthur Milton's a dangerous man. Seen his wife lately?"

"No—have you?"

Bliss turned. "No; I don't even know who she's living with."

The doctor's face hardened. "Would you remember you're speaking of a particular friend of mine?" he demanded.

Inspector Bliss allowed himself the rare luxury of a chuckle. "Oh, she's caught you, too, eh? She does find 'em!"

"Have you never heard of a woman having a disinterested friend?" demanded Lomond.

"Oh yes, there's one born every minute," was the harsh reply, and, seeing Wembury's disapproving eye on him: "You're a bit of a sentimental Johnny, too, aren't you, Wembury?"

"That's my weakness," said Alan coolly.

"That girl Lenley—she's in Meister's office, isn't she?"

Wembury smiled his contempt. "You've found that out, have you? There are the makings of a detective in you," he said, but Bliss was not perturbed by the studied insult.

"Sweet on her, they tell me. Very romantic! The old squire's daughter and the love-sick copper!"

"If you must use thieves' slang, call me 'busy'. Were you ever in love, Bliss?"

"Me! Huh! No woman can make a fool of me!" said Inspector Bliss, one hand on the door.

"It takes a clever woman to improve on God's handiwork. What are you doing down here, anyway?" retorted Alan rudely.

"Your job!" snapped Bliss, as he went out, banging the door behind him.

Chapter 42

Carter was intrigued.

"It's curious that the inspector doesn't know station routine, isn't it, sir?"

"Everything about Mr. Bliss is curious," said Alan savagely. "Bliss! Where he got his name from, I'd like to know!"

Lomond went to the door of the inspector's room, where Meister lay under the watchful eye of a "relief". He was rapidly recovering, the doctor said. As he returned, a policeman came in and whispered to Wembury.

"A lady to see me? Who is it?"

"It's Cora Ann Milton," said Lomond, again displaying that uncanny instinct of his. "My future bride!"

Cora Ann came in with an air in which defiance and assumed indifference were blended. "Say, is there something wrong with your date book, doctor?"

Alan regarded the old doctor suspiciously as Lomond took the woman's hand in his.

"There's something wrong with you. Why, you're all of a dither, Cora Ann."

She nodded grimly. "I never wait longer than an hour for any man."

Wembury looked up at this.

"Good Lord! I was taking ye to dinner!" gasped the doctor. "I was called down here and it slipped out of my mind."

Cora Ann looked round with every indication of distaste.

"I can't blame you. If I were called to a place like this my mind would slip a cog. So, this is a police station? My idea of hell, only not so bright!" She looked at Wembury. "Say, where's your fancy dress? Everybody else is in uniform."

"I keep that for wearing at parties," he smiled.

She shuddered.

"Ugh—doesn't it make you sick? How can you stay here? There must be something wrong with a man's mind who likes this sort of life."

"There's something wrong with you," said Lomond quietly. "There's a queer vacant look in your eye."

She eyed him steadily. "The vacancy isn't in my eye—I haven't had anything to eat since lunch!"

Lomond was all remorse. "You poor hungry mite—could you not eat by yourself?"

"I prefer to take my meals under the eye of a medical man," said Cora.

"I'm not so sure that it would be safe," he bantered. "Do you think I'll poison you?"

"You might poison my mind."

All the time Wembury was listening with undisguised astonishment. What was the doctor's game? Why was he making friends with this girl?

"Are you going to take pity on a poor hysterical female?" she demanded.

There was an element of desperation in her tone; it was as though she were making one last effort to. . .what? Alan was puzzled.

"I'd love to, Cora Ann, but—" Lomond was saying.

"But! But!" she mocked. "You're a 'butter', eh? Listen, Scottie, you won't have to pay for the dinner!"

He grinned at this. "That's certainly an inducement, but I've got work to do."

In a second her face had grown haggard. "Work!" She laughed bitterly, and with a shrug of her shoulders walked listlessly towards the door. "I know the work! You're trying to hang Arthur Milton. That's your idea of work! All right."

"Where are you going now, lassie?" asked the doctor, anxiously.

She looked at him, and her smile was a little hard. "It's too late for dinner. I think I'll go and have supper and a music lesson at the same time. I've a friend who plays the piano very, very well."

Lomond walked to the door and peered out into the fog after her. "That sounds like a threat to me," he said.

Alan did not answer immediately. When he spoke, his voice was very grave.

"Doctor—I wish you wouldn't make love to The Ringer's wife."

"What do you mean?"

"I mean—I don't want the possibility of two tragedies on my mind."

Carter, who had been into the room where Meister was lying, came back to his desk at that moment.

"How is he now?"

"He's all right, sir," said the sergeant.

Tramp, tramp, tramp!

Alan's keen ears had caught the sound of the measured march, the peculiar tempo of a man in custody, and he drew a long breath as Johnny Lenley, his arm gripped by a plain-clothes policeman, came through the door and was arrayed before the desk. There was no preliminary.

"I am Detective-Constable Bell," said the tall man. "This evening I was on the roof of 57, Camden Crescent, and I saw this man come up through a trap-door in the attic of No. 55. I saw him searching behind the cistern of 57, and took him into custody. I charged him with being on enclosed premises for the purpose of committing a felony."

Lenley stood looking down at the floor. He scarcely seemed interested in the proceedings, until he raised his head and his eyes found Wembury's, and then he nodded slowly.

"Thank you, Wembury," he said. "If I had the brain of a rabbit I shouldn't be here."

Carter at the desk dipped his pen in the ink. "What is your name?" he asked automatically.

"John Lenley." Silence and a splutter of writing.

"Your address?"

"I have no address."

"Your trade?"

"I'm a convict on licence," said Johnny quietly.

The sergeant put down his pen. "Search him," he said. Johnny spread out his arms and the tall officer ran his hands through his pockets and carried what he had found to the desk. "Who put me away, Wembury?"

Alan shook his head. "That is not a question to ask me," he said. "You know that very well." He nodded to the desk to call the prisoner's attention to the man who was, for the moment, in supreme

155

authority.

"Have you any explanation for your presence on the roof of 57, Camden Crescent?" asked the sergeant.

Johnny Lenley cleared his throat.

"I went after some stuff that was supposed to be planted behind a cistern. And it wasn't there. That's all. Who was the snout? You needn't tell me, because I know. Look after my sister, Wembury; she'll want some looking after, and I'd sooner trust you than any man—"

It was unfortunate for all concerned that Mr. Meister chose that moment to make his bedraggled appearance. He stared foolishly at the man in the hands of the detectives, and Johnny Lenley smiled.

"Hallo, Maurice!" he said softly.

The lawyer was staggered.

"Why—why—it's—it's Johnny!" he stammered. "You haven't been getting into trouble again, have you, Johnny?" He raised his hands in a gesture of despair. "What a misfortune! I'll be down at the court to defend you in the morning, my boy." He ambled up to the sergeant's desk. "Any food he wants, let him have it at my expense," he said loudly.

"Meister!" The word came like the clang of steel on steel. "There was no swag behind the cistern!"

Mr. Meister's face was a picture of wonder and amazement.

"No swag behind the cistern? 'Swag?' I don't know what you're talking about, my boy."

Lenley nodded and grinned mirthlessly.

"I came out too soon for you. It interfered with your little scheme, didn't it, Meister? You swine!"

Before Wembury could realise what was happening, Johnny had the lawyer by the throat. In a second four men were struggling in a heap on the ground.

As they rolled on the floor, the door of the charge room flung open, and Inspector Bliss appeared. He stood for a second, and then with one leap was in the thick of the scrum.

It was Bliss who flung the boy back. He walked to the prostrate Meister.

"Is he hurt?" he demanded.

White with rage, Johnny glared at the lawyer.

"I wish to God I'd killed him!" he hissed.

Bliss turned his hard eyes upon the prisoner.

"Don't be so damned selfish, Lenley!" he said coldly.

Chapter 43

Alan Wembury had only one thought in his mind as he walked from the police station, and that a supremely wretched one. Mary had to be told. Again, he was to be an unwilling messenger of woe. A fog was blowing up from the river, and lay so thick in some places that he had to grope his way feeling along the railings. In the dip of Lewisham High Road it was clearer, for some reason. Being human, he cursed the fog; cursed John Lenley for his insensate folly; but it was when he thought of Maurice Meister that he found it most difficult to control his anger. The base treachery of the man was almost inhuman.

He climbed up the stone staircase of Malpas Mansions and knocked at the door of Mary's flat. There was no answer. He knocked again, and then he heard an inner door open with the snap of a lock as it was turned back, and: "Is that you, Johnny? I thought you had the key."

"No, my dear, it is I."

"Alan!" She took a step back and her hand went to her heart. "Is anything wrong?"

Her face was twitching with anxiety. He did not answer until he had closed the door behind him and followed her into the room.

"Is there anything wrong?" she asked again.... "Is it Johnny?"

He nodded. She sank into a chair and covered her eyes with her hands.

"Is he. . .arrested?" she whispered.

"Yes," said Alan.

"For the forgery?" She spoke in a voice little above a whisper.

"For the forgery?" He stared down at her. "I don't know what you mean, my dear."

And she turned a white, bewildered face up to his.

"Isn't it for forgery?" she asked, in wonder; and then, as she realised her indiscretion: "Will you forget that I asked that, Alan?"

"Of course, I'll forget, Mary, my dear. I know nothing about a forgery. Johnny was arrested for being on enclosed premises."

"For burglary—oh, my God!"

"I don't know what it's all about. I'm a little at sea myself," said Alan. "I wish I could tell you everything I guess: perhaps I will, even if I am fired out of the force for it."

He dropped his hand gently on her shoulder.

"You've got to stand up to this, Mary; there may be some explanation. I can't understand why Johnny should have been such a lunatic.

157

I did my best to warn him. I still think there is a chance for him. After I leave here and have seen Meister, I'm going to knock up a lawyer friend of mine and get his advice. I wish he hadn't gone for Meister."

And then he told her of the scene at the police station, and she was horrified.

"He struck Maurice? Oh, he's mad! Why, Maurice has it in his power—" She stopped short.

Alan's keen eyes searched her face.

"Go on," he said gently. "Maurice has it in his power—?" And, when she did not speak: "Is it the forgery you are thinking of?"

She looked at him reproachfully.

"Alan, you promised—"

"I didn't promise anything," he half smiled, "but I'll tell you this, that anything you say to me is to Alan Wembury the individual, and not to Alan Wembury the police officer. Mary, my dear, you're in trouble: won't you let me help you?"

She shook her head.

"I can't, I can't! This has made things so dreadful. Maurice is so vindictive, and he will never forgive Johnny. And he was going to be so nice. . .he was getting us a little farm in the country."

It was on the tip of Alan's tongue to tell her the truth about the betrayal, but the rigid discipline of the police force was triumphant. The first law and the last law of criminal detection is never to betray the informer.

"It's a mystery to me why Johnny went to this house. He told some story about there being loot, the proceeds of an old burglary, hidden in a cistern, but of course there was nothing of the sort."

She was crouching over the table, her head on her hands, her eyes closed. He thought for a moment she was going to faint, and his arm went about her shoulder.

"Mary, can't I help you?" His voice was husky. He found a difficulty in breathing. "I don't care how you think of me, whether it is as the son of your old servant, as Inspector Wembury the police officer, or just Alan Wembury. . .who loves you!"

She did not move; made no attempt to withdraw from his encircling arm.

"I've said it now and I'm glad," he went on breathlessly. "I've always loved you since you were a child. Won't you tell me everything, Mary?"

And then suddenly she pushed him away and came to her feet,

wild-eyed, her lips parted as at some horrible thought.

"I can't, I can't!" she said, almost incoherently. "Don't touch me, Alan. . . .I'm not worthy of you. . . .I thought I need not go, but now I know that I must . . .for Johnny's sake."

"Go where?" he asked sternly, but she shook her head. Then she flung her hands out impulsively and caught him in a frenzied clasp.

"Alan, I know you love me. . .and I'm glad. . .glad! You know what that means, don't you? A woman wouldn't say that unless she. . .she felt that way herself. But I've got to save Johnny—I must!"

"Won't you tell me what it is?"

She shook her head. "I can't. This is one of the hard places that I've got to go through without help."

But he was not to be silenced. "Is it Meister?" he asked. "Is it some threat that he is holding over you?"

Mary shook her head wearily.

"I don't want to talk about it, Alan—what can I do for Johnny? Is it really a bad charge—I mean, will he be sent to penal servitude again? Do you think that Maurice could save him?"

For the moment Johnny's fate did not interest the police officer. He had no mind, no thought for anybody but this lonely girl, battered and bruised and broken. His arms went round her; he held her to his breast and kissed her red lips.

"Don't, please, Alan," she murmured, and realising that she had no physical strength to resist, he released her gently.

He himself was shaking like an aspen when he moved to the door.

"I'm going to solve a few mysteries—about Johnny and about other things," he said, between his teeth. "Will you stay here where I can find you? I will come back in an hour."

Dimly divining his purpose, she called him back, but he was gone.

Meister's house was in darkness when Alan struggled through the fog into Flanders Lane. The police officer on duty at the door had nothing to report except that he had heard the sound of a piano coming faintly from one of the upper rooms.

The policeman had the key of the gate and the front door, and, leaving the man on duty outside, Alan strode into the house. As he mounted the stairs, the sounds of a Humoresque came down to him. He tried Meister's door: it was locked. He tapped on the panel.

"What do you want?" asked Meister's slurred voice. "Who is it?"

"Wembury. Open the door," said Alan impatiently.

He heard the man growl as he crossed the room, and presently the door was opened. He walked in; the room was in darkness save for a light which came from one standard lamp near the piano.

"Well, what's that young blackguard got to say for himself?" demanded Maurice. He had been drinking heavily; the place reeked with the smell of spirits. There was a big bruise on his cheek where John Lenley had struck him.

Without invitation, Alan switched on the lights, and the lawyer blinked impatiently at him.

"I don't want lights. Curse you, why did you put those lights on?" he snarled.

"I want to see you," said Wembury, "and I would like you to see me."

Meister stared at him stupidly.

"Well," he asked at last, "you wanted to see me? You seem to have taken charge of my house, Mr. Wembury. You walk in and you go out as you wish; you turn on my lights and put them off at your own sweet will. Now perhaps you will condescend to explain your attitude and your manner."

"I've come to ask you something about a forgery."

He saw Maurice start. "A forgery? What do you mean?"

"You know damned well what I mean," said Alan savagely. "What is this forgery you've told Mary Lenley about?"

Drunk as he was, the question sobered the man. He shook his head. "I really don't understand what you're talking about." Maurice Meister was no fool. If Mary had told the story of the forged cheque, this bullying oaf of a police officer would not ask such a question. He had heard a little, guessed much—how much, Meister was anxious to learn.

"My dear man, you come here in the middle of the night and ask me questions about forgeries," he went on in a flippant tone. "Do you really expect me to be conversational and informative—after what I have experienced tonight? I've dealt with so many forgeries in my life that I hardly know to which one you refer."

His eyes strayed unconsciously to a little round table that was set in the centre of the room, and covered by a fine white cloth. Alan had noticed this and wondered what the cloth concealed. It might be Meister's supper, or it might be—Only for a second did he allow his attention to be diverted, however.

"Meister, you're holding some threat over the head of Mary Lenley, and I want to know what it is. You've asked her to do something which she doesn't want to do. I don't know what that is either, but I can guess. I'm warning you—"

"As a police officer?" sneered Maurice.

"As a man," said Alan quietly. "For the evil you are contemplating there may be no remedy in law, but I tell you this, that if one hair of Mary Lenley's head is hurt, you will be sorry."

The lawyer's eyes narrowed.

"That is a threat of personal violence, one presumes?" he said, and in spite of the effort to appear unconcerned his voice trembled. "Threatened men live long, Inspector Wembury, and I have been threatened all my life and nothing has come of it. The Ringer threatens me, Johnny threatens me, you threaten me—I thrive on threats!"

The eyes of Alan Wembury had the hard brightness of burnished steel. "Meister," he said softly, "I wonder if you realise how near you are to death?"

Meister's jaw dropped and he gaped at the young man who towered over him.

"Not at my hands, perhaps; not at The Ringer's hands, nor John Lenley's hands; but if what I believe is true, and if I am right in suspecting the kind of villainy you contemplate tonight, and you carry your plans through, be sure of one thing, Maurice Meister—that if The Ringer fails, I shall get you!"

Meister looked at him for a long time and then forced a smile.

"By God, you're in love with Mary Lenley," he chuckled harshly. "That's the best joke I've heard for years!"

Alan heard his raucous laugher as he went down the stairs, and the echo of it rang in his ears all the way down Flanders Lane.

He had a call to make—a lawyer friend who lived in Greenwich. His interview with that gentleman was very satisfactory.

Chapter 44

Alan Wembury came into the charge-room and glanced at the clock. He had been gone two hours.

"Has Mr. Bliss been in?" he asked.

Bliss had vanished from the station almost as dramatically as he arrived.

"Yes, sir; he came in for a few minutes: he wanted to see a man in the cells," said Carter.

Instantly Alan was alert. "Who?" he asked.

"That boy Lenley. I let him have the key."

What interest had the Scotland Yard man in Johnny? Wembury was puzzled. "Oh—he didn't stay long?"

"No, sir. Above five minutes."

Alan shook his rain-soddened hat in the fireplace. "No messages?"

"No, sir: one of our drunks has been giving a lot of trouble. I had to telephone to Dr. Lomond—he's with him now. By the way, sir, did you see this amongst Lenley's papers? I only found it after you'd gone."

He took a card from the desk and gave it to Wembury, who read:

Here is the key. You can go in when you like—No. 57.

"Why, that's Meister's writing."

"Yes, sir," nodded Carter, "and No. 57 is Meister's own property. I don't know how that will affect the charge against Lenley."

As he read a great load seemed to roll from Alan Wembury's heart: everything his lawyer friend had said, came back to him. "Thank God! That lets him out! It was just as I thought! Meister must have been very drunk to have written that—it is his first slip."

"What is the law?"

Wembury was no lawyer, but when he had discovered that the arrest had been made on Meister's property, he had seen a loophole. Johnny Lenley went at Meister's invitation—it could not be burglary. Meister was the landlord of the house.

"Was there a key?" he asked.

"Yes, sir." Carter handed the key over. "It has Meister's name on the label."

Alan sighed his relief. "By gad! I'm glad Lenley is inside, though. If ever I saw murder in a man's eyes it was in his!"

Carter put a question that had been in his mind all the evening. "I suppose Lenley isn't The Ringer?" he asked, and Alan laughed.

"Don't be absurd! How can he be?" As he spoke, he heard his name called, and Lomond ran into the charge-room from the passage leading to the cells. "Is anything wrong?" asked Alan quickly. "What cell did you put Lenley in?"

"Number eight at the far end," said Carter. "The door's wide open —it's empty!" Carter flew out of the room. Alan picked up the 'phone from the sergeant's desk.

"By God, Lomond, he'll be after Meister." Carter came into the room hurriedly.

"He's got away all right," he said. "The door is wide open, and so is the door into the yard!"

"Two of my men, Carter," said Wembury quickly, and then the number he had asked for came through.

"Scotland Yard?...Give me the night officer...Inspector Wembury speaking. Take this for all stations. Arrest and detain John Lenley, who escaped tonight from Flanders Lane police station whilst under detention. Age twenty-seven, height six feet, dark, wearing a—"

"Blue serge," prompted Sergeant Carter.

"He's a convict on licence," continued Wembury. "Sort that out, will you? Thank you."

He hung up the receiver as a detective came in.

"Get your bicycle and go round to all patrols. Lenley's got away. You can describe the man."

To the second man who came in: "Go to Malpas Mansions—Lenley lives there with his sister. Don't alarm the young lady, do you understand? If you find him, bring him in."

When the men had hurried out into the thick night, Alan strode up and down the charge-room. This danger to Meister was a new one. Dr. Lomond was going and collecting his impedimenta.

"How the devil did he get away?" Wembury put his thoughts into words.

"I have my own theory," said Lomond. "If you allow Detective Inspector Bliss too near a prisoner, he'll get away easily enough."

On which cryptic note he left.

He had to wait at the head of the steps to allow Sam Hackitt to pass in—and Hackitt did not come willingly, for he was in the hands of a detective and a uniformed policeman.

Alan heard a familiar plaint and looked over his shoulder.

"'Evening, Mr. Wembury. See what they've done to me? Why don't you stop 'em 'ounding me down?" he demanded in a quivering voice.

"What's the trouble?" asked Alan testily. He was in no mood for the recital of petty larcenies.

"I saw this man on Deptford Broadway," said the detective, "and asked him what he had in his bag. He refused to open the bag, and tried to run away. I arrested him."

"That's a lie," interposed Sam. "Now speak the truth: don't perjure yourself in front of witnesses. I simply said: 'If you want the bag, take it.'"

"Shut up, Hackitt," said Wembury. "What is in the bag?"

"Here!" said Sam, hastily breaking in. "I want to tell you about that bag. To tell you the truth, I found it. It was layin' against a wall, an' I says to meself,' I wonder what that is?'—just like that."

"And what did the bag say?" asked the sceptical Carter.

The bag "said" many damning things. The first thing revealed was the cash-box. Sam had not had time to throw it away. The sergeant opened it, and took out a thick wad of notes and laid them on the desk.

"Old Meister's cash-box!" Sam's tone was one of horror and amazement. "Now how did that get there? There's a mystery for you, Wembury! That ought to be in your memories when you write them for the Sunday newspapers. 'Strange and mysterious discovery of a cash-box!'"

"There's nothing mysterious about it," said Wembury. "Anything else?"

One by one they produced certain silver articles which were very damning.

"It's a cop," said Sam philosophically. "You've spoilt the best honeymoon I'm ever likely to have—that's what you've done, Wembury. Who shopped me?"

"Name?" asked Carter conventionally.

"Samuel Cuthbert 'Ackitt—don't forget the haitch."

"Address?"

Sam wrinkled his nose.

"Buckingham Palace," he said sarcastically.

"No address. What was your last job?"

"Chambermaid! 'Ere, Mr. Wembury, do you know what Meister gave me for four days' work? Ten bob! That's sweating! I wouldn't go into that house—'aunted, I call it—"

The 'phone rang at that moment and Carter answered it. "Haunted?"

"I was in Meister's room, and I was just coming away with the stuff when I felt—a cold hand touch me! Cold! Clammy like a dead man's hand! I jumped for the winder and got out on the leads!"

Carter covered the telephone receiver with his palm.

"It's Atkins, sir—the man at Meister's house. He says he can't make him hear—Meister's gone up to his room but the door's locked."

Alan went to the 'phone quickly.

"It's Mr. Wembury speaking. Are you in the house?. . . You can't get in? Can't make him hear?. . . You can't get any answer at all? Is there a light in any of the windows?. . . You're quite sure he's in the house?"

Carter saw his face change.

164

"What's that? The Ringer's been seen in Deptford tonight! I'll come along right away."

He hung up the receiver.

"I don't know how much of that cold hand is cold feet, Hackitt, but you're coming along to Meister's house with me. Take him along!"

Protesting noisily, Mr. Hackitt was hurried into the street.

From his hip pocket Wembury slipped an automatic, clicked back the jacket and went swiftly to the door.

"Good luck, sir!" said Carter.

Alan thought he would need all the luck that came his way.

Chapter 45

The car was worse than useless—the fog was so thick that they were forced to feel their way by railing and wall. One good piece of luck they had—Alan overtook the doctor and commandeered his services. The route led through the worst part of Flanders Lane—a place where police went in couples.

Wembury's hand lamp showed a pale yellow blob that was almost useless.

"Is that you, doctor?" he asked and heard a grunt.

"What a fearful hole! Where am I?"

"In Flanders Lane," said Wembury. He had hardly spoken the words before a titter of laughter came from somewhere near at hand.

"Who is that?" asked Lomond.

"Don't move," warned Alan. "Part of the road is up. Can't you see the red light?"

He thought he saw a pinkish blur ahead.

"I've been seeing the red light all the evening," said Lomond. "Road up, eh?"

Some unseen person spoke hoarsely in the fog. "That's him that's going to get The Ringer!" They heard the soft chuckle of many voices.

"Who was that?" asked Lomond again.

"You are in Flanders Lane, I tell you," replied Alan. "Its other name is Little Hell!"

The doctor dropped his voice.

"I can see nobody."

"They are sitting on their doorsteps watching us," answered Alan in the same tone. "What a night for The Ringer!"

Near at hand and from some miserable house a cracked gramophone began to play. Loudly at first and then the volume of sound decreased as though a door were shut upon it.

Then from another direction a woman's voice shrieked: "Pipe the fly doctor! 'Im that's goin' to get The Ringer!"

"How the devil can they see?" asked Lomond in amazement.

Alan shivered. "They've got rats' eyes," he said. "Hark at the rustle of them—ugh! Hallo there!"

Somebody had touched him on the shoulder.

"They're having a joke with us. Is it like this all the way, I wonder?"

Ahead, a red light glowed and another. They saw a grimy man crouching over a brazier of coke: a watchman. For a second as he raised his hideous face, Lomond was startled.

"Ugh! Who are you?" he demanded.

"I'm the watchman. It's a horrible place, is Flanders Lane. They're always screaming—it'd freeze your blood to hear the things I hear." His tone was deep—sepulchral.

"She's been hangin' round here all night—the lady?" he said amazingly.

"What lady?" asked Wembury.

"I thought she was a ghost—you see ghosts here—and hear 'em."

Somebody screamed in one of the houses they could not see.

"Always shoutin' murder in Flanders Lane," said the old watchman gloomily. "They're like beasts down in them cellars. Some of 'em never comes out. They're born down there and they die down there."

At that minute Lomond felt a hand touch his arm.

"Where are you?" he asked.

"Don't go any farther—for God's sake!" she whispered, and he was staggered.

"Cora Ann!"

"Who is that?" asked Alan turning back.

"There's death there—death"—Cora's low voice was urgent—"I want to save you. Go back, go back!"

"Trying to scare me," said Lomond reproachfully. "Cora Ann!"

In another instant she was gone and at that moment the fog lifted and they could see the street lamp outside Meister's house.

Atkins was waiting under the cover of the glass awning, and had nothing more to report.

"I didn't want to break the door until you came in. There was no sound that I could hear except the piano. I went round the back of the house, there's a light burning in his room, but I could see that, of course, from under his door."

"No sound?"

"None—only the piano."

Alan hurried into the house, followed by the manacled Hackitt and his custodian, Atkins and the doctor bringing up the rear. He went up the stairs and knocked at the door heavily. There was no answer. Hammering on the panel with his fist, he shouted the lawyer's name, but still there was no reply.

"Where is the housekeeper?" he asked. "Mrs. K.?"

"In her room, sir. At least, she was there a few hours before. But she's deaf."

"Stone deaf, I should say," said Alan, and then: "Give me any kind of key—I can open it," said Hackitt.

They stood impatiently by whilst he fiddled with the lock. His boast was justified—in a few seconds the catch snapped back and the door opened.

Only one big standard lamp burnt in the room, and this threw an eerie light upon the yellow face of Meister. He was in evening dress and sat at the piano, his arms resting on the top, his yellow face set in a look of fear.

"Phew!" said Alan, and wiped his streaming forehead. "I've heard the expression 'dead to the world', but this is certainly the first time I've seen a man in that state."

He shook the dazed lawyer, but he might as well have shaken himself for all the effect it had upon the slumberer.

"Thank Gawd!" said a voice behind. It was Hackitt's trembling voice. "I never thought I'd be glad to see that old bird alive!"

Alan glanced up at the chandelier that hung from the ceiling. "Put on the lights," he said. "See if you can wake him, doctor."

"Have you tried burning his ears?" suggested the helpful Hackitt, and was sternly ordered to be quiet. "Can't a man express his emotions?" asked Mr. Hackitt wrathfully. "There's no law against that, is there? Didn't I tell you, Mr. Wembury? He's doped! I've seen him like that before—doped and dizzy!"

"Hackitt, where were you in this room when you felt the hand?" asked Alan. "Take the cuff off."

The handcuff was unlocked, and Hackitt moved to a place almost opposite the door. Between the door and the small settee was a supper table, which Wembury had seen the moment he came into the room. So, Mary had not come: that was an instant cause of relief. "I was here," said Hackitt. "The hand came from there."

167

He pointed to the mystery door, and Wembury saw that the bolts were shot, the door locked, and the key hung in its place on the wall. It was impossible that anybody could have come into the room from that entrance without Meister's assistance.

He next turned his attention to the window. The chintz curtains had been pulled across; Hackitt had noticed this immediately. He had left them half-drawn and window and grille open.

"Somebody's been here," he said emphatically. "I'm sure the old man hasn't moved. I left the bars unfastened."

The door leading to Mary's little office room was locked. So was the second door, which gave to the private staircase to Meister's own bedroom. He looked at the bolts again, and was certain they had not been touched that night. It was a dusty room; the carpet had not been beaten for months, and every footstep must stir up a little dust cloud. He wetted his finger, touched the knob of the bolt, and although he had handled it that afternoon, there were microscopic specks to tell him that the doorway had not been used.

Atkins was working at the sleeping Meister, shaking him gently, encouraged thereto by the uncomfortable snorts he provoked, but so far, his efforts were unsuccessful. Wembury, standing by the supper table, looked at it thoughtfully.

"Supper for two," he said, picked up a bottle of champagne and examined it. "Cordon Rouge, '11."

"He was expecting somebody," said Dr. Lomond wisely and, when Wembury nodded: "A lady!"

"Why a lady?" asked Wembury irritably. "Men drink wine."

The doctor stooped and picked up a small silver dish, piled high with candy.

"But they seldom eat chocolates," he said, and Wembury laughed irritably.

"You're becoming a detective in spite of yourself. Meister has— queer tastes."

There was a small square morocco case under the serviette that the doctor moved. He opened it. From the velvet bed within there came the glitter and sparkle of diamonds.

"Is he the kind of man who gives these things to his—queer friends?" he asked with a quiet smile.

"I don't know." Wembury's answer was brusque to rudeness.

"Look, governor!" whispered Hackitt.

Meister was moving, his head moved restlessly from side to side.

Presently he became aware that he was not alone.

"Hallo, people!" he said thickly. "Give me a drink."

He groped out for an invisible bottle.

"I think you've had enough drink and drugs for one night, Meister. Pull yourself together. I've something unpleasant to tell you."

Meister looked at him stupidly.

"What's the time?" he asked slowly.

"Half-past twelve."

The answer partially sobered the man.

"Half-past twelve!" He staggered rockily to his feet. "Is she here?" he asked, holding on to the table.

"Is who here?" demanded Wembury with cold deliberation.

Mr. Meister shook his aching head.

"She said she'd come," he muttered. "She promised faithfully. . .twelve o'clock. If she tries to fool me—"

"Who is the 'she', Meister?" asked Wembury, and the lawyer smiled foolishly.

"Nobody you know," he said.

"She was coming to keep you company, I suppose?"

"You've got it. . . .Give me a drink." The man was still dazed, hardly conscious of what was going on around him. Then, in his fuddled way, he saw Hackitt.

"You've come back, eh? Well, you can go again!"

"Hear what he says?" asked the eager Hackitt. "He's withdrawn the charge!"

"Have you lost your cash-box?" asked Wembury.

"Eh? Lost. . .?" He stumbled towards the drawer and pulled it open. "Gone!" he cried hoarsely. "You took it!" He pointed a trembling finger to Sam. "You dirty thief. . .!"

"Steady, now," said Wembury, and caught him as he swayed. "We've got Hackitt; you can charge him in the morning."

"Stole my cash-box!" He was maudlin in his anger and drunkenness. "Bit the hand that fed him!"

Mr. Hackitt's lips curled.

"I like your idea about feeding!" he said scornfully. "Cottage pie and rice puddin'!"

But Meister was not listening. "Give me a drink."

Wembury gripped him by the arm. "Do you realise what this means?" he asked. "The Ringer is in Deptford."

But he might have been talking to a man of wood.

"Good job," said Meister with drunken gravity, and tried to look at his watch. "Clear out: I've got a friend coming to me."

"Your friend has a very poor chance of getting in. All the doors of this room are fastened, except where Atkins is on duty, and they will remain fastened."

Meister muttered something, tripped and would have fallen if Wembury had not caught him by the arm and lowered him down into the chair.

"The Ringer! . . ." Meister sat with his head on his hands. "He'll have to be clever to get me. . .I can't think tonight, but tomorrow I'll tell you where you can put your hands on him, Wembury. My boy, you're a smart detective, aren't you?" He chuckled foolishly. "Let's have another drink."

He had hardly spoken the words when two of the three lights in the chandelier went out.

"Who did that?" asked Wembury, turning sharply. "Did anybody touch the board?"

"No, sir," said Atkins, standing at the door and pointing to the switch. "Only I could have touched it."

Hackitt was near the window, examining the curtains, when the light had diverted his attention.

"Come over this side of the room: you're too near that window," said Wembury.

"I was wondering who pulled the curtains, Mr. Wembury," said Hackitt in a troubled voice. "I'll swear it wasn't the old man. He was sleeping when I left him and you couldn't get any answer by telephone, could you?"

He took hold of the curtain and pulled it aside and stared out into a pale face pressed against the pane: a pale, bearded face, that vanished instantly in the darkness.

At Hackitt's scream of terror Alan ran to the window. "What was it?"

"I don't know," gasped Sam. "Something!"

"I saw something, too," said Atkins.

Danger was at hand. There was a creeping feeling in Alan Wembury's spine, a cold shiver that sent the muscles of his shoulders rippling involuntarily.

"Take that man," he said.

The words were hardly out of his lips when all the lights in the room went out.

170

"Don't move, anybody!" whispered Alan. "Stand fast! Did you touch the switch, Atkins?" .

"No, sir."

"Did any of you men touch the switch?"

There was a chorus of Noes.

The red light showed above the door.

Click!

Somebody had come into the room!

"Atkins, stand by Meister—feel along the table till you find him. Keep quiet, everybody."

Whoever it was, was in the room now. Alan heard the unquiet breathing, the rustle of a soft foot on the carpet, and waited. Suddenly there was a flicker of light. Only for a second it showed a white circle on the door of the safe, and was gone.

An electric hand lamp, and they were working at the safe. Still he did not move, though he was now in a position that would enable him to cut across the intruder's line of retreat.

He moved stealthily, both hands outstretched, his ears strained for the slightest sound. And then suddenly he gripped somebody, and nearly released his hold in his horror and amazement.

A woman! She was struggling frantically.

"Who are you?" he asked hoarsely.

"Let me go!" Only a whispered voice, strained, unrecognisable.

"I want you," he said, and then his knee struck something sharp and hard. It was the corner of the settee, and in the exquisite pain his hold was released. In another second, she had escaped. . .when he put out his hands, he grasped nothing.

And then he heard a voice—deep, booming, menacing.

"Meister, I have come for you. . . ."

There was the sound of a cough—a long, choking cough. . . .

"A light, somebody!"

As Wembury shouted, he heard the thud of a closing door.

"Strike a match. Haven't any of you men torches?"

And when the lights came on, they looked at one another in amazement. There was nobody in the room save those who had been there when the lights went out, and the door was locked, bolted, had not been touched; the key still hung on the wall.

Alan stared; and then his eyes, travelling along the wall, were arrested by a sight that froze his blood.

Pinned to the wall by his own swordstick drooped Maurice

Meister, and he was dead!

From somewhere outside the room came a laugh: a long, continuous, raucous laugh, as at a good joke, and the men listened and shivered, and even the face of Dr. Lomond changed colour.

Chapter 46

It was an hour after Meister's body had been removed and Dr. Lomond was making a few notes.

He was the reverse of nervous. And yet twice in the last half-hour he had heard a queer sound, that he could not but associate with human movements.

"I'm going to see Mr. Wembury," he said to the waiting constable. "I'll leave my bag here."

"Mr. Wembury said he was coming back, sir, if you care to wait," Harrap told him. "The sergeant's going to make a search of the house. There ought to be some queer things found here. Personally," he added, "I'd like to have the job of searching the pantry or the wine-cellar, or wherever he keeps the beer."

Again, Lomond heard a sound. He went to the door leading to Meister's room and, pulling it open, stared. Alan Wembury was coming down the stairs.

"There are three ways into the house. I've found two of them," he said.

Atkins, who had been searching some of the lower rooms, came in at that moment.

"Have you finished?" asked Wembury.

"Yes, sir. Meister was a fence all right."

Alan nodded slowly. "Yes, I know. Is your relief here?"

"Yes, sir."

"All right. You can go. Goodnight, Atkins."

Lomond was looking at Wembury narrowly. He waited until the man had gone before he drew up a chair to the supper table.

"Wembury, my boy, you're worried about something—is it about Miss Lenley?"

"Yes—I've been to see her."

"And, of course, it was she who came into the room at that awkward moment?"

Alan stared at him.

"Lomond, I'm going to take a risk and tell you something, and there is no reason why I shouldn't, because this business has altered all

The Ringer stuff. What happened tonight may mean ruin to me as a police officer. . . and still I don't care. Yes, it was Mary Lenley."

The doctor nodded gravely.

"So, I supposed," he said.

"She came to get a cheque that Meister told her young Lenley had forged—a pure invention on Meister's part."

"How did she get into the room?" asked Lomond.

"She wouldn't tell me that—she's heartbroken. We took her brother, and although I'm certain he will get off, she doesn't believe that."

"Poor kid! Still, my boy—happy ending and all that sort of thing," said Lomond with a yawn.

"Happy ending! You're an optimist, doctor."

"I am. I never lose hope," said Lomond complacently. "So, you've got young Lenley? That laugh we heard—ugh!"

Wembury shook his head.

"That wasn't Lenley! There is no mystery about the laugh—one of the Flanders Lane people going home—normally tight. The policeman on duty outside the house saw him and heard him."

"It sounded in the house," said Lomond with a shiver. "Well, The Ringer's work is done. There's no danger to anybody else, now."

"There's always danger enough—" began Wembury, and lifted his head, listening. The sound this time was more distinct.

"What was that? Sounded like somebody moving about the house," said Lomond. "I've heard it before."

Alan rose. "There is nobody in the house except the fellow outside. Officer!"

Harrap came in. "Yes, sir?"

"None of our people upstairs?"

"Not that I know of, sir."

Wembury went to the door, opened it and shouted: "Anybody there?" There was no answer. "Just wait here. I'll go and see."

He was gone quite a long time. When he returned his face was pale and drawn.

"All right, officer, you can go down," he said shortly, and when the man saluted and went out: "There was a window open upstairs—a cat must have got in."

Lomond's eyes did not leave his face.

"You look rather scared. What's the matter?" he demanded.

"I feel rather scared," admitted Wembury. "This place stinks of death."

But the answer did not satisfy the shrewd Lomond.

"Wembury—you saw something or somebody upstairs," he challenged.

"You're a thought-reader, aren't you?" Alan's voice was a little husky.

"In a way, yes," said the other slowly. "At this moment you are thinking of Central Inspector Bliss!"

Wembury started, but he was relieved of the necessity for replying. There was a tap at the door and the policeman entered.

"It has just been reported to me, sir, that a man has been seen getting over the wall," he said.

Wembury did not move.

"Oh!. . .How long ago?"

"About five minutes, sir."

"Was that the cat?" asked Lomond satirically, but Alan did not answer.

"You didn't see him?" he asked.

"No, sir; it happened when I was up here," said Harrap. "Excuse me, sir; my relief's overdue."

Wembury snapped round impatiently. "All right, all right. You can go!"

There was a long silence after the man had gone.

"What do you make of that?" asked Lomond.

"It may have been one of the reporters; they'd sit on a grave to get a story."

Again, came the sound of footsteps—stealthy footsteps moving in the room upstairs.

"That's not a cat, Wembury."

The nerves of Alan Wembury were at breaking point. "Damn the cat!" he said. "I don't know what it is, and I am not going up to see. Doctor, I am sick and tired of the case—heartily sick of it."

"So am I," nodded Lomond. "I am going home to bed." He got up with a groan. "Late hours will be the death of me."

"Have a drink before you go." Alan poured out a stiff whisky with a hand that shook.

Neither man saw the bearded face of Inspector Bliss at the window or heard the grille open noiselessly as the Scotland Yard man came noiselessly into the room.

"Do you know, doctor," said Alan, "I don't hate The Ringer as much as I should."

Lomond paused with his glass raised.

"There are really no bad men who are all bad—except Meister — just as there are no really good men who are all good."

"I want to tell you something, Lomond"—Alan spoke slowly—"I know The Ringer."

"You know him—really?"

"Yes; well." And then, with fierce intensity: "And I'm damned glad he killed Meister."

Bliss watched the scene from behind the curtain of the alcove, his eyes never leaving the two.

"Why? Did he get Mary Lenley?" Lomond was asking.

"No, thank God—but it was only by luck that she was saved. Lomond, I—I can tell you who is The Ringer."

Slipping from the shadow of the curtains. Bliss came towards Lomond, an automatic in his hand.

"You can tell me, eh—then who is The Ringer?"

A hand stretched out and snatched at his hat.

"You!" said the voice of Bliss. "I want you—Henry Arthur Milton!"

Lomond leapt to his feet.

"What the hell—?"

No longer was he the grey-haired doctor. A straight, handsome man of thirty-five stood in his place.

"Stand still!" Alan hardly recognised his own voice.

"Search him!" said Bliss, and Alan stripped off the 'doctor's' overcoat.

The Ringer chuckled.

"Bliss, eh? It doesn't fit you! You're the fellow who said I knifed you when you tried to arrest me three years ago."

"So, you did," said Bliss.

"That's a lie! I never carry a knife. You know that."

Bliss showed his teeth in an exultant grin.

"I know that I've got you. Ringer—that's all I know. Come from Port Said, did you—attended a sick man there? I thought your woman knew I suspected you when she was scared that day at Scotland Yard."

Henry Arthur Milton smiled contemptuously. "You flatter yourself, my dear fellow. That woman—who happens to be my wife—was scared not because she even saw you—but because she recognised me!"

"That Port Said story was good," said Bliss. "You saw a sick man there—Dr. Lomond, a dope who'd been lost to sight for years and sunk to native level. He died and you took his name and papers."

"I also nursed him—and I paid for his funeral," added Milton.

"You tried to make people suspicious of me—you've got a cheek! It was you who let Lenley out of the cell!"

The Ringer inclined his head.

"Guilty. Best thing I ever did."

"Clever!" approved Bliss. "I hand it to you! Got your job as police surgeon by smoodging a Cabinet Minister you met on the boat, didn't you?"

The Ringer shuddered.

"'Smoodging' is a vulgar word! 'Flattering' is a better. Yes, I was lucky to get the post—I was four years a medical student in my youth—Edinburgh—I present you with that information."

Bliss was beside himself with excitement.

"Well, I've got you! I charge you with the wilful murder of Maurice Meister."

Alan could bear the gloating no longer.

"I say. Bliss—" he began.

"I'm in charge of this case, Wembury," said Bliss sourly. "When I want your advice, I'll ask you for it—who's that?"

He heard the patter of footsteps on the stairs. In another minute Cora Ann had flown into her husband's arms.

"Arthur! Arthur!"

"All right, Mrs. Milton. That'll do, that'll do," cried Bliss.

"I told you—I told you—oh, Arthur!" she sobbed.

Bliss tried to pull her away.

"Come on."

"One minute," said The Ringer, and then, to the girl; "Cora Ann, you haven't forgotten?" She shook her head. "You promised me something: you remember?"

"Yes—Arthur," she said, instantly all the suspicions of Bliss were aroused and he dragged the woman away.

"What's the idea? You keep off and don't interfere."

She turned her white face to his.

"You want to take him and shut him away," she cried wildly—"like a wild animal behind bars; like a beast—like something that isn't human. That's what you want to do! You're going to bury him alive, blot out his life, and you think I'll let you do it! You think I'll stand right here and watch him slip into a living grave and not save him from it."

176

"You can't save him from the gallows!" was the harsh reply.

"I can't, can't I?" she almost screamed. "I'll show you that I can!" Too late Bliss saw the pistol, but before he could snatch it from her hand she had fired. The Ringer collapsed into a settee.

"You little brute—Wembury!" yelled Bliss.

Wembury went to his assistance and wrenched the revolver from her hand. As he did so, The Ringer rose swiftly from the place where he had been lying limp and apparently lifeless, and walked out of the door, locking it behind him.

"My God! He's gone!" roared Bliss, and threw open the chamber of the revolver. "Blank cartridge. After him!"

Wembury rushed to the door and pulled at it. It was locked!

Cora was laughing.

"Smash in the panel," cried Bliss. "The key's on the other side," And then, to the girl: "Laugh, will you—I'll give you something to laugh at!" With a crash the panel split, and in another few seconds Wembury was flying down the stairs.

"Clever—clever; aren't you clever, Mister Bliss!" Cora's voice was shrill and triumphant. "But The Ringer's got you where he wants you."

"You think so—" said Bliss, between his teeth, and shouted for the officer on duty in the hall below.

"There's a car waiting for him outside," taunted Cora, "and a new disguise which he kept in the little room downstairs. And an aeroplane ten miles out, and he's not afraid to go up in the fog."

"I've got you, my lady!" howled Bliss. "And where you are, he'll be. I know The Ringer! Officer!" he shouted.

A policeman came through the door.

"I'm Inspector Bliss from the Yard. Don't let her out of your sight, or I'll have the coat off your back."

He ran out, stopping only to lock the door. Cora flew after him, but he had taken the key, and she turned, to see the policeman opening the long panel by the door. Then in a flash off came helmet and cape, and she was locked in the arms of this strange man.

"This way, Cora," he said, and pointed to the panel. "*La Via Amorosa.*"

He kissed her and lifted her through the panel. Presently it closed upon them. No man saw The Ringer again that night or for the many nights which followed.

Again the Ringer

Contents

Chapter 1: The Man with the Red Beard

To the average reader the name of Miska Guild is associated with slight and possibly amusing eccentricities. For example, he once went down Regent Street at eleven o'clock at night at sixty miles an hour, crippled two unfortunate pedestrians, and smashed a lamp standard and his car. The charge that he was drunk failed, because indisputably he was sober when he was dragged out of the wreckage, himself unhurt.

Nevertheless, an unsympathetic magistrate convicted, despite the conflict of medical evidence. Miska Guild went to the Sessions with the best advocates that money could buy and had the conviction quashed.

The inner theatrical set knew him as a giver of freakish dinner parties; had an idea that he gave other parties even more freakish but less descriptive. Once he went to Paris, and the French police most obligingly hushed up a lurid incident as best they could.

They could not quite hush up the death of the pretty chorus-girl who was found on the pavement outside the hotel, having fallen from a fifth-floor window, but they were very helpful in explaining that she had mistaken the French windows for the door of her sitting-room. Nobody at the inquiry asked how she managed to climb the balcony.

The only person who evinced a passionate interest in the proceedings was one Henry Arthur Milton, a fugitive from justice, who was staying at the hotel—not as Henry Arthur Milton, certainly not as "The Ringer", by which title he was known; indeed, he bore no name by which the English police could identify him as the best-wanted man in Europe.

Mr. Guild paid heavily for all the trouble he had caused divers police officials and came back to London and to his magnificent flat in Carlton House Terrace quite unabashed, even though some of the theatrical celebrities with whom he was acquainted cut him dead whenever they met him; even though the most unpleasant rumours surrounded his Paris trip.

He was a man of thirty, reputedly a millionaire three times over. It is certain that he was very rich, and had the queerest ideas about what was and what was not the most amusing method of passing time. Had the Paris incident occurred in London neither his two nor his three millions would have availed him, nor all the advocacy of the greatest lawyers averted the most unpleasant consequences.

★★★★★★

One bright November morning, when the sun rose in a clear blue sky and the leafless trees of Green Park had a peculiar splendour of their own, the second footman brought his breakfast to his bedside, and on the tray, there was a registered letter. The postmark was Paris, the envelope was marked "Urgent and confidential; not to be opened by the secretary."

Miska Guild sat up in bed, pushed back his long, yellowish hair from his eyes, bleared for a moment at the envelope and tore it open with a groan. There was a single sheet of paper, closely typewritten. It bore no address and began without a conventional preamble:

On October 18 you went to Paris, accompanied by a small party. In that party was a girl called Ethel Seddings, who was quite unaware of your character. She committed suicide in order to escape from you. I am called The Ringer; my name is Henry Arthur Milton, and Scotland Yard will furnish you with particulars of my past. As you are a man of considerable property and may wish to have time to make arrangements as to its disposal, I will give you a little grace. At the end of a reasonable period I shall come to London and kill you.

That was all the letter contained. Miska read it through; looked at the back of the sheet for further inspiration; read it through again.

"Who the devil is The Ringer?" he asked.

The footman, who was an authority upon such matters, gave him a little inaccurate information. Miska examined the envelope without being enlightened any further, and then with a chuckle he was about to tear the letter into pieces but thought better of it.

"Send it up to Scotland Yard," he commanded his secretary later in the morning, and would have forgotten the unpleasant communication if he had not returned from lunch to find a rather sinister-looking man with a short black beard who introduced himself as Chief Inspector Bliss from Scotland Yard.

"About that letter? Oh, rot! You're not taking that seriously, are you?"

Bliss nodded slowly.

184

"So seriously that I'm putting on two of my best men to guard you for a month or two."

Miska looked at him incredulously.

"Do you really mean that? But surely . . . . my footman tells me he's a criminal; he wouldn't dare come to London?"

Inspector Bliss smiled grimly.

"He dared go into Scotland Yard when it suited him. This is the kind of case that would interest him."

He recounted a few of The Ringer's earlier cases, and Miska Guild became of a sudden a very agitated young man.

"Monstrous . . . . a murderer at large, and you can't catch him? I've never heard anything like it! Besides, that business in Paris—it was an accident. The poor, silly dear mistook the window for her sitting-room door——"

"I know all about that, Mr. Guild," said Bliss quietly. "I'd rather we didn't discuss that aspect of the matter. The only thing I can tell you is that, if I know The Ringer—and nobody has better reason for knowing him and his methods—he will try to keep his word. It's up to us to protect you. You're to employ no new servants without consulting me. I want a daily notification telling me where you're going and how you're spending your time. The Ringer is the only criminal in the world, so far as I know, who depends entirely upon his power of disguise. We haven't a photograph of him as himself at Scotland Yard, and I'm one of the few people who have seen him as himself."

Miska jibbed at the prospect of accounting for his movements in advance. He was, he said, a creature of impulse, and was never quite sure where he would be next. Besides which, he was going to Berlin——

"If you leave the country, I will not be responsible for your life." said Bliss shortly, and the young man turned pale.

★★★★★★

At first, he treated the matter as a joke, but as the weeks became a month the sight of the detective sitting by the side of his chauffeur, the unexpected appearance of a Scotland Yard man at his elbow wherever he moved, began to get on his nerves.

And then, one night, Bliss came to him with the devastating news.

"The Ringer is in England," he said.

Miska's face was ghastly.

"How—how do you know?" he stammered.

But Bliss was not prepared to explain the peculiar qualities of Wally the Nose, or the peculiar behaviour of the man with the red beard.

When Wally the Nose passed through certain streets in Notting Dale, he chose daylight for the adventure, and he preferred that a policeman should be in sight. Not that any of the less law-abiding folk of Notting Dale had any personal reason for desiring Wally the least harm, for, as he protested in his pathetic, lisping way, "he never did no harm" to anybody in Notting Dale.

He lived in a back room in Clewson Street, a tiny house rented by a deaf old woman who had had lodgers even more unsavoury than Wally, with his greasy, threadbare clothes, his big, protruding teeth, and his silly, moist face.

He came one night furtively to Inspector Stourbridge at the local police station, having been sent for.

"There's goin' to be a 'bust' at Lowes, the jewellers, in Islington, tomorrer, Mr. Stourbridge; some lads from Nottin' Dale are in it, and Elfus is fencin' the stuff. Is that what you wanted me about?"

He stood, turning his hat in his hands, his ragged coat almost touching the floor, his red eyelids blinking. Stourbridge had known many police informers, but none like Wally.

He hesitated, and then, with a "Wait here," he went into a room that led from the charge room and closed the door behind him.

Chief Inspector Bliss sat at a table, his head on his hand, turning over a thick dossier of documents that lay on the table before him.

"That man I spoke to you about is here, sir—the nose. He's the best we've ever had, and so long as he hasn't got to take any extraordinary risk—or doesn't know he's taking it—he'll be invaluable."

Bliss pulled at his little beard and scowled. "Does he know why you have brought him here now?" he asked.

Stourbridge grinned.

"No—I put him on to inquire about a jewel burglary—but we knew all about it beforehand."

"Bring him in."

Wally came shuffling into the private room, blinked from one to the other with an ingratiating grin.

"Yes, sir?" His voice was shrill and nervous.

"This is Mr. Bliss, of Scotland Yard," said Stourbridge, and Wally bobbed his head.

"Heard about you, sir," he said, in his high, piping voice. "You're the bloke that got The Ringer——"

"To be exact, I didn't," said Bliss gruffly, "but you may."

"Me, sir?" Wally's mouth was open wide, his protruding rabbit's teeth suggested to Stourbridge the favourite figure of a popular comic artist. "I don't touch no Ringer, sir, with kind regards to you. If there's any kind of work you want me to do, sir, I'll do it. It's a regular 'obby of mine—I ought to have been in the p'lice. Up in Manchester they'll tell you all about me. I'm the feller that found Spicy Brown when all the Manchester busies was lookin' for him."

"That's why Manchester got a bit too hot for you, eh, Wally?" said Stourbridge.

The man shifted uncomfortably.

"Yes, they was a bit hard on me—the lads, I mean. That's why I come back to London. But I can't help nosing, sir, and that's a fact."

"You can do a little nosing for me," interrupted Bliss. And thereafter a new and a more brilliant spy watched the movements of the man with the red beard.

★★★★★★

He had arrived in London by a ship which came from India but touched at Marseilles. He had on his passport the name of Tennett. He had travelled third-class. He was by profession an electrical engineer. Yet, despite his seeming poverty, he had taken a small and rather luxurious flat in Kensington.

It was his presence in Carlton House Terrace one evening that had first attracted the attention of Mr. Bliss. He came to see Guild, he said, on the matter of a project connected with Indian water power. The next day he was seen prospecting the house from the park side.

Ordinarily, it would have been a very simple matter to have pulled him in and investigated his credentials; but quite recently there had been what the Press had called a succession of police scandals. Two perfectly innocent men had been arrested in mistake for somebody else, and Scotland Yard was chary of taking any further risks.

Tennett was traced to his flat, and he was apparently a most elusive man, with a habit of taking taxicabs in crowded thoroughfares. What Scotland Yard might not do, officially, it could do, and did do, unofficially. Wally the Nose listened with apparent growing discomfort.

"If it's him, he's mustard," he said huskily. "I don't like messing about with no Ringers. Besides, *he* hasn't got a red beard."

"Oh, shut up!" snarled Bliss. "He could grow one, couldn't he? See what you can find out about him. If you happen to get into his flat and see any papers lying about, they might help you. I'm not suggesting you should do so, but if you did . . . . "

Wally nodded wisely.

In three days, he furnished a curious report to the detective who was detailed to meet him. The man with the red beard had paid a visit to Croydon aerodrome and had made inquiries about a single-seater taxi to carry him to the Continent. He had spent a lot of his time at an electrical supply company in the East End of London, and had made a number of mysterious purchases which he had carried home with him in a taxicab.

Bliss consulted his superior.

"Pull him in," he suggested. "You can get a warrant to search his flat."

"His flat's been searched. There's nothing there of the slightest importance," reported Bliss.

He called that night at Carlton House Terrace and found Mr. Miska Guild a very changed man. These three months had reduced him to a nervous wreck.

"No news?" he asked apprehensively when the detective came in. "Has that wretched little creature discovered anything? By gad! he's as clever as any of you fellows! I was talking with him last night. He was outside on the Terrace with one of your men. Now, Bliss, I'd better tell you the truth about this girl in Paris——"

"I'd rather you didn't," said Bliss, almost sternly.

He wanted to preserve, at any rate, a simulation of interest in Mr. Guild's fate.

★★★★★★

He had hardly left Carlton House Terrace when a taxicab drove in and Wally the Nose almost fell into the arms of the detective.

"Where's Bliss?" he squeaked. "That red-whiskered feller's disappeared . . . . left his house, and he's shaved on his beard, Mr. Connor. I didn't recognise him when he come out. When I made inquiries, I found he'd gorn for good."

"The chief's just gone," said Connor, worried.

He went into the vestibule and was taken up to the floor on which Mr. Guild had his suite. The butler led him to the dining-room, where there was a phone connection, and left Wally the Nose in the hall. He was standing there disconsolately when Mr. Guild came out.

"Hullo! What's the news?" he asked quickly.

Wally the Nose looked left and right.

"He's telephonin' to the boss," he whispered hoarsely, "But I ain't told him about the letter."

He followed Miska into the library and gave that young man a piece of news that Mr. Guild never repeated.

He was waiting in the hall below when Connor came down.

"It's all right—they arrested old red whiskers at Liverpool Street Station. We had a man watching him as well."

Wally the Nose was pardonably annoyed.

"What's the use of having me and then puttin' a busy on to trail him?" he demanded truculently. "That's what I call double-crossing."

"You hop off to Scotland Yard and see the chief," said Connor, and Wally, grumbling audibly, vanished in the darkness.

The once red-bearded man sat in Inspector Bliss's private room, and he was both indignant and frightened.

"I don't know that there's any law preventing me taking off my beard, is there?" he demanded. "I was just going off to Holland, where I'm seeing a man who's putting money into my power scheme."

Bliss interrupted with a gesture.

"When you came to England you were broke, Mr. Tennett, and yet immediately you reached London you took a very expensive flat, bought yourself a lot of new clothes, and seemingly have plenty of money to travel on the Continent. Will you explain that?"

The man hesitated.

"Well, I'll tell you the truth. When I got to London, I was broke, but I got into conversation with a fellow at the station who told me he was interested in engineering. I explained my power scheme to him, and he was interested. He was not the kind of man I should have thought would have had any money, yet he weighed in with two hundred pounds, and told me just what I had to do. It was his idea that I should take the flat. He told me where to go every day and what to do. I didn't want to part with the old beard, but he made me do that in the end, and then gave me three hundred pounds to go to Holland."

Bliss looked at him incredulously.

"Did he also suggest you should call at Carlton House Terrace and interview Mr. Guild?"

Tennett nodded.

"Yes, he did. I tell you, it made me feel that things weren't right. I wasn't quite sure of him, mind you, Mr. Bliss; he was such a miserable-looking devil—a fellow with rabbit's teeth and red eyelids ..."

★★★★★★

Bliss came to his feet with a bound, stared across at Stourbridge, who was in the room.

"Wally!" he said.

A taxicab took him to Carlton House Terrace. Connor told him briefly what had happened.

"Did Wally see Mr. Guild?"

"Not that I know," said Connor, shaking his head.

Bliss did not wait for the lift; he flew up the stairs, met the footman in the hall.

"Where's Mr. Guild?"

"In his room, sir."

"Have you seen him lately?"

The man shook his head.

"No, sir; I never go unless he rings for me. He hasn't rung for half an hour."

Bliss turned the handle of the door and walked in. Miska Guild was lying on the hearthrug in the attitude of a man asleep, and when he turned him over on his back and saw his face Bliss knew that the true story of the chorus-girl and her "suicide" would never be told.

Chapter 2: Case of the Home Secretary

There were two schools of thought at Scotland Yard. There were those who believed that The Ringer worked single-handed, and those who were convinced that he controlled an organisation and had the assistance of at least half a dozen people.

Inspector Bliss was of the first school, and instanced the killing of Miska Guild in proof.

"He's entirely on his own," he said. "Even his helper in that case was an innocent man who had no idea he was being used to attract the attention of the police."

"By the way, is there any news of him?" asked the assistant commissioner.

Bliss shook his head.

"He's in London; I was confident of that—now I know. If you had told me, sir, a few years ago, that any man could escape the police by disguise, I should have laughed. But this man's disguises are perfect. He *is* the character he pretends to be. Take Wally the Nose, with his rabbit's teeth and his red eyes. Who would have imagined that a set of fake teeth worn over his others and a little colouring to his eyelids, plus the want of a shave, would be sufficient to hide him from me? I am one of the few people who have seen him without make-up, and yet he fooled me."

"Why do you think he is in London?"

Chief Inspector Bliss took out his pocket-case and, opening this, searched the papers it contained for a letter.

"It came this morning."

Colonel Walford stared up at him.

"From The Ringer?"

Bliss nodded. "Typewritten on the same machine he used when he wrote to Miska Guild—the 's' is out of alignment and the tails of the 'p's' are worn."

Colonel Walford put on his glasses and read:

"Michael Benner, now under sentence of death, is innocent. I think you knew this when you gave evidence against him at the Old Bailey, for you brought out every point in his favour. Lee Lavinski killed the old man, but was disturbed by Benner before he could get the loot. Lee left for Canada two days after the murder. Be a good fellow and help save this man."

There was no signature.

"What's the idea?" The commissioner looked up over his glasses.

"The Ringer is right," said Bliss quietly. "Benner did not kill old Estholl—and I have discovered that Lavinski was in England when the murder was committed."

The crime of which he spoke was one of those commonplace crimes which excite little interest, since the guilt of the man accused seemed beyond doubt and the issue of the trial a foregone conclusion. Estholl was a rich man of seventy, who lived in a small Bloomsbury hotel. He was in the habit of carrying around large sums of money—a peculiar failing of all men who have risen from poverty to riches by their own efforts.

At four o'clock one wintry morning a guest at the hotel, who had been playing cards in his sitting-room with a party of friends, came out into the corridor, and saw Benner, who was the night porter, emerge from the old man's room, carrying in his hand a blood-stained hammer. The man's face was white, he seemed dazed, and when challenged was speechless.

Rushing into the room the guest saw old Estholl lying on the bed in a pool of blood, dead. The porter's story after his arrest was that he had heard the old man's bell ring and had gone up to his room and knocked. Having no answer, he opened the door and went in. He saw the hammer lying on the bed and picked it up mechanically, being so horrified that he did not know what he was doing.

★★★★★★

Benner was a young married man and in financial difficulties. He was desperately in need of money and had tried that evening to borrow seven pounds from the manageress of the hotel. Moreover, he had said to the head porter, "Look at old Estholl! If I had half of the money that he has in his pocket I shouldn't be worrying my head off tonight!"

Protesting his innocence, Benner went to the Old Bailey, and, after a trial which lasted less than a day, was condemned.

"The hammer was the property of the hotel, and Benner, had access to the workroom where it was usually kept," said Bliss; "but, as against that, the workroom, which is in the hotel basement, was the easiest to enter from the outside, and the window was, in fact, found open in the morning."

"Is there any hope for Benner?"

Bliss shook his head.

"No. The court has dismissed his appeal—and Strathpenner is not the kind of man who would have mercy; old Estholl was, unfortunately, a friend of his."

The commissioner looked at the letter again, and ran his fingers through his hair irritably. "Why should The Ringer bother his head about Benner?" he asked, and the ghost of a smile appeared on the bearded face of the detective.

"The trouble with The Ringer is that he can't mind his own business," he said. "That little note means that he is in the case—he doesn't drop letters around unless he's vitally interested; and if he's vitally interested in Benner, then we're going to see something rather dramatic. By the way, the Home Secretary has sent for me in connection with this affair."

"Is he likely to be influenced by you, Inspector?" asked Colonel Walford dryly.

"If I agree with him, yes; if I don't, no," said Bliss.

He went back to his room to learn that a visitor had called, and before his secretary told him her name, he guessed her identity.

She was a pretty girl, despite the haggard lines which told of sleepless nights. She was dressed much better than when he had seen her at the Old Bailey.

"Well, Mrs. Benner," he said kindly, "what can I do?"

Her lips quivered.

"I don't know, sir … I know Jim is innocent. He's incapable of doing such a horrible thing. I called at the Home Office, but the gentleman wouldn't see me."

Again, Bliss looked at her clothes: they were obviously new. As though she read his thoughts: "I'm not in a bad way, sir—for money, I mean. A gentleman sent me twenty five-pound notes last week, and that paid off all poor Jim's debts and left me enough to live on for a bit."

"Who sent the money?" asked Bliss quickly, but here she could not give him information. It had arrived by post and was unaccompanied by any card or name.

"It might have been a woman who sent it?" suggested Bliss, though he knew better. "There was no letter at all?"

She shook her head.

"Only a piece of paper. I've got it here."

She fumbled in her bag and produced a strip of paper torn off the edge of a newspaper, on which was typed :

DON'T LOSE HOPE.

★★★★★★

The "s" was out of alignment, the tail of the "p" was faint. Bliss smiled to himself, but it was a grim smile.

"You're under distinguished patronage," he said ironically, and then, in a more serious tone: "I'm afraid I can do very little for you. I am seeing one of the officials at the Home Office this morning, but I'm afraid, Mrs. Benner, you'll have to resign yourself to——"

He did not finish his sentence, as he saw her eyes close and her face grow a shade paler.

Bliss pulled out a chair and bade her sit down; and somehow the sight of this woman in her agony brought a pang to a heart not easily touched.

"No hope?" she whispered, and shook her head in anticipation of his answer.

"A very faint one, I'm afraid," said the detective.

"But you don't think he's guilty, Mr. Bliss? When I saw Jim in Pentonville, he told me that you didn't think so. It is horrible, horrible! He couldn't have done such an awful thing!"

Bliss was thinking rapidly. He had a dim idea of The Ringer's methods, and now he was searching here and there to find the avenue by which this ruthless man might approach the case.

"Have you any relations?"

She shook her head.

"No brothers?"

Again, she gave him the negative.

"Good! Now, Mrs. Benner, I'll do the best I can for you, and in return I want you to do something for me. If the man who sent you that money approaches you, or if anybody who is unknown to you calls on you or asks you to meet them, I want you to telephone me here."

He scribbled down the number on a slip of paper and passed it across to her. "If anybody comes to you purporting to be from Scotland Yard, or to have any position of authority whatever, I want you to telephone to me about that also. I'm going to do what I can for your husband, and, though I'm afraid it isn't much, it will be my best."

It was half-past two when he arrived at the Home Office, and, by some miracle, Mr. Strathpenner had arrived. He was the despair of his subordinates, a man without method or system. There were days when he would not come to the office at all; other and more frequent days when he would put in an appearance an hour before the staff left, with the result that they were kept working into the night.

The Right Honourable William Strathpenner, His Majesty's principal Secretary of State, was a singularly unpopular man, both in and outside his party. He was pompous, unimaginative, a little uncouth of speech, intolerable. He had worn his way into the Cabinet as other men had done before him; not by genius of oratory or by political character, but the sheer weight of him had rubbed a place through which he had fallen, first to a minor office under the Crown, and then, by a succession of lucky accidents, to the highest of the subordinate Cabinet positions.

A thin man, short-necked, broad-shouldered, he had the expression of one who was constantly smelling something unpleasant. Political cartoonists had helped to make his face familiar, for his was an easy subject for caricature. The heavy, black, bristling eyebrows, the thick-lens spectacles, the bald head with the black wisps brushed across, his reddish nose—a libel on him, since he was a lifelong abstainer—made him unpleasant to look upon. He was almost as unpleasant to hear, for he had a harsh, grating voice and punctuated his sentences with an irritating little cough.

He kept Bliss waiting twenty minutes before he was admitted to the august presence; and there seemed no reason for the delay, for Mr. Strathpenner was reading a newspaper when he came in. He looked at the slip which announced the name of his visitor.

"Bliss, Bliss? Of course. Yes, yes, you're a police officer—ahem! This Benner case .... yes, I remember now; I asked you to see me—ahem!" He blinked across the table at Bliss, and his face had more than ever that unpleasant-smell expression.

"Now what do you know about this, hey? I haven't seen the Judge, but there's no doubt in my mind that this blackguard should suffer the extreme penalty of the law. This report, of course, is bunkum." He tapped the newspaper with his finger. "The usual bunkum—ahem! I don't believe in confessions—you don't believe in confessions?"

"Confessions, sir?" The inspector gazed at him in astonishment.

"Haven't you seen it?" Strathpenner threw the paper across the table. "There it is. Use your eyes .... third column ...."

★★★★★★

It was not in the third, but the fifth column, and the item of news was headed:

Hotel Murder Confession. Remarkable Statement by Red-handed Murderer.
Ottawa.

A man named Lavinski, who shot two policemen in cold blood in the streets of Montreal last night, when detected in the act of breaking into the Canadian Bank, and was shot by a third policeman, has made a remarkable statement before a magistrate who was called to his bedside at the hospital.

Lavinski is not expected to recover from his wounds, and in the course of his statement he said that he was responsible for the murder of Mr. Estholl, for which a man named Benner lies under sentence of death in London. Lavinski says that he made an entrance to the hotel knowing that Mr. Estholl carried large sums of money in his pocket, that he took a hammer intending to use the claw to open the door in case it was locked.

Estholl woke up as he entered the room, and Lavinski says that he struck him with the hammer, though he was not aware that he had inflicted a fatal injury. He then discovered that the dead man had a hanging bell-push in his hand, and fearing that he had rung it, he made his escape without attempting to search his pockets. The statement has been attested before a magistrate."

Bliss looked up and met the Home Secretary's gaze.

"Well? Bunkum, eh? You've had no official notification at Scotland Yard?"

"No, sir."

"I thought not; I thought not—ahem! An old trick, eh, Inspector? You've had that sort of thing played on you before. It won't save Benner, I assure you—ahem! I assure you!"

Bliss gaped at him. "But you're not going to hang this man until you get this statement over from Canada?"

"Don't be absurd, Inspector, don't be absurd! If a Secretary of State were to be influenced by newspaper reports where would he be, eh? Did you read the last paragraph?"

Bliss took up the paper again and saw, later:

"The man Lavinski died before he could sign the statement he had made before Mr. Prideaux."

"Let me tell you, sir"—Mr. Strathpenner wagged an admonitory finger—"His Majesty's Secretary of State is not to be influenced by wild-cat stories of this kind . . . . by newspaper reports, by—ahem —hearsay evidence as it were! What are we to do? I ask you! On the unsigned deposition of a—er—convicted murderer caught in the act. Release this man Benner?"

"You could grant him a respite, sir," interrupted Bliss.

Mr. Strathpenner sat back in his chair and his tone became icy.

"I am not asking your advice, inspector, ... If I lose my pocket-book or my watch I have no doubt your advice will be invaluable— ahem —to secure its recovery. Thank you, inspector."

He waved Bliss from the room. The detective went across to Scotland Yard, but Walford had gone. The only thing he knew was that the death warrant had not been signed. It is part of the Home Secretary's duty to affix his name to a document that will send a fellow-creature from this life, and one of the bravest men who ever sat in a Cabinet refused the second offer of the office for this reason.

Mr. Strathpenner, at any rate, was not in any way distressed by his duty. He had summoned the Judge who had tried the case to meet him the next day, and he went back to his house in Crowborough that night without a single qualm or misgiving.

★★★★★★

He was a widower; lived alone—except for a large staff of servants, which included a French *chef*, and he dined, a solitary figure in the big mahogany-panelled dining-room, a large German philosophical work propped up before him for he was an excellent linguist and had a weakness for shallow philosophies if they were propounded with sufficient pretentiousness.

He was so reading at the end of his meal when the visitor was announced. Mr. Strathpenner looked at the card suspiciously. It read:

Mr. James Hagger, 14, High Street, Crouchstead.

Now, Crouchstead was the West of England constituency which had the honour of being represented in Parliament by the Home Secretary, and, since he held his seat by the narrowest of majorities, he resisted the temptation to send the message which rose too readily to his lips.

"All right, show him in here."

He looked at the card again. Who was Mr. Hagger? Probably somebody very important in Crouchstead; somebody he had shaken hands with, probably. An important member of the Crouchstead Freedom Club, likely enough. Sir. Strathpenner loathed Crouchstead and all its social manifestations; yet he screwed a smile into his face when Mr. Hagger was ushered to his presence.

The visitor proved to be a very respectably dressed man, with a heavy black moustache which drooped beneath chin level.

"You remember me, sir?" His voice was deep and solemn. "I met you at the Freedom banquet. I'm the secretary of the Young Workers' League."

Oh, it was the Young Workers' League, was it, thought Mr. Strathpenner. He had almost forgotten its existence.

"Of course . . . . naturally . . . . sit down, Mr. Hagger. Will you have a glass of port?"

Mr. Hagger deposited his hat carefully on the floor.

"No, sir, thank you, I'm a lifelong abstainer. I neither touch, taste, nor handle. Of course, I realise that a gentleman like you has to have likker in the 'ouse. It's about this man Benner . . . . ."

The minister stiffened.

"We've been 'aving a talk, some of the leaders of the party in Crouchstead, and we've come to the conclusion it'd be a great mistake to hang that man——"

Mr. Strathpenner shook his head sadly. "Ah Mr. Hangar, you've no idea how deeply I have considered this subject, and with what reluctance I have been compelled, or shall be compelled, to allow the law to take its course. You realise that a man in my position . . . ."

He continued his justification in terms which he had applied before to stray members of Parliament who had strolled into his room in the House of Commons, and had expressed views similar to those

197

which Mr. Hagger was on the point of enunciating.

"Now, let us leave this—er—unpleasant subject. Will you take some coffee with me? By the way, how did you come?"

"I was brought up from the station in a fly," said Mr. Hagger. He was very apologetic.

"You quite understand, Mr. Strathpenner, that I had to do my duty. The committee paid my fare up, and I thought it'd be a good chance of seeing you. I've heard about your wonderful house, and I didn't want to miss the chance of seeing it."

Here he touched the Home Secretary on his soft side. The house had an historic as well as an artistic value; it was one of the innumerable John o' Gaunt hunting lodges that stud the county of Sussex. It was indubitably pre-Elizabethan. Mr. Strathpenner was prouder of his home than of any of his attainments. He led the visitor from room to room and was almost genial in his response the visitor's interest.

". . . . Haunted, of course—all these old places are haunted. There's a dungeon . . . . the previous owner used it as a coal-cellar! A Philistine, sir—a boor—ahem—or something objectionable. Come this way."

He opened a stout oak door and preceded his visitor down a flight of stone stairs; showed him not only the dungeon, which had been carefully restored to its earlier grimness, but a lower prison chamber, six feet by six, approached through a stone trapdoor.

"Let me show you . . . ."

He went before the other down the ladder.

"We have ringbolts here, almost worn through with age, where the unfortunate prisoners were chained. And yet the place is fairly well ventilated."

"It's a funny thing," said Mr. Hagger, as he carefully descended the ladder, "that the flyman who brought me up from the station told me to be sure to ask you to show me your dungeon."

"Extraordinary," said Mr. Strathpenner, not ill-pleased. "But the place has quite a local reputation."

★★★★★★

His Majesty's judges are not to be kept waiting. Sir Charles Jean, the senior Common Law Judge, looked at his watch and closed the case with a vicious snap.

"The Home Secretary said that he would be here at half-past four."

"I'm very sorry, sir," said the official who was with him. "I've been on the phone to Mr. Strathpenner. He left the house an hour ago and should be here at any moment. It's rather foggy, and he's a very nervous traveller."

"Where is his secretary, Mr. Cliney?"

"He has gone down to Crowborough with some documents for signature—he had only gone ten minutes when Mr. Strathpenner 'phoned through."

"I'm afraid I can wait no longer. I will see him in the morning. I hope you'll impress upon Mr. Strathpenner that there is, in my mind, a very grave doubt about Benner's guilt."

He might have added that he did not think that would have very much influence with the Minister, who had on a previous occasion ignored the recommendation of a judge.

He had hardly gone before the official heard the rasping voice and nervous cough of his chief, and hurried into the secretary's office.

"Sir Charles Jean, eh? And gone? Ahem! Well, well, well! I can't be at the beck and call of judges, my dear man. Or Ringer's either, my friend, eh?—ahem! Or Ringer's either!"

"Ringer's, sir?" said the astonished official.

There was a dry, rasping chuckle.

"Visited me last night, the scoundrel—ahem! That will be something to tell Mr. What's-his-name—Bliss. By the way, call him up and tell him that when I return from Paris on Friday, I should like to see him."

"Paris, sir?" asked the startled official. "There's a meeting of the Cabinet on Friday morning."

"I know, I know," testily.

He opened a portfolio, took out a sheet of paper and stared at it owlishly. The official saw the document and thought it a moment to pass along the message.

"Sir Charles asked me to tell you that he is very doubtful as to whether this man should be executed——"

But the other was scrawling his name.

"There will be a respite of fourteen days," he said. "The matter may come up for consideration next Wednesday after the arrival of the depositions from Canada."

He blotted the sheet and pushed it across to the under-secretary.

"The respite may be announced in the newspapers," he said.

★★★★★★

"I ought to have known," said Bliss ruefully, "that Strathpenner was the easiest man in the world to impersonate. The curious thing is, it did strike me when I was talking to him."

"How is he?" asked Walford.

"When they released him from his lower dungeon," said Bliss, with the ghost of a smile in his eyes, "he was slightly insane, but not, I think, quite so insane as Mr. Hagger of Crouchstead, who is no longer a life-long abstainer. Mr. Strathpenner used the lower dungeon as a wine cellar, and they had to live on something. They might be living there still if The Ringer hadn't been obliging enough to send me a wire."

Chapter 3: The Murderer of Many Names

1

Mr. Ellroyd arrived in England six months after the Meister murder, when the police of the world were searching for one Henry Arthur Milton, "otherwise" (as the police bills stated in eighteen languages) "known as 'The Ringer.'"

They translated "The Ringer" variously and sometimes oddly, but, whether he saw it in Czecho-Slovakian or in the Arabic of Egypt, the reader knew that this Henry Arthur Milton was a man who could change his appearance with the greatest rapidity.

Perhaps not quite so readily as Mr. Ellroyd could and did change his name.

In Australia, which was his home, he was Li Baran; in Chicago he was Bud Fraser, Al Crewson, Jo Lemarque, Hop Stringer, and plain Jock. Under these pseudonyms he was wanted for murder in the first degree, for he was a notorious gunman and bank robber.

In New York he bore none of these names, but several others. Canada knew him as a bigamist who had married under three different names, one of which was the Hon. John Templar-Statherby.

He came to England from Malta (of all places in the world), and he came handicapped with a Ringer complex. Now the vanity of the criminal is a matter which has formed the subject of many monographs, and Joseph Ellroyd, in spite of his poise, his middle age, and his undoubted philosophy, was vain to a degree.

He wanted the publicity of The Ringer, and in his first unlawful act (which was the daylight hold-up of the Streatham Bank) he publicly identified himself with The Ringer.

If you think it extraordinary in a man whose one desire in life should have been to preserve a modest anonymity and pursue his own peculiar graft, attracting as little attention to himself as possible, you make no allowance for his complex, or, as Superintendent Bliss said, for his desire to put the police on the wrong track. Bliss was wrong.

Joe's chief urge was vanity.

He derived immense satisfaction from the sensation which resulted. "Again The Ringer!" said a flaming headline. The phrase tickled Mr. Ellroyd. His second *coup* was a little less spectacular—the smashing of an hotel safe. But what it lacked in news value as a piece of craftsmanship (though the haul subsequently proved to be a large one) was compensated by the three words scrawled across the safe door: "Again The Ringer!"

A month later Mr. Joe Ellroyd went to his bedroom to change for dinner. He was staying at the Piccadilly Plaza Hotel, for he was a gentlemanly man and a classy dresser. He entered the room switching on the light and closing the door.

When he turned, he looked first into the muzzle of a large Browning pistol and then into the completely masked face of the man who held it.

"Ellroyd your name is, isn't it?"

Joe blinked at the gun, and his hand dropped carelessly to his pocket.

"Keep 'em up!" said the stranger. "This gun doesn't make much noise, and I could catch you before you fell. My name is Henry Arthur Milton—I am wanted by the police for killing a gentleman who deserved to die."

"My God—'The Ringer'!" gasped Joe.

"The Ringer—exactly. You are using my name to cover certain vulgar robberies—you are wanted for other and worse offences in various parts of the world. I object to my name being used by a cheap skate of a gunman. I have a greater objection to its use by a thief. I have taken a lot of trouble to find you, and my original intention was to hand you over to the mortuary keeper. I am giving you a chance."

"Listen, Milton——" began Joe.

"I am warning you. I shall not warn you again. If you are a wise man you will not need a second warning. That is all. Step over here—and step quickly!"

Joe obeyed. The man moved to the door, and the lights went out.

"Don't move—you're against the window and I can see you."

A second later the door opened and closed. There was the sound of a snapping lock.

Joe, breathing heavily, went cautiously forward, turned on the lights and tried the door. It was, as he suspected, locked. But there was a telephone . . . .

Before he picked up the instrument, he saw the cut of trailing wires.

"The Ringer!" he breathed, and sat down heavily on his bed, wiping the cold perspiration from his face. It was remarkable that there was perspiration to wipe, for Joe was the coolest man that ever shot a policeman.

For two years after Joe lived without offence, as he could well afford to do, for he was a comparatively rich man.

And then one day in Berlin . . . .

★★★★★★

"*Auf wiedersehen!*"

The perfect stranger, with the elaborate friendliness which is too often the attribute of his kind, flourished his hat extravagantly.

"So long!" said Henry Arthur Milton, coldly indifferent.

Why this sudden activity? he wondered. He passed out on to the Friedrichstrasse and nobody would imagine that he was in the slightest degree concerned with the big fat man he had left at the entrance to the *bahnhof*. His fingers said "snap!" to a watchful taxi-driver.

"*Kutscher!* Do you see that gentleman in the black coat with the fur collar?"

"Most certainly: the Jew!"

Arthur Milton nodded approvingly and opened and closed the door of the taxi once or twice in an absent-minded manner.

"Is that insight or eyesight?" he asked.

"I know him," said the *Kutscher* complacently. "He is from Frankfort and his name is Sahl—a dealer in sausages."

Mr. Milton inclined his head.

"A local industry," he said lightly. "Now, my friend, drive me to the Hôtel Zweinerman und Spiez."

It was a very comfortable taxi: Berlin is famous for the luxury of these public vehicles, but it *was* a taxi. There was nothing remarkable about it except that its driver had ignored the summons of half a dozen of the passengers who had arrived by the Hamburg express, and had instantly responded to the signal of Henry Arthur Milton. But there was no spring lock on the door—he had tried that before he got in. And the driver was following the conventional route.

Mr. Milton stroked his dark toothbrush moustache. His colouring gave him a somewhat saturnine appearance. His black glossy hair, his heavy black eyebrows, a marked lugubriousness of expression, corrected the attractions of good features and rather nice eyes.

Before the barrack *façade* of the hotel the cab stopped. Milton gripped his suitcase and alighted.

"Wait for me, I shall be five minutes."

The hotel porter stood at the open door of the cab, his face set in the hospitable smile for which he was engaged. He sought to secure the suitcase, but was frustrated.

"Is Mr. Pffiefer in the hotel?"

The porter would see—immediately. Arthur Milton followed him into the hotel; but when the porter, having inquired, discovered that Mr. Pffiefer's name did not appear in the guest list, and turned to inform the elegant Englishman, he had vanished. There was an elevator opening from the vestibule, and into this Arthur Milton had stepped.

Truthfully speaking, quite a number of so-called coincidences are interpretable into inevitable effects of quite logical causes. The Hôtel Zweinerman, for example: one gravitated there naturally. Englishmen were swept into the Zweinerman as by some mystic force.

As to the second floor—Mr. Milton chose the second floor because thereon were large and often unoccupied suites. He knew the hotel this way and that way, as the saying goes, and he knew that the largest, the most expensive suite usually reserved for plutocrats in a hurry was that which was to the right front of the elevator. So that, if there had been any English plutocrat rushing through the capital in mad haste, No. 9 would be his suite.

He tried the door of No. 9, opened it boldly, as a man might who had made a genuine mistake. It was a large bedroom, floridly decorated, furnished heavily. The room was empty; obviously it had not been occupied for some days—obviously, at any rate, to Henry Arthur Milton, who had the gift of observation.

There was a small calendar on the mantelpiece, an oxidised silver frame with a day in large letters. The day was "*Mittwoch*," 7th, which was Wednesday—it was now Friday, the 9th, but the chambermaid had not turned the little knob which would bring the calendar up to date.

Between the bed and the bathroom door was a writing-table—an unusual position, for the writer would sit in his or her own light. And on the table was a pale pink blotting-pad, which Milton would not have favoured with a second glance—only the writing was in English.

He reconnoitred the bathroom before he made any other inspection of the pad. From the bathroom a second door gave access to a sitting-room. Escape was a simple matter.

Detaching the top sheet of blotting-paper, he carried it to the bathroom and bolted the door. There was no mistaking the "B" or the firm, masculine "M"—they were not in German or Latin handwriting.

Milton read slowly.

"Suffering snakes!" he breathed.

It was the name of the man to whom the letter was addressed which excited his profanity. The significance of the florid preamble did not come home to him until he read, later, the London telegram in the *Deutsche Allgemeine Zeitung*.

"Bless my soul!" said Mr. Milton, and, going into the bathroom, locked the door. A hot, wet towel wiped his eyebrows from existence (they had taken him an hour to fix before he left Hamburg); the toothbrush moustache yielded instantly to the same treatment. Opening his suitcase, he took out a light fawn coat and a shapeless hat . . . .

★★★★★★

There went down the lift a man with a somewhat vacuous expression. He wore large rimless glasses and a vivid necktie. His face was hairless, his head so closely cropped that it might have been shaved. In the vestibule he saw the big sausage-maker from Frankfort interviewing the manager. With him was another detective.

Milton shuffled up to the reception clerk, grief in his voice and tone.

"I have brought for the gentleman of No. 9 an account. But he is gone."

"Account!"

A reception clerk dealing with nobodies is altogether a different person from a reception clerk dealing with somebodies.

"You should have brought it when the gentleman was here," he grumbled. Nevertheless, he turned the pages of a book. "Mr. Smith, 249, Doughty Street." he said in English.

"Do not give addresses!"

His companion was obviously in authority. The book closed with a bang.

"Write!" he barked.

Mr. Milton shuffled forth humbly.

The cab-driver who had brought him to the Zweinerman stood guard in the doorway.

"I want a cab—" began the hairless man, peering short-sightedly through his glasses.

"Engaged!"

The new Mr. Milton passed into the street. Near the Tiergarten he bought the Government newspaper, and then he understood what all the bother was about:

THE RINGER IN BERLIN!
The So-Infamous English Criminal Traced, to Germany . . . .

("Good Lord!" said Henry Arthur Milton, and read on):

Henry Arthur Milton, an English criminal, is believed to be in hiding in Berlin. Following an atrocious robbery and murder near London, the miscreant escaped to Germany, and has had the audacity to address a letter to Chief-Central Superintendent of Police Bliss . . . .

("They never get our titles right," he murmured):

. . . . deriding the police efforts to capture him. That letter was posted in Berlin! The Ringer, as he is called, is a master of the art of disguise and owes his name (Ringer of Changes) to that fact. The crime for which he is now sought by the Berlin police is . . . .

(The Ringer read on and on, a set grin on his face):

. . . . Hitherto The Ringer has killed, but has never robbed. Man, after man he has slain for some wrong done either to himself or to humanity. But robbery has never before been his object . . . .

"Dear me!" said Henry Arthur Milton, still smiling mirthlessly. "That is certainly amusing! Joe has forgotten something!"

He left Berlin by the night train on a passport which described him as Eric Ressermans, a native of Munchen. He went on board the English boat as Joseph Sampson, of Leeds. But that was not the name that he wrote in the guest book at the Craven Street Hotel.

He spent the whole of the next day examining the files of a newspaper for particulars of the interesting crime with which his name had been associated.

2

It was half-past two o'clock on a wet, cold morning when the mail van from London came out of the Great West Road and turned towards Colnbrook and Slough. A motor scout on duty at the juncture of the roads saw from his shelter the red-painted motor-van pass. It skidded as it turned (he afterwards stated), and he thought he heard the driver laugh.

The mail van was late, but once out of the West Road, speeding would be impossible until Slough was passed. The road winds and turns abruptly and is rather narrow. Moreover, ahead of the driver was the narrower street of Colnbrook.

The van had travelled to within a mile of that village when the driver saw a red lamp in the road and jammed on his brakes. Ahead of him, in the light of his headlamps, he saw a man in shining oilskins, who was pointing to the side of the road.

He stopped the car, and, as he did so, the solitary wayfarer came out of the glare of the lamps into the patch of darkness level with the driver's seat.

"What is the matter?" It was the guard inside the van.

"Get down!"

The driver saw the automatic in the stranger's hand—saw it was pointed at him, and gripped the lever . . . .

It was the sound of the shot which brought the guard leaping to the road, revolver in hand. He was alive when the police found him two hours later. The van had been driven into a field near the end of the Colnbrook by-pass. He told his fragment of tale, but was dead before the magistrate arrived to take his statement.

There were two clues, so attenuated that Superintendent Bliss rejected the one and was baffled by the other.

A motorcycle with sidecar had passed through Colnbrook at five minutes after three. It had been driven by a man in a brown leather coat who was talking to somebody in the sidecar—evidently a woman—for he addressed her as "my dear girl." To the police officer who saw him he shouted "Goodnight." Ten minutes later he should have been in Slough, but was not seen in that town. There was, however, an explanation for this: he might have turned off on to the Windsor Road.

The second piece of evidence was on the mail van itself. Scrawled in chalk along the side were the words: "Again The Ringer!"

Mr. Bliss read this and his bearded lips curled derisively. He might sneer at this piece of bravado, but the country had for the moment lost its sense of humour. Newspaper columns protested at the "immunity of this arch-assassin." None the less, Mr. Bliss maintained his opinion.

******

Colonel Walford, Assistant Commissioner of Police, leaned back in his padded chair, a wandering quill toothpick between his teeth, and listened.

"If it is The Ringer, then he has changed his method," said Superintendent Bliss. "You know, sir, that he has never killed except to fulfil some crazy vendetta of his—he's a man of means .... why, you've told me the same thing a score of times!"

Colonel Walford shifted uneasily in his chair.

"Well .... yes. But you can't get over the fact that the words 'Again the Ringer' were written in chalk on the mail van, that they were found scribbled on the safe door of the Rugeley Hotel—and you remember that Streatham robbery .... Still ...."

He was of two minds: Mr. Bliss had one.

"'Again The Ringer'!" he scoffed. "As if Milton would descend to that kind of tomfoolery! He has killed people—but there has been a reason behind it. He is a self-appointed executioner of nasty men."

The colonel shook his grey head.

"I don't know—this letter from Berlin in which he confesses he was the murderer .... giving details which only he could know ...."

He shook his head again.

But Bliss was not convinced.

"One always gets these sham confessions—there was enough published the morning after the murder to supply a mischievous busybody with all the information he required. The problem to me is: how did the murderer know that there was a registered package containing 160,000 American dollars in the van? I only found that out yesterday."

"Dollars? Why on earth?"

"The package was from the London Textile Bank to a Mr. Elliott, of Long Hall, near Slough. It was insured with underwriters, so that only the insurance people will be the losers."

"But why dollars?"

Bliss could supply an explanation. Mr. Elliott, a wealthy and a self-made man, dabbled in the fine arts. There was in the country at that moment the newly-discovered Maltby Velasquez. It was the property of a French dealer, who had stipulated, in view of the erratic behaviour of his native currency and an ingrained suspicion of sterling, that payment should be made in dollars.

"The picture has been bought to all intents and purposes, and was to have been delivered yesterday. I am seeing Mr. Elliott tonight."

"And if you see The Ringer——" began Walford.

"The Ringer? Huh!"

As he walked down the corridor a messenger handed him a telegram. Bliss read and nodded. On the whole, he was not sorry to get the intimation this telegram contained.

Mr. Forsythe Elliott, being a public-spirited man, might well have complained that none of the theories so ingeniously advanced by him in letter, even by telegram, had been accepted. Or, if the police had acted upon them, certainly there had been no acknowledgment of the inspiration.

He had seen Bliss for a few minutes.

"He treated the matter quite casually," he reported to his saturnine young secretary. "You might imagine that a double murder and robbery was an everyday occurrence! I have no wish to be hard on the police, but I do think . . . ."

What Mr. Elliott did think he related at length.

And then, to his annoyance, coming back from a brisk country walk, his servant informed him that Mr. Bliss had not only arrived, but had been in the house for the greater part of an hour. Later he saw the bearded figure strolling aimlessly across the lawn, and wagged his finger in playful admonition, though in truth Mr. Elliott was very annoyed indeed.

"You said six," he said reproachfully. "Well, have you a clue? You look tremendously mysterious."

"I cannot afford to be mysterious," said the man from London quietly. "I have just been having a chat with your secretary."

"An extremely able young man," said Elliott.

"Young?" The bearded man shook his head. "He's not so young as he appears. Would you call him reliable?"

The eyebrows of Mr. Forsythe Elliott rose in amazement.

"Reliable? Well, I have had him for the greater part of six months."

"Then he must be reliable."

There was a touch of irony in the tone.

Mr. Elliott was all for dropping such unimportant matters as his secretary; was, indeed, ready to repeat and amplify the theories that he had already propounded.

"Obviously it is The Ringer," he said. "I have made a very careful study of this man. In fact, I have read every scrap of information I can beg, borrow, or buy."

"My view is," continued the undaunted master of Long Hall, "that he escaped from this country after the last affair, went to Germany—you, of course, know all about the letter, because it was addressed to you, according to the newspapers—and, being hard up—these fellows are invariably gamblers—he has returned and is living somewhere in this neighbourhood."

But his hearer gave him no encouragement. Not that Mr. Elliott required such a stimulus.

"My secretary says—and Leslie is something of a motorcyclist—that this wretched assassin probably never uses the roads at all, but takes to the field paths."

"You surprise me," said his audience politely.

★★★★★★

In the few minutes he had alone with his secretary later Mr. Elliott expressed his utter lack of faith in the official police. The young man did not answer. Mr. Elliott thought he looked a little nervous. He had never known him so jumpy before. That night at dinner:

"You know The Ringer?"

"Very well indeed."

"He interests me tremendously" (Mr. Elliott was almost enthusiastic). "Although I cannot afford to lose so large a sum—as a matter of fact, I don't lose it at all, but if I did the fact that The Ringer was responsible gives the crime a certain cachet. Now, my theory ..."

It was difficult even to contend against theories, for surely there was no atmosphere better calculated to put a man in good humour, even with the crankiest of cranks, than the raftered dining-room of Long Hall.

The cloth had been removed, the super-polished surface of the dark table reflected the long-stemmed port glasses. Mr. Elliott reached out and helped himself to another cigarette from the silver box and lit it with the glowing end of the first.

He was tall and broad-shouldered; good-looking in his rugged way. The untidy hair was streaked with grey; he looked all that he confessed himself to be—a man of the people who had come to fortune by his own industry. In every sense he was a contrast to the young man who sat on his left, gloomily absorbed in his own dark thoughts.

Leslie Carter's voice said "public school." His face was moulded more finely than his employer's, his hands were more shapely, his movements had something of an athletic grace. The sombre man sitting opposite, twisting the end of his little beard to a point, noticed that from time to time Mr. Elliott shot a puzzled glance at his secretary. And Leslie Carter's attitude throughout the meal had been a little puzzling. He had scarcely spoken a word, hardly raised his eyes from the plate, though his *vis-à-vis* had been the second prettiest girl Mr. Bliss had ever seen.

Sullen—sulking about something—worried? The visitor was not sure.

".... the third crime of the character committed during the past three months," Forsythe Elliott was saying; "and all occurring within a radius of twenty—say thirty—miles. That can only mean that our friend The Ringer has his headquarters in Berkshire."

"It was not The Ringer."

The other man shook his head emphatically, was about to say something else, but stopped himself. Instead, he looked swiftly from his host to the secretary, and Mr. Elliott understood. Presently: "You might tell them to have the car ready for Mr. Bliss."

The young man looked up with a start.

"All right," he said, and rose.

When he had gone the visitor drew his chair nearer to where Elliott sat.

"What is his financial position?" asked Bliss.

Elliott shrugged his broad shoulders.

"He's always broke—that kind of kid always is."

"Have you asked him whether he told anybody about the money coming to you?"

His host shook his head. "No; I have had no opportunity. He had to go to Germany—his brother, who is in Hamburg, sent for him."

"He went to Germany—when?"

Elliott considered. "The day after the robbery. In any event, I should have let him go, but it happened that I went off to Paris to fix up about the picture. I should, in the ordinary course of events, have taken the money with me."

His guest tugged at his little beard.

"In Berlin, eh? The murder was committed on Monday night—he could have reached Berlin by Wednesday—the date the letter was posted—he could have been back here on Thursday. When did your secretary return?"

Mr. Elliott was obviously uncomfortable.

"Yesterday—Friday. But, good heavens! You don't suggest ....?"

"I'm not suggesting anything," said the other. "I am merely following the avenues of possibility. The fact is that I have already spoken to your secretary .... do you mind if I talk to you outside? I have a strong objection to talking in a room."

Elliott went to the door.

"I hate wasting good wine, but I suppose you don't mind."

Elliott turned to see him looking admiringly at the ruby glass.

"Here's destruction to The Spurious Ringer!"

The host came back to the table and poured wine into his half-empty glass.

"That, Mr. Bliss, is a toast I can drink. At the same time, I'm not so sure that you're right."

He carried his argument into the night and past the waiting car. At the far end of the lawn were three high firs, and it was not until they reached these that Elliott stopped. He might not have stopped even then, but he stumbled over a coiled rope that lay on the grass.

"What the devil——" he checked himself and asked: "Now, what do you want to say about Leslie?"

"His brother was not ill—the telephone message which you passed on to him was a hoax. And a blundering hoax. Did you notice how worried he was at dinner?"

"I did notice," admitted Elliott, and the other laughed.

"He's worried because he found a small cottage on your estate that is supposedly empty, but which contains the motorcycle and side-car that the robber and murderer has been using. He put these two facts together—the fake phone message from London which took him to Germany in order that he might be incriminated, and the discovery of the cycle. Probably he has found out something else. I hadn't time to ask him."

"He told you this?"

"Yes, Joe, he told me this."

Joe Ellroyd (Forsythe Elliott was almost the toniest *alias* he had ever used) turned to fly, but a hand gripped his arm, and he felt curiously weak.

"You're doped, Joe—that last toast was my mercy! You went to Berlin and wrote a letter to Bliss. I found the blot of it—that was a coincidence. But I should have found you anyway. I think I warned you once before . . . ."

★★★★★★

In the house a telephone bell rang, and the secretary answered it.

"Mr. Bliss? But Mr. Bliss is here, in the grounds with Elliot . . . .!"

Bliss, at the other end of the wire, spoke quickly.

"I had a wire telling me not to come tonight. 'Phone the local police and have them up as quickly as you can . . . . got a gun? Take it, arm the servants and search the grounds."

He himself arrived an hour later, but neither Elliott nor his visitor was found. It was not until the dawn came and showed the still figure swinging on a branch of the highest fir that Elliott's absence was explained.

When they got him down, they found a half-sheet of paper and a ten-pound note pinned to the dead man's sleeve.

Please give the banknote to the public hangman and offer him my apologies for this invasion of his province.

There was no signature—but Inspector Bliss knew the writing.

Chapter 4: A Servant of Women

Once upon a time, in those absurd days of war, when the laws governing the sanctity of human life were temporarily suspended, a flying officer, making a reconnaissance to the north-west of Baghdad, saw the solitary figure of a man lying in the desert land. By his side was a dead camel.

The flying officer, whose name was Henry Arthur Milton, dipped down to take a closer view, and as he did so he saw the man's hand raised feebly as though signalling for help.

Captain Milton shut off his engines, having found a likely landing-place, and five minutes later was examining the wounded man, a person of some importance, to judge by the trappings of his camel and his own raiment.

He was wounded in the shoulder, half delirious with thirst, and proved to be one Ibn el Masjik. He had been wounded in a skirmish with British troops, and after the rescuer had made him comfortable El Masjik had a request to make.

"I am the chief of a fighting clan and I could not survive the disgrace of being taken prisoner. Therefore, I ask you as a favour that you take me to the city of my father, and I will give you my parole that I will not fight against your people, nor shall any of my tribe fight."

Milton spoke Arabic as though it were his mother-tongue. He was also a man of unconventional habits, and although he had no more authority to carry out the wishes of his prisoner than he had to take upon himself the command of the British Army in Mesopotamia, he did not hesitate.

His aeroplane made a journey of a hundred and seventy miles, landed within half a mile of the walled city of Khor, and at some risk to himself (for the local inhabitants were unaware of his errand of mercy) delivered the wounded man to the care of his friends.

"Come to me when this war is ended," said Ibn el Masjik; "and, though all the world be against you, I shall be for you. If you are poor, I will make you rich. My father's city is for your asking."

This time he spoke in English, for he had in his youth been educated at a preparatory school in Bournemouth, his father being a rich man with a leaning to Western ideals.

Henry Arthur Milton remembered this promise some years later, when he was hard pressed, and for six months was the guest of Ibn el Masjik, whose father was now dead. Mr. Milton saw the administration of an Eastern city and a Near Eastern people who snapped their scornful fingers at authority which was too far away to be effective.

This white-walled city stood on the edge of the wilderness, and time had passed it by. Raiding parties went out unashamed and returned laden with booty and slaves. Milton saw men and women sold in the market-place, saw life unchanged from what it had been in the days when Mahomet's uncle was guardian of the Kaaba, and the Prophet's disciples were praying in Medina.

One night, Henry Arthur expostulated about certain practices, and the thin, ascetic face of Ibn el Masjik lit up in a smile. He tossed a half-smoked cigarette into a silver vase, lit another, and settled himself more comfortably on the cushions.

★★★★★★

They were in the dining-room of his palace—a tall, bare apartment, with lime-washed walls and vivid, silken colourings—and a Circassian girl sat at his feet and ate sweetmeats noisily.

"My friend," he said, "it is a far cry to Bournemouth, Hampshire. Slavery is merely a name for service, and it is a matter of form whether it takes the shape you see here in Khor or in some dingy northern town where men and women have to leave their beds at the sound of a whistle and hurry through rain and sleet to the prison-houses you call factories. My slaves are more pleasantly treated: they have the sunshine; they are well fed: they sleep in their own houses."

He was perfectly frank about the traffic. There was a little port on the Red Sea where one could buy, under the very noses of a British administration, this kind of artisan—at a price.

"Not always can I buy what I desire," he explained. "My women ask me all the time for such a man, and where may he be found?" He sighed heavily. "Yes, the West is creeping upon us, and Kemal's new law concerning women has reached even here."

He shrugged his shoulders, smoothed his white silken robe more decorously about his knees, and smiled reminiscently.

"I do not object. There is a piquancy in the new custom which is very amusing. And we differ from most other tribes in that our women are never veiled, and have rights of choice."

After Milton came back to Western Europe, he frequently corresponded with his blood brother, and at the back of his mind he always had Khor as a final sanctuary in case things went wrong.

The police might suspect that Henry Arthur Milton, whom they called The Ringer, had many homes, but they did not know where. There was, for example, a villa on the outskirts of Cannes, very convenient for a man who wished to make a rapid exit from one country to another. He rented a small flat overlooking the little *Sok* in Tangier; he had certainly a house which was a semi-detached residence in Norbury, and here he spent a greater part of his time than any of his enemies imagined.

There was a small garden at the back of the house which he cultivated, and across the dividing wall it often happened that he discussed with his neighbour such mundane matters as the depredations of cats.

He had few opportunities, for Captain Oring, that grey-bearded man who had dreamed for forty years of a shore life was captain of a small tramp vessel which traded between London and Suez. He was not only captain but part proprietor, he and his sons holding three-quarters of the shares in this little vessel.

One of the "boys" was his chief officer, another his chief engineer, a third attended to the business end in London. He had, also, a daughter, a floridly-pretty girl, who kept the home for her brother and did an immense amount of housework in such time as she could spare from the pictures.

On an occasion when The Ringer was absent from London the girl disappeared. Her father was at sea, and it was from him, months later, that The Ringer heard the story.

Captain Orin did not tell him coherently—it was not the sort of story that a father could tell straightforwardly—and Henry Arthur Milton listened to the broken narrative with a cold-bloodedness which was his chief characteristic.

"My boy found her after a lot of trouble … she's with my sister now, in the country. Naturally, I've tried to find the people, but what chance had I got in London? I can't go to the police . . . . I don't want her name in the papers, do I? If I ever meet this man . . . ."

"You won't," said The Ringer. "But perhaps I shall—I travel about a lot."

(In the neighbourhood he was registered as Mr. Ernest Oppenton, and his profession was described as "commercial traveller.")

Captain Oring went away to sea, with his sons and his grief and his patched-up little steamer; and Henry Arthur Milton had certain urgent business which took him to Berlin—so urgent that you might imagine that the matter of Lucy Oring had entirely slipped from his mind.

But nothing ever escaped him, and on his return to London he became a great frequenter of that type of West End club which appears on and is struck from the register so very rapidly that you might not know it had ever existed.

He overheard a little; waiters told him something. It is extraordinary how confidential an Italian waiter will become to a man who speaks his language. Women told him most of all, for he paid for drinks with great munificence.

On a certain afternoon a scene was enacted at one of the great London termini which was so commonplace that only very keen observation would have noted it as being out of the ordinary.

The nice-looking old lady, with the white hair and the cameo brooch, saw the train come slowly along the platform of Victoria Station, and moved nearer to the barrier.

Presently, the passengers began to trickle past the ticket-collector, not in the hurried way of suburban season-ticket holders, but with the leisure which is peculiar to travellers from a distance. She watched carefully, and after a while she saw the pretty girl with the black suitcase. She was dressed in dark brown and carried in her other hand a bunch of autumnal flowers.

The nice old lady intercepted her.

"My dear, are you Miss Clayford? I thought so! I am Mrs. Graddle. I thought I would come along and see you safely across London."

The girl nodded gratefully.

"I was wondering what I should do. Are you from the agency?"

The nice old lady smiled.

"Oh, dear no! But a friend of mine at the agency keeps me informed about the engagements. I like to do what I can for young people. Now, you must come along and have tea with me. I understand it is a perfectly awful place you are going to! Forty pounds a year for a nursery governess is scandalous! And in a little country village where there is nothing to see and nothing to do . . . .!"

215

She rattled on as she accompanied the girl through the booking-hall to the station yard, and Elsie Clayford listened dismally. Forty pounds a year was a small sum, but she understood that her new employers were very nice people, and that the home was comfortable. It was her first engagement.

"I'd like you to stay a few days with me," said Mrs. Graddle, as she signalled a cab. "I've got a lovely little house in St. John's Wood, and we have young society. I have already telephoned to Lady Shene, and she agrees. You might do a theatre or two . . . ."

Elsie had not the vaguest idea who Mrs. Graddle was. She guessed that the old lady was a member of one of those organisations which undertake the care of young girls. It was a matter for satisfaction that such societies existed.

For instance, as she had met her white-haired guardian, she had noticed a lank-looking man with long black hair and large horn-rimmed spectacles; and this sinister-looking individual had looked at her so oddly that she felt a queer little thrill of fear. And now he was standing at her elbow as the cab drew up at the kerb.

"Get in, my dear," said Mrs. Graddle, as Elsie pushed in her suitcase. The girl obeyed, and the old lady was following when the man with the spectacles caught her arm, and, drawing her gently aside, shut the cab door.

"King's Cross," he said to the driver, and, still holding Mrs. Graddle's arm, he pushed his head through the open window space. "Your train leaves at 5.32. Lady Shene will probably meet you at Welwyn Station. Have you money for the cab fare?"

"Ye-es," said the panic-stricken Elsie.

"Good. Don't talk to people unless you know them; especially angelic old birds like this one."

He waved the cab on.

"What's the idea?" demanded Mrs. Graddle, breathlessly.

The man had already called another cab.

"Get in," he said; and she obeyed tremblingly. The man followed.

"I've told him to drive through the park. I'll drop you at the end of Birdcage Walk."

"I've a good mind to give you in charge!" There was a whimper in the old woman's voice. "Who do you think you are?" He did not answer this question.

"You've been convicted twice—once in Leeds and Manchester,"

216

he said; "and for a number of offences. You get acquainted with some-body in a registry office who keeps you supplied with information regarding the movement of servants. I understand that you're not above touting and using the cinemas to discover stage-struck girls."

"You can't prove anything," she interrupted. "And even if you arrest me—but you're not going to do a thing like that."

She opened her bag with trembling fingers, groped in the interior and took out a wad of bank-notes.

"Be a good man and don't make any trouble," she pleaded.

The Ringer took the notes from her hand, counted them deliberately.

"Sixty-five pounds doesn't seem a very adequate bribe," he remarked.

She opened an inner purse, and sorted out two notes, each for a hundred pounds.

"That's all I've got." Old Mrs. Graddle was inclined to be hysterical. "You 'busies' can't keep your noses out of anything!"

The Ringer tapped at the window and the cab stopped. It was now raining heavily, and there were few pedestrians about.

"Have you any children?" he asked.

"No," she said quickly.

"Apart from the beastliness of your job, do you ever realise what it feels like to be a father or a mother, to be waiting and hoping for somebody to come back . . . . to be uncertain about their fate?"

"I don't want any argument with you," she said, with surprising savagery for so picturesque an old lady. "You've got your money, and that's all you care about! I've got no children!"

"I think you're right," he said, cryptically; and opened the door for her.

"Let him drive on to the Tube station," she demanded; but he shook his head.

"You can get out and walk. You'll be wet through, probably, and die—and if you do, I shan't stop laughing!"

She said something which no angelic old lady should have said. The Ringer smiled. As she moved quickly towards Parliament Square, he paid the cabman.

"Turn round and go back," he said, slipped on a mackintosh which he carried over his arm, took off his glasses, and wiped away his small moustache before the cabman had turned the nose of his machine in the other direction. He was taking no risks—the more so since he was well aware for what destination Mrs. Graddle was bound.

In the circumstances she went to a lot of unnecessary trouble in taking an Underground train to South Kensington and doubling back by taxi. Eventually she reached her pleasant home in St. John's Wood in a condition of semi-exhaustion.

It was a very nice house, with a beautiful dancing floor; this was necessary, for Mrs. Graddle gave select parties. The peculiar servants she employed were decorating the ballroom when she arrived, but she was not interested in the coming festivities of the evening.

★★★★★★

She went upstairs to the small study, where her son was eating greasy toast and reading the evening newspaper.

"Hullo! Did you get her?" he asked pleasantly.

He was a lethargic man of thirty, heavy-featured, heavy-eyed, and decidedly plump. On one finger he wore a diamond ring of great value; stones sparkled from his ornate cravat. He listened while she told her breathless story, stroking his small moustache.

"That's pretty bad," he said. "Who was he? Do you know him? A 'busy'? It's awkward—damned awkward! They know about the Leeds and the Manchester affair too; that's rotten!"

He had reason for his perturbation. Only by the skin of his teeth had he succeeded in keeping clear of the Manchester charge, and it would have been much more serious for him than for his mother.

"What are you scared about—I paid the feller, didn't I?" She rang the bell viciously, and when the servant came: "We shan't want the room for that girl; she's not coming," she snapped, and when the servant had closed the door: "For God's sake don't sit there shaking like a jelly, Julian! There's nothing to be afraid of!"

But Julian thought there were many things to be afraid of, and enumerated a few.

"I've been dreading this," he quavered, "ever since that Oring girl was found. Let's go down into the country, mother—what about Margate? We could stay there for a month or two till this affair blew over——"

"It has blown over," she interrupted, and went upstairs to change from her street clothes, which were most uncomfortably damp.

Julian Graddle never felt less like following his legitimate profession. He had to go into the West End to attend to two clients for he was a ladies' hairdresser—an extremely useful trade to his mother: for women gossip to one another. They talk of servants who are leaving

218

them, of girls who have got into scrapes. Some of his mother's best "finds" had been located by Julian in the course of his working day.

He was certainly not at his best after a series of sharp admonitions from his best client—a lady whose temper was by no means equable at the best of times, and he came to his second call more rattled than ever. The next day he had to attend at the shop which employed him, and he lived on tenterhooks, growing bolder, however, as the day progressed without a sign of a policeman.

In the evening, as he was leaving, the clerk at the desk handed him a slip of paper.

"Miss Smith, 34, Grine Mews, telephoned for you specially."

He frowned at the paper, but the time was convenient. "Six-thirty," said the note. "Miss Smith, very urgent. Pay on completion of work."

He was not at all surprised to be called to a mews. So many fashionable people had converted garages into artistic flats, and in the course of a normal week he made acquaintance with at least three.

The occupant of 34, Grine Mews, was obviously terminating her occupation. There was a board displayed, informing the world that "this handsome and commodious flat" was to let. He knocked at the narrow door, which was immediately opened.

"Come in," said a man's voice pleasantly. "Are you the hairdresser? Miss Smith has been waiting for you."

★★★★★★

Julian stumped wheezily up the steep stairs. They were uncarpeted, and so was the landing. There was also the queer smell which attaches to houses that have been long unfurnished. Possibly Miss Smith was only just moving in, and was the victim of that enticing notice.

His conductor opened a door.

"This way. It is rather dark, but I'll get a light."

Julian entered unsuspectingly. The door slammed behind him—then there was a click, and a bare lamp hanging from the ceiling glowed dimly. The room was empty of furniture; the floor and mantelpiece were covered with dust. Over the little window a heavy horse-rug had been fastened with forks.

"Don't move," said the stranger.

His face was covered with a half-mask: a habit of The Ringer's when he was not wearing disguise.

"If you raise a bleat, I shall shoot you through the stomach, and you will die in great agony," he said, calmly; and Julian's face went green at the sight of the pistol in the man's hand.

219

"What—what——?" he began.

"Don't ask questions. Go through that doorway."

Like a man in a dream, the prisoner obeyed. The inner room had a rickety table and a dark-coloured sofa, evidently left by a former tenant. On the table was a glass of red wine, and to this The Ringer pointed.

"Drink," he said, curtly.

The man turned an agonised face to him.

"Is it poisoned?" he whimpered.

"No, but I will tell you very frankly it is drugged. I'm not going to kill you—I promise you."

Julian gulped down the draught.

"Who are you?" he asked hollowly.

"People call me The Ringer," said Henry Arthur Milton.

It was the last word Julian Graddle remembered.

★★★★★★

That night The Ringer had a long consultation with Captain Oring.

"He is the man all right, so we need not distress your daughter by bringing her up to identify him. Where is your ship lying?"

"She's lying at Keeney's Wharf, Rotherhithe," said Captain Oring, pondering the problem before him. "If I thought this was the man——"

"He is the man; but you're to do nothing drastic. He is to be kept alive and in good health. You will arrive at El Sass on the 23rd as I reckon the time—a day or two more or less doesn't matter, because you will be expected. You will arrange to hand him over at night to a crew of Arabs who will come out in a boat for him. Here is the money for his passage—two hundred and sixty-five pounds. His mother is paying the fare."

His two sons were with Captain Oring, and one of them spoke.

"If this is the man, Mr. Oppenton, we don't want any payment. I'd like to take the swine and beat his head off, but if you say no—well, your word goes."

What really was to happen to the man was explained before, in the middle of the night, they went down to the little garage at the end of the garden, where Mr. Julian Graddle was sleeping soundly, and bundled him into an old car. He was taken to Keeney's Wharf when the night watchman was dozing, and laid in a bumpy berth in a very uncomfortable little cabin …

To Ibn el Masjik The Ringer wrote a letter, and sent it overland by a series of aeroplane posts. It began:

From his friend Arthur, to Ibn el Masjik, the servant of God, on whom be peace!

I have thought much over the trouble which you confided to me, and of Certain Ones in your house who desire to follow the Western custom, making their hair short like men. Also, that you can find none in your city who may do this service for you.

Now, El Masjik, I am sending to you a man very skilful in such things: a slave who has no protection of the law, and you shall keep him in your house all the days of his life, and I ask only that he be a servant to women, such an one as they may beat with their slippers.

On the fourteenth day of the month of the Pilgrimage a little steamer shall come to the port of El Sass and you shall send . . .

He gave the most minute instructions for the disposal of Mr. Julian Graddle—instructions that he knew would be obeyed to the letter.

A fortnight later he saw an advertisement in the agony columns of three daily newspapers:

Will Julian Graddle, who disappeared from London, please communicate with his anxious and sorrowing mother?

And when he read this The Ringer laughed. He had read such appeals before, addressed by parents who sought daughters. And where those daughters had gone, and why they did not answer, the angelic Mrs. Graddle knew best.

Chapter 5: The Trimming of Paul Lumière

"It is not for me, sir, ever to say anything which suggests criticism," said Chief Inspector Mander with great diffidence: "the only thing I say is that possibly The Ringer has become too specialised a problem with you. You are, as it were, living too near to the subject."

Superintendent Bliss chewed on a quill toothpick thoughtfully. He disliked Mander extremely—but he was not singular in that.

Mander had very nice manners, spoke the King's English with a certain refinement of tone, looked well in evening dress, had fine company manners, and was suspected of employing his superiority in these respects to secure the rapid promotion which had come to him.

You searched his records without finding any great accomplishment. He had figured in a few unimportant cases, and had had charge of a murder—but the murderer had given himself up to justice, and had made a full confession to the local divisional inspector before Mander came on the scene; so, there was no merit in that.

But he had, however, a wonderful knack of appearing clever to the right people. Bliss was not the right person. He never thought Mander was clever: invariably he referred to Inspector Mander in terms that were neither complimentary to the inspector nor commendable in himself.

Bliss was going to the south of France, partly on business, partly on holiday. He had not the slightest doubt in his mind what Mander was after; he had a malignant pleasure in the thought that, if there was one man at Scotland Yard to whom he would like to hand over The Ringer case it was Mr. Mander, he of the aristocratic nose and the fair moustache.

"All right—take control while I am away. I'll arrange for my clerk to turn over anything that comes. It isn't going to be an easy job for you."

"So, you have found," said Mander, with a smile.

"So, *you* will find, Inspector," replied Bliss emphatically.

He had not left London before he saw in the columns of a daily newspaper that:

"Chief Inspector Mander had assumed control of The Ringer case during the absence of Superintendent Bliss."

Mander was strong on publicity.

On the following day a letter arrived at Scotland Yard. It was addressed to Superintendent Bliss, and those who were in the habit of handling his correspondence had no doubt as to who was the writer.

"The Ringer? Rubbish! Why does he write? Does he write to Bliss?"

The man took the letter with a contemptuous smile and tore open the envelope. The letter was written on just that coloured paper which The Ringer invariably used.

Mr. Paul Lumière is a man for whom I have no affection. He began life as a common thief; he is a sweater of labour, a trickster; and he once treated a friend of mine very badly—not so badly that he deserves the shades, but badly enough to deserve robbing.

I purpose taking from him the sum of £30,000—or its equivalent. This will be the price offered to Randwell and Coles, the Bond Street jewellers, for a diamond and emerald chain. After the chain has been acquired by its purchaser it will be acquired by me.

"Who is Paul Lumière?" demanded Mander. His immediate subordinate went forth to make enquiries. There was, he discovered, no Paul Lumière in any of the available directories.

"Sheer braggadocio!" said Mander, who had a line of classy words. "I suppose this is the sort of thing that impresses Bliss."

"Whenever The Ringer sends that kind of letter he follows it up with a *coup*," warned the sergeant.

Mr. Mander made derisive noises.

He was working in his office that night when the sergeant, who had gone off duty hours before, walked into his room.

"I've found Paul Lumière," he said; and, producing an evening newspaper from his pocket, he pointed to a paragraph which he had marked:

"Mr. Paul Lumière, the American millionaire, who arrived from New York last week, is buying Old Masters for his private gallery, and yesterday bought a lovely example of the early Flemish school for a thousand guineas from Messrs. Theimer, of Grafton Street."

Mander was instantly alert.

"Get on to the principal hotels, and find out where he is staying."

It was not difficult to locate Mr. Lumière. He had a suite in London's most crowded hotel. When Mander put through a call he found that the millionaire, who went early to bed, had retired to his room, and was not to be disturbed. Nor, when Mander made a personal call, did he have any greater success.

★★★★★★

He decided to call the next morning, but before he made his visit, he dropped in at the Bond Street jeweller's whose name had been mentioned in the letter.

The head of the firm was in the south of France, and he saw the managing director.

"Mr. Paul Lumière? Oh, yes. We have had some negotiations with him. He is buying some jewellery from us—the Alexandria necklace, to be exact." And then, suspiciously: "Is there anything wrong about him?"

"Oh, nothing, nothing!" said Mander, impatiently. Like all men of his peculiar mentality, he resented being asked questions. "He is all right—a millionaire or something. I am merely looking after his interests, I don't mind telling you—I shall probably have to tell you later, in any case—that an attempt is being made to rob him; and I want you, when the time comes, to afford me all the assistance you possibly can."

The managing director was naturally curious, but Inspector Mander was not in the mood to satisfy that curiosity.

He called in at Scotland Yard to look through his letters before going on to the Revoy Hotel, and found that Mr. Paul Lumière had made matters very easy.

There was a note from him, enclosing a letter of introduction. It bore the printed letter-head of Police Headquarters in New York City.

Dear Sir,

May I personally commend to your care Mr, Paid Lumière, of this city? Mr. Lumière, who is going to Europe, has for some months past been the recipient of threatening letters from The Ringer.

There may be nothing to this, but I happen to know that Mr. Lumière has, for some reason or other, incurred the animosity of this man. Will you he good enough to give Mr. Lumière any assistance he may require?

Sincerely,

E. B. Sullivan.

The covering note was a formal invitation asking Bliss to call, and a few minutes after reading these epistles Inspector Mander was shown into the millionaire's suite.

Mr. Lumière was a tall, not ill-looking man, with a short, grey moustache and a mop of iron-grey hair. He had a nervous little trick of screwing up his mouth every few seconds, but apparently this was no evidence of any apprehension so far as The Ringer was concerned.

"Sit right down, Captain—I'm glad to know you. Say, who is this bird, The Ringer? Milton, eh? Never met him, but I'm not scared—no, sir . . . ." He talked rapidly, continuously. Mander, who was not averse from hearing himself talk, waited impatiently for the opportunity.

He received the impression that The Ringer and the cause of his vendetta was not unknown to Mr. Lumière. Once or twice the millionaire referred vaguely to "this girl Fleitcher," but who "this girl Fleitcher" was he did not explain.

"The only thing I know," said Mander, "is that he has threatened to rob you. He says that you are buying jewellery to the value of thirty thousand pounds——"

Lumière's jaw dropped. "Well, I'll be——, the Alexandriff necklace! A hundred and fifty thousand dollars. Now, how in hell did he know that?"

★★★★★★

Mr. Mander was not in a position to answer the inquiry.

"I want you to do me this favour: Whenever you go to Randwell and Coles ring me up and I will go with you. If you take money——"

"Am I crazy?" demanded the other, contemptuously. "I'll pay with a banker's draft if I pay at all. But I'll certainly tip you on when the negotiations reach that point. What do you think of that picture——?"

For the next ten minutes he talked of his recent purchases—the sitting-room was littered with works of art that he had been offered or had bought.

Mr. Mander returned to his office with a fixed smile. For once in his life The Ringer had made a mistake. He had a different type of man to deal with from Bliss.

Bliss was tired, lived too near the problem of The Ringer to adjust himself instantly to every new development. A fresh brain, a fresh outlook, and methods which, Mr. Mander flattered himself, were a little out of the ordinary, would produce results for which Superintendent Bliss had groped in vain.

In his exhilaration, he sat down and wrote a long letter to the absent superintendent, telling him just how the case was developing, and giving him a bare outline of the measures, he was taking to meet and defeat the machinations of Henry Arthur Milton. He wrote:

"Naturally, I shall take no chances. Lumière has promised that in no circumstances will he make the purchase without notifying me."

He made a second call upon Randwell and Coles, and had a long conference with the manager.

"You understand that when Mr. Lumière buys this necklace it is to be taken by two trustworthy assistants to him at the hotel. In no circumstances must he buy it here and take it away with him. I will arrange that you have four of the best men from Scotland Yard to escort your salesmen. It would be better perhaps, if you came yourself to take the banker's draft. You can have the detectives to guard you back to Bond Street."

The manager laughed.

"A banker's draft wouldn't be of much use to The Ringer," he said; and then: "Perhaps you would like to see the article which Mr. Lumière is trying to buy. We're asking thirty-five thousand, but I think the purchase price will be nearer thirty; naturally, we're after the best price we can get, but he's a very shrewd man and knows more about precious stones than most people I have met."

He unlocked a safe in his private office and took out a tray on which lay a long and dazzling chain of diamonds and emeralds.

"Some of these stones weigh eight carats. Those three emeralds"— he pointed with his little finger—"are worth something like £5,000 in the open market. As a matter of fact, we get very little profit, because the value of this chain, which came to us from Russia, is in the stones and not in the setting."

★★★★★★

Mander interviewed the assistant commissioner and gave him particulars of the steps he had taken to safeguard the chain.

"It comes down to a question of system," he graciously explained. "I am a great admirer of the work of Superintendent Bliss, but it has always struck me as being a little haphazard, and left open all sorts of avenues of escape.

"In this case, I purpose, if you have no objection, utilising the full strength of the Yard. I shall have the hotel surrounded by detectives; I shall have men in every corridor; and if The Ringer can get in or out, he will be a much cleverer man than I gave him credit for."

The assistant commissioner, who had a very high regard for the genius of Bliss, listened coldly.

"One thing you must be careful about, Inspector, is a possible confederate—probably a woman," he said. "The Ringer is a quick and efficient worker."

Mr. Mander smiled.

"I also have some sort of reputation, sir," he said; and the assistant commissioner was too polite to ask for particulars.

Mander, in his way, was very thorough. He took a census of every room occupied at the hotel and paid particular attention to the guests whose rooms were adjacent to Mr. Lumière's suite. The room adjoining Lumière's own bedroom was occupied by a Miss Gwerth Stacey, who had arrived at the hotel on the same day as Lumière. She was an American and a physical culture expert. Lumière, who confessed that he had had several chats with her, said she was a fanatic on the question of hotel fires.

She told him that she never went into an hotel without making a survey of her position and discovering the quickest way of leaving the building—a quite unnecessary precaution so far as the Revoy Hotel was concerned, for in every room there was a fire alarm.

"Trail her up," said Mander to one of his subordinates. "She's the most suspicious-looking individual in the hotel."

All the trailing, however, revealed no more than that she attended lectures on hygiene and physical culture which were being delivered at that period by a Swedish authority. She had apparently one or two professional friends in London with whom she occasionally went to supper and a dance.

But Mander was taking no risks: he instructed a woman detective to make this athletic lady her especial care. He chose the five best detectives at the Yard and gave them detailed instructions as to what they were to do in certain emergencies, and, in addition, earmarked four reliable men to accompany the jeweller to the hotel.

That pilgrimage of commerce came on the very day he completed his arrangements. A telephone message brought him to the jewellers' and he interviewed the managing director in his private office.

"We have agreed to a price, and Mr. Lumière is taking possession of the chain this afternoon at half-past four."

That was all Mander wanted to know.

He put into movement the machinery he had created to circumvent Scotland Yard's cleverest and chiefest enemy. Plain-clothes officers were detailed to watch every railway terminus: a corps of watchers was distributed about the hotel; and at four o'clock, when the jewellers' manager stepped into a car that waited in Bond Street, four stalwart detectives closed in on him and entered the machine with him.

At the entrance to the hotel were two police officers in uniform. In the corridor on Mr. Lumière's floor two detectives, Mander's most reliable officers, were awaiting them.

The inspector was with Mr. Lumière when the treasure arrived, and the millionaire chuckled as he saw this unusually large party crowd into the room.

"Lock the door," said Mander, authoritatively, and his order was carried out.

The jeweller took a case from his inside pocket, laid it on the table, and opened the cover. Under the overhead light of the glass chandelier the beautiful rope flashed into a thousand hues.

"You've got a bargain, Mr. Lumière," said the manager.

The purchaser shrugged his shoulders.

"I'm not so sure that it's a great bargain," he said, good-humouredly. "At any rate, you have your money."

He took a banker's draft from his pocket and handed it to the jeweller, who examined it carefully and slipped it into his pocket-case.

"What do you intend doing with this piece of jewellery?" asked Mander. "I presume you're going to put it into the hotel safe?"

★★★★★★

Mr. Lumière smiled and shook his head.

"I've something more secure than any hotel safe in my room," he said. "Nobody knows about it but myself, and I can only assure you that I will put it in a place that not even you and your detectives could find."

Mander frowned at this.

"Why not——" he began.

"My friend," said Mr. Lumière, quietly, "I trust nobody! If you do not know where I have placed it, and none of your intelligent officers—one of whom may be The Ringer for all I know—sees where it goes, I have only myself to blame if it is lost."

He took up the case, walked quickly into his bedroom, and closed the door.

The jeweller looked at the detective and chuckled.

"I shouldn't be surprised it he's right," he said. "These people who are in the habit of carrying stones are very seldom robbed."

Mander was in something of a quandary; he had no authority to demand that he should be shown where the jewels were hidden, and the suggestion which was thrown out by Lumière that one of his men might possibly be The Ringer gave him a moment's uneasiness. He was so impressed that he had them lined up and looked closely at one after the other. They were clean-shaven, and none of them bore the slightest resemblance to the description he had had of this notable individual.

"I suppose it's all right——" he began.

And then he heard a cry in the corridor outside, and a quick scamper of feet. Instantly he was outside the door, in time to see a woman flying along the corridor, pursued by the two detectives. She turned an angle of the wall, and fled to the stairs.

Mander dashed back into the room and tried the door of Lumière's bedroom; it was locked.

"Are you there . . . . Mr. Lumière?"

He tapped on the panel, but there was no answer. He shouted

again, and then flung all his weight against the door. The lock was a stout one, and did not budge.

"Come here, two of you fellows!" he shouted, savagely; and two of the heaviest detectives applied their shoulders to the door. There was a crack, and a crash, and the door flew open.

The room was empty. It was a large bedroom, from which led two other doors, one apparently into the bathroom and the other to the corridor. This, they found, was unlocked. There was no sign of Lumière, nor of the diamond rope.

The windows were fastened, and exit from here would have been almost impossible, for the suite was on the fourth floor, and there was a sheer drop; and there was no means by which even a cat could have climbed down.

Mander's face was very pale. He realised that something had happened, something that might be very unpleasant to himself. He rushed into the corridor in time to see the two detectives bringing back a protesting and dishevelled young lady, whom he recognised as Miss Stacey.

She was incoherent with wrath. It was a long time before she could make any understandable statement.

"Now come across, my girl—you were working with The Ringer," said Mander, when he had taken the girl into the sitting-room. "He handed you the stuff and you bolted with it—where is Mr. Lumière?"

"Are you crazy?" she demanded, shrilly. "Who is The Ringer, anyway? The fire-bell went, and I ran downstairs. Just as I had got to the hall, these two . . . ."

******

Mander looked at her incredulously.

"Fire-bell?" he said. "There's been no fire alarm."

"The fire-bell went, I tell you," she insisted, "and the indicator dropped, and the red light burnt."

He followed her into her room and discovered that she had spoken only the truth. The bell was still ringing; a red light glowed at the side, and the indicator which dropped at the ringing of the bell showed plainly.

He returned to Lumière's room, stunned with amazement. By this time, the hotel staff had gathered. Nobody had seen any sign of Mr. Lumière.

"What is that door?" He pointed to a plain door opposite the bedroom of the missing man.

229

"That is the baggage lift," said the valet.

Mander made his way quickly down the stairs to the hall. His policemen were still on guard at the door, but they had seen no sign of the missing millionaire.

He was about to turn into the manager's office when he heard a well-remembered and much-disliked voice.

"Have you lost him?" He spun round on his heels, to meet the unpleasant smile of Superintendent Bliss.

"I came back this afternoon, after I had your letter," said Bliss, in his deliberate way. "I gather you've had some trouble?"

By this time Mander was nearly hysterical.

"I've had no trouble," he almost shouted. "I took every precaution. I have had every entrance guarded—"

"Go back to the Yard and leave this case to me, will you?" said Bliss.

★★★★★★

It was late that night when a miserable detective inspector was summoned to his superintendent's office. He found Bliss chewing at a half-smoked cigar.

"Sit down, Mr. Mander," Bliss's voice was icily polite. "In the first place," he said, "let me explain why I came back from Nice. When I got your letter, I pretty well knew that The Ringer was purposely taking advantage of your innocence. He knew I'd left London—you saw to that! And when he addressed the letter to Bliss, he knew very well that Mr. Mander would open it.

"It was the cleverest little *coup* that he'd ever planned, and I've not the slightest doubt—this may bring a little comfort to you—that he would have tried it on me, and possibly have succeeded. Do you know the firm of Randwell and Coles?"

"I know they are jewellers, that is all," said Mander, unhappily.

"Randwell and Coles," said Bliss, "are names which cover the identity of a very rich man who changed his name some years ago to Chapman. It was previously Lumière, and when The Ringer told you that he was going to rob Lumière, that was the Lumière that he meant."

"And who was the other Lumière?"

He saw Bliss smile, and his jaw dropped.

"The Ringer?" he squeaked.

Bliss nodded.

"The millionaire in his suite at the Revoy was our dear friend. To get possession of the thirty thousand pound necklace was a very simple matter, with a forged bank draft, always supposing that he could find a mug at Scotland Yard who would vouch for him. He found one. You left the unfortunate jewellers no doubt as to the *bona fides* of Mr. Lumière. If you had cabled to New York, to Mr. Sullivan, of the police department, you would have discovered that Mr. Sullivan died last year; and if you had ever seen a letter-head from Police Headquarters at New York you would also have known that the heading of the letter you received was printed in London.

"As to the fire alarm—I'm not so sure that that wasn't as clever as anything The Ringer has ever attempted. He knew all about this girl who was living next door; knew exactly her horror of fires, and she served him rather well, because at the psychological moment, by inserting a steel needle through the plaster of the wall and short-circuiting the fire alarm, he was able to send that timorous female flying for her life with the two people who had been set to watch the passage running after her.

"That gave him the opportunity he wanted. He slipped into the luggage lift, went down into the basement; he had his quick-change ready, and was out through the service entrance before you could say 'knife'!"

Mr. Mander said nothing.

"The Ringer isn't easy, is he?" asked Bliss, maliciously.

Chapter 6: The Blackmail Boomerang

There was a man who had an office in Chancery Lane, who de-scribed himself as The Exsome Domestic Agency. His ostensible busi-ness was the placing of domestic servants in new situations, and he specialised in that type of servant who had reason for not applying to his or her late employer for the indispensable "character".

He did not advertise this fact, either in the newspapers or on his nice note-heading, but it was pretty well known that he would supply necessary credentials for a consideration.

"This man (or woman) we know to have been employed, by Mr. Hackitt, who is now in India. Mr. Hackitt left England in a hurry, but in a letter to us he spoke in the highest possible terms of . . . ."

Mr. Exsome was very friendly with his clients. He would talk to them, drink with them, and sometimes learn important facts. Mr. Ex-some had another Agency which called itself the Secret Service Bu-reau. In this capacity he was a private detective, and, as such, would call upon the late employers of his servant clients.

Was it true that Mrs. Z— had once entertained Mr. Y— in the absence of her husband? Was she aware that there was a blackmailer trying to make capital out of the knowledge? And would she leave everything in the hands of the Secret Service Bureau—at a fee to be settled later?

Mrs. Z—, in a panic would agree, and from time to time would pay the exorbitant fees of her "protector". In this way "Skid" Exsome made a very large income.

His intimate associates called him "Skid" because he had the knack of side-slipping most of the dangers that came his way.

He had a lovely house near Egham, a flat in Maida Vale, and ran the most expensive of cars. For these luxuries two people had paid with their lives (Mrs. Albany's suicide will be remembered), and hundreds had paid in cash. To build his own house he had broken many; to provide for the jewels with which his phlegmatic wife bedecked herself many jewels had been sold and many little properties mortgaged.

Mr. Exsome had never been convicted—he had "skidded" most effectively.

Mrs. Leadale Verriner once employed a butler who vanished one morning with the contents of her jewel-case. She was out hunting at the time, and returned to find her flimsy safe ripped open and property to the value of £3,000 gone. It was not until after she had communicated with the police that she remembered that there were other things in the case besides jewellery.

She did not go grey or haggard. She was a sane and wise as well as a pretty woman. She went to Scotland Yard and interviewed Bliss and told him all about Bobbie, who was now in India, and about her grumbling, difficult and jealous husband. She did not tell Mr. Bliss very much about the letters that Bobbie had written; but the superintendent was a man of the world and a good guesser.

When the butler was arrested, he was interviewed at Scotland Yard. Most of the jewellery had been disposed of; the letters, he said glibly, he had destroyed. "Threw them into the fire," was his explanation.

"I hope you did, Cully," said Bliss, who knew the butler's record rather well. "You'll get five for this job; but if, when you come out, you put the black on this lady I'll undertake to get you another fourteen."

"If I drop dead this minute," said Cully virtuously, "I burnt them letters."

He did not drop dead that minute, proving beyond any doubt

whatever that Providence gives a miss to the most tempting invitations.

Cully got a three, and, coming out, looked for another job. The Exsome Agency was pretty well known in Dartmoor, and to Mr. Exsome he went. That gentleman also knew Cully's record and treated him most kindly. In the course of a couple of lunches, and an evening spent at a music-hall and worse, Cully made mysterious references to letters.

The next day he brought them to the office and "Skid" read them very carefully. He checked up Mrs. Leadale Verriner's social and financial position, discovered that she had an income of her own of two thousand a year, and that her husband was even better off.

He bought the letters, after some bargaining, for £320, and they immediately came within the operations of the Secret Service Bureau ....

Mrs. Verriner listened without comment to the apologetic "detective" who called upon her.

"No, it isn't your late butler," said Mr. Exsome. "I've taken a great deal of trouble to seek out that unfortunate man. He told me he threw them away, at a spot where the man who has approached me found them."

She was a little haggard now, possibly because Bobbie was married, and had written long, incoherent, rather foolish letters explaining his treachery and how everything was for the best.

Mr. Exsome waited for her to speak and then went on: "This man wishes to get to Australia and start life afresh——"

"It is a very common excuse, isn't it?" she asked coldly, and Mr. Exsome knew that she was going to be very difficult—the kind of woman who would go to the police if she was not handled rightly. He proceeded to handle her rightly.

He rose from his chair with a certain brusqueness.

"Well, madam, I've done all I possibly can, and there the matter ends so far as I am concerned. This blundering fool of a man may very well approach your husband, though why he should I don't know. But, as I say, these people are perfect fools——"

She signalled him to sit down again, and thenceforward she began to pay and pay, and one by one the letters were returned to her—all except the only one that counted.

On the loneliest corner of her pretty little Berkshire estate was a small cottage, rented by a French artist, who spent occasional weekends at the place. He kept no servants, for the simple reason that his language could not be understood.

Mrs. Verriner had had one or two talks with this long-haired gentleman with the twirling black moustache, and in his florid, extravagant way, he had placed his demesne—which cost him a pound a week—at her disposal.

Soon after Mr. Exsome began to draw on his new source of revenue she took the Frenchman at his word—to his undisguised amazement.

"I have people coming to see me whom I don't wish to receive at the house," she said. "It would be very convenient, Monsieur Vaux, if I could tell them to come here. Naturally, I would arrange these meetings while you were away."

"Why, *certainement!*" smiled her tenant. "When I am in residence, I will elevate to this little flagpole a small tricolour. Madam, I place in your hands the key of my little *château!*"

When the flagstaff was bare, she strolled across to the cottage, unlocked the back door, and in the very plain sitting-room furnished with sketches, finished and unfinished, she listened to Mr. Exsome's newest explanation.

★★★★★★

On a balmy spring evening Mr. Exsome was smoking a fragrant cigar in his Maida Vale flat. The letter came by hand, which puzzled him. It was typewritten and bore a typewritten signature:

"I have discovered that you are a professional blackmailer. I do not like blackmailers, professional or amateur. Find another occupation. I shall not warn you again."

The typewritten signature was "The Ringer," and Mr. Exsome's jaw dropped, for just then the newspapers were full of the recent exploits of that criminal.

His complacent wife came in soon after.

"Why, Ernie, you're looking very pale. What's the matter?" she asked. "Got your income tax assessment——"

She could be heavily jocular.

"Shut up!" he snarled.

Now, even he knew that it would take a big skid to avoid The Ringer; but he was on a good thing in Mrs. Leadale Verriner, had indeed only touched the edge of her resources. In a foolish moment of confidence, she had told him she would be very rich when her uncle died, and her uncle, as Mr. Exsome had already discovered, was nearer to eighty than seventy. This time he was out for big money, and it looked reasonable odds on his getting what he wished. As for The Ringer——

Going out that evening to the car that waited at the door, he saw a newspaper boy who carried an amazingly cheering poster: "The Ringer Located."

He bought a paper, his hand so trembling that he could hardly see the print; presently he found the item and learnt little except what he had discovered on the poster.

★★★★★★

Once upon a time a certain unpleasant gentleman was consigned by The Ringer to a hot little town set in the wastes of the Arabian desert, for offences which need not be particularised. And there for three months he performed the office of hairdresser and head shingler to the women of one Ibn el Masjik.

One day he conceived the idea of setting forth the story of his wrongs in a long, long letter to the Foreign Minister of Great Britain, and, by bribery and corruption, persuaded a camel-driver named The Accursed (for some ancient sin of his forefathers) to carry the letter to a civilised place. He also wrote to his mother, but that letter was lost the night our accursed camel-driver got drunk in Benarim and the unveiled women with whom he was spending the evening went through his turban in the hope of finding money to pay them for the trouble of throwing him out of the window.

The letter reached Whitehall and was sent across to Scotland Yard. Inspector Bliss was hardly stirred by the fate of Mr. Julian Graddle, but he was tremendously interested in certain sequences of cause and effect. Somebody had been indiscreet; a wronged father (who was also a seagoing captain and Mr. Graddle's custodian) had spoken highly of his neighbour who had engineered the kidnapping.

Bliss had something to go on. A police tender raided a house in Norbury. The Ringer escaped by the back door of a tiny garage as the tender halted at the corner of the street. He was in his respectable car with a heavy red moustache and a heavier pipe; he passed Bliss, and the superintendent did not give him more than a glance.

That evening every private police wire radiating from the instrument room at Scotland Yard carried the duplication of this message:

"Very urgent: very urgent. Hold brown Buick two-seater T.D. 7418. Seen ten minutes ago Great West Road stop Staines report Slough report Maidenhead report Beading report stop Arrest and detain driver of car stop Dangerous carries firearms stop Report Bliss

Scotland Yard."

"I think," said Inspector Mander, fingering his fair moustache, "that this is where we get him."

A buoyant soul was Inspector Mander. Failure was so normal a condition that a very recent and flagrant misfire of his, which would have crushed most men, had not more than momentarily depressed him.

Superintendent Bliss regarded him with an unfriendly eye.

"You will be interested to learn that the car has been discovered in Epping Forest, which is exactly opposite the direction to that in which he was seen moving. And if you want an afternoon's occupation you will probably work out the route he followed. I have already done so, but you are so much cleverer than I that you may be able to show me a point."

✶✶✶✶✶✶

The next clue Scotland Yard received was from the Berkshire police. There was, apparently, living on the estate of Mrs. Leadale Verriner, a French artist who occupied his bungalow only during the week-end. In his absence, as he learnt when he returned rather earlier than usual, some unauthorised person had been living in the bungalow and had been sleeping in a room which the artist did not use. He left behind a small map on which two routes were traced in red ink one leading to the south of England and one—and this explained the disposition of the car—through Hounslow, Hampton, and by a circuitous route to North London.

"I'd better go down and see this Frenchman and have a look at the cottage," suggested Mander.

"Do you speak French?" asked his chief, coldly.

"No, sir, but I can make myself understood——"

"The question is whether he'll make himself understood. Leave him to the Berkshire police."

Mrs. Leadale Verriner got to know of the burglary from her tenant, and at first, she was a little alarmed.

"I will tell you the truth, my dear madam. At first, I said nothing because I thought it was your friend! You are a lady; I have placed my house at your disposition. What is more likely than that you should say: 'Very good, you shall sleep here tonight. I am sure my friend Mr. Vaux would not object.' And would I object, madam? Most assuredly I would not!

"But when I hear of this Ringer, I say, 'Ha, ha!' I do not fear this

Ringer—I snap my fingers at him and say '*Pff!*' I search the little room and what do I discover? The map. This, I think, is strange. And then I find a revolver—I do not tell the police about that! I think I will keep that revolver for myself, though I am not nervous truly! But it is a souvenir. And then I find you have been away in London, so your friend could not have been here, and I speak to the police."

She bit her lip thoughtfully. She was growing rather peaked; there were dark shadows under her eyes. She had been to London to negotiate a mortgage on a house she owned in Wiltshire. And her husband was growing suspicious—an easy process—of the real cause for her clandestine meetings with Mr. Exsome in the artist's cottage.

"You don't think he came—while my friend was here, that he was in the house all the time?"

He shook his head and smiled.

"He would not be so ungallant," he said, so archly that she stiffened.

★★★★★★

Exsome was growing more and more requiring. The few hundreds that were to send the unknown owner of the letters to Australia had been succeeded by a demand for a thousand. Her husband's present suspicion was but a foretaste of the attitude he would adopt if the letters ever came to his notice. She had got to the point where she could not sleep; she was making her last desperate effort to satisfy the rapacity which Mr. Exsome interpreted in terms more suave.

Exsome waited patiently. He knew to the minute when to put on the screw and when to release it. Frantic letters were coming to him from his victim telling him the progress she was making in the rather protracted negotiations which were going on between herself and a lawyer. Early one afternoon he received a wire:

"Meet cottage eight o'clock. Bring letters. Cash ready."

It was a large sum he had demanded—the ultimate squeeze. Thereafter any further demands would drive her to Scotland Yard, and Mr. Exsome knew just where to stop.

He got the letter out of his safe, put it in his pocket, and was on the point of going to the little club in Soho, where one can bet race by race, when an urgent telephone call came through for him.

★★★★★★

There are more than eighteen thousand constables in the Metropolitan Police Force, and it would be very remarkable if there were not one or two crooks among them. One of these had been fired out of Scotland Yard for malpractice, but had kept in touch, through a friend, with a great deal that was happening at police headquarters, and he was a very useful servant to Mr. Exsome.

"It's Joe," said the voice, and when Joe spoke in a tone so urgent that his voice was almost unrecognisable, Mr. Exsome sat up and took notice.

"Anything wrong?" he asked quickly.

"I've just had it straight," said the speaker rapidly. "Bliss has got information against you. Somebody's raised a squeak—name of Lynn."

Mr. Exsome nodded. He remembered the Lynn case—the son of a wealthy member of the Stock Exchange who had got himself into very serious trouble and had, in consequence, enriched Mr. Exsome's treasury to an incredible amount.

"Is there a warrant?" he asked.

"There will be tomorrow. You'll be under observation from to-night."

"Thank you, Joe," said Mr. Exsome gratefully.

He was prepared for such a crisis. His bank was only a few doors from the flat in which he lived. He arrived there twenty minutes before closing time, and drew so substantially upon his balance that the manager had to be sent for to make delivery from the private vault.

He went back and saw his wife. She had a private account of her own and needed no provision.

"I shall be away for a few months," he said, and she accepted his hasty departure philosophically.

He read the telegram again. He would go by train to Windsor, taking his bicycle, would cross Windsor Great Park, and reach the cottage in the twilight. The bicycle would get him to Slough and the main Western line . . . . there was a boat leaving Plymouth for a French port that night. By the time the warrant was issued he would be well away.

Everything worked according to plan. He rode at his leisure through the deserted park, and came to the cottage a quarter of an hour before the time of his appointment. There was nobody in sight on the road. He passed through the garden gate and made a circuit of the house. Near the hedge which separated the artist's little garden from the park somebody had been digging. A deep trench had been cut—he was only faintly interested in this.

He pushed at the back door—it was open. So, the lady had arrived! He left his bicycle against the wall and entered, closing the door softly behind him. The door of the sitting-room was ajar, and a light was burning.

"Well, madam——" he began cheerfully as he entered.

"Shut the door," said the pleasant-faced man who was sitting at the other side of the table.

★★★★★★

Mr. Exsome stopped and stared.

"You don't know me?" The stranger smiled. "You'll be interested to learn that you're one of the few people who have ever seen The Ringer without his make-up."

"The Ringer?" croaked Exsome, and his face went green.

"Don't run—I can shoot quicker than you can move."

His right hand was caressing a Browning.

"Won't you sit down?"

The blackmailer sank back into a chair. He was speechless, could only gape at Judgment.

"You've had a fair warning, I think?" He asked the question in a pleasant, conversational tone. "I've been on your trail for quite a long time, but you've been so clever that it's been a little difficult to identify you, and I've been rather busy myself lately," He smiled. "And then I happened to be staying here. I've got one or two little bolt-holes, you know—they're rather necessary.

"When Mrs. Verriner said she had a friend to meet I feared the worst; but, then, I'm not a censor of morals. Curiosity and interest induced me to stay in the house one day when you came—you never know what you may learn of value if you listen hard enough. Of course, I am so much of a gentleman that if it had been a vulgar love affair, I shouldn't have listened at all. But it wasn't a vulgar love affair; it was a vulgar blackmailing affair. Did you bring the letter?"

Exsome nodded dumbly.

"Put it on the table. Throw on to the table also the money you drew from the bank. I phoned you this afternoon and got you on the run—oh yes! I know all about Joe; that was only natural, for I made a very thorough inquiry about you and your connections."

He waited a little while, and then said sharply: "The letter and the money!"

Exsome obeyed; and then he found his voice.

"Is that all you want?" he asked huskily.

The Ringer shook his head.

"I want something more. I've been looking up your cases. I don't suppose you ever think of them—they're not nice, are they? Do you remember that unfortunate lady who was found with her head in a

239

gas oven? And the girl who walked into a pond and stayed there? And that elderly clergyman who went a little wrong in his head after you'd taken sixteen hundred pounds out of him? Now, take only those few cases."

Mr. Exsome remembered them rather well. The memory of them was very vivid at that moment. Perhaps for the first time he was seeing another point of view.

"That's all," said the Ringer, and rose. "Let's go outside."

******

The morning mail brought Mrs. Leadale Verriner two letters—one from the lawyer regretting his inability to arrange the mortgage; the other (and this was registered) a letter three years old, and she nearly fainted.

With it was a slip of paper which said:

I shall not trouble you again. All the money I received from you I have paid into your London account.

Bewildered, yet half-swooning with joy, she pushed the letter into the grate.

Ten minutes later her banker rang her. The money had arrived by post.

"Only your name written on a postcard was with the banknotes."

Her husband was in town. That afternoon she saw the tricolour flying and strolled across to the cottage. The Frenchman was in his garden, a long cheroot between his teeth, and he greeted her volubly.

"Here is your key, Monsieur Vaux," she said in her excellent French. And then, with a smile: "You were very busy yesterday afternoon. One of my gardeners told me he saw you digging frantically!"

She looked round the garden; there was no sign of the trench the gamekeeper had reported, but the earth had been turned and a new oval garden-bed had appeared amid the rank grass.

"There I shall plant forget-me-nots," said Mr. Vaux, "which shall remind of one small service which I was able to render you, madam."

She thought he was referring to the key. He was, in point of fact, thinking of something quite different.

Chapter 7: Miss Brown's £7,000 Windfall

Mr. Gilbert Orsan was an industrious writer: he might not, perhaps, rival that inventor of tales who, if rumour does not lie, produces a novel a week and a play a fortnight. And he certainly could not be credited with the fabulous income of that restless man; for Mr. Orsan was not paid for his contributions to journalism. He wrote letters on genealogy and the thriftlessness of the poor, and similar cheerful subjects.

As to the thriftlessness of the poor, he might claim to be an authority. The rents due to him were sometimes, on the aggregate, as much as a thousand pounds in arrears. He owned a very considerable amount of house property in the south, east, north, and west of London.

Sometimes the most unpleasant things were said about him—both as landlord and employer. For he was also the proprietor of the Orsan Stores, which had branches in every part of the metropolis. He invariably wrote about these outcries against his humanity as "carefully engineered". He referred to them as "artificial grievances", and put them down to "the unscrupulous agitations of Communists."

Communism was a great blessing to Mr. Orsan. He ascribed all criticism to the "growing spirit of lawlessness engendered by the pestiferous doctrines of Moscow."

Yet, if the truth be told, there were thousands of people who hated Moscow and Mr. Orsan with equal ferocity.

Lila Brown should have been one of these, but she was too sore at heart to hate any but herself.

Yet Mr. Orsan had behaved very generously to her. As he said in his god-like way, These Things Happen, and there was no sense in Making Mountains out of Molehills. She ceased to be Mr. Organ's housekeeper-secretary and went to live at Schofields boarding-house at Hythe, on four pounds a week, which was little enough to keep two people, even though one of the two lived on an exclusive diet of milk and patent barley.

★★★★★★

A quiet man went to live at Schofield's. He was of uncertain age, rather good-looking, and his hair was greyish at the temples. He had one trick of inviting and inspiring confidence, and another of making people talk about things that they could never dream they would ever discuss with their nearest friends. And he loved babies, and handled them beautifully—he had once "walked" an Edinburgh hospital.

So, in the course of the quiet weeks when Superintendent Bliss was seeking him in every part of England except Hythe, the engaging man learned all about Mr. Orsan and his *ménage*, and the little passage that led from the garage to the study, which Mr. Orsan used when he took friends to the house who could not go more openly without endangering his reputation for sanctity.

And Miss Brown showed him his portrait signed "Gilly", which was both intimate and anonymous. For she had reached the stage where she had to tell somebody or die.

The nice man was sympathetic and understanding, and, since his mind was on results rather than causes, he gave her no cause for embarrassment.

Mr. Orsan lived in a beautiful house overlooking Hyde Park, but on its unfashionable frontier. His connection with his business was a very slight one. For two hours a day he attended his head office and dictated reproofs to the various heads of departments, watched salary lists with the eye of an eagle, punished the petty defalcations which are the common experience of storekeepers, told his general manager the story of how he started life with nothing and by his industry and application to business had amassed a fortune—and then went back to his room, the windows of which looked across the budding green of trees, and composed the letter or the lecture (for he was in demand as a speaker at literary societies) which occupied his attention at the moment.

This writing-room was a lovely saloon, all gold and jade green, with a great marble fireplace, and it was famished in Empire style. It was very unlike the cupboards where his shop assistants slept, and bore no comparison with the hovels in which his tenants lived and died.

Mr. Orsan was strong for gentility, and the footman who took a card to him wore knee breeches, with the golden tassels of aiguillettes dangling from his shoulders. Mr. Orsan read the card, fingered his greying side whiskers, rubbed his bristling black eyebrows, and pursed his lips.

"Superintendent Bliss? Who the deuce is Superintendent Bliss? Show him in, Thomas."

Bliss entered and instantly annoyed the great man by expressing, by his attitude and manner, less deference and respect to him than he felt was due from a public servant. Bliss put his hat on the floor and sat down uninvited—an objectionable action to Mr. Orsan, who was strong for proper behaviour.

"Well, sir," he said impatiently, "I presume you wish to see me about that defaulting cashier of mine? I would much rather you saw my general manager. I do not, as a rule——"

"I haven't come to discuss defaulting cashiers, Mr. Orsan," said Bliss brusquely. "My visit is in regard to a letter you wrote which was published in this morning's *Megaphone* dealing with the criminal classes and the urgent need for extending capital punishment for felonies."

******

Mr. Orsan sat back in his chair, put the tips of his fingers together, and inclined his head more graciously. That Scotland Yard should take notice of his views on criminals was especially flattering.

"Of course, of course! I had forgotten that," he said. "I think you will agree with me, Inspector—or Superintendent, or whatever you are—that the only way to deal with the habitual criminal—"

"I'm not even asking you for your views on the habitual criminal," said Bliss, who had no finesse.

Mr. Orsan hated being interrupted, and showed it.

"In your reference to criminals," Bliss went on, unconscious of the fact that he had ruffled the magnate, "you spoke of a certain man, The Ringer. You said it was disgraceful that the police allowed this criminal to remain at large and that his crimes had gone unpunished."

"And I hold to that opinion," said Mr. Orsan firmly. "I suppose it has rubbed you up the wrong way at Scotland Yard. Well I'm afraid I can't help that. As a public man, writing on a matter of national interest, I must speak the views which, as I feel, are generally held."

Bliss laughed.

"It is very interesting to read your views, Mr. Orsan, but we aren't very much troubled by them. Scotland Yard is there to be kicked, and if we weren't kicked, we should think something unusual was happening. I merely came to warn you that it is a very dangerous thing to mention this man or to draw attention to yourself in the way you have, especially in view of the fact that we have reason to believe he has been staying at Hythe recently."

Mr. Orsan frowned. Hythe? It had a familiar sound.

"Why at Hythe?" he asked.

"There is a young lady at Hythe who calls herself Mrs. Tredmayne, but is, I believe, a girl named Brown who was recently in your employ. I don't know whether she has any grievance against you; I only know that to all appearances she has reasonable grounds for grievance. She was once your secretary-housekeeper—rather a pretty girl——"

"I know all about Miss Brown," snapped Orsan. "A very nice—er—young lady who had the misfortune to . . . . . Well, I don't wish to discuss it with you, and——"

"It is unnecessary to discuss it at all, Mr. Orsan," said Bliss in his hard, metallic voice. "It would take more than Miss Brown to shock Scotland Yard. The only point is that if the man who was living in the same boarding-house at Hythe was The Ringer, then there is every reason for you to expect trouble. I think it is very undesirable that you should call attention to yourself and your antagonism to The Ringer."

Mr. Orsan rose and towered over the detective.

"Let me tell you, Mr. Bliss, that I am surprised to hear you offer such a suggestion! Is it not my duty as a citizen to denounce this man—aye, and to denounce the police for their laxity in their treatment of him?

"So far from avoiding any reference to The Ringer, I shall make it the subject of my next letter to the *Megaphone*—the editor of which is a personal friend of mine," he added significantly, as though that statement conveyed a terrible threat.

Bliss shrugged his shoulders and rose, picking up his hat. "Does it occur to you that it would be a simple matter to use you as a bait to catch this man?" he asked. "Or that it might make our task considerably easier if we encouraged you to denounce, as you call it, The Ringer?"

★★★★★★

That had not occurred to Mr. Orsan; it did not occur to him now. After Thomas had shown the visitor from the premises Mr. Orsan pushed aside the sheet on which he had been inscribing his remedies for poverty (remedies which did not include decent housing and higher wages) and, ringing for his secretary, gave orders that every available piece of data concerning Henry Arthur Milton, better known as The Ringer, should be accumulated for reference. Having done this he began a letter to the editor of the *Megaphone*, which began:

> Sir,—When Pliny the Younger spoke of that "indolent but agreeable condition of doing nothing," he surely had in view the attitude of the police towards "the biggest rascal that ever walked on two legs" (see Pliny's letters)—The Ringer. . . .

He wrote with vehemence, with passion, with a tremendous sense of importance. He called for an instant investigation of police methods, he hinted that Scotland Yard was not sacrosanct, and introduced such Latin tags as *Non sibi sed patriae*, to justify his own energy, and *Quis custodiet Ipsos custodes*, to explain the inaction of the police.

His letter did not create a furore: little bits of it were cut out by the gentleman who "made up" the *Megaphone* in order to allow space for a dog-racing advertisement; but it certainly attracted attention. At

244

Scotland Yard Bliss read the letter and grinned mirthlessly.

"It is a pity," he said, "that the old man forgot that 'Those whom the gods destroy write letters to the newspapers'."

Inspector Mander smiled his disapproval of the flippancy.

"There's a lot in what he says," he stated.

Mr. Bliss turned cold eyes upon his incompetent assistant.

"There's a lot in what you say, and yet you're hardly worth listening to," he said unkindly.

Two days after the epistle was published the inevitable letter came to Mr. Orsan. It was typewritten, posted in the north-west district of London, and began without conventional introduction.

"You're a very amusing letter-writer. Are you as good a debater? I am thinking of giving a Christmas dinner to all your unfortunate tenants, and I have taken the Herbert Hall for that purpose. At nine o'clock in the evening I am prepared to appear on the platform and debate with you the question of Capital Punishment. Show this to Bliss. Reply through the advertisement columns of the *Megaphone*."

It was signed, in a flourishing hand, "Henry Arthur Milton."

"Swank," said Mr. Orsan vulgarly.

He telephoned through to Scotland Yard, and was infuriated when Bliss, with the greatest coolness, invited him to call on him.

"I shall be at home all the afternoon," repeated Mr. Orsan.

"So, shall I," was the reply. "Call at three o'clock. I may be able to give you exactly ten minutes."

Swallowing his pride, the magnate drove down in his limousine to Scotland Yard and suffered the indignity of being kept waiting for a quarter of an hour before ho was admitted to the bare business-like office where Superintendent Bliss worked.

The detective took the letter and read it through.

"Well?" he asked, when he had finished. "Are you going to take up the challenge?"

"Take up the challenge?" Mr. Orsan stared at him. "Do you seriously suggest that this man will come to the Herbert Hall to debate . . . . it's preposterous!"

"If he says he'll come to the Herbert Hall, he'll come," said Bliss. "Exactly what will happen to you I don't know, but I should imagine something unpleasant. You'd better put the advertisement in, and I will do my best to keep you from harm."

Mr. Orsan was not frightened; he was merely surprised. "Do you mean to tell me, Inspector——"

"Superintendent," murmured Bliss.

"Does it really matter what you are?" asked Mr. Orsan impatiently. "You are a public servant, which is all that concerns me. Do you really mean to tell me that you take this balderdash seriously?"

"I certainly do, and I advise you to do the same."

★★★★★★

In the course of the next few days Mr. Orsan attained to the eminence of a public figure. Another letter from him, which quoted that received from The Ringer, was published in every newspaper in the land.

It was ascertained that the Herbert Hall, which is one of the largest in London and is situated in South Kensington, had been engaged through an agent for the use of an unknown patron, who had paid the rent in advance; and that a large firm of caterers had received orders to provide refreshments for three thousand people. They also had been paid in cash.

There was some suggestion that the proprietors of the hall should cancel the letting, in the public interest, but Scotland Yard got busy to prevent this. Mander interviewed the owners of the hall and the caterers and told them to let matters stand as they were.

He himself was, at his own request, put in charge of the police arrangements.

"I want this chance, chief, to wipe out the mistake I made over the Lumière case," he pleaded. "I shall make no mistake here."

Bliss was unwilling to do this, but Mander's appeal was seconded by a high authority, for the inspector had made many useful friends, and in the end Bliss yielded.

"It's a chance for you, Mander, but it's very nearly your last chance," he said. "I hate putting you in charge, and I doubt if I'd do it if I wasn't convinced that whoever tackles The Ringer at this little Christmas party of his will get it in the neck."

Mander smiled.

"If he's a man of his word he'll have to be a magician to get away."

"He's a man of his word, all right. Take the case, and God help you."

It was not difficult to secure guests at this party. Mr. Orsan's tenants lived in solid blocks, in little mean streets where every house looked like the other, in tenements which had been up to date in the 'seventies and were no longer up to date. To every occupier came an invitation, printed on a private press. Mr. Orsan became famous. He was pointed out in restaurants as the man who would meet The Ringer in debate.

Superintendent Bliss had made only one suggestion to his subordinate.

"I advise you to have four doctors within reach of the platform and an ambulance ready to rush Orsan to the hospital," he said.

"Why four?" asked Mander.

"Two for each of you," snarled Bliss, and again Mr. Mander smiled.

"If he turns up, I'm a Dutchman."

"You are what you are and nothing can alter you," said Bliss bitterly.

It was on Christmas Eve that Mr. Orsan received the second letter.

"Do not fail me. If you do not turn up, I shall wait for you on the platform for ten minutes, and no longer."

But, for the moment, Mr. Orsan was not concerned about The Ringer. A new protagonist had appeared in the field. He had received a communication from a Mr. Arthur Agnis, and not only a communication, but a call.

Mr. Agnis, a shock-headed, bearded man, was a strenuous opponent of capital punishment. He had, he said, argued against capital punishment wherever the English language was spoken, and he came with the request that if The Ringer did not turn up, he might be allowed to argue in his stead. He seemed a respectable man, was well dressed, and treated Mr. Orsan with the greatest deference. Moreover, he arrived in his own car.

"My point is this, sir," he said. "You're being taken down to the Herbert Hall, and it is pretty clear that The Ringer will not appear—it's a hoax, if ever there was one. Why not let us have the debate?"

It seemed a very good idea, especially as Mr. Orsan had his speech already in type.

As a matter of precaution, he communicated with Scotland Yard.

"Arthur Agnis!" said Mander softly. "By gad!"

He got on the telephone to Orsan.

"By all means, let him come," he said. "Where does he live?"

"I didn't trouble to ask him," said Mr. Orsan. "He is telephoning me tonight to get my decision. He seems a very charming and well-spoken man."

"He would be!" said Mander, smiling to himself.

There were certain arrangements to be made. Mounted police were drafted to control the crowd of curious onlookers that surrounded the hall; policemen in plain clothes were called for duty by the thousand, and orders were given that only ticket holder were to be admitted.

"Don't forget," warned Bliss on Christmas afternoon, when he met his subordinate at the Yard, "that Henry Arthur Milton does not depend upon wigs and beards. When he impersonates a man, he is that man. His voice, his gestures, his tricks of speech—he has the whole box of tricks."

"Trust me," said Mander.

"I'd rather not," replied Bliss, and left the man to his fate.

The ticket-holders began to queue up as early as four o'clock in the afternoon. By seven the hall was packed, and the tables which had been set on the floor and in the galleries were filled. A band had been engaged to keep them occupied and amused; there was to be dancing after the debate.

At half-past eight Mander, accompanied by four armed officers, went to Orsan's house and was shown up into his beautiful library-sitting-room. When they went in the urbane gentleman looked up over his glasses and pointed to chairs.

"Sit down, please. I want to finish this letter to the *Megaphone*."

He wrote steadily for a quarter of an hour, then put down his pen, blotted the paper, and, collecting the sheets together, folded them into an envelope.

"It has occurred to me that this man might be—er—a suspicious person."

"That's already occurred to me, sir," said Mr. Mander. "You needn't worry about him. The moment he gives his name at the door he will practically be surrounded by police. We have left a space in front of the platform so that he can come forward, because we want to see just what he is going to do."

"He's not likely to do anything—rash, is he?" asked the other nervously.

"Trust me, sir," said Mander. It was a favourite expression of his—and, happily, the man he guarded did not know the right answer.

★★★★★★

The car was waiting at the door, and in this the five were driven to the Herbert Hall and admitted at a private entrance. As the hands of Mr. Orsan's watch pointed to nine its wearer walked forward on to the platform with his bodyguard, and the audience, forgetting, in the cheer of the blessed feast, their natural and year-long grievance against their oppressor, cheered in the sycophantic way of tenants saluting their landlord.

He went nervously to the platform and stood with folded hands, waiting. There was a deathly hush; privileged reporters who had been admitted made a brief examination of the hall, wondering whence The Ringer would come.

Then there was a stir; a bearded man strode into the beam of the limelight, which was focused, by Mander's orders, not on the figure standing on the stage, but upon the space where the debater would take his position.

"As The Ringer hasn't come," he began, in a high-pitched voice, "I'd like to take issue with you, Mr. Orsan, on the subject of capital punishment. I've got a few notes here——"

He reached for his hip pocket. Before he could withdraw its contents a cloud of detectives surrounded him. Before anybody in the hall realised what was happening, he was whisked away.

"I think that's all, air," smiled Mander. "I shouldn't advise you to stay any longer; we don't want to take any unnecessary chances."

He left to the bodyguard the task of escorting the charge to safety, and dashed off to interrogate his bearded prisoner. Mr. Agnis was livid of face, violent of tongue.

"You pull my beard again," he screamed, "and I'll beat the head off you! All England shall ring with this outrage!"

"It's a real beard," muttered one of the detectives to Mander, "and he's got papers on him that prove he's what he says he is."

The inspector examined these quickly. A horrible mistake had been made.

"Why did you come here at all?" he asked.

"Because I was invited here," howled Agnis. "I was brought down from Manchester. A gentleman gave me twenty-five pounds to come and debate the question of capital punishment with old Orsan."

The eyes of Mander and his second-in-command met blankly.

"Anyway," said Mander after a while, "that disposes of The Ringer. I said he'd never come, and he hasn't. Now, if anybody looks silly over this business it's Bliss."

He went back to Scotland Yard and found Bliss waiting impatiently for news.

"Why the hell didn't you telephone?" said the superintendent savagely when he told the story.

He was out of Scotland Yard, flying to Mr. Orsan's house, before

Mander could think of an adequate reply.

One of the resplendent footmen admitted him.

"Yes, sir, Mr. Orsan is at home; he's been home some time."

"Where is he?"

"In his writing-room, sir."

But Orsan was not in his writing-room. He was not in his bed-room. Eventually they found him trussed up in a small box-room at the top of the house, gagged and handcuffed, and there he had been since three o'clock that afternoon, when The Ringer went for him through a private passage leading from the garage, before he made himself up at his leisure in Mr. Orsan's own bedroom, wearing Mr. Orsan's own clothes (even Mr. Orsan's own watch), and had appeared on the platform at the Herbert Hall.

He had not gone alone. The library safe had been forced; some seven thousand pounds' worth of negotiable securities had been taken. How negotiable they were Miss Brown could have told them, for a month after the robbery she received bank-notes to their full value, with a line of writing which ran:

"A present from Horace."

Which was curious, because she knew nobody named "Horace."

Chapter 8: The End of Mr. Bash—The Brutal

"Bash" was really clever. He stood out from all other criminals in this respect. For the ranks of wrongdoers are made up of mental deficients—stupid men who invent nothing but lies. They are what the brilliant Mr. Coe calls in American "jail bugs". The English criminal, because he does not dope, becomes a pitiable and whining creature who demands charity, and the American criminal develops into a potential homicide.

Bash was a constant, but not, in the eyes of the law, an habitual criminal. He had never been charged because he had never been caught. He was an expert safe-breaker and worked alone.

He might have been forgiven, and, indeed, admired by scientific and disinterested students of criminology for his burglaries, for he had none of the nasty habits of part-time burglars, which means that he was never in the blue funk that they were. But Bash earned his name of infamy from a practice which neither police nor public ever forgave. He was never content to work with the knowledge that there was a watchman sleeping peaceably on the premises he was supposed to guard.

He would first seek out the unfortunate man, and, with a short and flexible life-preserver, beat him to insensibility. The same happened to several unhappy servants. He spared neither man nor woman. He had suspected of doing worse than bludgeon, but no complaint had been made public.

It was Inspector Mander who suggested that Bash was a name by which one Henry Arthur Milton might be identified. He developed his thesis with great skill but little logic, and Mr. Bliss, on whom the interesting theories were tried, listened with a face that betrayed none of the emotions he felt.

"He has got the same methods as The Ringer; in many ways he has the same identity—nobody knows him——"

"He may be Count Pujoski," suggested Bliss.

"Who is he?" asked Mander, interested.

"I don't know—nobody knows. There isn't such a person," said Bliss calmly. "If the fact that you don't know two people proves that you know one means anything, how much easier it is not to know three!"

Mander pondered this, having no sense of humour.

"I don't see how——" he began.

"Get on with your funny story," said Bliss.

But Mr. Mander had run short of arguments.

"I often wonder why you don't write a pantomime (Bliss could be foully offensive) or a children's play! The Ringer! Good God!" All his contempt was comprehended in that pious ejaculation.

"The only connection I see," said Bliss, "is the possible connection between The Ringer and our bashing friend. The newspapers have got hold of the story of what happened to Colonel Milden's parlour maid, and that is the sort of thing that will make The Ringer see red. If he isn't too busy putting the world right in other directions and he gives his mind to Mr. Bash, we shall be saved a lot of trouble."

Bliss had discovered by painful experience that The Ringer had extraordinary sources of information; it was pretty certain that he was, in some role or other, in the closest touch with the great underworld of London. It was equally certain that none of the men he employed had the least idea of his identity.

There was a reward offered for his capture, and the average criminal would sell his own brother at a price—especially if he were certain that no kick was coming from the associates of the man betrayed.

Who was Bash? At least a dozen men in London must know—the

receivers who fenced his stolen property, close confidants who had at some time or other worked with him. But these would never tell.

There were times when Superintendent Bliss sighed for the good old days of the rack and the thumb-screw. What they would not squeak to the police, however, they might very well tell to a "sure-man".

★★★★★★

In Penbury Road, Hampstead, was a small detached house with a tiny garden forecourt and a narrow strip of garden behind. Here dwelt Mr. Sanford Hickler, a man of thirty-five, athletic, sandy-haired, slightly bald. He was both arty and crafty, and his house in Hampstead was full of arty and crafty objects—ancient dower chests that might have dated back to the Middle Ages and certainly came from the Midlands.

Mr. Hickler had greeny wallpaper and yellowy candlesticks, and his study was littered with junk that he called "pieces". Some of these pieces he had picked up in Italy, and some he had picked up in Greece; most of them would hardly be picked up at all. And there were a few maternity homes for the *lepidoptera* family hanging on the wall, which were distinguished by the name of tapestry.

Mr. Hickler's hobby was literature. He was a graduate of a famous university, and he knew literature to be something that was no longer manufactured. He studied literature as one studies a dead language or the ruins of Ur. It did not belong to today. With the passing of the years his mind had broadened. He had come to the place where the works of the late Mr. Anthony Trollope were literature.

He was sitting one evening reading the sonnets of Shakespeare when there was a knock at the door, and his maid, who was also his cook, came in. She had just put on the brown uniform and the coffee-coloured cap and apron which were the visible evidence of her transition.

"A Mrs. Something or other to see you, sir. She came in a car."

Mr. Hickler put down his sonnets. "Mrs. Something or other came in a car? What does she want?"

"I don't know, sir—she said it's about books."

"Show her into the drawing-room," he said. A great many boring people went to see Mr. Hickler about books. He had a local reputation as a poetaster.

"Very good."

He put a slip of paper to mark his place in the volume he had been reading, and went up the short, narrow passage to the tiny room, more arty and crafty than any of the others, since it was furnished with one settle, a spinet, two Medici prints, and a rush carpet. And there he saw a figure that was out of all harmony with the aesthetic surroundings. The lady was big, squat, and old-fashioned; a more revolting figure he never hoped to see. Her hair was obviously dyed; a large and fashionable hat sat at a large and unfashionable angle over her spurious locks. Her face was powdered a dead white, and she exhaled a perfume that made Mr. Hickler shudder.

The modishness of her headgear was discounted somewhat by the length of her skirt and the antiquity of her fur coat.

"No, thank you, I won't sit down," she said in a shrill voice. "You're Mr. Hickler? Will you see this for me, please?"

He took the book she offered to him in her large, gloved hand, and saw at a glance that it was a veritable treasure—the very rare Commentaries of Messer Aglapino, the Venetian. Turning the leaves reverently, he peered down at the print, for the lights in his house were so shaded that it hardly seemed worthwhile to have lights at all.

"Yes, madam, this is a very rare book—probably worth three or four hundred pounds. I envy you our possession."

He handed the book back with a courteous little bow.

"Mrs.——?"

"Mrs. Hubert Verity. You probably know our family. They are Shropshire people. I only wish my nephew was Shropshire in spirit as well as in birth."

She raised her black eyebrows and closed her eyes. Evidently her nephew was not especially popular.

"Won't you sit down?" he asked.

She shook her head.

"I prefer to stand."

Her high-pitched voice was very painful to the sensitive ears of Mr. Hickler.

"I don't know why I should trouble you with my affairs; but I never could stand a miser, and Gordon is a miser. My dear husband was thoroughly deceived by him or he would never have left him thirty thousand pounds, which was quite as much as, if not more than, he left me.

"I've had a lot of misfortune owing to these terrible Stock Exchange people who tell you shares are going up when they're really going down—and well they know it! And when I went to my nephew today to ask him for a trifling loan—I must put The Cedars in a state of repair, with dear Alfred coming back from South Africa in the spring—he showed me his pass-book!

"I could have laughed if I wasn't so enraged. I said to him: 'My dear boy, do you imagine that I am a fool? Do you think I don't know you well enough to know that you keep your money fluid, like the miser that you are!' It was a dreadful thing to call one's own nephew, but Gordon Stourven deserves every word. I could tell the Income Tax Commissioners a few things about Gordon."

She tossed her grotesque head and simpered meaningly. And then she looked at the book.

"Three hundred pounds . . . .and I want the money very badly. I suppose you wouldn't like to buy it?"

The book was worth five hundred at least, but Mr. Hickler hesitated. His inclination was to buy; his sense of discretion told him to temporise.

"I am not in a position now to buy the book," he said, "but if you would give me the first offer, perhaps I could take your name and address."

She gave the name of her house in Kensington.

"I shall be out of town until next Wednesday week. I go to Paris for my dresses."

She said this importantly, and Mr. Hickler did not laugh.

"I like you: you're businesslike. If Gordon Stourven had half your straightforwardness life would be ever so much more enjoyable. That man is so mean that he will not have a telephone in his office. I said to him: 'My dear boy, do you imagine I'm coming through this horrible city to Bucklersbury and climbing to the top floor of a wretched office building just to see you?' In fact, I offered to pay for the telephone myself . . . . "

★★★★★★

Mr. Hickler listened, apparently without interest; and later accompanied the lady as she waddled to her car. She insisted upon leaving the book behind, and for this concession he was grateful.

He waited till the car had disappeared and then he went back to the house, closed the door, and took the volume into his sitting-room, turning the pages idly. Somebody had been looking through it that very day: there was a bookmark—a credit slip from the Guaranty Trust, of that day's date, and it showed the exchange of a draft for 180,000 dollars into English currency.

Mr. Hickler turned the slip over and over. The book had been in the possession of Mr. Gordon Stourven; and here was Mr. Gordon

Stourven's name scribbled in pencil on the top of the slip. A man who dabbled in cash finance, obviously, and a wealthy man. It was all very interesting, all very foreign to the art and the craft and the aestheticism in which Mr. Hickler lived his normal life.

The next day business took him to the City, and he drove down in the cheap little car that he permitted himself—the car that has its hundred-thousand duplicates up and down the land. There were two blocks of offices in Bucklersbury, but the first he entered was the one he sought.

Mr. Gordon Stourven's name was painted in black on one of the many opalescent slides that filled an indicator. He lived on the fifth floor and his number was 979. Mr. Hickler took the elevator, toiled down the long corridor, and after a while stopped before a door on the glass panel of which was "Gordon Stourven", and, in smaller characters at the bottom left-hand corner:

"The Vaal Heights Gold Mining Syndicate.

The Leefontein Deeps.

United American Finance Syndicate."

Since the panel also announced that this was the general office, he turned the handle and stepped in.

An L-shaped counter formed a sort of lobby, in which he waited until his tapping on its surface brought a bespectacled and unprepossessing young lady.

"Mr. Stourven's out," she said promptly and hoarsely. "He's gone to lunch with his aunt."

Mr. Hickler smiled faintly.

"I had better wait and see him," he said, and held up a little parcel. "This book is the property of the lady and I wish to return it."

She looked at him for a long time before she decided to lift the flap of the counter and invite him across the linoleum-covered floor to a small inner office. She pulled a chair from the wall.

"You'd better sit down," she said jerkily. "I don't know whether I'm doing right—I've only been at this place for two days. The young lady before me got sacked for pinching—I mean stealing—I mean taking a penny-halfpenny stamp. You wouldn't think anybody would be so mean, would you? But she was—he told me himself! And he's worth thousands. I'm going myself today."

"I'm sorry to hear that," smiled Mr. Hickler.

"I'm only staying to oblige him," explained the bespectacled girl. "He mislaid his keys this morning and the way he went on to me about it was a positive disgrace. Why should I pinch anything out of his old safe?"

★★★★★★

Hickler did not encourage conversation. He very badly wished to be left alone. Presently his desire was gratified.

There was the safe, embedded in the wall. Curious, he mused, what faith even intelligent people have in five sides of masonry! It was an American safe that grew unfashionable, except among the burglaring classes, twenty years before. He examined it thoughtfully. Two holes drilled, one below and one above the lock. . . . even that wasn't necessary. A three-way key adjustment would open that in a quarter of an hour.

He stepped to the door softly and looked through a glass-panelled circle in the opaque glass. The girl was at her desk, writing laboriously, her mouth moving up and down with every figure she wrote. He put his hand in his hip pocket and took out his little cosh—a leather-plaited life-preserver.

The girl could be dealt with very expeditiously; but the danger was too great. Stourven might return at any moment. He took another and a closer scrutiny of the safe and smiled. Then he went to the desk and examined the memoranda and the papers.

The only thing that really interested him was the carbon sheet of a type-written letter—and a letter so badly typewritten that he guessed it was the work of the disgruntled young lady with spectacles. It was addressed to a Broad Street Trust Company and bore that day's date.

> Dear Mr, Lein,—I am prepared to close the deal tomorrow and will meet you at your lawyer's as arranged, I do not agree with you that I have a great bargain. The property must be developed—it seems to have fallen into a pretty bad state of disrepair. In the circumstances I do not think that £18,700 is a very attractive price. However, I never go back on my word, I quite understand that lawyers require cash payments, and in any circumstances my cheque wouldn't be of much use to you, for I keep a very small balance at the bank.

Mr. Hickler replaced the letter carefully where he had found it. He had not removed his gloves since he left his house. It was a peculiarity of Mr. Hickler that he never removed his gloves except in his own home. People thought it was because he had been nicely brought up, but that was not the reason.

He went into the outer office, still carrying the book.

"By the way, I don't think you should have invited me into Mr. Stourven's private office. If I were you, I shouldn't say you took me there." He smiled benignantly at her.

Yes, he was glad he didn't have to tackle this bespectacled imbecile. She looked like one of those thin-skulled people with whom one might easily have an accident; and she was wiry and vital—the sort of shrimp who, if one didn't get her at the first crack, would scream and raise hell.

On his way downstairs he stopped to inquire at the janitor's office whether there were any offices to let and what were the services. The janitor told him.

"By the way, what time do the cleaners start their operations?" he asked.

This was rather an important matter. The hours the office cleaners arrived and left very often determined an operation.

They came on at midnight, explained the porter. So many of the offices were let to stockbrokers, who in the busy season worked very late. There were two entrances to the building; the other was an automatic lift, which tenants could operate themselves, the general elevator going out of action at 9 p.m.

All this Mr. Hickler learned, and more. There were two offices to let in the basement. The porter very kindly took him down and flattered them to their face.

"No, sir, I go off at six, but we've got a night man on duty. We have to do that because we've a great deal of property and money in this building. One of our tenants, Mr. Stourven, was asking me that very question this morning. He's only been here a fortnight himself—he came from somewhere down in Moorgate. A very nervous gentleman he is too." The porter smiled at the recollection.

Mr. Hickler, who was paying the closest attention to the accommodation of the offices, explained that he thought of founding a small literary society in the City for clerks who, in the hours so crudely devoted to the mastication of beef-steak pudding, might enrich their souls with an acquaintance with the *soufflés* of Keats.

The porter thought it was a very good idea. He did not know who Keats was, but had a dim notion that he was the gentleman who had found a method of destroying beetles and other noxious friends of the pestologist.

★★★★★★

257

The little car went back to Hampstead at a slow rate, was garaged in the tiny shed at the end of the garden before Mr. Hickler went into his house, stripped his gloves and gave his mind to the evening's occupation.

He was clever, very clever, because he devoted thought to his trade. He applied to a "transaction" such as tonight's the same minute care, the same thought, the same close analysis as he gave to a disputed and obscure line of one of the earlier English poets.

Nobody knew very much about him; nobody guessed why he had called his tiny cottage "The Plume of Feathers". Even the bronze ornament above the knocker on his door, representing, as it did, such a feathery plume, did not explain his eccentricity.

Yet the name of his house was one of the most careless mistakes he ever committed, and if there had been the remotest suspicion attached to him, if Scotland Yard had been even aware of his existence, the Plume of Feathers would have been illuminating—for it is the name of an inn immediately facing Dartmoor Prison, an inn towards which Mr. Hickler had often cast wistful eyes on his way to the prison fields.

He was not Mr. Hickler then; he was just plain James Connor, doing seven years' penal servitude for robbery with assault, to which sentence had been added a flogging, which he never forgot.

He was prison librarian for some time; cultivated his fine taste in *belles lettres* with the grey-backed volumes of the prison library. Only two men in London knew of his connection with that dreadful period of inaction. One of them, as Bliss rightly surmised, was the greatest of the fences—great because he had never betrayed a client and had never been arrested by the police.

Mr. Hickler expected a telephone call concerning the book, but it did not come. At half-past seven he put a small suitcase and a rough, heavy overcoat in the back of his car, and drove by way of Holloway to the Epping Forest road. Here, in seclusion, he made a rapid change of clothes; drove back to Whitechapel, where he garaged the car, and made his way to Bucklersbury on foot.

The only evidence that the activity of the human hive was slackening was discoverable in the fact that one of the two doors which closed each entrance was already shut. He awaited his opportunity, stepped briskly into the deserted passage, found the automatic lift, and went up to the top floor. The corridor here was, except for one lamp, in darkness. There was no light in any of the offices, and that was a great relief.

258

Mr. Stourven's outer door was, of course, locked, but only for about three minutes. By that time Mr. Hickler was inside and had shot the bolt. He did not attempt to put on the lights, preferring the use of his own hand-lamp.

Both the outer office and the inner office were empty. He made a quick examination of the cupboards, tried the windows—he was free from all possibility of interruption.

Setting his lamp on the floor, he took the remainder of his tools from his pocket and set to work on the safe—the easiest thing he had ever attempted. In twenty-five minutes, the key he had inserted some thirty times gripped the wards of the lock. It went back with a snap. He turned the brass handle and pulled open the heavy door of the safe.

He was on his knees, peering into the interior. He had scarcely time to realise that the safe was empty except for thousands of fragments of thin glass before he fell forward, striking his head on the edge of the safe.

★★★★★★

Bliss had a letter. It was delivered by a district messenger, and he knew it was from The Ringer before he opened it. It came to him at his private residence.

You will find our friend Bash in office No. 979, Greek House, Bucklersbury. He is, I should imagine, quite dead, so he will not be able to tell you how splendid an actor I am. I went to see him at his artistic little place in Hampstead—my most difficult feat, for I had to keep my knees bent all the time I was talking to him in order to simulate dumpiness. You should try that some time.

I persuaded him to burgle a safe in my office. Inside the safe I smashed, just before I closed the door, a large tube of the deadliest gas known to science. I will call it X.3 and you will probably know what it is. It was then in liquid form, but, of course, volatilised immediately to a terrific volume.

And the moment he opened the door he was dead, I should imagine, but you might make sure. And you had better take a gas mask. You are too good a man to lose.

There was no signature but a postscript.

Or why not send Mander without a gas mask?

Chapter 9: The Complete Vampire

There was a skid on the road out of St. Mary Church which, since it came before no court and involved no drawing of plans for the further bewilderment of a dazed jury, need not be described in too great detail.

It is sufficient to say that motorcar A took a hairpin turn at thirty-five miles an hour, saw motorcar B proceeding in the opposite direction at about the same pace, and swerved to avoid a collision, both cars being on the wrong side of the road, but A being more on the wrong side than B.

Dropping all alphabetical anonymity, the Hon. Mr. Bayford St. Main's car kept its balance and suffered no harm, but the other waltzed round in its own length, turned turtle into an over-flooded ditch, and its one occupant would most certainly have been drowned if Bay had not had the wit and the muscle to effect a rescue. His strength was as the strength of ten, not because his heart was pure, but because he was terribly exhilarated over his engagement, and even more exhilarated as a result of a lunch he had had with his rather parsimonious father at Torquay.

"Go easy with that Napoleon brandy, my boy! That cost me a hundred and eighty shillings a bottle—and I only got it as a special favour from a *maître d'hôtel* at Monte Carlo."

"Everybody does," said Bay.

Straddling the ditch, he lifted the car sufficiently to allow the imprisoned man to escape.

"Dreadfully sorry—I don't know whose fault it was," said Bay with great politeness. The victim smiled weakly.

"Lots of people have predicted various ends for me," he said, "but nobody suggested that I should die in a ditch."

He was—he announced this with rather ridiculous pomposity—Marksen, the explorer.

"Good Lord!" said Bay, in tones of awe.

He had never heard of Marksen the explorer, but he knew exactly the tone that the moist man expected.

"I'd better take you back to Babbacombe in my car," he began, but at this point the gardener came on the scene. He and his mistress had witnessed the accident from the crest of the high bank which was in the main the real cause of the accident.

"If you'll come up to the house, sir, madam will telephone to Babbacombe to a garage and you'll be able to dry yourself."

Mr. Marksen agreed gratefully, but the tall young man who had overturned him insisted upon returning to the nearest point of civilisation to obtain the necessary breakdown gang. They shook hands soberly at the foot of the stone steps which led from the roadway to madam's invisible demesne.

"I hate to say the trite thing, but you've saved my life—undoubtedly," said Mr. Marksen, whose dignity nothing could ruffle. "To think of the perils I have endured, the dangers I have passed, and then to find myself in a Devonshire ditch . . . ."

"Yes, yes; deuced awkward," replied Bay hastily. He had a wholesome dread of scenes.

"Someday I shall be able to repay you, Mr. St. Main," said Marksen.

He followed the gardener into beautifully-ordered grounds. There were close-cropped lawns and flower beds ablaze with the joyous banners of spring, and a red-roofed little house, just as picturesque as a modern house can be when it is masquerading as an old house. Here was a very stately lady of sixty who wore silk mittens, a white cap, and on the bosom of her black alpaca dress, a large ornament which was cameo on the one side and a hand-painted photograph on the other.

It was a beautifully furnished little house, and when Mr. Marksen had enjoyed a hot bath and had attired himself in the brand-new suit of the gardener (rashly purchased for the funeral of an aunt who took a turn for the better the day the clothes were delivered), Mrs. Reville Ross (this was the name of his hostess) conducted him from room to room, exhibiting her treasures with immodest pride.

There were certain incongruous features which Mr. Marksen could not fail to observe. A cheap crayon enlargement of a cheaper kind of photograph seemed out of place in the sunny drawing-room.

"My dear husband," said Mrs. Ross proudly. "He was killed on the railway but was insured. My daughter." She turned the big cameo to reveal the highly coloured portrait of a pretty girl of sixteen. "You must have heard of her." She mentioned the name of a famous American cinema star. "English!" said Mrs. Ross in triumph. "Everybody thinks she's American. She'd lose her job if it was known she was Betty Ross. I've got a piece of newspaper somewhere—American newspaper—where she says she's never been to England. She comes over secretly every year to stay with me for a month. She worships me, that girl. She bought this house—I got my own servant, shooter, gardener, car—everything. Nothing's too good for me."

261

Mr. Marksen listened and was interested. He had been interested ever since he had heard the old lady speak in the good old English of Limehouse and realised that the chatelaine of the pseudo-Elizabethan house was not all that she appeared to be.

Coincidences belong to real life rather than to fiction, and there are three coincidences in this story—one of which does not count; the gardener's name was Fate—Herbert Arthur Fate.

Superintendent Bliss, of Scotland Yard, might have fashioned a poem on this odd fact.

★★★★★★

Nobody would suspect Mr. Bliss of poetical leanings, yet in truth he was, if not a student, a lover of the more robust forms of poetry.

He invariably referred to Louise Makala as "the lady called Lou," and on two occasions had spoken with her for the good of her soul. Louise was not easily impressed, less readily scared: Superintendent Bliss certainly did not frighten her—she regarded him as a bore, thought once that he was on the sentimental side, and attacked him on that flank, only to, discover that what she had thought was mush was really a rigid sense of decency.

Lou had a flat in Grosvenor Street, a magnificent apartment, with an impressive approach. She had a butler and a couple of footmen; a night and a day chauffeur; a cottage in the country which bore the same resemblance to a cottage as a hunting-box bears to a tin of sardines; a flat in the Etoile, and a small house in Leicestershire where she kept half a dozen hunters. She was the most beautiful creature that Bliss and the majority of men had ever seen—to have seen her was the principal experience of any man's day, and her occupation in life, reducible to modern terms, was vampire. Her victims were many and they were all immensely rich. She did not select them: they did their own selection.

"Who is that lady?" asked the Honourable George Cestein of the hotel porter at Felles Hotel.

The hotel porter told him she was Miss Blenhardt, that her father was a very rich Australian, and that she had, at the moment, the best suite at the hotel.

The Honourable George followed her from the hotel and picked up the glove, handkerchief, or whatever it was she dropped, and within twenty-four hours . . . .

"Either you sign a cheque for twenty thousand pounds or I will scream and send for the police."

George had no more than kissed her, but why, oh why, had he chosen his own private suite at the Margravine Hotel for this attention? He stared at her horrified. Her dress was torn, her hair dishevelled —but these artistic touches were her very own handiwork. George raved but made a quick decision. Louise's own maid put in an appearance. The open cheque was signed and cashed, George threatening to go immediately to Scotland Yard. She had heard such threats before, would hear them again. The substantial fact was a roll of notes valued at £20,000.

★★★★★★

The first time she met Bliss she had a moment of panic, but it did not last very long. "Do you know Sir Roland Perfenn?" he asked her sternly. And she laughed. For Sir Roland is a Privy Councillor and a great ecclesiastical lawyer, and he was the last person in the world to bear evidence of his very heavy loss.

"Does he say I do?" she asked coolly, and of course Bliss would have to say "No" to that.

"It has come to my notice . . . ." he began, and told the story of the all-too-gallant Sir Roland.

"Produce your Sir Roland, dear my Mr. Bliss," she said. "It is a fairly simple matter—if I remember rightly, his name is in the Telephone Directory."

But Bliss was not in a position to accept her advice. He could, however, talk to her like a father.

"So far you've only caught men who dare not squeal and who would rather pay than look foolish. But sooner or later you'll catch a man who looks like a gentleman and talks like one—but isn't! And you'll go to the Old Bailey, and when the Judge asks what is known about this woman, I shall step up on to the witness stand and say 'This lady is a notorious blackmailer,' and you'll go down for twenty years."

She only laughed.

"When a general loses a battle he's finished," she said, "and if a lion-tamer makes a mistake he's mauled … and, Mr. Bliss, if you pull that one about the pitcher going often to the well, I'll scream for help! No—if I make a mistake I'll pay. But I shan't make a mistake. Will you have a cocktail?"

Bliss smiled grimly and shook his head. She was sitting on the arm of a big and expensively covered settee, and she drooped her head on one side and into her fine eyes came a quizzical smile.

"Instead of warning me you ought to ask my help," she said. "I think I'm the only person in London who could catch The Ringer for you!"

Bliss winced at this: he thought the remark a little indelicate in view of The Ringer's more recent success.

"Mind that he does not catch you!" seemed a feeble retort in the circumstances, but she did not gloat over the weakness of his *tu quoque.*

"The Ringer! Good heavens! If Scotland Yard was officered by women he would have been caught years ago! I wish he would try me—look!"

She went to the fireplace and produced something from no-where—she did not trust him sufficiently to show him the tiny marble-faced door of the wall cupboard.

"Have you a licence for that pistol?" asked Bliss professionally, and she laughed.

"Don't be silly! Of course, I have! And I can use it! I really did live in Australia for two years—I was married to an imitation squatter. He had *delirium tremens* for six months in the year and was recovering the other six. We lived on a lonely station and I was taught gun work by a man who had killed three policemen in the State of Nevada. If I give you The Ringer what do I get—a medal?"

He shook his head.

"It will stand in your favour when you come in front of a Judge," he said.

Lou was very amused.

She made her big mistake six months after this conversation. It was in the matter of "Bay" St. Main—who was young and harum-scarum, and was, as we know, engaged to be married to Rendlesham's youngest and richest daughter. Let us do justice to Bay—when he was invited to a convenient snuggery to take tea with this beautiful chance acquaintance, he had no more in his mind than the possibility of a thrilling lark. He had the vanity of a normal young man, which meant that he was vainer than the average woman; and that this lovely creature should so readily succumb to the kind and admiring glances he shot at her was distinctly flattering.

Quite a number of people thought that the tall, fair-haired and classical-featured Bay was immensely wealthy. His father was worth a million, but his father liked to see his money stay home with him. Bayford's allowance was absurdly small—he realised very clearly that the chance of his father's helping him honour a cheque for fifteen thousand pounds was a poor one.

As a matter of fact, he didn't really think at all; he was in that condition of horror and shock which inhibits thought. He could stare, pale-faced, at this lovely being in her self-made dishevelment, and when he did speak his words were ludicrously inadequate.

"Why, you—nasty creature!" he squeaked. "I didn't! I just kissed you. I think you're foul to—to make such a suggestion—I really do!"

Louise had no more regard for youthful horror than for middle-aged vituperation. She stated her terms for the second time.

"Fifteen thousand? I haven't got fifteen thousand pence———"

And then he remembered and gasped. That morning his father-in-law-to-be had placed to his credit exactly that sum. Bay was buying a partnership in an underwriting business—thirty thousand was the purchase price. Pa St. Main's half was to come on the morrow. Bay was to hold a one-third interest of the whole. Louise had very accurate information about the financial standing of her cases.

"Don't talk nonsense," she said. "I know your credit to a penny. You have over sixteen thousand in the Piccadilly branch of the Western Bank."

It was now that Bay St. Main's brain began to function, and he reviewed dismally the possible items of embarrassment. Item No. 1 was St. Main Senior, who already leaned towards devoting his fortune to the establishment of Sailors' Institutes—he had in his early youth served before the mast. Item No. 2 was Lord Rendlesham, a High Churchman who virtuously deplored the laxity of the age. Item No. 3 was Inez Rendlesham, very lovely and austere and intolerant of vulgarity. It was difficult to discover any expression of popular activity, from cross-word puzzles to shingling, that did not come into that category.

And, thinking, Mr. St. Main grew paler and paler.

Eventually he signed the cheque and waited, imprisoned with the enchantress, until the money was drawn. During that time, he told her incoherently what he thought of such women as she. Lou, who had heard everything that could be said on the subject much more eloquently put —Sir Ronald had once moved the Court of Arches to tears—listened and did not listen.

She was too bored to tell him just what was her point of view. She could have recited her formulae without thinking. Men are born robbers, unscrupulous, remorseless, pitiless. She stood for avenging womanhood. Men must pay sometimes. *Etcetera*. What she did say was:

"Yours is a sad case—you might apply to the police or you might find The Ringer and tell him all about it. I'd love to meet him."

Which was very foolish of her.

The time came for the return of the maid and his release. He hurled at her one tremulous malediction, but he did not invent the fiction that he was a close personal friend of the chief commissioner. For this she was frankly grateful.

★★★★★★

Mr. Bayford St. Main went out into the busy street and walked aimlessly, unconsciously westward. To whom should the news be broken? To his father? He closed his eyes and shuddered at the thought. To Rendlesham? Picturing Miss Rendlesham's comments, he had a vision of a broken icicle—irregular and frigid lengths of speech, cold, cutting-edged.

His mind searched frantically for rich relations, for wealthy and philanthropic friends. There was nobody in the wide world to whom he could appeal.

"Why—Mr. St. Main, I declare!"

Bay had turned and blinked owlishly at the man who had laid an almost affectionate hand on his arm.

"Hallo .... Mr.—um—eh—Marksen, of course." Bay gripped at the murmured reminder, though who Mr. Marksen was—"Oh, yes, the—um—I hope you weren't fearfully ill after that car business?"

He made an instant appraisement of his companion. Mr. Marksen might be very rich—some of these exploring johnnies are: they find buried cities and unbury them, and dig up all sorts of gold things. Unless, of course, they go exploring the North Pole, when they have to be supported by public subscriptions. He looked rather like that kind in his well-worn golf suit, his foul and massive briar pipe, his gold-rimmed spectacles, and little yellow moustache. He had grown the last since they last met, thought Bay. Here, however, he was wrong. Mr. Marksen had the moustache before the accident, but had lost it in the ditch—and his spectacles.

"I could have sworn I saw you coming out of Lethley Court. I used to have a friend who lived in that hotel, and somebody was telling me the other day that—um—quite a notorious—um—person lived there. A lady called .... well, well, well, it is no business of mine."

Bay looked at his companion aghast.

"A—a lady?" he stammered.

"More or less," said Mr. Marksen, "more or less. A friend of mine got into serious trouble over—um—a perfectly innocent folly, and I

266

was able to help him; but you couldn't be interested——"

Bay was more than interested—he was enthralled. "Come round to my flat, will you?" he asked urgently.

Mr. Marksen looked at his watch and hesitated before he said "Yes."

★★★★★★

Remember always that Bliss spoke the truth when he said that The Ringer did not merely dress, but lived the part he played.

His insatiable curiosity had brought him on to the track of the lady called Lou. He had been standing within six feet of the entrance to the Lethley Court Hotel when Lou and her victim had driven up, but not being quite sure of the method, had missed the maid when she went out to cash the cheque. There was no question at all in his mind when, eventually, Bay had staggered out of the hotel with a face the colour of chalk. Curiously enough, it was only then that he recognised his rescuer. Perhaps Bay's face was that colour after he had fished a brother motorist from beneath an overturned car.

Bay had his apartment near Bury Street, and the man in the golf suit strode by his side, smoking his big pipe furiously, and spoke no word until they were alone in the sitting-room which looks out upon Ryder Street.

"I'm going to tell you something," said Bay with a desperate effort to be philosophical. "I've been fearfully, badly caught—naturally, you'll think I'm a fearful cad and all that sort of thing, but I swear to you that I hadn't any idea of anything—you know what I mean?"

Happily, Mr. Marksen knew what he meant, otherwise, from the disjointed narrative which followed, he might have gained only the scrappiest idea of what Mr. Bayford St. Main rightly described as his fearful predicament.

"Fifteen thousand—humph!" said Marksen. "And the money isn't yours? Do you mind if I say 'humph' again? I don't know what it means, but it seems the correct thing to say. Anyway, I will get the money back."

Bay gaped at him.

"How? .... when?"

"I'll ask her for it; the cheque will come to you tonight."

Mr. St. Main did not believe him.

"You need not worry about whether the cheque will be honoured or not —it will be," said Mr. Marksen thoughtfully. "The only doubt I have in my mind is whether she has an heroic streak. You wouldn't be able to tell me much about that. If she has that slither of theatrical heroism in her make-up, everything may be deucedly complicated. However . . . . did she say anything when you were rude to her?"

Bay tried to think.

"Yes—she said I might apply to that johnny who is always doing something ghastly—The Ringer, that was the feller! She said she'd love to meet him."

"Dear me," said Mr. Marksen, shocked. "Whatever will she say next?"

He ambled out without a word of farewell. Bay was not in a condition to protest at his abrupt exit.

★★★★★★

The lady called Lou rarely left her Grosvenor Street flat after dinner. The theatres and the fashionable restaurants knew her not. Invariably she dined at home, sometimes alone, sometimes with one she had marked for treatment. The vanity of men! Seldom did a victim tell his dearest friend of his experience. There was an occasion when she had caught in successive weeks two close friends neither of whom was aware of the other's misfortune.

This night she had dined alone, and had retired to her beautiful little drawing-room to draw cheques and to examine accounts. Her overhead bill was a heavy one. There was the flat and an apartment very occasionally used, but which was sometimes very handy.

She was, by the ordinary tests, a strictly proper lady. Her "cases" might call her blackmailer—they could not truthfully call her worse. She was businesslike, cool-blooded, and a shrewd investor in real estate; never drank, seldom smoked, and certainly never gambled. So methodical was she that when the second footman came into the room and announced that the Marquis de Crevitte-Soligny was waiting in the little sitting-room, she was thrown off her balance, and consulted her engagement book with a puzzled expression.

"The Marquis de Crevitte—? Show him in, Bennett."

He might be a friend of a friend; the visit a consequence of an enthusiastic description.

She did not know the tall, white-haired man with the trim, grey moustache, who bowed over her hand. He was handsome, tall, soldierly, and in the lapel of his faultless evening coat was the red rosette of an *officier*.

"Madame does not remember me?" he asked in French.

She shook her head. "I ask a thousand pardons, but I do not, *Monsier le Marquis*."

"Good!"

This time he spoke in English, turned slowly and, walking to the door, locked it with great deliberation.

In an instant she was at the fireplace, the marble-faced cupboard swung open, but before her hand could close on the butt of the automatic——

"Don't touch that. I am covering you with an ugly little pistol that fires shot—it would not kill you, but it would make such alterations to your face that you would be compelled to go out of business. Turn!"

She turned, empty-handed.

"Who are you?" she asked, and she saw him smile.

"I am the man you expressed a desire to meet—The Ringer!"

She stared at him incredulously.

"The Ringer? That's a wig, is it?"

He nodded. "Sit down, sister brigand! You caught a young friend of mine today for fifteen thousand pounds."

Not a muscle of her face moved.

"I'm afraid you're talking about something that I do not—understand—" she began.

He laughed softly and laid the squat pistol on the table, drew up a chair, and sat down.

"This is going to be a longer business than I thought, Mrs, Rosler."

Now he had got beneath her guard, for he saw her wince.

"I'm not blaming you for preying on naughty-minded men. You deserve all that they lose. You choose them with such care that I can only admire you——"

There was a knock. The Ringer moved silently to the door and as silently turned the key.

"Come in," said Lou breathlessly. Pink spots burnt in her two cheeks —there was a light in her eyes that stood for triumph. It was Bennett, the footman.

"Mr. Bliss, madam."

She looked at The Ringer steadily; he was standing by the table, his hand hiding the pistol.

"Show him up," she said steadily.

Before he could speak the door was opened wider; evidently Bliss was on the landing waiting. He glanced from the girl to the immaculate-looking foreigner.

"I can see you later, Miss Makala—it isn't very important."

"But no," protested The Ringer. "It is I who am *de trop*."

269

"You can wait where you are." Her voice was hard. She stood now close enough to the half-closed cupboard door to reach for the gun, when Bliss crossed between them.

The Ringer shrugged his shoulders delicately. "I am in the way, but it does not matter—this gentleman is——?"

"Inspector Bliss, of Scotland Yard!"

The Ringer inclined his head.

"An extraordinary coincidence! You shall advise me, Inspector. In Devonshire there is an old lady who lives in a nice house—but she is under the impression that her daughter is Miss Stella Maris, the famous cinema star! And her daughter is no such person! Now should one leave the poor lady in her illusion? Or should one say to her: 'No, madam—your daughter is . . . . whatever she is'?"

Lou's face was whiter than any of her victims had been; the hand that came to her quivering lips shook perceptibly.

"I don't know exactly that I am concerned," said Bliss brusquely; and then to Lou, lowering his voice: "I can get my business over in a minute, Miss Makala. Have you ever met a man named Marksen?"

He described Mr. Marksen even as she was shaking her head.

"We believe it is The Ringer—he has been making inquiries about you, and every description we have had is the same. Do you know any private detective of that name?"

"No," she said.

Bliss turned to scrutinise the other occupant of the room. That gentleman was gazing at himself in a mirror, gently smoothing his moustache.

"Who is this gentleman?" he asked.

She cleared her voice.

"The Marquis de Crevitte-Soligny," she said in a low tone. "I have known him for years."

Bliss stayed only long enough to give her instructions as to what she must do if Mr. Marksen called. She listened with apparent absorption.

They heard the street door close on the detective.

"Now," said The Ringer cheerfully, "I want you to draw a cheque for fifteen thousand pounds payable to Bayford St. Main."

"And if I don't——?" she challenged.

He smiled in her face.

"I shall go and tell your mother what a naughty girl you are," he said softly, "and that her darling daughter, so far from being a rich cin-

270

ema star, is a low little vamp—and that, I think, would hurt her more than the death of her dear husband."

He was watching for the effect of this piece of mimicry and saw her face go livid and the fires of hell come into her eyes.

"Don't insult my dear mother!" she breathed.

And then he knew that he had won—he had discovered where the blackmailer could be blackmailed.

★★★★★★

"Lou's gone out of business," reported Bliss. "She's sold up her flats and gone to live in Devonshire somewhere. I'll bet The Ringer scared her!"

He had: but not in the way Mr. Bliss thought.

Chapter 10: The Swiss Head Waiter

There was a broad streak of altruism in the composition of Henry Arthur Milton, whose other name was The Ringer. There was, perhaps, as big a streak of sheer impishness. At Scotland Yard they banked on his vanity as being the most likely cause to bring him to ruin, and they pointed out how often he had shown his instant readiness to resent some slight to himself. But Inspector Bliss, who had made a study of the man, could not be prevailed upon to endorse this view.

"He chooses the jobs where his name has been used in vain because they give him a personal interest," he said; "but the personal interest is subsidiary."

It was never quite clear whether the Travelling Circus offended through the careless talk of "Doc" Morane or whether there was an unknown and more vital reason for the events at Arcy-sur-Rhône.

Now, as a rule, systematic breakers of the law are so busy with their own affairs that they do not bother their heads about the operation, much less speak slightingly of their own kind. But the Travelling Circus were kings in their sphere, and were superior to the rules which govern lesser crooks. There were three of them: Lijah Hollander, Grab Sitford, and Lee Morane. Li was little and old, a wizened man. Grab was tall and hearty, a bluff, white-haired man, who was, according to his own account, a farmer from Alberta. "Doc" Morane was a tough looker, broad and unprepossessing, ill-mannered. Whether he had ever been anything but a doctor of cards nobody knew or cared.

The Doc was the leader of the gang and had a definite part to play. Little Li Hollander supplied one gentle element, Grab the other; it was the Doc who got rough at the first suggestion of a victim that the game was not straight. Mr. Bliss had expressed the view before that The Ringer controlled the best intelligence department in Europe; apparently, he should have included the Western Ocean.

★★★★★★

The s.s. *Romantic* was sixteen hours from Southampton and the smoke-room was almost empty, for the hour was midnight and wise passengers had gone early to bed, knowing that they would be awakened at dawn by the donkey engines hoisting passengers' baggage into the tender at Cherbourg. A few of the unwise had spent the evening playing poker, and among these was a newspaper man who had been to New York to study the methods of Transatlantic criminals—he was the crime reporter of an important London newspaper. He was a loser of forty pounds before he realised exactly what he was up against, and then he sat out and watched. When the last flushed victim had gone to bed, he had a few words to say to the terrifying Doc and his pained associates.

"Forty pounds, and you can give it back tonight. I don't mind paying for my experience, but I hate paying in money."

"See here,"—began the Doc overpoweringly.

"I'm seeing here all right," said the imperturbable scribe: "that's been my occupation all the evening. I saw you palm four decks and it was cleverly done. Now do you mind doing a bit of see—here? There's a Yard man comes on board at daybreak. I'm the crime reporter of the *Megaphone*, and I can give you more trouble than a menagerie of performing fleas. Forty hard-earned pounds—thanks."

The Doc passed the notes across and, dropping for the moment his role of bully-in-chief, ordered the drinks.

"You've got a wrong idea about us, but we bear no malice," he said when the drinks came. "The way you were going on I thought you might be that Ringer guy!" he chuckled amiably. "Listen—if The Ringer worked in the State of New York he'd have been framed years ago. He tried to put a bluff on me once, but I called him. That's a fact—am I right, Grab?"

Grab nodded.

"Surely," he said.

The report of this conversation was the only evidence Bliss had that there was any old grudge between The Ringer and the Circus. Very naturally he could not know of the subsequent conversation on the Col de Midi.

"No, I never met him—we had a sort of 'phone talk. I was staying at the Astoria in London," the Doc went on, his dead-looking face puckered in a smile. "If I'd met him, I don't think there would have been any doubt about what'd have happened—eh, Grab?"

The white-haired Grab agreed. He was a living confirmation of all that the Doc asserted, guessed, believed, or theorised.

That was about the whole of the conversation. The Circus left the boat at Cherbourg and travelled south, for this was the season when rich Englishmen leave their native land and go forth in search of the sun. Doc and his friends lingered awhile in Paris, then took separate trains for Nice. Here they stayed in different hotels, packed up a parcel of money which had once been the exclusive property of a bloated Brazilian, missed Monte Carlo—Monte does not countenance competition—and went, by way of Cannes and San Remo, to Milan. Milan drew blank, but there are four easy routes into Switzerland.

"There's a new place up the Rhône Valley full of money," said Doc. "They threw up two new hotels last fall, and they've opened a new bob run that's dangerous to life and limb. The Anglo-Saxon race are sleeping on billiard tables and parking their cash in their pockets."

★★★★★★

A week later . . . .

"Mr. Pilking" came into the Hotel Ristol, stamping his boots to rid them of the snow, for a blizzard was sweeping down the Rhône Valley and the one street of the little village of Arcy-sur-Rhone was a white chasm through which even the sleighs came with difficulty.

He was a big, florid man, red-faced, white-haired, and he wore a skiing suit of blue water-proofed cloth. He had left his skis leaning against the porch of the hotel, but he still carried his long ash sticks.

Mr. Pilking stopped at the desk of the *concierge* to collect his post, and clumped through the wide lounge to his room. His post was not a heavy one; the guests at the hotel knew him as a business man with large Midland and Northern interests; not even on his holidays could he spare himself, he often said—but his post was very light.

Arcy-sur-Rhône is not a fashionable winter resort. It lies on a shelf of rock, a few thousand feet above the Rhône Valley, and is not sufficiently high to ensure snow, but at an elevation which appeals to people whose hearts are affected by higher altitudes. There is generally a big and select party at the Ristol in January, for Arcy has qualities which not even St. Moritz can rival. The view across the Lake of Geneva is superb, the hotel is so comfortable that its high charges are tolerable, and it can add to its attractions the fact that in all its history

273

it had never consciously harboured an undesirable in the more serious sense of the word. The skiing was good, the bob run one of the best in Switzerland; it enjoyed more than its share of snow, and the hotel notice-boards were never disfigured with that hateful notice *Patinage Fermé.*

★★★★★★

As to whether or not Mr. Sam Welks was altogether desirable, there were several opinions. He was a stoutish man who wore plus-fours all day, never dressed for dinner, talked loudly on all occasions, and was oracular to an offensive degree. Mr. Pilking saw him out of the corner of his eye as he passed. He was standing with his back to a pillar, his waving hands glittering in the light of the electroliers—for Mr. Welks wore diamond rings without shame.

". . . . Gimme London! You can say what you like about scenery and that sort of muck, but where's a better scene than the Embankment on a spring day, eh? You can 'ave your Parises an' Berlins an' Viennas; you can 'ave Venice an' Rome. Take it from me, London's got 'em skinned to death, as the Yankees say. An' New York . . . .! Why, I've made more money in London in a week than some of them so-called millionaires have made in a month o' Sundays! There's more money to be made in dear old London . . . ."

He always talked about money. The dark-haired head waiter, who spoke all languages, used to listen and smile quietly to himself, for he knew London as well as any man. The head waiter was new to Arcysur-Rhône; he had only been a week in the place, but he knew every guest in the hotel. He had arrived the same day as Mr. Pilking and his two friends who were waiting for him in his ornate sitting-room.

Doc Morane looked up as Grab came clumping into the room.

"Look at Grab!" he said admiringly. "Gee! I've got to go play that she-ing game—I was a whale at it when I was a kid. Maybe, I'll take Sam out and give him a lesson!"

Old Li Hollander, nodding over an out-of-date visitors' list, woke up and poured himself a glass of ice water.

"We're dining with that Sam Welks man tonight, Grab," he said. "I roped him into a game of bowls after lunch, and he wanted to bet a hundred dollars a game. I could have beaten him fifty, but thought I'd give him a sweetener. That man's clever!"

The Doc was helping himself to whisky.

"I like a clever guy," he said, "but I don't like head waiters who remind me of somebody I've seen before."

Grab looked at his leader sharply.

"All head waiters look that way," he said. "Maybe we've seen him somewhere. These birds travel from hotel to hotel according to the season. Do you remember that guy in Seattle, Doc, the feller you had a fight with when you were running around with Louise Poudalski?"

★★★★★★

The Doc made a little face. The one person in the world he never wished to be reminded about was Louise Poudalski, and if there was a memory in that episode which grated on him, it was the night in a little Seattle hotel when a German floor waiter had intervened to save Louise from the chastisement which, by the Doc's code—even his drunken code, for he was considerably pickled on that occasion—she deserved. He often used to wonder what had happened to Louise. He had heard about her years ago when he was in New York—she was keeping house for a Chinaman in New Jersey, or was it New Orleans?

"Louise," said Li reminiscently, "was one of the prettiest girls——"

"Shut up about Louise," snarled the Doc. "Are we sweetening this Welks man tonight or are we giving him the axe?"

Grab was for sweetening; but then, in matters of strategy, Grab was always wrong. Li thought that Sam Welks was a "oncer".

"These clever fellows always are. Let 'em win, and they stuff the money into their wallet and tell you they know just when to stop, and that the time to give up playing is when you are on the right side. Soak him tonight and maybe you'll get him tomorrow. The right time to watch a weasel is the first time."

Doc Morane agreed, and Li, dusting the cigar ash from his waistcoat and brushing his thin locks, went down in search of the sacrifice.

Mr. Welks was talking. There seldom was a moment when he was not talking; and Li saw, hovering in the background, the new head waiter, a tall, dark man with a heavy black moustache.

Mr. Welks was in a truculent mood. The manager of the hotel, in the politest possible terms and with infinite tact, had suggested that it would be a graceful compliment to the other guests if he conformed to the ridiculous habit of dressing for dinner.

"Swank!" Mr. Welks was saying to his small and youthful audience—the young people of the hotel got quite a lot of amusement out of studying Mr. Welks at first hand in preparation for giving life-like imitations of him after supper.

"It's what the Socialists call being class-conscious. It's the only thing I have ever agreed with the Socialists about. I have lived in Ley-

275

tonstone for twenty-three years man and boy, and I have never dressed for dinner expect when I have been going out to swell parties—why should I here, when I am out on an 'oliday? It's preposterous! I pay twenty shillings in the pound wherever I go. I am paying seventy-five *francs* a day for my soot, and if I can't dress as I like I'll find another hotel. I told this manager—I'm John Blunt. What's the idea of it? Why should I get myself up like a blooming waiter?"

Mr. Hollander thought he saw a faint smile on the face of the head waiter, though apparently, he was not listening to the conversation.

"That's my view entirely," said Li. "If I want to dress, I dress; if I don't want to dress, I don't dress."

"Exactly," said Mr. Welks, kindling towards his supporter.

★★★★★★

Li took him by the arm and led him to the bar.

"If there's going to be any fuss, I'm with you," he said. "And that gentleman, Mr. Pilking, a very nice man indeed, although an American (Li was born in Cincinnati) he holds the same opinion."

They drank together, and Mr. Welks gratefully accepted the invitation, extemporised on the spur of the moment, that he should dine in Mr. Pilking's private room that night.

The Doc and Pilking strolled providentially into the bar to confirm this arrangement, and for an hour the conversation was mainly about Mr. Welks, his building and contractor's business, the money he made during the war, the terrible things that happened to competitors who did not profit by Mr. Welks's example, his distaste of all snobbery and swank, his clever controversies with the Board of Trade, and such other subjects as were, to Mr. Welks, of national interest.

It was after he had drifted off that a curious thing happened which was a little disquieting. The three shared in common a sitting-room, out of which opened on the one side Grab's bedroom and on the other side the Doc's. Li had his bedroom a little farther removed. The Doc went up to his room to make a few necessary preparations for the dinner and the little game which was to follow. He pushed down the lever handle of the sitting-room door, but it did not yield, and at that moment he heard the sound of a chair being overturned. There should have been a light in the sitting-room, but when he stooped to look through the keyhole there was complete darkness.

He went along to the door of his own bedroom and tried that. This, too, was bolted on the inside. The Doc retraced his footsteps to Pilking's room. Here he had better luck. The door was unfastened, and he entered, switching on the light. The door communicating between the bedroom and the sitting-room was wide open. He went in, turned the switch, and walked to the door, which, to his surprise, he found unbolted. He passed through the door leading to his own bedroom, and here he had a similar experience, the door opening readily.

There was no sign of an intruder, no evidence that anything had been disturbed. If the chair had been overturned it had been set on its feet again. He opened the door of the long cupboard, which might conceal an intruder, but save for his clothes suspended on hangers, it was empty.

Returning through the sitting-room, he went out into the corridor. As he did so he saw a man come, apparently from the stairs, stand for a moment as if in doubt, and then, catching sight of the Doc, turn swiftly and disappear—not, however, before Doc Morane had recognised the dark-haired headwaiter.

★★★★★★

Very thoughtfully he returned to his apartment and made another search. Nothing, so far as he could see, had been disturbed. He locked the doors and opened a suitcase which stood on a small pedestal. There must have been over a hundred packs of cards in that case, each fastened with a rubber band and each representing half an hour's intensive arrangement. These had no appearance of having been disturbed. He relocked the grip and went slowly back to his companions, and at the earliest opportunity told them what had happened.

"Somebody was in the room," he said, "and I pretty well know who that somebody was."

Elijah was obviously worried.

"Maybe that waiter is an hotel 'tec," he said. "Up at St. Moritz the Federal people sent a couple of 'tecs into one of the hotels and pinched the Mosser crowd."

Mr. Sam Welks did not go to his host's room that night unprepared for the little game that was to follow. It was Li who had suggested it. "Mr. Pilking was not particularly keen," he said. He didn't like playing for money; one wasn't sure if the people who lost could really afford to lose.

The talkative Sam had bridled at the suggestion—this was over cocktails before dinner.

"Speakin' for meself," he said, "I don't worry about people losin'. If they can't afford to lose, they shouldn't play. That foreign-lookin' waiter feller had the nerve to tell me not to play cards with strangers.

I told him to mind his own business. I never heard such cheek in my life! If anybody can catch me, good luck to 'em! But they couldn't. I've met some of the cleverest crooks in London, an' they've all had a cut at me."

He chuckled at the thought.

"Bless your life! When a man's knocked about in the world as I have it takes a clever feller to best him. See what I mean? It's an instinct with me, knowin' the wrong 'uns. I remember once when I was stayin' at Margate . . . ."

They let him talk, but each of the three was thinking furiously. It was Doc Morane who put their thoughts into words.

"That waiter was frisking the apartment," he said, "and that means no good to anybody. We'll skin this rabbit and get away tomorrow if he looks like squealing——"

"He'll not squeal," said the saintly Li, who was the psychologist of the party. "He wouldn't admit he'd been had. The most he'll do is to ask for a No. 2 *séance*, but I'm all for getting while the road's good. This is going to be one large killing!"

★★★★★★

The dinner in the little *salon* was a great success. Grab, who was something of a gourmet, had ordered it with every care.

Under the mellowing influence of '15 Steinberger Cabinet, Mr. Welks grew expansive. He wore his noisiest plus-fours, and, as a further gesture of defiance against the conventions, a soft-collared shirt of purple silk.

"You've got to take me as I am," he said, "as other people have done before. I don't put on side and I don't expect other people to. My 'ome in Leytonstone is Liberty 'All-I don't ask people who their fathers was—were. I could have been a knight if I'd wanted to be, but that kind of thing doesn't appeal to me. Titles—bah!"

The time came when the dinner table was wheeled out into the corridor and a green-covered table was brought into the centre of the room. Again Mr. Pilking made his conventional protest.

"I don't like playing for money. Although I know you two gentlemen, I don't know Mr. Welks, and I've always made a rule never to play with strangers."

He said this probably a hundred times a year, and it never failed to provoke the marked victim.

"Look here, mister," said Welks hotly, "if my money's not good enough for you, you needn't play! If it comes to that, I don't know you. Money talks—hear mine!"

He thrust his hands into his pockets and took out a thick roll of Swiss bills, and from a pocket cunningly placed on the inside of his plus-fours, a thicker wad of Bank of England notes.

"The Swiss are milles—which means a thousand—an' these good old English notes are for a hundred. Now let's see yours!"

With a perfect assumption of hesitancy, Mr. Puking produced a goodly pile and his companions followed suit.

For the first quarter of an hour the luck went in the direction of Mr. Welks—which was the usual method of the Travelling Circus.

Unseen by any. Doc Morane "palmed" a new pack. The substitution was made all the easier by the fact that Welks was separating the larger from the smaller notes which represented his inconsiderable winnings.

"Cut," said the Doc, offering the pack.

"Run 'em," replied Mr. Welks, professionally.

★★★★★★

Something went wrong with the hand. Welks should have held four queens and the Doc four kings. These latter appeared in Doc Morane's hand all right, and the betting began.

Li threw in his hand when the bidding reached six hundred pounds. Grab retired at eight hundred. The Doc brought the bidding to a thousand.

"And two hundred," said Mr. Welks recklessly.

Doc Morane made a rapid calculation. This man was good for a few thousands if he was gentled.

"I'll see you," he said, and nearly collapsed when the triumphant Mr. Welks laid down four aces.

Li took the pack from the table, and with a lightning movement dropped it to his lap as he slipped a new pack into its place. Li was the cleverest of all broad-men at this trick.

"Run 'em," said the Doc as the pack was offered to him.

This time there could be no mistake. The four knaves came to him, and he knew by Li's nod and Grab's yawn that they each held one ace, king and queen. Mr. Welks drew two cards-which was exactly the number he should have drawn. The Doc knew that he now held two kings and three tens.

They bid up to eight hundred, which was more than any sane man would bet on a "full house."

"I'll see you," growled Doc Morane.

Mr. Welks laid down a small straight flush.

"You'll have to take a cheque," said the Doc when he recovered.

"I'll take the cash you've got and a cheque for the rest," said Welks. He was a picture of fatuous joy. "I'm a business man, old boy, but I know something about poker, eh?"

That ended the party; they were too clever not to accept his invitation to the bar for a celebration. The three went upstairs together and Doc Morane locked the salon door.

"Somebody was in here before dinner, planting new decks of cards," he said. "Did you lamp that head waiter? I'll fix that bird!"

"What are we going to do?" asked Li fretfully. "Do we get or stay?"

"We're not leaving till we get that money and more," said Grab savagely. "What do you say, Doc?"

Doc Morane nodded. "Me an' Welks are like brothers," he said, significantly. "We're going she-ing on the Midi slopes tomorrow morning, and I'll hook him for tonight. You fellows stay home and fix those cards."

★★★★★★

A little railway carried a small and cold party to the skiing fields early the next morning. Because the upper stretches of the line were snowed under the party descended on the Col de Midi, which is a razor-backed ridge which mounts steeply up to the precipice face of the Midi Massif.

Mr. Welks was no mean exponent of the art, and led his companion up the snowy slopes. And all the time he sang loudly and untunefully the vulgar song of the moment.

The head waiter had not been in the train. Once or twice the Doc looked round to make sure. He saw a Swiss guide signalling frantically, but nobody seemed coming their way, and when Mr. Welks pulled up after an hour's laborious climb they were alone.

"You're not a good skier, my friend," he said pleasantly.

The Doc wiped his perspiring forehead and growled something.

"A little farther," said Mr. Welks, and went on.

The Doc noticed that he went tenderly along the crest of a snowy cornice, but did not understand why until he had passed and, looking back, saw that they had passed a snowy bridge over a deep chasm.

"Dangerous, eh?" Mr. Welks smiled gleefully. "You can take off your skis."

"Why?" asked the Doc, frowning.

"Because I ask you."

The Doc took off his skis: he invariably did what he was told to when the teller covered him with a Browning pistol.

Mr. Welks lifted the skis and threw them into the chasm.

"On the other side of this ridge is Italy," he said pleasantly. "That is where I am going. What will happen to you I don't know. It is impossible to walk back. Perhaps the headwaiter—who is the best detective in Switzerland—will rescue you. He was going to arrest you, anyway. By the way, it was I who planted the cards last night."

"Who are you?" The Doc's white face was whiter yet.

Mr. Welks smiled.

"My wife had a little friend in Seattle-one Louise Poudalski. Remember her?"

Before Doc Morane could reply, The Ringer was flying down the Italian slope, his skis raising snow like steam . . . .

Chapter 11: The Escape of Mr. Bliss

There was an incident on the Oxford and Henley Road, which may be recorded as a matter of interest, since it marked the introduction of Superintendent Bliss to Silas Maginnis.

Mr. Bliss, who was (despite certain poetical tendencies) a great realist, always believed that the name "Silas" was the imagining of story-writers. All his life he had never met a human being who bore such a name; never once had he written "Silas" on any charge sheet.

Naturally, he knew that Silas Maginnis had arrived in the neighbourhood. The ruined chapel of Chapel-Stanstead, a veritable Norman relic which, to the discredit of the county, had been allowed to fall into decay, was now made whole, thanks to the generosity of an American philanthropist—and to a variety of other causes.

It had stood in a swampy marsh, but when the Wollingford Brick Company had begun operations on an adjoining property, and the Wollingford District Council had made certain improvements to the banking of a little river which ran through the shallow valley of Wollingford, the land became automatically drained, and there stood high and dry the four walls of the chapel, a couple of arches intact and eight little pillars.

Said the vicar of Wollingford: "You should see the chapel, Mr. Bliss: it is rather beautiful, and I don't suppose that it cost more than a thousand to restore. Mr. Mountford—he's the American who paid for the restoration—has fixed up a caretaker who is almost as interesting as the chapel! My curate is holding a service there next Sunday. Go along and see the chapel—and Silas!"

But Superintendent Bliss was not a churchman. He went to Wollingford at week-ends solely for the purpose of recreation.

He liked to spend his weekends out of town. He had a cottage between Oxford and Newbury and some forty-five acres of indifferent land which he inherited from an aunt. In addition, he had the shooting rights over a couple of hundred acres. This latter cost him no more than a gun licence, for the owner of the shoot was a wealthy and grateful man to whom Bliss had once rendered a very important service.

On Saturday mornings the detective could be seen, with a gun under his arm and a lurcher at his heels, loafing along likely hedges, a pipe between his bearded lips and an ancient and battered hat on the back of his head. Here he touched a new life and found new interests which helped to dispel the cobwebs with which his drab work at Scotland Yard encumbered his brain.

Sometimes he met the vicar of Wollingford, an elderly man but a deadly shot, and occasionally he foregathered with Mr. Selby-Grout, a middle-aged man who had recently acquired Wollingford Hall and the lordship of the manor. He was a taciturn man of fifty, grey-haired and heavy-moustached, whose principal occupation in life was shooting.

Sometimes, as they sat in the pale spring sunlight discussing lunch, Bliss would talk of his work, and if the question of Mr. X arose it was because a foreign bank in which Mr. Selby-Grout had an interest had been victimised.

The lord of the manor was rather scornful on the subject of restored chapels.

"It's a pity these damned Americans haven't something better to do with their money," he growled. "I haven't seen the church, but the other day I saw the half-witted verger, or sexton, or whatever he is . . . . He has Church Cottage—the Yankee bought that, too. Silas something. Have a look at him. He's madder than the Yankee who put him there."

A week after this Mr. Bliss met Silas Maginnis.

★★★★★★

Mr. Mander strolled into his chief's office on the following Friday afternoon, and he took with him an elaborately drawn map of England and a brand new theory about The Ringer.

The day being what it was, Mr. Bliss had no desire to read maps or examine theories; his little car was waiting in the courtyard, and, in addition to a suitcase in which he had packed the newest book that a subscription library could supply, the car carried a market basket in which was packed a weekend's supply of provisions.

Being independent of trains and time-tables, he settled down with resignation to listen.

"Fire ahead, but keep it short," he said.

Inspector Mander spread the map.

"For three months nothing has been heard or seen of The Ringer," he said impressively. "My view is that he is still in England——"

"Your view is probably supported by the fact that I had a letter from him yesterday. I seem to remember that I told you," said Bliss wearily. "I presume that all these crosses in black ink are intended to show the scenes of his activities, and the crosses in red ink where he is most likely to appear next."

"They are all near a railway station——" began Mr. Mander, anxious to avert the demolition of his "theory."

"Everything is near a railway station in England," said his superior coldly.

He glanced at the map, and was irritably amused to note that a certain village in Oxfordshire bore an extra large red cross.

"Why Wollingford?" he asked.

Here Mr. Mander could elaborate his theory.

"You have had three letters from him recently," he said, with the deliberation of one who is revealing a great discovery. "One was posted in the Paddington district, one was posted at Reading, one was posted at Cheltenham. I have been studying these postmarks very carefully, and I have compared them with a timetable. They all coincide with the theory that this man is operating from somewhere near Oxford."

Bliss glanced at the figures on the sheet of paper which his subordinate placed before him. It was true that he had received three letters written by the portable typewriter which was part of The Ringer's baggage.

One had warned him about the impending departure of a gentleman who had swindled a very large number of shareholders, and who was packing his bag to catch the Air Mail when Bliss descended on him; another was a sympathetic inquiry after the health of the superintendent, who had been knocked over in Whitehall by a motor-lorry without any serious damage; and the third bore reference to some statement attributed to Bliss in connection with one of The Ringer's most daring exploits—"a statement which I am sure that a man with your peculiar sense of fairness could not have made," said the writer politely.

And, since all the documents in the case of The Ringer went automatically to Inspector Mander, he had seen these three letters, and, less from their contents than their superscription, had evolved his great idea.

Bliss pushed the note back and shook his head.

"Your time-table tells me nothing except that you are most industrious when you are pursuing dud clues," he said crushingly. But it took a lot to crush Mr. Mander.

★★★★★★

At the moment Scotland Yard was less interested in The Ringer than in a gang which was engaged in the forging and uttering of letters of credit on an extensive scale.

The master criminal is supposed to be a figment of the novelist's imagination-and usually he is; but somewhere in England was a brilliant criminal who, with the aid of a small printing press, was literally coining money.

Complaints had flowed into Scotland Yard for eighteen months: they came from places as far apart as Constantinople and Stockholm. Twice, the agents of Mr. X. had been caught, but the police were unable to trace the head of the business, except that all the evidence pointed to the fact that he operated from England and worked through a super-agent in Paris.

Bliss was thinking of Mr. X. as his little car sped down the Great West Road. There had come to him that week the faintest hint of a whisper that one Elizabeth Hineshaft might lead him to the forger; but Elizabeth, when she was interviewed at Holloway Prison, had shown no enthusiastic desire to offer information. She was rather a pretty woman, and he knew no more of her friendships than that she had many.

She ran with Bossy Clewsher, a great organiser of spieling clubs, who had made more than a fortune out of high-class gambling hells in Mayfair and Regent's Park, and would have made another when he opened a similar club in the very heart of the West End if it had not been for the activities of Bliss.

He arrested Bossy one unpleasant night and took Elizabeth in the same net. Unfortunately for this lady, she was in possession of a small portfolio—it was between overlay and mattress.

It is rather difficult to explain what that portfolio contained, or how she came to possess it. One does not wish to cast reflections upon the character of under-secretaries of State, especially middle-aged under-secretaries who ought to have known better. She was a very attractive girl, and even budding statesmen do incomprehensively stupid things.

There would have been no harm in it if the papers in the portfolio were plans of a new submarine fleet or a scheme for attacking the Russian fleet, or such things as are usually stolen in stories.

The documents actually contained in that flat leather wallet were letters written by the leaders of two parties dealing with a possible fusion of party interests. Mr. Z was the intermediary and had been promised Cabinet rank if he pulled off the deal, so that when he discovered his loss, he was not unnaturally agitated. His advertisement:

LOST: Probably in a taxicab between Birdcage Walk and Maida Vale, a red leather portfolio containing papers of no value to anybody but the owner, etc.

—appeared in every newspaper.

★★★★★★

Mr. Bliss found the portfolio and unwittingly became involved in the highest kind of politics.

Lawbreakers are not severely punished for stealing Cabinet secrets, and it is quite possible that Elizabeth might never have had that particular piece of stealing brought up against her. Only, with the portfolio was found a flat case containing a large number of small phials containing a narcotic favoured by drug addicts, and, with this evidence that she had a fairly large clientele.

She was an old offender, though young in years. There were seven distinct counts to her indictment, and when these were supported by a record of five convictions her sentence was inevitable. She was sent down for the term of five years, and when somebody in the public gallery heard the Judge deliver judgment he burst into tears.

"Find the weeper," said Bliss after this had been reported to him; but the quest was unsuccessful.

The whisperers of the underworld hinted in their vague way that Elizabeth was well beloved. She certainly lived in the style of one who had unlimited sources of income; her jewels were worth thousands, and her flat was furnished regardless of cost.

If you ask why, in these circumstances, she bothered her head to peddle dope, there is this reply: that criminals are all a little mad. Did not the notorious Al Finney, with twenty thousand in the bank, go down to the shades for a cheap swindle that could not have netted him more than fifty pounds?

★★★★★★

Bliss was musing on these queer inconsistencies when his car drew up at a small garage on the outskirts of Colnbrook. He invariably stopped here for a week-end supply of petrol. The garage keeper knew him and came out with a letter in his hand.

"It was left here an hour ago," he said.

"For me?" demanded Bliss in surprise, and then, when he saw the typewritten envelope: "Who left this?"

The man did not know. He had found the note stuck to the door with a glass-headed pin, such as photographers use to hang up films.

He tore open the letter. It consisted of six typewritten lines:

Take the Reading road. It is a long way round, but safer. I don't know exactly what they are preparing for you, but it is something unpleasant. And I don't want you to die.

The Ringer! There was no doubt about that typewriting. Bliss smiled grimly. So Mander had been more or less right. The Ringer's headquarters were somewhere in this neighbourhood.

When his petrol tank was filled and three extra tins loaded into the back, he resumed his journey. West of Maidenhead he had two alternative routes: he could pass through Henley; he could follow the main road to Reading, as The Ringer advised. He chose Henley and whatever danger lay beyond.

It was quite dark now, and, clear of Henley town, he switched on his headlights, stopped the car, and, taking an automatic from his handbag, laid it on the seat beside him.

Wollingford lies off the main road. He came to the place where he had to turn and slowed down. Invariably he came this way. The road was narrow and for a mile was between high hedges. Presently his headlamps revealed the little Norman chapel, and in its shadow the tiny cottage where the "crazy" caretaker lived. He passed this, followed the sharp turn of the lane, and then suddenly his foot went down on the brake.

Standing in the middle of the road, and in the glare of the headlamps, was a figure with outstretched arms. Bliss stared at the twisted face, the wide eyes, the foolishly-smiling mouth, and his hand dropped to his gun. For a second, he experienced a little thrill of apprehension, but the man was unarmed.

"What do you want?" he demanded, and stepped down from the car.

The stupid face contorted into a leering smile. "He told me to stop you, master ... the big man on the bicycle. He took me from my cottage and said, 'Stand there and stop him.'"

His voice was uncannily shrill, and when he chuckled Bliss felt a cold shiver run down his spine.

"He came on a bicycle .... it made noises like a devil .... *bing-bang!* And he said, 'Stay there—I cannot cut the wire!'"

"The wire?"

The strange figure turned, and, pointing into the darkness, chuckled again.

Bliss found an electric torch and walked down the road. He had not far to go. A stout wire had been fastened across the road a few feet from the ground. It was just high enough to miss the little windscreen and catch the driver.

When he walked back to the car the mad-looking caretaker had vanished. Getting into the car, he backed it until he came to the caretaker's cottage, and, getting down, he knocked at the door. There was no answer. Bliss was puzzled and more than a little perturbed.

He drove on to where the wire was stretched, stopped long enough to cut it and throw the loose end over the hedge, and reached his own cottage a very thoughtful man.

He locked all the doors carefully before he retired and slept till late the following morning. Almost the first person he saw after breakfast was Mr. Selby-Grout. He was leaning over the cottage gate, a big pipe between his strong teeth, his gun resting against the gate.

"Hullo!" he boomed. "What about Henfield Wood?"

It was only then that Bliss remembered that he had accepted an invitation to shoot over the man's land.

On the way across the fields he related what had happened the previous night, and Mr. Selby-Grout listened with a frown.

"I should think the crazy brute put the wire there himself," he said. "I saw him this morning snooping round my house—in fact, he was in my library when I came down. How on earth he got there I don't know. He said he'd made a mistake and came through the wrong door. He often comes up to the house to beg food from the servants. By gad, there he is!"

Bliss turned his head and looked. They were nearing the plantation which was known as Henfield Wood, and he caught a glimpse of a figure disappearing behind a belt of bush.

"There he goes!"

A man was running across the open towards a cut road which formed a boundary to the property. Bliss saw him leap a low hedge and disappear, apparently into the earth.

"I'd like to take a shot at the devil!" growled the owner of the land.

It was some time before he recovered his equanimity. They walked a little way into the wood, and then both men loaded.

"I'll bet he's frightened away every feather of game," said Mr. Selby-Grout; and then, most unexpectedly: "Did you ever hear of a woman called Elizabeth Hineshaft?"

"Yes—I see you've been reading the newspapers," smiled Bliss. "I got her a term of penal servitude this week."

"Oh, you did, did you?"

Click!

It was the sound of a gun-hammer falling, but Bliss did not look round.

Click!

"What's wrong?"

Selby-Grout was staring at the gun in his hand. His face was white and streaming with perspiration; the hand that held the gun was shaking.

"I don't know . . . . that fellow rattled me," he said hoarsely.

He was trembling from head to foot.

"For God's sake, what is wrong with you?"

The man shook his head. "Let's go back."

They walked for a long time in complete silence.

"I'd give a lot of money to know if he is working with The Ringer," said Bliss, speaking his thoughts aloud.

The gun dropped from the nerveless hand of his companion. For a second, he swayed as though he were about to fall, and Bliss gripped him by the arm.

"The Ringer!" His breath came in gasps, " . . . . my library—he was there—chequebook on my table——!"

At eleven-thirty that morning a handsome-looking limousine drew up before the Leadenhall Street branch of the Western Counties Bank, and a man in the livery of a chauffeur interviewed the manager. He had a letter bearing the note-heading of Wollingford Hall.

The letter was written in Mr. Selby-Grout's characteristic handwriting. He needed thirty-three thousand pounds in cash. It was not unusual that Mr. Selby-Grout should make large withdrawals. The cheque which accompanied the letter was duly honoured.

The manager of the Western Counties afterwards remarked to his assistant that Mr. Selby-Grout's account was hardly worth keeping. No sooner did big sums come in than they were withdrawn. Subsequently he repeated this to Superintendent Bliss, and showed him some significant figures, but this was after Bliss returned to Scotland Yard and found a long typewritten letter awaiting him.

My dear Bliss,—

You are under a great obligation to me—twice have I saved your life! Honestly, I did think that your Mr. X. was waiting to shoot you on the Henley road. You see, I know all about his romantic love affair with Elizabeth.

I only discovered the wire too late to remove it. I guessed that he was staging a shooting accident; for a week he has been rehearsing that accidental shooting—holding his gun first one way and then another.

Eventually I think he decided to shoot you while the gun was under his arm. He became quite an adept at this method, and you will find certain trees in the wood simply peppered with shot.

So sure was I that I took a haversack full of dud cartridges with me this (Saturday) morning to his library—he keeps his guns and cartridges in that noble apartment—and made an exchange. Otherwise you would be dead.

I also borrowed a blank cheque—the notepaper I have had for a week.

Yes, I was the American who restored the chapel—by letter. I appointed myself caretaker. I had to live in the neighbourhood without exciting suspicion. I have been after Mr. X.—whose real name is Whotby—for the greater part of a year. You will find his printing press in his dressing-room.

Why do I betray my fellow criminal? Does dog eat dog, you ask? Alas! he does! It is for your dear sake that I give him away—your life is too precious to risk.

Think well of me, your benefactor.

P.S.—I should not have saved Mander.

Mr. Bliss was not as flattered by these gracious references to his life as he might have been. On the other hand, he agreed about Mander.

Chapter 12: The Man with the Beard

The trouble with Mr. Bliss, from the point of view of the Yard, was that he tried to do too much himself. He had, moreover, a furtive and secret method of working, consulted nobody, and seldom informed even his immediate superior that he was taking on some especial task until the moment was ripe for an arrest.

An example of his methods was the case of the brothers Steinford. London had become flooded with forged ten-shilling notes—ten-shilling notes being much easier to pass than the pound variety. He took the case himself, and immediately it vanished as a subject of discussion; when the conferences were called and the forged bills came up for examination. Bliss would content himself with saying: "Oh, yes, I'm seeing to that." No further comment was made.

He took a journey or two into the Midlands, went down into Wales, to interview a man serving a sentence, and, with his assistance, found a gentleman named Poggy, who kept a baked potato-can and lived in East Greenwich.

But the solution of the mystery was never revealed. Nobody was arrested, and when the forgery was mentioned in Mr. Mander's private office he would look at his sycophantic sergeant, and they would raise their eyebrows together and smile. All of which indicated a deep disparagement of Mr. Bliss and his methods.

In the Rowley murder case, it was the same. Bliss didn't bother to look for the tall, dark man who had been seen in the neighbourhood of Mr. Rowley's house, but scoured London to find an old carpet slipper, the fellow of that which had been left behind in the kitchen of Mr. Rowley's house on the night of the murder.

In this case, of course, he was successful; but, as Mr. Mander often said, it is the exception which proves the rule.

★★★★★★

There appeared in the pages of a popular weekly periodical an article entitled: "Can The Ringer Be Caught?" Its author was described as "the greatest living authority upon this super-criminal." His name was modestly withheld. It described certain exploits of Henry Arthur Milton, and dealt with the failure of those who were responsible for his capture. One passage ran:

There is no doubt that those engaged in the search are either stale or inefficient. Contemporaneously with his activities, a strange inertia seems to have settled on the officers in charge of the various cases.

Now, every man has his favourite word, and, the less literate he is, the more frequently it is employed. Mr. Bliss, who had read many reports written by the officer, knew that "contemporaneously" was a great pet with Inspector Mander. If he had a second fancy it was for "inertia", and these words occurred many times in the article.

He rang the bell, and the messenger came. "Ask Mr. Mander to see me, please," he said.

Inspector Mander arrived cheerfully, but at the sight of the periodical spread out on the superintendent's desk he changed colour.

"Have you read this article, Mander?"

Mr. Mander cleared his throat.

"No," he said boldly.

"An interesting one—you should take it home and study it," said the icy voice of Superintendent Bliss. "It is full of queer English, and is obviously written by a man who, in addition to being a fool and disloyal to his superiors, is also extremely illiterate."

Bliss did not look up, yet a furtive glance told him that Mr. Mander's face had gone a deep red.

"He says, amongst other things," Bliss went on, "that—well, I'll read it:

The Ringer is not so clever as people think he is. By a series of lucky chances, he has escaped detection; but, sooner or later, the one man at Scotland Yard whose name perhaps is less known to the public than the officer who is associated with The Ringer and his nefarious acts will bring him to justice.

"I gather from this rather involved sentence that there is a super-intelligence at Scotland Yard. Do you happen to know whose it is?"

"No," said Mander loudly.

Bliss folded the paper, picked it up, as though it were some noxious and evil-smelling thing, with the tips of his finger and thumb, and dropped it carefully into the wastepaper basket.

"It isn't the paper," he explained, "it's the article that makes me sick. I can only say that whoever wrote that article is a very bold man. It is a challenge to The Ringer, and I have never known him to ignore a challenge. I shall be interested to see if the writer is still alive at the end of next week because it contains some very rude references both to The Ringer's courage and his genius."

There was a silence, which, with an effort, Mr. Mander broke.

"Who do you think wrote it?" he asked, a little huskily.

Bliss shook his head. "Obviously an hysterical woman," he said icily, fished the periodical from the wastepaper basket, and handed it to his subordinate. "Read it—it will give you a laugh."

★★★★★★

There were, apparently, people who agreed with the writer of the article. Mr. Mander lived in Maida Vale, and it was his practice to travel home by Tube. Police-Constable Olivan, who stepped into the Tube compartment with him one night, was among the number. He grinned, touched his helmet, and, with an apology, sat down by the side of the inspector.

Mr. Mander was not averse from being saluted by policemen: he was one of those men who believe that detective-inspectors should carry a gold badge or something equally distinguishing, so that common individuals should not rub elbows with him without realising the honour his presence gave them.

"Do you mind if I smoke, sir?"

Police-Constable Olivan was obviously going off duty; he carried a rolled waterproof cape between his knees, and he took the liberty, after consulting the inspector, to light a clay pipe.

"Oh, yes, sir, I recognised you; I've seen you in several big cases," he said, a smile on his rubicund face. "It's a funny thing—I was only talking to our sergeant this morning about you, sir, if I might be so bold."

Mr. Mander inclined his head graciously to indicate that Police-Constable Olivan could be as bold as he liked, so long as the talk was complimentary.

"I read a bit in the paper—I forget the name of it—about this Ringer, and I said to my sergeant: 'I bet the gentleman that feller means is Mr. Mander.'"

"I haven't read the article, constable," said Mr. Mander.

"You ought to, sir," said the other earnestly. "It's the talk of our division. Do you know what I think, sir, if I might say so without being disrespectful to my superiors? I think a flat-footed policeman could catch that Ringer better than some of the people that's taken an 'and in it."

"I wouldn't say that," demurred Mr. Mander.

The constable nodded.

"Naturally you wouldn't, sir; I understand the police service very well. I've been twenty-three years a constable. They offered to make me a sergeant when I'd done seven years' street-duty, but I wouldn't look at it.

"I haven't got the education," he added explanatorily, "and I can't be bothered to go to school with a parcel of young policemen."

"So, you think that you could catch The Ringer, eh?"

Mander looked at the police officer with an amused smile.

"Good Lord, no, sir!" the man hastened to excuse himself. "All I say is that if I was assistant to a gentleman like you–somebody that gave me confidence–we'd run him to earth in a week–if you'll excuse my saying 'we'."

He took out his pipe, looked round the compartment as though to be sure that there was nobody near enough to hear him, and bending towards Mr. Mander, said in a low, confidential voice: "I don't mind telling you, sir, there's a man keeping a money-lender's business near where I live who might be The Ringer. He's only been in the place about two months; he's seldom at home, and when he does come home it's always at night."

"What does he look like?" asked Mander, interested.

"He's got a little beard, rather like Mr. Bliss, sir. I don't even know whether he's a money-lender. I know he's got the premises that old Isaacstein used to have: but there it is!"

Constable Olivan grew confidential about himself. He had been married seventeen years, and nobody had a better wife, unless, he added hastily, Mr. Mander was married. Mr. Mander denied that happy state.

It was easy to see that Police-Constable Olivan was tremendously interested in the high politics of the police force. Mander glowed under the enthusiastic admiration of his subordinate.

"If I'd had any sense," said the policeman, "I'd have gone into the C.I.D. years ago. It's too late now. It fairly makes me writhe when I see fellows getting away with it as they are every day. Look at those ten-shilling forgers: nothing's been done about it! In our division they say that there's going to be a lot of changes at Scotland Yard, and, with all due respect, sir, I think it's about time."

Mr. Mander thought so too.

"Where is this house where the mysterious Ringer lives?" he asked flippantly.

The constable drew a little plan on the palm of his hand.

"I'll ride on with you and take a look at the place," said Mr. Mander, and Olivan nearly dissolved with gratification.

"If any of my mates saw me with you, sir," he said humorously as they left the station, "it'd be a rare feather in my cap! But only two of our division live round here. It's hard to find a house . . . ."

As they trudged through the dark streets he enlarged upon every policeman's grievance, which is mainly confined to the question of pay and allowances.

They came at last to a narrow crescent, where houses stood shoulder to shoulder. They must have been built in the 'sixties, and they bore the unmistakable stamp of the 'sixty architects' atrocious minds. Flights of stone stairs led up to the front doors; there was a little narrow basement, protected by railings; and above the level reached by the stone stairs was another floor.

"That's my house." The police-constable pointed. "When I say it's my house, I mean I've got three rooms there." He thought a moment and added a kitchenette; he was evidently not a fast thinker. "If you'll come along, sir, I'll show you the other place."

Half-way along the crescent the houses were divided by a narrow lane, about wide enough to take the wheels of a cart.

"That's the house." He pointed to the corner premises. "And this is what always strikes me."

He led the way down the passage. On the right was a wall the height of a tall man's chin, and over this Mander commanded an uninterrupted view of a back garden. At the end of the garden was a solid-looking building which, Olivan explained, comprised the premises of a firm of electrical instrument makers, the entrance being in the street running parallel to the crescent.

Except for one window set upon an upper floor, the back of the premises which showed on to the garden of the mysterious stranger was black.

"See that window?" said Olivan impressively. "I'll tell you something about that, sir. I came home rather late one night, suffering from insomnia or indigestion, as the case may be, and I had a walk round and a smoke. I come along this very passage, and what do you think I saw? A ladder up to that window! That's funny, I thought. I didn't know that this fellow had moved into the house then. I continued my stroll, and when I come back the ladder wasn't there!"

He said this dramatically. Mr. Mander scratched his chin.

"Electrical instrument makers, eh?" he said thoughtfully. "I'd like to have a little private investigation here, constable. What time are you off duty tomorrow night?"

"Seven o'clock, sir. It's about eight by the time I get home."

"Could you meet me at the end of this street at half-past eight?" suggested Mander. "I don't want you to be in uniform—you understand?"

"Quite, sir," said the constable gravely. "You want the whole thing to be private."

"And I don't want you to mention the fact to any of your friends, your sergeant, or your inspector. In fact, this is a private matter between ourselves. If I pull off anything, you may be sure you won't be the loser."

"Very good, sir."

Constable Olivan saluted. He insisted upon walking with Mander back to the end of the street.

"There's a lot of bad characters around here, sir, and, although I know you're quite capable of looking after yourself, I shouldn't like anything unpleasant to happen in our neighbourhood." Which was very thoughtful of him.

★★★★★★

When Mander got to the office next morning he found Bliss had already arrived and had twice sent for him. With a little sinking of heart, his mind instantly flew to his ill-timed literary effort; but Superintendent Bliss had evidently forgotten all about that unhappy lapse.

"The Ringer is in London," he said. "I had a 'phone message from a call-box this morning, and, although I was able to locate the box in the Kingsland Road, I haven't been able to track the gentleman. I want to warn you."

Mr. Mander was startled.

"Warn me, sir? Why?"

"Because I have an idea that you are immediately concerned," said Bliss grimly. "If you feel you'd like to go after this gentleman, you're at perfect liberty to do so. I have a couple of cases which will occupy all my tune and probably take me out of town a good deal."

Mr. Mander smiled.

"I don't know that there's much to go on," he said. "A telephone message from the north of London doesn't give us a great deal of assistance."

Bliss looked up at the ceiling.

"I seem to remember reading an article in which the writer said that the big mistake they were making at Scotland Yard was in waiting for definite clues. I also seem to remember that there was some talk of anticipating The Ringer's movements and working out a theory as to what he would do next."

Mander coughed. "Yes, I read the article," he said awkwardly. "Nonsense, I call it."

"Damned nonsense, I should call it," said Bliss; and for a moment his subordinate hated him, for he loved that little article, the composition of which had occupied so much of his time.

He considered the matter all the morning. The telephone message had come from North London, and that fitted with Constable Olivan's theory. He might be wildly guessing; at the same time, luck runs in curious grooves, and who knew if that stolid man might not be the instrument for bringing Mander's name prominently before the world as the single-handed captor of The Ringer?

It was an old trick of The Ringer's, too, to call up Scotland Yard.

★★★★★★

When Mander met his new assistant that night he had half formulated a working theory.

Constable Olivan in mufti was less imposing than Constable Olivan in uniform. He wore a purplish suit, a silver watch-guard decorated with athletic medals, and on his feet a pair of white gymnasium shoes. "He's in the 'ouse, sir." Olivan was in a state of excitement.

"He come up in a taxicab and let himself in with a key. I'll tell you something, sir: I've been making a few inquiries in the neighbourhood, and that house is practically unfurnished.

"He's got one little bedroom where he sleeps, and all the other rooms are empty. They took old Isaacstein's money-lending sign away yesterday, so he's not in that business. Isaacstein was the fellow who was pinched for receiving about; two months ago."

They made their way to the passage and took up a position near the wall. After an hour their vigilance was rewarded. There came the click of a door opening, and presently Mr. Mander espied a dark figure stealing through the garden towards the building at the end. He waited some time, then heard a thud, like the sound of a door closing.

Ten minutes passed, and then Mander, with the assistance of the constable, climbed over the wall and went stealthily in the direction of the building.

There was nobody in sight. The man, whoever he was, had vanished, and after a little search Mander discovered where he had gone.

Near the wall of the instrument maker's little factory was a wooden trapdoor, and when Mander tried this he found it was unbolted. He peered down into the darkness, but could see and could certainly hear nothing. Replacing the trap, he returned to his companion.

"He may be just an ordinary burglar," he said. "I want to make sure before reporting."

He gave Olivan his private address and telephone number, and the constable volunteered to keep watch until two o'clock in the morning, after which, "nature being what it is," as he reluctantly confessed, he could not maintain the surveillance.

It was a little after eleven when Mr. Mander reached his home, and he had hardly entered the hall of the respectable boarding-house where he had his residence when the telephone bell rang.

"For you, Mr. Mander," said the landlady, bustling out from the sitting-room which she called an office.

Mander went in. It was Olivan's excited voice.

"Excuse me, sir. He come out of the house and I trailed him. He went to one of the public telephones in the street and I heard him call Victoria 7000—isn't that Scotland Yard?"

"Yes, yes," said Mander impatiently. "Did you hear what he said?"

"No, sir. He shut the door after he gave the number."

Mander thought quickly.

"Ring me up in ten minutes' time. I'm going to get on to the Yard."

In a few minutes he was connected with his own office, and after a little delay found somebody who could give him information.

"Yes, there's been a message through from The Ringer tonight. I don't know how genuine it was. I wrote it out and, as a matter of fact, I was just going to call you up to give it to you. I'll get it now."

"What was it about?" asked Mander impatiently. "Anyway, it doesn't matter, so long as you're sure it was from The Ringer. Do you know where the call came from?"

The officer in charge had taken the precaution of locating the message. It must have been the very box from which the spying Olivan had seen the man telephone.

In ten minutes, Constable Olivan came through.

"Wait for me," said Mander. "I'll pick you up near the wall. And listen, Olivan; don't mention this to a soul—not to anybody in the division, or to any police officer you meet or may know. . . ."

"Trust me, sir," said Olivan's reproachful voice.

★★★★★★

The taxicab that carried Inspector Mander of Scotland Yard to the rendezvous did not move fast enough for him. He jumped out, paying the driver at the corner of the street and, hurrying along, met Olivan.

"I thought I told you——" he began.

"Excuse me, sir," said the police officer, "in a case like this I've got to do me own thinking. I thought I'd have to have a consultation with you, and what's the good of doing it just outside his garden, where he might be hearing every word?"

The intelligence of this reply was rather staggering.

"Yes, of course."

Mander seldom admitted that he was wrong, but he did so now.

"Well, where is he?"

"In the factory, sir. He's made two journeys, and the last time, sir, I saw him take a gun out of his pocket and look at it before he put it back. It was an automatic, I'm sure, because I heard the jacket come back."

Now to do Mr. Mander every justice, he was not deficient in courage, and the fact that he might confront an armed Ringer did not in any way deter him, the more especially as he had also brought an automatic from his house in preparation for any such emergency, and he was a fairly good shot.

He gave his instructions in a low voice as they walked rapidly towards the passage.

"I'll go into the factory and you keep guard in the garden. You haven't got your police whistle?"

"Yes, I have sir," said Olivan proudly. "I brought that with me in case——"

"You're an extremely intelligent man, constable," said Mander graciously. "If you hear me shout blow your whistle—not before, you understand? When I've got him, I don't mind who helps to put him inside. If there's any credit going for this job, I want it myself."

"I think we ought to have it, too," said the constable. If Mr. Mander noticed the "we", he did not contest the claims of his humble friend to recognition.

There was no sound in the garden when Mr. Mander was assisted over the wall. He went straight to the trap-door, opened it, and flashed down the light of an electric lamp. There was a flight of stone steps, and down this he went, extinguishing the lamp before he moved into the vault-like passage which apparently ran under the factory.

He heard a queer sound: a distant whirr, a thud. Along he crept and turned into another passage which ran at right angles, not daring to use his lamp. And then, stretching out his hand to feel his way, he touched a human shoulder. Instantly he grappled with the unknown. The rough hair of a beard brushed his face as he gripped the intruder's throat.

"Go quietly," he shouted. "I've got you, and the house is surrounded by police!"

He heard the sound of running feet and then silence. "I want you——"

Something hard and violent caught him under the jaw and he staggered back.

"I've got you covered; don't move!"

As he spoke, he flashed the lamp upon the bearded man.

It was a very dishevelled Inspector Bliss.

★★★★★★

Next morning there was a discussion at the Yard.

"Naturally, the constable did not blow his whistle when he heard you shout," said Inspector Bliss with exaggerated politeness, "because the constable was Henry Arthur Milton, who had been playing you for the sucker that you are!

"Could you not choose some other time to make your dramatic appearance than the moment when I had located the printing works of the biggest gang of forgers that has ever operated in London? Happily, I had phoned through to Scotland Yard for my reserves, and the most important of the gang were caught.

"Why do you imagine I spend my nights in an empty house if I hadn't some reason for it? It took me three months to locate that factory. It took you three minutes nearly to bust up three months' work! However, I'm bearing you no malice. The Ringer caught you, and that is my complete satisfaction."

As Mr. Mander walked towards the door Bliss called him back.

"You ought to write an article about this adventure of yours," he said offensively.

Chapter 13: The Accidental Snapshot

People have the most unlikely hobbies. Mrs. Gardling occupied her moments of leisure with photography. She had a small studio at the back of her house in Hampstead: it was one partitioned half of a garage that had been built to house four cars. Mrs. Gardling had only one car, though she could have afforded more.

Her favourite subjects were flowers, and she was dealing with some perfect Easter lilies in an exquisite Venetian vase that night when The Ringer, who was fleeing for his life, broke into her garage in his search for petrol.

He came out of complete darkness through the partition door into the blinding light of photographic lamps just as Mrs. Gardling was making an exposure. She saw him for a second before his hand closed over the switch and turned out the lights. But she saw him, as few people had ever done, without disguise.

As the lights went off, he heard a drawer being pulled out and something hard scrape along the wood.

"Don't move or I'll shoot!" she said, and heard him laugh and the door slam behind him.

By the time the police came he had vanished. They told her they were pursuing a motorcar thief, but they did not tell her who that thief was because they were chary of talking about him and the news-papers getting to know that they had so nearly caught the man they were seeking.

So Mrs. Gardling cherished that photographic negative of Easter lilies rather as a curiosity than from its intrinsic value. Henry Arthur Milton, for his part, was quite unaware that this deadly thing was in the possession of a lady against whom he found it necessary at a later period to operate.

★★★★★★

The Ringer was in Berlin, a favourite haunt of his. Superintendent Bliss had a letter from him bearing a Charlottenburg postmark. The letter began, as usual, without formality:

> There is a lady with a club in Hogarth Street, Soho, on whom it might be worth your while to keep an eye. I thought of dealing with her myself because her baseness (doesn't that word look queer?) had not brought her within the purview of the law. I think she might be very gently "moved on."
>
> She dispenses drink in prohibited hours—a mild offence, but sufficient to put a check to her other activities. (Name: Mrs. Erita Gardling (born Demage). Address: The Red Monk Club, Hogarth Street. Previous conviction at Manchester, March 7, 1921, conspiracy to defraud. Six months second division.

Henry Arthur Milton was an exasperating man, and nothing distressed Mr. Bliss as this habit of putting the police under an obligation to him. He knew, before the wire he addressed to the Manchester police was answered, that The Ringer's data were exact. The matter was handed to the divisional police, a raid was staged, and in due course Mrs. Gardling appeared before a police magistrate and was sent to prison with hard labour for three months.

Ordinarily this would have been a harsh sentence for selling liquor after hours, but the police found many things which were not described or even hinted at in The Ringer's letter. The amenities of the club were apparently much more extensive than desirable.

Who it was that had betrayed the fact that the raid was made at the instigation of the notorious criminal, Bliss found it difficult to discover. He was a stickler for official secrecy, and it is no exaggeration to say that when Mrs. Gardling turned round as she was leaving the dock and said, in a voice vehement with fury: "You can tell your friend The Ringer that he'll be sorry he ever interfered with me," Bliss was furious.

The divisional inspector denied that he had revealed the part The Ringer had played; the other detectives in the raid were equally emphatic, though it was one of these who had light-heartedly taunted Mrs. Gardling with the name of the informant.

Mrs. Gardling was a rich woman who had afforded to marry her daughter into respectable society. How madam obtained her wealth was no mystery. She ran profitable side-lines to the club business, and many a cheque for a large amount had gone into her bank as the price of her silence about certain disreputable happenings to which she was privy.

When she was waiting to be removed to Holloway, she saw the detective who had given her the identity of the informer, and he was rather agitated because his chief had had an unpleasant interview with Bliss and had passed the kick down.

"For the Lord's sake, Mrs. Gardling, don't mention the fact to anybody that it was I who told you The Ringer squeaked on you."

She, who should have been wilting in shame, was boiling with anger.

"I'd like to know that fellow!" she said, incoherent in her justifiable annoyance. "I'd spend ten thousand pounds to get him! Oh, yes, of course I've heard of him, you fool—who hasn't?"

"It's a curious thing," said the loquacious officer of the law, "that the only time I ever met you before, Mrs. Gardling, was the night he broke into your house and pinched petrol——"

She stared at him.

"The Ringer? Was that man The Ringer?" she gasped. "Your people said it was a burglar——"

"Car thief," he corrected, rather satisfied with the sensation he had created. "Yes, that was The Ringer. It's a regular coincidence! He busts your house and now he's bust you!"

But Mrs. Gardling wasn't thinking of coincidences.

She had permission to see her well-married daughter before the removal to Holloway.

"Annie," she said, "go up to 'The Linnets' and in the studio you'll find a black tin box full of negatives. Take it to the bank and ask the manager to keep it locked up till I come out."

"Aren't you going to appeal, mamma?" asked her daughter.

"I'll be out quicker by saying nothing," she said. "And get the lease of that house in Maddox Street; we can wangle a licence for it—we'll call it 'The Furnace Club'. I thought that out last night."

★★★★★★

So, passed to a prison laundry in North London the famous Mrs. Gardling, and her mind during the period of her incarceration was equally divided between plans for her new club and methods by which she could bring to justice the man she loathed.

It was unfortunate to some extent that Annie, her daughter, desired most passionately to assist her mother in her material rehabilitation. The well-married one was a bright girl, brisk and businesslike, and too well she knew the power of the Press. Her mother had been absent for a month when she sent out a little helpful propaganda for the Furnace Club.

She was not a particularly clever writer, but, as some of us know, it is not necessary to be clever to be interesting, and the news editor of the *Weekly Post-Herald*, scanning the typewritten effusions she sent to him, and scanning them with an apathetic eye, came upon a paragraph which quickened his interest. He rang a bell and sent for a reporter.

"Call on this woman and see what there is in the story." He blue-pencilled the paragraph.

During the following week there appeared an interesting column. "The Ringer's Vengeance," it was headed, a little hectically, and it told the story of the midnight visit, When Mrs. Gardling was photographing flowers.

"My mother has often spoken to me of the man's face which had appeared on the negative, but because she has always had a sympathetic heart towards the unfortunate, she never brought this picture to the notice of the police,

"I have no doubt at all that The Ringer concocted these stories about my mother, who is perfectly innocent of all the dreadful things which have been said about her. ..., "

In the course of the article it was stated that the interesting negative was in a safe place and that "more would be heard of it."

Curiously enough, Bliss did not give the article a great deal of attention, and the only thing which really interested him was the revelation that the Furnace Club was to be opened in the near future under the care and management of the well-married daughter.

As for this lady, she realised that she had said a great deal too much and refused all further interviews, quaking a little as to what would be the effect upon her fond mother when that resolute woman came out of prison.

She could hardly consult her husband on the matter, for Mr. Leppold, that dark, handsome man, was not on speaking terms with his mother-in-law, and whenever her name obtruded into the conversation, he invariably excised it.

"Don't talk to me about that old so-and-so," was his favourite expression.

Ann Leppold bridled but was silent. Mrs. Gardling had been very rude to Alfred, though undoubtedly her exasperation had cause. He had first appeared at the club as Count Giolini. He wasn't a count at all—this fact was not discovered until after the marriage.

In other respects, she had little to complain of; he was a well-off man, had a beautiful flat off Jermyn Street, lived expensively, presented jewels to his wife, and took her away every year to Monte Carlo, Deauville, and other fashionable resorts.

She often wondered what his business was, for, although he claimed to be something in the City, he had no office, and spent most of his time in the West End of London. Whatever it was, it did not keep him very busy. He was never away for more than a few days at a time, and, generally speaking, his life was quiet and inoffensive.

She spoke to him about The Ringer but he was rather uninterested. Most of the evenings at home he spent reading the newspapers, the City pages being of special significance, for he was a frugal man who had invested well and hoped someday to retire and live in Paris, a city for which he had a great affection, though he seldom went there.

She was an avid reader of newspapers herself, but confined her studies to those fascinating episodes which are revealed in the courts of law.

One night—it was about a week before her mother was sent to prison—she laid the paper down on her knees.

"It's perfectly awful the way these robberies are going on, Alf," she said. "One of these gangs took over forty thousand pounds' worth of diamonds from a place in Hatton Garden on Sunday, and got away without leaving a trace. I think the police must be in it. Now, if I were the police——"

"You're not," snapped her husband from behind his newspaper; "and the best thing you can do is to shut up."

Annie closed her lips firmly. When she had been married somebody had given her a book entitled How to be Happy though Married, and she had learned the lesson of bearing and forbearing.

At Scotland Yard they accepted this succession of burglaries with philosophic calm. The police were only human, and if shop-owners refused to take elementary precautions, such as employing watchmen or buying safes which offered six hours' resistance to the best of burglars, that was their look-out.

The police did all they possibly could, and followed a routine which is usually very effective. But Scotland Yard had neither second sight nor the power of divination.

"It might be Lewing or Martin or Crooford," speculated Mr. Bliss, "or it may be that Paris gang that come over specially for these jobs."

The gangs which operate from foreign cities are the most difficult to trace. Paris is seven hours from London, and, supposing that one of the gang were in London, making all the preliminary investigations, completing the time-table, and getting together the necessary apparatus and tools, they could arrive on Saturday evening, and leave on Monday morning with the bulk of their loot.

"The thing to do is to find the caretaker," said Bliss.

By this he referred to the one member of the gang permanently established in London.

★★★★★★

Mr. Leppold did not even read the interview with his wife in the *Weekly Post-Herald*, he merely saw her name in a column of print and admonished her.

"The advice I give to you, my girl, is to keep out of the public eye. There's no reason why you should go shoving yourself forward into the limelight."

"I am doing something for my poor, dear mother," said Mrs. Leppold hotly, "and I've a good mind to get that box out of the Northern and Southern——"

Mr. Leppold became instantly interested.

"Does your mother bank at the Northern and Southern?"

"She has for years," said Annie complacently, because the Northern and Southern is rather an exclusive banking company. "She keeps all her papers—what are you laughing at?"

"I wasn't laughing," said Alt Leppold as he took up his newspaper again; but she gathered, from the fact that the sheet shook convulsively, that he was lying.

"What's the joke?" she demanded.

"Something I read in the paper," was his reply.

After she had gone to bed, he went into his study and put through a call to Paris. For six minutes he spoke cryptically. He often spoke over the Paris wire, and he always spoke cryptically.

The next day he went to the south of London and had tea with a bearded army pensioner who was a widower and lived alone in two rooms in a model dwelling, and had a grievance against society, particularly that eminent section of society represented by the Stewards of the Jockey Club.

"They ought to warn off . . . ."

He named a number of eminent trainers whose horses had not won that afternoon at Hurst Park. This bearded man backed horses on a system, though his employers would have dropped in their tracks if they had even suspected his favourite recreation. If he had not backed horses, Mr. Leppold would never have got to know him.

He soothed the disgruntled punter with certain alluring prospects.

"You stay on for a month, then off you pop to South America or South Africa or anywhere you like. There's five thousand pounds—more than you'd earn in fifty years——"

"I should lose my pension," said the man, looking at him from under his beetling black brows. "And what about my good name?"

"You'll lose that anyway," said Mr. Leppold coolly. "The first time your boss knows that you owe money to bookmakers your name will be mud. I'm paying you five hundred pounds on account," he went on, counting out the notes. "I trust you, and you've got to trust me. I'll knock twice on the side door, like this." He sounded a Morse B on the table. "All you've got to do is to let us in."

The man moved uncomfortably.

"What about tying me up?" he suggested.

"You needn't worry about that," said Mr. Leppold, secretly amused. "We'll stick an alibi on to you that you couldn't blow off with dynamite."

The man gathered up the money, and after Mr. Leppold had left put it in a safe place. He thought the scheme was a very simple one, that detection was impossible. The prisons of Great Britain and the United States are filled with men who have harboured similar illusions.

★★★★★★

When Mr. Leppold got home that night he found his wife a preening piece of self-importance.

"I've had a letter from dear mother," she said, "about that Ringer."

For once he did not silence her.

"What about that Ringer?" he demanded.

"It's his photograph that mother took. I've been talking on the phone to Scotland Yard." (Mr. Leppold blinked, but said nothing.) "A gentleman named Bliss said it's most important, and I'm to get the photograph tomorrow and take it to him. It appears they haven't got a picture of this fellow, and I might get the thousand pounds reward."

"Good luck to you, my girl!" said Mr. Leppold heartily. "That fellow ought to be hung—he double-crossed a friend of mine." He did not particularise the friend or the circumstances.

He was in a very cheerful mood throughout the dinner, of which he partook sparingly, for one thinks most quickly on an empty stomach. After the meal was over, he went to the study, locked the door, and took from a safe a small leather packet of tools and put it into his overcoat pocket.

He could afford to be cheerful, for he was embarking upon one of the easiest jobs he had ever undertaken.

At half-past ten o'clock he arrived at a bar near Shaftesbury Avenue, and saw, without any apparent recognition, the two men who had arrived from Paris that night. Ten minutes later he walked out of the saloon and the two men followed him. At a convenient place he stopped to light a cigar, and they came up with him.

"The thing's sweet," he said. "There's enough foreign currency in the vault to make it worthwhile—about seven thousand pounds in Treasury notes and eighteen thousand in banknotes."

"Is it a dead shop?" asked one.

"No," said Mr. Leppold, "it's live. The assistant manager lives over, but he's gone into the country to see his mother who's ill."

How Mr. Leppold obtained all these details is entirely his own business.

He walked down a side street, tapped at the private door of the bank, and it was opened instantly. He was hardly inside before the other two joined him. The door was locked.

"What about this tying up?" asked Mr. Leppold of the bearded man, but the watchman showed no inclination to submit to any tying.

"You can tie me before you go," he urged. "I'd like to see how you do the job."

Leppold, who was a man of few words, nodded. He had no need of a guide; he opened the steel grille leading to the vault and went down the stone steps, followed by three men; the key of that grille was the one duplicate he possessed.

At the end of a short passage was another grille. Workmen had been here, and great oblong cavities had been chiselled in the stone.

"They're putting a real safe door on," explained Mr. Leppold, and added: "About time!"

The bearded watchman gaped at the three experts as they attacked the lock. In an hour it was removed and the heavy steel-barred door swung open. A light burned in the arched roof and showed the contents of the vault. Stacked in three lines were a number of deed boxes, and at the sight of these Mr. Leppold, who had a grim sense of humour, chuckled.

"Half a minute," he said.

He walked quickly along till he came to a deed box, and this he tapped with his knuckle.

"Ma's," he said sardonically.

It bore the initials "S. A. G.," Mrs. Gardling's Christian names being Sarah Ann.

"My missus is going to get a thing out of there tomorrow that'll do The Ringer a bit of no good."

"What about this money?" said one of his companions impatiently, and for half an hour they were working industriously, collecting and sorting.

★★★★★★

The three men wore overcoats and each overcoat was cunningly pocketed. They were swift workers all, and the money was disposed of almost as soon as it was brought into view.

307

"Now I think we'd better tie up whiskers," said Leppold, and produced a rope from his pocket.

They looked around, but the bearded man was not in the room. They saw him, however, on the other side of the grille; he had a black box, which was open, and at the moment they came in sight of him he had produced a dark-looking negative and was holding it up to the light.

"Who locked this gate?" demanded Mr. Leppold.

The watchman looked round.

"I did," he said calmly. "You left the key in the lock, which was rather foolish."

"Well, unlock it, quick!" He was carrying in his hand the small kit of tools with which they had forced the downstairs lock.

Suddenly the watchman's arm shot through the grating, and there was an automatic attached to it. The muzzle pressed against Mr. Leppold's stomach.

"Hand over those tools!"

The dazed man obeyed.

"And if any of you pull a gun," said the 'watchman' calmly, "you'll know less about the cause of your death than the coroner who sits on you."

"Who the hell are you?" asked Leppold.

"My name is Henry Arthur Milton, vulgarly called The Ringer," said the other. "And, by the way, if you want the real night watchman, you'll find him tied up in the manager's office—really tied up. And the least you can do is to tell the police that you did the tying."

"I've been trailing that ancient sinner for a few days; I was, in fact, in his bedroom when you were discussing tonight's little adventure. He was a little surprised when he got the signal on the door an hour too soon."

He folded the negative and carefully put it in his pocket.

"Give my love to mamma," he said, as he moved out of view and out of range.

Mr. Leppold never forgave him that, and even in the morning, when the police arrived, he was still brooding upon the insult.

Chapter 14: The Sinister Dr. Lutteur

Inspector Mander had a great friend—at least, Miss Carberry was not as great a friend as he could have wished her to be.

He thought Scotland Yard was the most interesting place in the world and talked about it all the time. She had a weakness for musical comedy, and the more respectable kind of night clubs, where the orangeade sold after licensed hours really is orangeade. When he talked of crime she was bored. When she told him of the perfectly marvellous dance records that had recently been issued, he tried to bring the subject back to crime.

She frequently met a distinguished stranger, who would have taken her to musical comedies and night clubs, but was afraid he would get her a bad name, so they dined at nice little restaurants instead. She called him Ernest, which was not his name, though she was unaware of the fact. As to her apathy in the matter of Scotland Yard's activities, she was not to be blamed.

There is nothing romantic about crime. To be a successful detective does not require a super-intelligence, but the power of reducing your mind to the lowest possible level of intelligence. The great detectives are those who are able to lower their mentality to the level of the men whose ill-work they are endeavouring to counteract.

This was the thesis of an impromptu lecture which Superintendent Bliss delivered to his crestfallen subordinate.

"The trouble with you, Mander," he said, "is that you try to be clever. Instead of being your natural self and establishing contact with the normal criminal mind you waste the time you should devote to sleeping in working out theories based, as far as I can gather, upon those sensational detective novels which were so popular twenty years ago. I have a feeling that you are writing a monograph on cigar ash."

Mr. Mander writhed under the accusation.

"A criminal of the type I am looking for," Bliss continued remorselessly, "does not wear evening dress or frequent the more fashionable restaurants of the West End. You are more likely to find him in a public-house near the Elephant and Castle, and there is no need for you to employ logic or deduction. All you have to be is a good listener, for Libby is the type of man who makes a serial story of his adventures."

"I wasn't exactly looking for Libby," said Mr. Mander, stung to defence. "I had a theory about The Ringer——"

Superintendent Bliss groaned.

"Libby is a common and a cheap maker of counterfeit coins," he said. "He is a sordid, ten-conviction criminal. If you are under the impression that The Ringer has the slightest association with that type of individual you are greatly mistaken."

But here Mr. Bliss was to some extent wrong.

The incidence of the underworld, the real cheap, hard-labour men, never failed to interest Henry Arthur Milton. His view of the lower strata of law-breakers was no more flattering than were those of Superintendent Bliss; but, as it happened, he was at that moment especially absorbed in the career of quite a number of very poor people, most of whom gained their livelihood by illicit means.

★★★★★★

The Ringer was lodging at a house in Enther Street, Lambeth—rather larger than the ordinary type of poor house—a place kept scrupulously clean, where the scrubbing brush sounded most of the day. His landlady was Mrs. Kilford, a widow. She had two daughters, one of whom, Nelly, was both pretty and curious. The prettiness he recognised; her curiosity he discovered when she went up to his room one morning with a cup of unpalatable tea and lingered at the door to discuss her affairs.

".... Of course, he's much older than me, but quite refined. Mother says he ought to come to the house, but he won't. He's terribly shy."

"Blushing lad," said Henry Arthur Milton, who was in a cheerful mood.

He had no particular business in London at the moment except to avoid the attentions of people who wished to see him very badly. He was certainly not passionately interested in the love affairs of his landlady's daughter. More exhilarating was the knowledge that right opposite him lived one called Libby, who was a maker of counterfeit coins; for The Ringer had an especial grudge against manufacturers of half-crowns, who rob little tradesmen and other people to whom half a crown is quite an enormous sum of money.

He was returning home rather late one night when he saw Nelly at the corner of the mean street in which he lived. She was talking to a man who was a head taller than she and who, when he came abreast, turned his face so that Henry Arthur Milton could not see it very distinctly. As he passed, he heard Nelly say: "But I have never been a lady's maid."

He expected her the next morning to offer her confidence, but she was remarkably silent. A week later her mother told him tearfully that Nelly had run away and married Mr. Hackitt. The only consolation so far as The Ringer could gather was that the marriage had been most properly performed at a registrar's office and a copy of the marriage certificate had been forwarded to the landlady.

More amazingly, the bride announced that she and her husband were going to Paris for their honeymoon.

"Which is in France," explained the landlady unnecessarily.

★★★★★★

The Ringer could not spare a corner of his mind to be occupied by Nelly's love affair. He dismissed the matter and devoted his entire attention to the undoing of Libby.

He himself never attempted to usurp the functions of the law. If a criminal committed an offence for which the law could punish him, he was satisfied that the machinery of Scotland Yard should be put in motion.

One night, on information received, the Flying Squad descended on Mr. Libby and removed him with a hundredweight of metal, a number of excellent dies and electro-plating apparatus, and when the affair was cleared up Superintendent Bliss decided to comb the neighbourhood for the informant, who, he knew, was The Ringer. But that gentleman had anticipated some such move and had disappeared.

It was in the Strand between eleven and twelve one night when the theatre crowds were turning out and the roadway was a confusion of cars, taxicabs, and omnibuses that he saw and recognised Nelly's mysterious lover. There was no need to see his face; The Ringer remembered people by their backs, their walk, the movement of their hands, and he was as well satisfied that this man was Hackitt as though he were identifying him from a studio portrait.

Mr. Hackitt had no right to be in London; he should have been in Paris on his honeymoon. He certainly had no right whatever to be wearing a top hat and a coat obviously made by a good tailor. He was alone, moving in the leisured manner of one who was walking by preference. And by his side was a lady who was not Nelly.

Since it was the business of The Ringer to know the affairs of his enemies, he recognised the lady as a Miss Carberry, who was friendly with Inspector Mander. If she had not been "attached" to Inspector Mander he would not have known her at all.

"But how perfectly fascinating!" said The Ringer.

★★★★★★

It was a few days after this that the centre of his interest changed to Esher.

The nursing home of Dr. Lutteur in that village was a beautiful if modest house situated in ample grounds, and if the doctor's clientele was not large it was exclusive. He was an extremely agreeable gentle-

311

man, who went out of his way to make his clients comfortable and happy, and there were few establishments which could equal it in point of comfort and up-to-date equipment. He was a fairly wealthy man, unmarried, had no hobbies but his work, and was beloved by his patients and the few people who were admitted into the limited circle of friendship.

He could afford to pick and choose his patients, and if he showed a preference for those who promised to give him the least trouble he could hardly be blamed.

Mr. Roos, his new patient, was hardly the kind he would have chosen, for Mr. Roos was rather hearty, not to say boastful—a noisy man, and the doctor disliked noisy men.

"An aunt of mine came to you, doctor, about four or five years ago. She wrote out to me in South Africa and said you'd looked after her better than any other doctor she'd ever had, and you're the man for my money!"

He had had a nervous breakdown on the ship; in fact, his condition was such that he was nearly landed at Madeira, he said.

"Cash is no object to me. I can promise you this—that if you take me in, you're not going to be bothered with visitors, because I don't know anybody in this damned country and don't want to!"

He exhibited certain signs of nervousness; his hands shook, his face twitched at odd intervals; the shrewd Dr. Lutteur diagnosed the case as the after-effects of heavy drinking. But he did not like noisy people, or hearty people, or people who talked loudly of their vast possessions.

Nevertheless, he gave a bed and a room to his new patient, prescribed a diet, and was agreeably surprised to discover that Mr. Roos was content to lie in bed and read newspapers and showed no inclination to disturb his other patients.

There were three, the most interesting of whom was an elderly lady who had been under his care for two years. Mr. Roos saw her once in the garden being wheeled about in a bath-chair, a pale, severe woman who regarded him with the greatest suspicion. A surly gardener, who had been rude to her for picking his spring flowers and had been given a week's notice by the doctor, said her name was Timms—Miss Alicia Timms.

Roos had been there the greater part of the week when a visitor called. It was the afternoon, when the patients were resting in various parts of the grounds, and when Mr. Roos found it rather difficult to prevent himself from falling asleep, for the weather was warm, the silence, the fragrance of the fresh spring air, all things combined to induce that pleasant state of coma which attends a good luncheon. The doctor's study was under his bedroom, and the shrill voice of the woman pierced with startling distinctness the quiet of the house. He heard her angry protestations, heard the doctor's frantic request for silence, and then the voices sank to an indistinguishable rumble of sound, which only occasionally rose to audibility.

Mr. Roos had risen that day and was lying fully dressed upon his bed. He gathered up his book and his spectacles and went into the grounds, whence he saw the station fly carrying the visitor down the drive towards the main road. Dr. Lutteur's three prize patients were dozing; the disgruntled gardener was very wide awake.

"I shan't be sorry to leave here, anyway," he said. "You never see anybody but a lot of old people, and you don't see them long before one of 'em pops off! We've only had one patient here that didn't peg out."

"Thank you, my cheery soul," said Mr. Roos.

But the gardener insisted, with a certain gloomy satisfaction, on the high mortality of patients at Dr. Lutteur's house.

"Naturally, they die because they're old. I suppose he's a pretty good doctor but you can't make old people young, can you? The only one that didn't die here was an old gentleman who was taken away by his relations. And they know they're going to die—they're always making their wills.

"That old lady over there. Miss Timms—she's worth pots of money! Mind you, I respect her; she's left every penny to a lady's maid who used to look after her. I know because I witnessed the will and I had a good look at it because the old lady had a sort of fainting fit after she'd signed."

"Do you remember the name of the lady's maid?" asked Mr. Roos, carelessly.

The gardener looked up at the sky for inspiration.

"Yes, Hachett or Hackitt, or some such name. The last old lady that died here left all her money to a woman called—I forget her name; the only thing I do remember about her is that she fell in the river and was drowned about six months after she'd drawn the money. And then there was an old gentleman named—I don't remember his name—who left fifty thousand pounds to a girl whose father he knew when he was a boy.

"I was telling this to the young lady who came down here yester-

313

day when the doctor was at Bagshot; a nice-looking girl she was, very much like that young lady who came in the cab to see the doctor about an hour ago."

Late that night, when the patients were asleep, or should have been asleep, the girl who had called earlier in the day came to the house. Mr. Roos, lying full length on the floor, with a small microphone fixed to his ear, listened with the greatest interest to the more or less confused conversation.

". . . . Well, I may be curious, but I've found *you* out. . . . followed you to Waterloo Station. . . . What is the meaning of it? . . . ."

Later she became less truculent, agreed to something or other. Mr. Roos heard the words "little house."

He could not have heard it all, because when he learned, two or three days later, that the doctor was called away on business to Paris and had left a locum tenons to look after the inmates of the home he was taken by surprise.

The patient left the nursing home within an hour of receiving this information; but it took a long time for him to locate the doctor.

The quietness of Enther Street, Lambeth, was disturbed by a loud scream. The hour was 2 a.m. and in this drab neighbourhood a midnight scream was not an unusual phenomenon. At the corner of the street two policemen had met at the limit of their respective beats, and they were, contrary to regulations, smoking. One turned his head in the direction of the sound and remarked casually that somebody was "getting a lacing." They waited expectantly for the second and the successive cries, but they did not come.

Now a succession of such screams is normal. One shrill cry of horror that has no companion has a sinister significance. The two officers walked slowly down the street. They saw a window open and a tousled head stuck out.

"Next door," said the owner of the head—a man. "That's the first noise the new people have made since they've been here. Half a tick. I'll come down."

These police officers were not unused to the ways of the officious informant: they were rather amused. The man came out from his front door wearing an overcoat.

"There's a man and a woman live there; they moved in last Monday. Nobody's seen either of 'em. My missus, though, saw 'em move in—brought their furniture in a motor-van one night when it was raining. Nobody's ever seen 'em go out."

One of the police looked up at the mean face of the house. It consisted of two floors, the ground and the upper. A tall man with a fishing rod could reach the guttering of the slate roof. There were two windows above, a door and a window below—the kind of brick box you can have for a few shillings a week.

"Well," said the officer of the law, with the profundity of his kind, "you can't do anything to people because they don't come out of their houses."

The neighbour agreed, and there the party might have dispersed, the policemen to their interrupted smoke, the householder to his bed, only the second policeman saw a light in the upper window. It flickered up and down, grew to yellow brightness, and sank to a dull red.

"That room's on fire!" he said, and whipped out his truncheon.

The hammering on the door awakened the street. A panel smashed and a gloved hand went in, groping for the lock. As the door was flung open a great cloud of smoke rolled forth.

"Get the people out of the other houses, Harry!" spluttered the officer. "Mr. What's-your-name, run to the fire alarm at the corner."

He blundered into the house, felt his way up the stairs and threw open the door of the front room. The heat of the blazing floor drove him back, but he saw the woman lying half on and half off the smouldering bed. Bracing one foot upon a burning rafter, he reached out and dragged her through the flames.

It was a superhuman task to carry the weight down those narrow stairs that sagged under him. He blundered once on the landing and nearly fell. Presently he staggered out into the open. The fire engines arrived at that moment. The ambulance arrived a few minutes later, and they laid the woman on a stretcher and rushed her to the nearest hospital.

She was still living, in spite of the knife wound in her side, but died after admission. She was young and rather pretty.

The policeman telephoned to his superior and went back to pursue his inquiries, the affair having occurred on his beat.

Inspector Mander reported to his chief the following morning.

"It's a very ordinary case. A man named Brown knifed his wife, and in the struggle the lamp must have overturned. We haven't got Brown yet, but I've circulated his description."

Bliss had read the official report furnished by the divisional inspector.

"Apart from the fact that nobody knows that his name is Brown, and nobody has ever seen him, and that the floor was sprinkled with petrol, and that the house was deliberately set on fire, your account and prognostications seem fairly accurate. The case had better go to Lindon. It is in his area."

All day long detectives and firemen searched amid the blackened *débris* for the missing man. But he was some distance away and very much alive.

Dr. Lutteur sat in his study, a medical work propped up on the table before him, a long cigar between his even white teeth. He closed the book, put it away on a shelf, and drew from a drawer of his desk a sheet of foolscap paper. He read this carefully, then he rang the bell. A nursing sister answered it within a few minutes.

"Oh, sister, about Miss Timms; she's been bothering me all day about making a new will."

"She only made one a month or so ago," said the nursing sister. "Didn't she leave all her money to a woman called Hackitt?"

The doctor nodded.

"Apparently she's changed her mind," he said. "She wishes now to leave it to the daughter of an old friend of hers, a Miss Carberry. I've got the name in the will." He pointed to the document. "Will you come along and witness it?"

The nursing sister looked dubious.

"She doesn't seem to be in a condition to make a will. Do you think it's wise——" she began.

"It amuses her. She'll probably change her mind again in the course of a few days," said the doctor calmly. "Let us go up and get her signature while she's still awake. The night sister can witness it as well as you."

The clock was striking one; the doctor had locked away the new will in his safe, had risen and was preparing for bed when a perfect stranger rang the bell of the nursing home. He had come in a car and had three companions. Lutteur looked at the bearded face and wondered where he had seen it before.

"My name is Superintendent Bliss, of Scotland Yard," said the caller in cold and even tones. "I am inquiring into the death of a woman called Brown, who was murdered in Enther Street, Lambeth. I am also inquiring into the death of two other women who were legatees of estates left by former patients of yours. I shall ask you to accompany me to the Kingston Police Station."

It was all very formal and meaningless. Weeks after, when Dr. Lut-

316

teur was awaiting execution, he could not quite understand what had happened.

★★★★★★

"Lutteur's system," explained Mr. Bliss to Inspector Mander, "was a very simple one. He ran a nursing home, and there is no suggestion that any of the patients who died in his charge were the victims of foul play. They died natural deaths, but he chose his patients rather well. He scoured the country, looking for wealthy women without any near relations.

"By some means he persuaded them to go into his home—we found the most marvellous collection of literature, with expensive photographs of the grounds, and the treatment rooms—and, once there, the rest was a fairly simple matter.

"He first of all chose the legatee. Then, either by the administration of a drug which destroyed their will power or by his personal magnetism he induced them to make a will in favour of his nominee. Whether he married the nominee in every case I do not know. He certainly married Mrs. Kilford's daughter and killed her when he discovered that she knew who he was. He would have done the same with the girl Carberry——"

"Carberry?" said Mander. "I know a girl called Carberry. By the way, how did you get on to this story, chief?"

"Information received," said Bliss diplomatically. "And don't call me chief!"

Chapter 15: The Obliging Cobbler

Doctors are credited with an aversion for their own medicines. It was because of this aversion that Henry Arthur Milton found himself with two feuds on his hands. The first of these was with two brothers named Pelcher. They were specialists, but nobody referred to them by that title. The police called them "The Two"; damaged householders found descriptions which varied in their vitriolic quality according to their wealth of vocabulary.

Marlow Joyner, the latest of their victims, lay in bed with his head heavily bandaged, and told, haltingly and painfully, the story of his experience to a select audience consisting of a London police magistrate, Superintendent Bliss, and two police stenographers. For Mr. Marlow Joyner was on the danger list, and the doctors said that it was going to be a toss-up whether he ever left his bed alive. Happily, as it proved, the doctors were wrong, but it was touch and go for a week.

Bliss took the deposition back to Scotland Yard.

"I don't know which I'd rather take, The Two or The Ringer, but I know which would be the greatest loss to society."

"Maybe The Two is The Ringer?" suggested Inspector Mander hopefully.

Bliss turned his cold eyes upon the fatuous man.

"The Ringer has adopted many disguises," he said, "but I cannot remember that he has ever appeared at one and the same time as two people—except to the hopelessly intoxicated."

In a sense, the Superintendent was right, in a sense, wrong. There was an occasion when The Ringer was three men, but, as the greatest of tale-tellers has said, "that is another story."

★★★★★★

What was a secret to Scotland Yard was no secret to The Ringer, who, through his peculiarly effective organisation, was able to bring home to these two respectable young men—they lived in the suburbs and in their spare time cultivated roses—responsibility for their many acts.

For five weeks he sought evidence which would convince a police magistrate, but this was difficult to come by, and in the end, he decided that this was a matter for "private treatment."

In the early hours of the morning the two brothers were picked up in the street in which they lived and rushed to the hospital.

They were as terribly bludgeoned as any of their victims had been, and it was eight weeks before the first of them was convalescent. They gave no information to the police except that they had been attacked by "a gang of toughs." Neither told the story of the solitary man who accosted them late one night.

"You've heard of me—I am The Ringer, and I'm rather annoyed with you two thugs . . . ."

While they had been debating how best to deal with the man—naturally, they were disinclined to make trouble so close to their own home—something hit the nearest. It might have been a rubber truncheon; the victim wasn't sure. His brother, who rushed to the rescue, had no doubt at all that it was something effective. The blow that caught him did not stun him, but knocked him out. When he awoke, he was in the one bed and his brother was in the next. They were released from hospital at last and reached, spontaneously, a common agreement.

"From what you and I know, Harry," said one, "we ought to get this bird."

The second feud was developed more violently, in a fashionable Viennese *café*, when "Kelly" Rosefield missed the man he hated with his first shot. The strange man in the black wideawake hat fired the second, and Kelly went down with a bullet in the bony part of his shoulder. The curious thing about it was that the successful marksman was entirely in the right.

Kelly used to beat up his woman partner when he felt that way. They lived in an expensive block of flats; the interfering gentleman who stole in upon them one night—Kelly had most carelessly left the flat door open—lived in the apartment beneath. What he did to the wife-beater was a subject for comment, commiseration, and explanation among Mr. Rosefield's friends for many a day.

Kelly explained his injuries variously. He had been knocked over by a car, he had fallen against a lamp standard, he had been thrown when riding a spirited blood horse. And in all these prevarications he was assisted by the woman called Carmenflora, who had most reason to gloat over his enlarged countenance.

Carmenflora was more bitter than her man; and when the matter ended as it did, and Kelly was lying in hospital—nobody quite certain as to the brand of spiritual consolation appropriate to his condition— Carmenflora went forth and looked for the interfering gentleman.

But Henry Arthur Milton knew that other people were looking for him. You cannot shoot off automatics in Viennese restaurants, fashionable or unfashionable, without inviting the attention of the local constabulary. He faded to Berlin.

Four months later he was entering his London hotel and came face to face with Carmenflora, who recognised him. She said nothing, but he caught the flicker of her eyes, read their story, and, going up to his room, packed his handbag, 'phoned for his bill, and was out of the hotel in half an hour.

Therefore, there were three people looking for The Ringer or 18,004, if the active and intelligent members of the Metropolitan Police Force be included.

There were people who called The Ringer clever. He never laid claim to any such title. He was painstaking, thorough, left nothing to chance, examined his ground with the finicky care of a very conscientious staff officer.

He did not believe in luck, good or bad, and found no excuse for such failures as he had. He had his vanities, but they were of a harmless sort, judged by the meaner ones common to humanity.

"I'll get that feller if I have to wait fifty-five years," said Kelly extravagantly.

Now Kelly was, by the Scotland Yard standard, a pretty bad man. He was a thief and an associate of thieves, and, with the assistance of his partner, who was courteously described as his wife, he had cleaned up considerable sums of money, mainly from susceptible young men, for Carmenflora was pretty and could be very, very attractive.

Bliss heard of his arrival and sent a polite sergeant to inquire if he was staying long in London.

"I'm a British subject and you can't deport me," said Kelly hotly. "I'm here on private business."

"We can't deport you further than Wormwood Scrubs," said the police sergeant gently, "but that's one of the foreign countries you'd hate to visit, Kelly. And that's just where you'll be if I find you giving nice little supper parties to young gentlemen."

Kelly winced at that, for the previous night he had entertained the impecunious son of a millionaire. Most millionaires' sons are impecunious, but their fathers will pay almost anything to keep the family name out of the newspapers. But this was the merest side-line.

"If it hurts you to see somebody else getting a free drink——" he began.

The polite sergeant became impolite very suddenly.

"Let's fan you for that old gun of yours," he said, and Kelly submitted to the outrage. As he could afford to do, for his automatic was well hidden.

When the visit was reported to Bliss, the superintendent was rather interested.

"I've just had a report through from the Austrian police," he said. "Kelly's been shot up by somebody and Blunthall advances a theory that the somebody was The Ringer. If that is so The Ringer is in London."

He sent for Mander, who had his uses.

"I have an idea that we may get a line to The Ringer through Kelly," he said. "And there's another little matter which I'd like you to clear up. You remember the two brothers Pelcher, who were admitted to the Lewisham Hospital pretty well beaten up about six months ago?"

Mander remembered.

"I want them kept under observation. I don't say they are The Two, but the information I have from the divisional inspector has made me a little suspicious. If they are The Two then that is The Ringer's work also."

"They seem fairly respectable men: they are both working in the City——" began Mander.

"That doesn't make them respectable," said the superintendent.

★★★★★★

Kelly was a wealthy man. He could afford to live in the best hotel; he could afford to employ private detectives in his search for the man he loathed. He could also have afforded to have given his "wife" and partner complete control of her jewellery; but, like so many of his kind, he was mean to an extraordinary degree. For example, in all their Continental journeyings his wife invariably travelled second-class, while he lorded it in superior accommodation.

But his chief eccentricity was in relation to the jewels. His vanity demanded that his lady should appear beautifully and, indeed, extravagantly bedecked. Her necklace, her diamond bracelet, her rings and brooches he carried in a long case which fitted into his hip pocket. Every evening before dinner the jewels were given to her; every night, on her retirement, they were taken away and safely stored in the case.

There was an excellent reason for this. A previous partner, who had slaved for him and whom he had misguidedly trusted with jewellery, had disappeared, carrying with her about two thousand pounds' worth of portable property.

He was "serving out" the evening allowance of adornment, when the floor-waiter knocked at his door and told him there was a man who wished to see him. Kelly, whose mind ran to detectives, asked for a description, and was relieved to learn that the caller was an elderly gentleman.

"Gentleman" was perhaps an exaggeration; he was obviously a working man; he confessed to being a cobbler—a mender of old shoes—a grey-haired man, shabbily attired, who wore spectacles and a bristling, iron-grey moustache. He was obviously nervous, and would not speak until the partner had been peremptorily ordered into the next room.

"It's about a lodger of mine, sir," said the cobbler nervously. "I don't want to interfere with anything I ought not to interfere in. I've lived in the same house for twenty-five years and I've never owed anybody a shilling, let alone got myself mixed up in any scandal. This lodger of mine . . . ."

The lodger had been staying with him three weeks—a quiet man, who only went out in the evenings—a perfectly natural thing to do, since he was, as he said, a night watchman.

"But I've had my suspicions of him," said the cobbler-landlord, who gave his name as Hays; "and the other night, after he went out, I opened his bedroom door with one of my keys and I found the table covered with plans of this hotel.

"I didn't know it was this hotel," he went on, "but it happens to be the only hotel in the street."

"Plans?"

★★★★★★

The cobbler felt in his pocket, produced a transparent sheet of paper and smoothed it out on the table.

"Here you are, sir," said Mr. Hays, and pointed to an inscription—"Kelly's room." And then a cross: "Wife's jewels kept here."

Kelly looked and gasped. The cross marked exactly the place where in the daytime the jewellery was securely locked in a dressing-trunk.

"I said to myself," proceeded Mr. Hays, "this man must be a burglar, and my job is to go along and warn the gentleman——"

"What's he like?" asked Kelly, easily.

Mr. Hays's description was not very graphic. There were one or two points which left no doubt in the mind of Kelly who the burglar was. He made a few rapid inquiries. The cobbler lived alone in a small house on the outskirts of Finchley.

"He's out all night, is he?" said Kelly thoughtfully. "What about letting me in after he's gone one night?"

Mr. Hays hesitated and murmured something about the police.

"Never mind about the police, old boy," said Kelly, producing a convincing number of Treasury notes.

The next morning, he gave his orders to his partner.

"You get back to Vienna by the first train and wait for me. I'll be returning in a day or two."

"What have you got on?" she asked, not unused to these sudden fits.

His answer was offensive.

That afternoon he paid his bill—his wife had already taken every bit of baggage and he could stroll forth unencumbered to the rendez-vous.

He was not the only person who had received a visitor the night before. The brothers Pelcher were playing a peaceful game of dominoes in their ornate, over-decorated little drawing-room when the maid-of-all-work announced Mr. Hays.

"Hays? Who's Hays, Harry?" asked one of the other, but the information was not forthcoming.

Mr. Hays was a cobbler, a greyish man with a bristling moustache and a nervous manner. He had a small house in Finchley and a lodger . . .

"It's not for me, gentlemen, to put my nose into other people's affairs. I am a respectable, law-abiding citizen, as you gentlemen are. But I read the papers, and I got a headpiece that can put two and two together."

He paused, but the two silent men did no more than stare at him in their normally unfriendly manner.

"If you're not the two gentlemen who was knocked about one night some months ago, then I've made a mistake and I won't trouble you any further—I mean, two gentlemen named Pelcher . . . . I read it in the papers. I keep a Press cutting book of things like that."

"It's a curious thing that this lodger of mine should have been looking over my shoulder as I was a-reading that bit about you two gentlemen being beaten up. 'Why do you keep that?' said he, laughing. When I told him I always pasted up horrors, he said: 'There's one thing they didn't tell the police—they didn't say anything about Henry Arthur Milton.'"

Both the brothers looked up quickly.

"Did he say any more?" asked Harry.

The cobbler fondled his unshaven chin.

"Yes, he did, sir, and that's why I've come to see you. He said: 'Those two fellers ought to have been settled, and one of these days I'm going down to have a look at them.'"

At their invitation, he described his lodger. The brothers looked at one another, and then Harry began to ask questions. When he was through with his inquiries he said to Hays: "If we gave you a couple of quid, what about going to the pictures tomorrow night and lending us the key of your house? You say he don't go out till ten?"

"Eleven," corrected Mr. Hays.

★★★★★★

For five pounds the cobbler surrendered the key. Kelly had paid twice that amount for the key's duplicate.

For the greater part of the night the brothers discussed possibilities. Said one: "If we leave him in the house this old bird will put up a squeak. On the other hand, if we get in quiet and drop him somewhere, there will be no squeak at all, and nobody can swear that we went in."

There was agreement here. The second of the ferocious fraternity suggested knocking off a car. They found one the next night: a doctor's *coupé*, standing outside a house to which he had been called; and they drove cheerfully to the place of judgment.

It was a tiny house, with a tiny garden; and if the brothers had searched diligently in the untidy forecourt, they would have discovered a board announcing that "this desirable residence" was to let.

This had been taken down by the cobbler when he had obtained possession of the premises a week before. He had apparently spent very little in furniture; for, although the passage had a narrow strip of carpet, the stairs were bare.

"The room at the head of the first flight of stairs," murmured one brother to the other before they inserted the key. "Have you got your rubbers on, Harry?"

Harry nodded. He had already covered his feet with snow boots.

They went in and closed the door noiselessly behind them. Harry went first up the stairs and paused by the closed door at the head. Somebody was inside. They heard a slight noise. Harry took out his life-preserver with a mirthless little grin, and gently turned the handle.

"Who's that?" said a voice from the dark interior. The occupant of the room, unfortunately for himself, was silhouetted against the uncurtained window. Harry saw the gun with the bulging silencer at the end, and threw himself aside. There was a flash of light, a loud "*plop!*" and before the man with the pistol could shoot again the life-preserver got home.

★★★★★★

Two men got down from a car near Burlington Gardens, and each walked in a different direction. That, in itself, was a suspicious circumstance if it had been observed that at this hour—it was nearly ten—Burlington Gardens is more or less deserted save for cars that are taking a short cut to Regent Street.

A constable observed the machine, a closed car of American make, noted that the lights were on, and jotted down mentally the hour at which he saw it. When he returned from the perambulation of his beat the car was still there.

Burlington Gardens is not a parking place; there was no restaurant or hotel which might justify this "obstruction". He took the number and waited for the owners to reappear. He was relieved towards midnight and passed on the information and complaint to the officer who took his place.

At two o'clock the car had not been moved, and its occupants had not appeared. The only person who saw the two men was a night wanderer, an elderly vagrant, who subsequently gave information to the police.

At a little after three the sergeant to whom the matter was reported went up to the car and looked inside. In the light of his lamp he saw a motionless figure huddled on the floor, its head on its chest. He jerked open the door. . . .

By the time the ambulance arrived they had laid the unfortunate man flat on the pavement. He was living—was to live for many years, though his appearance was never quite the same again.

The battered Kelly had a story to tell the police, and he spoke with difficulty.

". . . . two fellers. . . . one of 'em was The Ringer! . . . . He took my jewel-case from my hip-pocket ... my watch and chain ... about eighteen hundred quid. . . ."

The two brothers, who had separated in Burlington Gardens, met again at the corner of the street in which they dwelt. They had walked in single file within sight of one another until they were within easy reach of home, and then they joined up.

"I'm betting this feller doesn't use a cosh again for years."

"Is he dead, Harry?" asked his companion.

"It wasn't worth killing him," said Harry, complacently. "I want to have a look at that case as soon as we get indoors. I'll bet there are sparklers there, worth thousands. And as for money . . . ." His fingers closed on a thick wad of notes that he had neither counted nor examined.

They opened the door of their modest dwelling and walked into the drawing-room. Harry went first. "Clear!" he shouted.

Before the brothers could reach the door, it was opened, and the front garden seemed more or less filled with constabulary.

★★★★★★

"Robbery with violence is one of the most serious offences that can be committed," said the judge, in passing sentence upon the two dazed young men. "Your unfortunate victim is still in hospital, and, although he is a man of evil character, and one has the gravest doubts as to the origin of the property you stole, society must be protected. You will be kept in prison with hard labour for eighteen months, and will each receive twenty-five lashes with the cat-o'-nine-tails."

The extraordinary thing was that neither Kelly, the prosecutor, nor the brothers Pelcher ever mentioned the author of their misfortune.

Chapter 16: The Fortune of Forgery

The man who reclined with his arms upon the parapet, looking down upon the dark water, was shabbily dressed. A "down-and-out", thought Henry Arthur Milton, smoking an after-dinner cigar, and promenading in the unexpected warmth of an early spring night along the embankment.

He saw the man make a sudden jump upwards, gripped him by the arm, and swung him round.

"If you go into the water I shall have to jump in after you," said The Ringer pleasantly; "which means that I shall be very wet, very uncomfortable, and attract attention which I have no desire to attract."

The man was trembling from head to foot. His thin, unshaven face was gaunt and hollow. The shabby collar about his throat was frayed and ragged at the edges.

"I am very much obliged to you," he said.

It was the voice of an educated man, and his thanks were mechanical. He was obviously a gentleman; none but a gentleman would have received such a piece of unwarranted interference without resentment, without whining his troubles and his woes abroad.

"Come for a little walk," suggested The Ringer.

The man hesitated.

"I do not want any money," he said, "or charity of any kind."

The Ringer laughed softly. "And I am not at all in a philanthropic mood," he replied.

He was, in truth, in a pretty bad temper. It was his peculiar complex and eccentricity that he hated reading letters to the editor in the daily newspapers abusing the police for their failure to arrest him. There had been three in a morning journal, and that which annoyed him most had been written by one Ferdinand Goldford, of Crake Hall, Bourne End.

The Ringer had his own views about coincidences. He regarded them as part of the normal processes of life. For example, if he picked up a ten-*franc* piece in the Strand he would expect to pick up a five-*franc* piece in the Lewisham High Road on the same day. He did not think such things were remarkable, and was only astounded when they did not happen.

★★★★★★

The coincidence in this case was that he was very annoyed with Mr. Ferdinand Goldford, and that he should have rescued this human wreck from self-destruction.

"I think you ought to know," said the shabby man walking by his side, "that I was released from prison this morning, after serving two months for burgling a house in the country. I broke in to get what I thought was my own. The chief witness against me was the butler, who does not know me. The rest of the family are abroad."

"I hope they were having a good time," said The Ringer politely. "And as to your having been released from prison, believe me, I am so grateful that I have never been admitted into one that you may regard me as a spiritual complement."

The name of the wayfarer was Lopez Burt. He had once been an officer of a cavalry regiment in India. Mr. Milton was not surprised to learn this. He had been the heir-presumptive of a rich and eccentric father, whose eccentricities took serious shape while Burt was in India. He had left the whole of his fortune, no inconsiderable amount, to a cousin.

Lopez Burt might have contested the will, but he was not in a position, until months afterwards, to discover that his father had been "rather strange" in his manner for two years before his death, that he had lived with the fortunate cousin, and had made a new will at a period when he was quite incapable of any intellectual effort.

"I'm not kicking," he said philosophically. "The poor old governor came a cropper on his head in the hunting field, and was never the same after that. The Goldfords kept this fact from me——"

"The who-fords?" asked The Ringer, immensely interested. "Not, by any chance, the Goldfords of Crake Hall, Bourne End?"

The man walking by his side nodded.

"That's the place I burgled," he said, almost cheerfully. "I came an awful mucker in the army. You see, I got into debt, never dreaming but that I should have pots of money someday. Then there was some trouble over card debts, and I had to clear out.

"There was a lady in it, too," he added vaguely, "but I needn't mention her. Anyway, I landed in England with about fourpence-ha'penny, and after that ... well, I hadn't any desire to see the Goldfords and throw myself upon their tender mercies. And I hadn't the evidence

327

then about the governor being of unsound mind. Sounds like an old lag's story, doesn't it?"

The Ringer shook his head. "It sounds remarkably unlike any old lag's story that I've heard," he said. "I have a top floor flat in the Adelphi. Will you come up and have a bite and a bath?"

"No," said the other, with emphasis.

The Ringer shook his head.

"Then I'm afraid I shall have to give you a punch on the nose," he remarked regretfully. "I am rather touchy on the subject of people refusing my invitations."

He heard the man chuckle.

"All right, I'll take your charity. I'm so hungry that I haven't any spirit left. My last meal was a piece of bread I scrounged from a garbage tin last night. That sounds picturesque, but it wasn't."

★★★★★★

The Ringer had a new furnished flat, which he had taken from a gentleman who had gone to Canada for a year: a pleasant, simply-furnished apartment, with hair carpets and stuff covers, and two or three cupboards containing valuables tightly locked—the usual "let".

"There is the bathroom." He threw open the door and switched on the light. "You had better eat something terrifically digestible. Try some sandwiches. I have a supply sent in to me every day."

He found a suit of clothes, a shirt, a collar, a pair of old shoes and the requisite *etceteras*, opened the bathroom door and threw them in on to the floor.

"Thank me when you come out, but don't be effusive," he said, and went out to hunt up sheets for the bed in the spare room.

At two o'clock in the morning The Ringer, who was a very good listener, came to the subject which was nearest his heart.

"These Goldbugs—Goldfords, is it?—seem to be a pretty unpleasant family."

He looked up at the ceiling thoughtfully and whistled.

"I suppose you've none of your former belongings? Have you any letters from your father?"

Lopez Burt looked at him quickly. "Why do you ask that? Yes, I have quite a lot. They are in a box at my old army bankers, with one or two other documents of no particular value."

The Ringer nodded.

"Is it possible to get those letters?"

Again, Burt cast an odd look at his host.

"Will you tell me what the idea is?" he asked quietly.

Henry Arthur Milton stretched back in his chair and looked past him.

"I think I ought to tell you that I'm clairvoyant," he said. "Most of us are. The moment I saw you I had a feeling that you were the heir to a great fortune, and I naturally wondered why a man so favoured by the gods was contemplating such an early retirement from life."

"Great fortune!" scoffed the other. "What rot you're talking!"

The Ringer inclined his head graciously.

"That's one of my weaknesses," he said. "The truth is, I am talking rot! I have absolutely no knowledge in regard to the law affecting wills and such things. I presume that your cousins are now enjoying their ill-gotten gains and are rolling in wealth. How much money was there?"

"Seventy thousand pounds," said the other with a wry face. And then, with a shrug of his thick shoulders: "What does it matter?"

"How was the money left?" interrupted The Ringer.

"It had been left in equal parts to Mr. Ferdinand Goldford, Miss Lena Goldford, his sister, and Mr. Anthony Goldford, his brother. The funny thing about it was that the names were not specified.

★★★★★★

"The poor old governor simply wrote, 'To the children of my late brother-in-law, Tobias Goldford', and that is where the dispute came in."

"Dispute?" said The Ringer quickly. "Was the will disputed?"

His visitor made a grimace of weariness.

"Don't let us talk about it."

"But I very much want to talk about it," said The Ringer. "Hasn't the will been made absolute, or whatever happens to these things?"

"Probate hasn't been granted—no. I thought of popping in, but a lawyer fellow I met on my tramp to London told me I hadn't a dog's chance. The trouble is that there's a fourth son by a former wife of Tobias, and in persuading the old man to make the will they'd forgotten all about him.

"He's been in South America and he claims to have a share. Old Tobias, by the way, was married the first time in South America and had this one son. There was a devil of a delay while they collected evidence. Naturally, the other Goldfords were furious with this fellow, and there have been all sorts of lawsuits——"

"Is Ferdinand Goldford a very offensive man?" asked The Ringer

329

gently.

"He's an utter cad," was the prompt reply.

"I *am* clairvoyant," murmured Henry Arthur Milton, and a beatific smile dawned on his face.

Next morning The Ringer was early abroad pursuing his inquiries. He saw a copy of the will; it had been witnessed by two old servants of the deceased man, and was signed three months before his death. The Ringer returned from Somerset House primed with this information.

"Who was Jessica Brown and William Brown?" he asked.

"You mean the witnesses to the will?" Mr. Burt stopped in the middle of a very hearty breakfast to look up in some surprise. "You've been pretty early at the job!"

"Where are they to be found?"

"In Heaven," said Lopez Burt grimly. "They only survived the poor governor by about five months. My lawyer pal—by the way, I met him in prison again—told me that there might be a chance of upsetting the will if they were alive. They were a nice old couple. They used to write to me regularly in India. They knew me when I was a child. I suppose I've dozens of their letters——"

"Are they in the box, too?" asked The Ringer quickly.

Lopez Burt considered.

"Yes; I don't think there is anything but letters."

"Splendid!" said his host. "This morning you will go along and collect that box and bring it here."

★★★★★★

A week later a smart-looking man of middle age, with an iron-grey moustache, alighted from an expensive motorcar before the porch of Crake Hall, and the florid Ferdinand, who had been playing clock golf on the lawn, loafed across to discover the identity of the visitor.

"Good morning," said the caller brusquely. "I'm Colonel St. Vinnes. Is Burt anywhere about?"

"Burt?" said Ferdie in amazement. "Do you mean my cousin, Lopez Burt? Good Lord! I thought everybody knew about him. He got into serious trouble in India and had to clear out——"

"I know, I know," snapped the other. "But that was before the Lal Singh affair—the lucky young devil! If he wastes that fortune, I'll never forgive him. I thought he had come back from America——"

Ferdinand Goldford was very much interested. Money fascinated him.

"Is that old Lope you're talking about?" he asked, not concealing his astonishment. "Got a lot of money, has he? We haven't heard from him."

The colonel's face expressed astonishment. "He's not here, then? Dear, dear, dear, that's extremely awkward!"

Ferdinand was impressed.

"Won't you come in?" he invited, and the visitor followed him through the large square hall into the drawing-room, and found himself being introduced to Ferdie's brother and sister—florid replicas of Ferdie, with the same fresh, round faces and small, blue eyes. Mr. Burt had described them as "pig-cunning", and this was not an inapt description.

"Friend of old Lope's," said Ferdinand loudly, as though he were prepared in advance to drown their protests. "Colonel—um——"

The visitor supplied his name.

"Old Lope's made a lot of money . . . . in America now."

Mr. Goldford spoke rapidly. They eyed the visitor suspiciously, incredulously. Apparently, the idea of Lope making money was a paralysing one.

"The point is," said the colonel, looking at his watch, "how can I get in touch with him? I had a cable saying that he would call here in the course of the day, but I've got to go back to London. Is it possible for me to leave a letter for him?"

It was not only possible, but Ferdie was most anxious to facilitate the process.

"Come this way, Colonel."

They passed down a broad passage into a lovely old room, the walls covered with bookshelves.

"This was the old fellow's library. We don't use it much now. Here's a table; there is no ink, but perhaps you'd like to use my fountain-pen?"

The colonel had a pen of his own. Ferdie bustled out to get the necessary stationery. He came back in a few minutes and explained that this room was seldom used.

"Too many books, too smelly, too dismal," he said, as he laid the paper before the visitor. "We can't clear it out till this will business is settled. That ought to happen in a couple of weeks."

"It seems rather a nice library," said the colonel, glancing round.

Ferdie smiled. "Don't you believe it! There isn't a book here worth reading. Look at 'em?"

Certainly, the bookshelves had a very solid appearance. There was one filled with ancient tomes, the covers of which were considerably dilapidated.

The colonel wrote his letter, with Mr. Goldford standing over him. He had sharp eyes and could read "My dear Lope" and "terribly sorry I missed you . . . ." but he really wasn't trying hard to discover the contents of the letter. That could easily be steamed open after this military-looking gentleman had left. Indeed, the colonel was hardly out of the grounds before the family were perusing the four-page letter that he had written.

"Nothing—absolutely nothing," said Ferdinand, and his brother agreed.

Certain shares were referred to, but not specifically mentioned. Ferdie re-sealed the letter and put it aside for his cousin when he called.

★★★★★★

"What do I do now?" asked Lopez Burt, when The Ringer joined him at dinner that night in the little Adelphi flat.

"You will emulate the rabbit who laid low, and maintain a discreet silence," said Henry Arthur Milton. "I am thoroughly enjoying this little adventure. You went to the tailors?"

Lope nodded.

"It wasn't as ghastly as I thought," he replied, "and I'm getting almost used to ready-made clothes. They didn't fit me very well in prison. They're making a few alterations and delivering them tonight. I suppose you realise I have already spent over a hundred pounds of your money?"

"You will spend more," said The Ringer cheerfully. "As soon as your clothes arrive you will pack them, take a taxi and drive to the *Ritz-Carlton*. I've already reserved your room in advance. When you get there you will write to your lawyer, Mr. Stenning—Stenning and Stenning, isn't it?

"You will say that you have arrived, and you'll be glad if he will come to dinner one night. He won't come, because he's one of those old gentlemen who never go out. I have written to him already."

"You've written to him?" said the other incredulously. "Why?"

"You promised to ask no questions," said The Ringer, with one of his rare smiles. "All I want you to do is to establish the fact that you're living in luxury somewhere in London."

Lopez Burt shook his head in bewilderment.

"I don't know what the idea is——" he began.

"Don't try. All you have to do is to sit tight and wait for good fortune," said The Ringer. "I didn't like Mr. Goldford before I saw him. Why, I cannot explain. When I saw him I loathed him. I made a few inquiries—some tradesmen are very talkative—and there's no doubt that these people descended on your unfortunate father at a period when he was unable to resist their influence.

"He was not staying with them, as you supposed. They were staying with him. It is an extraordinary piece of good luck that they are constantly dismissing and engaging servants."

"Where's the luck in that?"

But The Ringer did not explain.

"Another bit of good luck," he went on, "was that there was no stationery in the library. If there had been, I should have taken another course."

"I'm not going to ask any more questions," said Lopez Burt. "You've been a brick to me, and if ever I can repay you——"

"Not only can you repay me, but you will. I'm trusting you to say nothing about myself. Here is an address in Berlin: I want you to keep that by you and never lose it. As soon as you're in a position to do so you can send me £6,000, which I shall regard as commission well earned."

Lopez Burt smiled.

"You'll have to wait a very long time for that!" he said.

"Not so long," said The Ringer cryptically.

★★★★★★

That morning, Mr. Samuel Stenning, the senior partner of Stenning and Stenning, received a letter. It was addressed to him personally, expressed, and certain words in the ill-written and illiterate communication were heavily underlined.

"... I could tell you things that are going on at old Mr, Burt's place that would make your hare stand up on end! I know what happened before he died, when he sent for old Mr, Brown and had a long talk with him ... he wasn't daft then.

"He came down to the libery and I see him put something in a book. It was on the third shelf, it was called *Concrudence*. I often wanted to look and see what it was, but I never had a chants.

"I'll bet it was something about the Goldfords, who are a miserable lot of people and don't deserve to live in the house of a gentleman. I'll bet this thing he put in the *Concrudence* was a showing up for the Goldfords."

333

The letter bore the signature "A Friend." Mr. Stenning was not unused to anonymous letters, and ordinarily would have dropped it in the waste-paper basket; but he, too, disliked the Goldfords exceedingly, and had been secretly pleased when a new heir had appeared on the scene and had disputed their share of their ill-won possessions.

Unfortunately he had been a semi-invalid in the south of France when the will was made, and had no knowledge of its circumstances; but he was satisfied in his own mind that old man Burt was not in a condition to dispose of his property, and if he had had the slightest evidence on which the will could have been opposed he would have combed the earth for Mr. Burt's unfortunate son.

It was a remarkable coincidence that that morning he should receive a note from the *Ritz-Carlton* announcing the arrival of Lopez Burt in London.

"Humph!" said Mr. Stenning. "That's queer!"

He turned the matter over in his mind all day, and the following morning, instead of going to the office, he and his clerk went down in his car to Bourne End. Mr. Goldford was not so surprised to see him as he had imagined he would be.

"Good morning, Mr. Stenning. Have you seen anything of Lope?"

"I believe he is in London," said Stenning, himself astonished. "Did you know?"

Ferdinand grinned.

"No, I haven't heard from him. Somebody called here for him yesterday and left a note. You might give it to him if you see him. Is anything wrong?"

"No; I've had some information on which I feel compelled to act," said Mr. Stenning. "Have you found any documents belonging to your uncle?"

A look of alarm came to the round face of Ferdie. "Documents?" he squeaked. "No—what documents could there be?"

"Has the place been searched thoroughly?"

"We've had his desk and boxes opened, and most of the letters he left behind were sent to your office," said Ferdinand. "There has been nothing else. What do you expect?"

"Can I look in the library?"

Ferdinand hesitated.

"Certainly," he said.

He went in first and must have communicated the news to his brother and sister, for when Mr. Stenning and his clerk reached the drawing-room their reception was a chilly one.

"What's the idea of all this nonsense?" asked Ferdinand irritably.

"What documents could he have left? I know you don't think he was in his right mind, but there's the will, signed and witnessed——"

"By two people who are now dead," said Stenning drily.

Ferdinand's face flushed an angry red.

"That doesn't invalidate the will, does it?" he demanded angrily.

"Of course, they're dead. You saw them when they were alive; didn't they tell you that Mr. Burt was perfectly normal …?"

"What's the use of arguing, Ferdie?" said the shrill voice of his sister. "Let's go in and see the library."

The lawyer and his clerk accompanied the family into the gloomy room. Stenning walked up and down, examining the books on the third shelf. Presently his hand went up. It was Cruden's *Concordance*.

"I am informed there is something here," he said.

He took down the book, laid it on the table, and it opened on a faded sheet of paper. Ferdie saw the heading, gasped, and his jaw dropped.

"Good God!" he said.

It was headed "The Last Will and Testament," and was written in the crabbed hand of old Mr. Burt. The lawyer read the document carefully. It revoked all former wills, and "particularly the will I made on the seventeenth of February last, and which I now regard as being neither just nor equitable," and left the whole of his property to Lopez Henry Martin Burt, "my dear son."

The signature was undoubtedly that of the dead man. Beyond any question the witnesses were those who had witnessed the other will— and it had been made three weeks later!

"I'll dispute this," stormed Ferdinand, pale and quavering. "The thing's a forgery—there are no witnesses——"

"The same people witnessed the will in your favour," said the lawyer with quiet malice. "I am afraid this document will make a great difference to you."

He put the will in his pocket. For a second Ferdie's attitude suggested that he would take it from him by force.

"It's a forgery!" he bellowed. "I'll dispute it, by God! if I have to spend every penny …"

"You haven't many pennies to spend of your own, Mr. Goldford," said the lawyer acidly.

★★★★★★

335

Seven months later Lopez Burt enclosed an open draft for six thousand pounds in a letter he posted to an address in Berlin. He wrote:

"I don't know exactly how it all happened, but the Court have upheld my claim. I am still mystified as to how you knew of the other will—that is the greatest puzzle of all.

"The document was undoubtedly in my father's handwriting, and I could swear to the signatures of the two witnesses. . . .

"Do you remember asking me to get the box from the bank? You must have seen a lot of my father's writing there, and also the letters from the two servants.

"If you'd seen the will also you would have agreed that there was no question as to the authenticity of the document."

The Ringer purred at this. He was rather proud of his draughtsmanship, and he had reason to be. He had forged that will in four hours, which was something of an achievement.

Chapter 17: A "Yard" Man Kidnapped

Government Departments keep a sharp eye on post-prandial oratory. They do not like their servants, high or low, to talk shop in their leisure hours. Certainly, they strongly discount anything that has the appearance of being criticism of superiors; and Inspector Mander overstepped the bounds when, at a police banquet, and in the course of proposing such an innocuous toast as "The Ladies," he made a reference to The Ringer.

"People sometimes criticise us because notorious criminals remain at large," he said. (The quotation is from the *Outer London News and Suburban Record*.) "I am not so sure that we have done all we might have done, or that the right methods have been employed to bring him under arrest. This man is not only a menace to society, but a mark of reproach against our administration."

If Bliss had not disliked him so intensely, he would have broken Inspector Mander. It was the knowledge that he actively loathed this cocksure officer that induced him to excuse his error. Nevertheless, Inspector Mander stepped upon the carpet before a very high official and spent a most uncomfortable ten minutes, during which he did most of the listening.

It was three days after the publication of Mander's speech in a weekly newspaper that Bliss received a letter from The Ringer.

"I am rather tired of Mander, and I think I will put him where he belongs. Fools rather terrify me because they have the assistance of

Providence—which is distinctly unfair.

"You may tell Mr. Mander from me that before the end of the week has passed I shall get him."

Bliss sent for his subordinate.

"Read this," he said.

Mander read and forced a smile, but the superintendent knew that he was none too happy.

"He has never threatened you before, has he?" asked Bliss.

Mander laughed, but there was no real mirth in it.

"That kind of bunk doesn't scare me," he said. "I've been threatened by——"

"By The Ringer?" asked Bliss maliciously, enjoying the officer's discomfiture.

Mander moved uneasily in his chair.

"Well, no, not by The Ringer, but—er—I don't take very much notice of that."

And then he brightened visibly.

"You can see, chief, that this fellow's scared of me, and——"

"Excuse me a moment while I laugh," said Bliss sardonically. "Scared of you! What job are you on now?"

Mr. Mander was dealing with a case of car-stealing. He had got on the track of a fairly important organisation which, if it did not actually steal, certainly played the part of a receiver. Bliss listened and nodded.

"You ought to be safe," he said. "You've got Sergeant Crampton working with you; he's a pretty intelligent man."

Mander winced.

"The Duke of Kyle——" he began, and the nose of Mr. Bliss wrinkled.

"The Duke of Kyle is a great authority on the breeding of pigs and nothing else—oh, yes, I read his letter in the *Monitor*, praising your speech. That nearly got you hung. But he's no authority on The Ringer."

The Duke of Kyle was one of those peers who had very little occupation in life other than the breeding of pigs and the inditing of letters to newspapers. He had written his unqualified approval of Mr. Mander's speech, and had, moreover, suggested fantastical and not even novel methods for bringing The Ringer to justice. Bliss had read and had feared for his Grace.

★★★★★★

That night Mander was at Notting Dale Police Station, pursu-

337

ing his inquiries, and was coming down the steps when a beautiful limousine drew up at the door and a lady in evening dress stepped down. She was fair-haired and very beautiful; her hands sparkled with diamonds; from her ears hung two glittering stones.

"Can you tell me where I can find Inspector Mander?" she asked, and Mander, susceptible to feminine charms, lifted his hat. "You're he? Mr. Bliss said I should find you here."

"Is anything wrong, madam?"

The lady nodded; she seemed a little breathless, considerably agitated.

"It is about my car," she said, lowering her voice, "a *coupé*. It was stolen this afternoon while I was shopping in Bond Street. Somebody enticed the chauffeur away. . . . It isn't the loss of the car. I wonder if I could speak to you alone? Could you come back to Berkeley Square with me?"

Mander gave instructions to his men and followed the lady into the luxurious, delicately-perfumed interior. She was silent for a while.

"It isn't the loss of the car," she said again, "but I foolishly left my handbag in the pocket. There are letters that—it's very difficult to tell you this—that I—I wish to recover. I can speak to you confidentially?"

"Certainly, madam," said Mander.

His proximity to such a fragrant, lovely being was a little intoxicating.

"The duke and I are not on very good terms, but there has never been a question of—divorce. These letters will make a tremendous difference to me. Is it true that such things can be recovered through the—the underworld?"

Mander smiled. "They say so in books, and it has happened in real life," he said, "but it has never been my experience."

If Inspector Mander had been a little more experienced he would have returned a different answer.

"They're compromising letters, I suppose?"

"Compromising? Yes—well, I suppose they are. They're from a boy—my cousin. Oh dear, oh dear!" She wrung her hands in despair.

"I'll try to get them for your grace," said Mander gallantly.

He did not know which duchess this was. His acquaintance with the peerage was slight and sketchy, and the only member he knew was an impoverished lord who occasionally found himself on the verge of prosecution.

She opened a little flap in the car before her and took out a jewelled cigarette case—in that half-light the diamond monogram sparkled brilliantly.

"Do smoke."

He took a cigarette and politely offered her a light to the cigarette she put between her red lips. There was a little microphone attachment at the side of the car, and she pressed a button. Mander saw the chauffeur bend his head towards the earpiece.

"Drive round the park for a little while before you go to Berkeley Square," she commanded.

In the light of his match Mander had seen the ducal coronet and a "K". The Duchess of——? Kyle, of course!

"The trouble with Bertie is that he's very indiscreet," she said. "He writes letters . . . ."

Mander, who had settled himself more comfortably in the corner of the car, most unaccountably fell asleep at this juncture.

★★★★★★

The ringing of the telephone bell brought Bliss from his bed and into the cold room where the instrument was. Detectives are human, and they never quite get accustomed to being awakened at half-past three in the morning.

"Mander? What do I know about Mander? Why? Ring him up, my dear man," he said testily.

"He's not in his house, sir. We haven't seen him since he went away with the lady."

Bliss was instantly wide awake.

"Which lady?"

The man at the other end of the 'phone told him of the car that called at Notting Dale.

"It's the Duke of Kyle's car," said that same Sergeant Crampton in whose intelligence Bliss had expressed his unbounded faith. "We found it abandoned on Hampstead Heath. It had been stolen from his Grace's garage."

"Have you searched it?"

"Yes, sir. We found rather an important clue—a lady's card, with a few words scribbled in pencil."

"Bring the car round and pick me up," said Bliss, and was waiting in the street before the police tender came in sight.

By the light of the headlamps he examined the card. In a woman's hand was written:

The Leek. First left, first right—Stillman.

"Now, look at this, sir," said the sergeant.

He switched on the lights inside the car, which was upholstered in fawn. The tiny carpet on the floor was of the same colour, but near the left-hand door was a large red patch, and on the padded upholstery on the near side of the car a larger patch level with a man's head.

"It's blood," said the sergeant. "I saw him go off, and that's the seat he occupied."

The local inspector of police was present at the examination.

"What is The Leek? Is there such a place near here?"

The inspector shook his head.

"No, but Stillman is the name of a house agent. He lives in Shardeloes Road. I've sent one of my men to wake him. He ought to be up by now: will you come round?"

They drove round to Shardeloes Road and found a sleepy, middle-aged man.

"The Leek is a cottage—I always call it The Leek; that was the former name of it. It's an empty house on the edge of the heath."

He took the card, examined it, and nodded.

"That's right. A lady asked to see it and I gave her the directions. That's the handwriting of my clerk."

"Have you the keys of this place?"

"Yes, at my office. If you wait, I'll dress."

★★★★★★

They waited while he dressed, accompanied him to his office in the steep hill street, and, crossing the heath, dipped into a depression. The road ran for some distance through an avenue of trees, at the end of which were three or four houses. Mr. Stillman stopped the car at the first of these, and the detectives jumped out.

It was a gloomy-looking little house with a forecourt behind the high wall. They passed into the garden through a wicket gate, and Sergeant Crampton, using his lamp, led the way. Presently he stopped.

"Look at this," he said.

On the stone flags were certain red stains, which were still wet. A little farther along were others. When they reached the door, they found it half open.

Bliss went ahead with Crampton into the musty-smelling house, his lamp searching the walls carefully. There was blood on the floor, blood on the walls; the trail led him upward to the front room.

Here the evidence of tragedy was almost complete. There were bloodstains everywhere, but if there was no sign of the body there was evidence of a struggle, for one of the walls was spattered red, and near the door he found the sanguinary print of a gloved hand.

He made a careful scrutiny of every room, but apparently only the front room had been visited by Mander and his captor.

At four o'clock they were coming out of the house, when a car drove up and a man stopped out. Crampton went to interview him, and returned with the information that it was the Duke of Kyle's secretary.

"I had to telegraph to his Grace about the car being stolen," he said. "His Grace is very much upset. The Ringer visited him last night."

"Where?" asked Bliss quickly.

"At Clane Farm—it is near Sevenoaks. His lordship has a large pig-breeding establishment there," said this middle-aged gentleman.

Apparently, the duke had been retiring for the night, when somebody had tapped on the window of his study; he had drawn up the window, and seen a strange and to him, a terrifying face.

"He was armed," said the secretary, his voice quaking. "He made the most terrible threats to his Grace. He said he was bringing a Mr. Mander to stay with him that night, and that they would both be found in the same condition in the morning."

"Did he notify the police?" asked Bliss.

"No, sir," The secretary shook his head. "His Grace is a very courageous man. It was very curious that I should have been getting on to him at the moment that he was trying to get into communication with me. He told me he was sitting up all night, and that he would be heavily armed."

Bliss noted down the exact location of the pig farm.

"Can you get on to his Grace and tell him that we're coming down almost immediately?" he asked. "I want to make an examination of this road."

After Mr. Whistle—for such was his peculiar name—had departed the detective began a systematic search for further clues.

The path outside was of gravel, and, although there were stains which had the appearance of blood, they were not sufficiently definite or informative to help very much. Fifty yards along the road, however, Bliss made a discovery. It was a large piece of bloodstained satin, rolled up and thrown on one side. From here the evidences of tragedy were clear to the naked eye. They followed the track of the tell-tale spots across the Heath until they came to the edge of a pond, where they had ceased.

Bliss observed that the pond was within easy walking distance of the place where the car had been found, and this puzzled him. If Mander had been killed, why had not the body been immediately disposed of? Why had it been taken to the house?

This was not the only thing that puzzled him. The detectives probed into the water with their sticks, but at the place where the track ceased the water was deep. Bliss gave instructions that the pond was to be dragged, but did not wait to see the result.

★★★★★★

Ten minutes later the police car was speeding across Westminster Bridge on its southward journey.

Daylight broke before they reached Clane Farm. It was rather a difficult place to locate, and Bliss regretted that he had not brought the secretary with him. They found it at last and saw that there were strange activities, for in the narrow lane they met three men beating the hedges and obviously searching for something. Bliss stopped the car and was addressed by the red-faced leader:

"Are you the police?" he demanded. "That's quick work. I only telephoned you a quarter of an hour ago."

"I'm from Scotland Yard," said Bliss. "What's the trouble?"

"Trouble?" roared the man, going red in the face. "Pride of Kent's been stolen. He couldn't have got out of his pen——"

"Who's Pride of Kent?"

"The finest hog in the country," said the man. "He's taken every first prize, and I wouldn't have lost him for a thousand pounds. When his Grace hears about it there's going to be trouble."

"When was he lost?"

"Last night. He was in his sty, and he couldn't have got out by himself," said the man. "One of these villagers must have come up and stolen him. If we catch him there's going to be trouble. I wouldn't be surprised if he'd been killed. You found blood, didn't you, Harry?"

"Yes, sir, I found blood," said the man he addressed. "It were near the old building."

"Where is his Grace?" asked Bliss.

The man stared at him.

"His Grace? Why, he's in Scotland."

The eyes of Mr. Bliss opened.

"In Scotland? Are you sure?"

"Yes, I'm sure," said the man impatiently. "I had a letter from his Grace yesterday. At least, not from his Grace, but from his secretary, Miss Erford."

Superintendent Bliss did not so much as wince. "Is there a Mr. Whistle?"

The man had never heard of Mr. Whistle.

★★★★★★

Bliss regretted even more that he had not brought the "secretary" with him, though he had no doubt that that gentleman would have found a very excellent excuse for remaining in London.

"There are lots of people who didn't like Pride of Kent," the man proceeded. "Some of these pigmen had a grudge against him because he was a bit savage; but he was the best hog in the county, and I don't know what his Grace will say if I can't find him."

"Where was this pig kept?" asked Bliss.

The Pride of Kent lived in a handsome mansion which many of his Grace's tenants might have envied. It was a low building, before which was an ample yard, where the joy of the piggery could rest at his well-fed ease. A steel grating was unfastened and the pigman explained just how impossible it was for anybody but an educated porker to let himself out.

"My theory is that it happened last night," said the man. "There was a van seen in the lane——"

"What is this?" said Bliss, and, stooping, picked up a round tin. It was half-filled with a brown, treacly substance. "Have you seen this before?"

The foreman shook his head. There was a small label on the tin, a wafer of paper, and on this was written the word "Poison."

"The Ringer is about the most thoughtful man I have ever met with," said Bliss bitterly, for he recognised the queer "n" that Henry Arthur Milton invariably made. "We'll have that for analysis," he said. "I suppose the Pride of Kent was rather fond of sweet things? I thought so. This looks to me like golden syrup—and something else! I can well understand why he didn't put up a squeak."

The pigman did not see the grim jest.

"What is that over there?" asked Bliss. He pointed to a range of buildings, each with its little front forecourt.

"We keep the young pigs there. They are his last litter," said the pigman proudly. "You won't find a better lot in Kent or anywhere else."

The forecourts were filled with little porkers, all engaged at that moment in their morning meal. At the second pen Mr. Bliss paused. In one corner was a round felt hat sadly battered and slightly gnawed.

"I think I'd like to go in here," said Bliss, and stepped in among the terrified little pigs, who scampered in all directions save one—this was significant. They did not go into the dark little house where they slept at night. One or two did approach the entrance, but turned and fled instantly.

★★★★★★

Bliss stooped low and passed through the door. The man who sat propped up in one corner bound hand and foot and scientifically gagged stared pathetically into the eyes of his chief.

"Come in here," called Bliss, and the two detectives who were with him followed.

It took them some little time to unfasten his bonds, but presently Mr. Mander staggered out into the light and was stimulated with brandy.

He had nothing to say; he could only babble about a beautiful lady, and somebody who carried him on his back. His most distinct recollection was facing the tiny eyes of a dozen little pigs, who resented his intrusion into their sleeping-quarters.

"Queer, isn't it?" said Bliss absently. "He said he'd put you where you belonged. I won't be so uncomplimentary as to say that he did."

"This woman was one of the prettiest——"

"I have met Cora Ann Milton before, but I didn't know she was in England," said Bliss; "and I don't suppose she is this morning."

One of the servants of the house came hurrying towards him.

"There's a telephone message for you, sir——"

Bliss waved him aside.

"I know all about it. They've found the body of the Pride of Kent in the pond at Hampstead. I know exactly where the bloodstains came from. I'm pretty sure I know where that unfortunate hog was killed."

LEONAUR

ALSO FROM LEONAUR

AVAILABLE IN SOFTCOVER OR HARDCOVER WITH DUST JACKET

THE EMPIRE OF THE AIR: 1 *by George Griffiths*—*The Angel of the Revolution*—a rich brew that calls to mind Verne's tales of futuristic wars while being original, visionary, exciting and technologically prescient.

THE EMPIRE OF THE AIR: 2 *by George Griffiths*—*Olga Romanoff or, The Syren of the Skies*—the sequel to *The Angel of the Revolution*—a future Earth in which nation states are given full self determination when the Aerians, the descendants of 'The Brotherhood of Freedom,' who have policed world peace for more than a century, decide they are mature enough to have outgrown war.

THE INTERPLANETARY ADVENTURES OF DR KINNEY *by Homer Eon Flint*—*The Lord of Death, The Queen of Life, The Devolutionist & The Emancipatrix.*

ARCOT, MOREY & WADE *by John W. Campbell, Jr.*—The Complete, Classic Space Opera Series—*The Black Star Passes, Islands of Space, Invaders from the Infinite.*

CHALLENGER & COMPANY *by Arthur Conan Doyle*—The Complete Adventures of Professor Challenger and His Intrepid Team-*The Lost World, The Poison Belt, The Land of Mists, The Disintegration Machine* and *When the World Screamed.*

GARRETT P. SERVISS' SCIENCE FICTION *by Garrett P. Serviss*—Three Interplanetary Adventures including the unauthorised sequel to H. G. Wells' *War of the Worlds*-*Edison's Conquest of Mars, A Columbus of Space, The Moon Metal.*

JUNK DAY *by Arthur Sellings*—". . . . his finest novel was his last, Junk Day, a post-holocaust tale set in the ruins of his native London and peopled with engrossing character types . . . . perhaps grimmer than his previous work but pointedly more energetic." *The Encyclopedia of Science Fiction*

KIPLING'S SCIENCE FICTION *by Rudyard Kipling*—Science Fiction & Fantasy stories by a Master Storyteller including 'As East As A,B,C' 'With The Night Mail'.

DARKNESS AND DAWN 1—THE VACANT WORLD *by George Allen England*—A Novel of a future New York.

DARKNESS AND DAWN 2—BEYOND THE GREAT OBLIVION *by George Allen England*—The last vestiges of humanity set out across America's devastated landscape in search of their dream.

DARKNESS AND DAWN 3—THE AFTER GLOW *by George Allen England*—Somewhere near the Great Lakes, 1000 years from now. Beneath our planet's surface tribes of near human albino warriors eke out an existence in a hostile environment.

LEONAUR

ALSO FROM LEONAUR
AVAILABLE IN SOFTCOVER OR HARDCOVER WITH DUST JACKET

THE FIRST BOOK OF AYESHA *by H. Rider Haggard*—Contains *She & Ayesha: the Return of She.*

THE SECOND BOOK OF AYESHA *by H. Rider Haggard*—Contains *She and Allan & Wisdom's Daughter.*

QUATERMAIN: THE COMPLETE ADVENTURES—1 *by H. Rider Haggard*—Contains *King Solomon's Mines & Allan Quatermain.*

QUATERMAIN: THE COMPLETE ADVENTURES—2 *by H. Rider Haggard*—Contains *Allan's Wife, Maiwa's Revenge & Marie.*

QUATERMAIN: THE COMPLETE ADVENTURES—3 *by H. Rider Haggard*—Contains *Child of Storm & Allan and the Holy Flower.*

QUATERMAIN: THE COMPLETE ADVENTURES—4 *by H. Rider Haggard*—Contains *Finished & The Ivory Child.*

QUATERMAIN: THE COMPLETE ADVENTURES—5 *by H. Rider Haggard*—Contains *The Ancient Allan & She and Allan.*

QUATERMAIN: THE COMPLETE ADVENTURES—6 *by H. Rider Haggard*—Contains *Heu-Heu or, the Monster & The Treasure of the Lake.*

QUATERMAIN: THE COMPLETE ADVENTURES—7 *by H. Rider Haggard*—Contains *Allan and the Ice Gods, Four Short Adventures & Nada the Lily.*

TROS OF SAMOTHRACE 1: WOLVES OF THE TIBER *by Talbot Mundy*—55 B.C.--an adventurer set during the Roman invasion of Britain.

TROS OF SAMOTHRACE 2: DRAGONS OF THE NORTH *by Talbot Mundy*—55 B.C. —Caesar plots, Britons war among themselves and the Vikings are coming.

TROS OF SAMOTHRACE 3: SERPENT OF THE WAVES *by Talbot Mundy*—55 B.C.--Caesar is poised to invade Britain—only a grand strategy can foil him!.

TROS OF SAMOTHRACE 4: CITY OF THE EAGLES *by Talbot Mundy*—54 B.C.—Rome—Tros treads in the streets of his sworn enemies!.

TROS OF SAMOTHRACE 5: CLEOPATRA *by Talbot Mundy*—Tros and the Roman Empire turn to the Egypt of the Pharaohs.

TROS OF SAMOTHRACE 6: THE PURPLE PIRATE *by Talbot Mundy*—The epic saga of the ancient world—Tros of Samothrace—draws to a conclusion in this sixth—and final—volume.

Lightning Source UK Ltd.
Milton Keynes UK
UKHW010637040321
379777UK00001B/128